C000184902

Robert A Rees

A SEASON
IN THE SUN

Robert Rees

Matador
9 Priory Business Park,
Wistow Road, Kibworth Beauchamp,
Leicestershire. LE8 0RX
Tel: 0116 279 2299
Email: books@troubador.co.uk
Web: www.troubador.co.uk/matador
Twitter: @matadorbooks

ISBN 978 1788037 174

British Library Cataloguing in Publication Data.
A catalogue record for this book is available from the British Library.

Printed and bound by Printed and bound by CPI Group (UK) Ltd, Croydon, CR0 4YY
Typeset in 11pt Minion Pro by Troubador Publishing Ltd, Leicester, UK

Matador is an imprint of Troubador Publishing Ltd

For Deborah and Madeleine, my two favourite maidens

ENGLAND

1
A Day Out

In the afternoon sun, the bowler turned and started his run in. All eyes in the ground followed him, save one pair.

"These bloody binoculars are hopeless, Henry!"

Henry Fanshawe repressed a chortle. "Ollie, I often find it helps to take the lens caps off first."

The slightly drunken figure on his right pondered this advice and attempted to remove the caps whilst balancing a pint of cold lager in a large plastic cup on his knees.

When the inevitable happened, Henry and the surrounding group of clients and friends let out a rousing cheer.

As the applause died away, the Honourable Oliver Winterton Smythe adjusted his blazer, handed the now soaked binoculars to Henry with careful dignity and stretched back in his seat to sleep in the sun.

Henry Fanshawe returned to the cricket. The bowler was accelerating towards the wicket, arms cycling in readiness to release the ball. Henry smiled a contented smile. There was very little in the world, he thought, that was more fun than the first day of the Lord's Test. And this year he had managed to wangle use of the Fanshawe Global Securities Box for the occasion. The room was dotted with some of his favourite clients, but most present were friends, in particular friends from the firm's cricket club, the Unmentionables.

It made for an interesting mix. In the corner, a rather polite and quiet Japanese client watched with absolute concentration and, Henry suspected, minimal understanding of what was happening on the pitch. A loud sharp-suited American from Fanshawe's Trading was determined to explain to him why baseball was a better game.

In addition to the group he had assembled for this most old-fashioned of City working days, other acquaintances had poked their heads round the door at regular intervals. Henry, being Henry, had invited them in for a chat and copious amounts of alcohol. Several had stayed for so long that they were unable to find their way back to their seats and, in one case, even to find the way out of the box. All in all, he thought, it was the perfect sporting event. Cricket, a bar tab of almost infinite possibilities, and a short cab ride home to his flat in Victoria when, as always, he and his mates were turfed out many hours after play had ended.

Henry returned to the match. The bowler was nearly at the crease. Henry had always appreciated the art of bowling. He was a decent amateur spinner and still enjoyed the odd outing for the Unmentionables even though he was now over fifty. Many of the players were taken from that large proportion of the firm to whom he had once taught the business. He liked nothing better than picking promising candidates from the back office and turning them into successful financiers. And he was very good at it. It made him one of the more popular figures at Fanshawe's, and as he grew older, he was proud of that.

4

On the field of play, the batsman, having limbered up by the crease, prepared to face his first ball. The ground held its breath.

It was not a good one, and the batsman, rolling back on his heels, opened his body and cut at it with all his monumental strength. It sped through the air for a certain six towards the Fanshawe box. Henry, in a moment of cold certainty, realised it was heading straight for Ollie's slumped head.

With a speed that belied his years, he leapt onto his seat, and as the ball passed over the first row of his guests, he lunged to grab it out of the air, inches in front of his friend's cranium. He then fell heavily into Ollie's lap, wakening him from his slumbers, and depositing the rest of the now warm beer over those perfectly creased trousers. The Honourable opened an eye and surveyed the man kneeling in front of him.

"Henry, old boy, I know you like to look after your clients, but one can go too far!" Oliver then resumed his nap, blithely unaware that he had been mere inches from severe brain damage or worse.

Henry picked himself up, and to a chorus of "Jolly good catch!", "Well done old boy!", "Henry saves the day!" (and one, "Why did you bother?") accepted another beer and turned back toward the cricket.

Another wicket. England were looking good for the win. All the boring bankers were back in the office and Henry and his mates were at Lord's. Nothing to do this evening except sleep it off and look forward to a relaxed weekend of almost complete inactivity. This schedule, for Henry, was as close to perfection as made no difference.

* * *

The next morning found Henry reclining in a large leather armchair in his Victoria mansion flat, a piece of toast and marmalade in one hand, and a large cup of coffee in the other.

The furniture, which Henry had collected over his lifetime, clearly bore the mark of his bulk. Leather armchairs (once purchased as a job lot from the Reform Club) dominated the space, illuminated by pools of light from Victorian standard lamps. At night, these left the rest of the room in a cosy religious gloom. In between the paintings on the walls stood large mahogany bookcases, stuffed full with an eclectic mix of titles, some of which Henry had read, and some of which he felt he ought to read. By the window, a slightly outdated music system occupied most of a polished oak table. And against the table leg stood, propped up and gleaming, a tenor saxophone.

As he was mulling over life in general, a large crash by the door made him start out of his chair. It was the post being pushed through the letter box – more of a small thump really, but to someone in Henry's hungover state, it sounded like a twenty-one gun salute that for reasons of economy had been combined into one shot.

"Bill, bill, bill, wealth management circular, venture capital fund offer." He smiled ruefully.

Upon throwing most of the post into the sometime-never pile on his desk, his eye was caught by one letter that stood out. With a sudden curiosity, and ignoring the remainder of the pile, Henry picked it up.

The colourful stamp depicted a plant which Henry did

not immediately recognise. At the same time it seemed strangely familiar. Neither was the currency obvious to him, though it did strike a soft chord somewhere within his memory banks. The crude postmark illustrated what appeared to be a pair of large female buttocks. Henry opened it and pulled out the contents.

Still bleary-eyed from the evening before, he found it difficult to focus. He slid out the letter, and when he put on his reading glasses, the words 'Kirby & Kirby' stood out in large black letters.

Messrs Kirby & Kirby
Attorneys at law
1 Victoria St
Victoria, Mahé

Dear Sir,
We are charged with the sad task of informing you of the recent death of your Aunt Esmeralda. Mrs Fanshawe was, you will be happy to know, active to the last and remained at the centre of affairs in St Christol right up until her unfortunate accident with the tractor and the town bus that ended her life. As executors to her will, we should be most grateful to you if you could contact us as soon as possible. It contains a number of matters which should be of great interest to you.

Your sincerely

Xavier Kirby MA (Cantab)

Like sunlight pouring into a room when a curtain is abruptly drawn, realisation flooded into Henry. Aunt Esme, of course! He recalled his wonderful, if slightly mad, Aunt Esme from the Seychelles. One of the younger Fanshawes had been sent out to oversee a new office for the cinnamon trade in this outpost of the empire in the early 1900s, and bewitched by the beauty of the islands, and also, it was rumoured, by the beauty of many of its inhabitants had elected to remain when the company had been forcibly nationalised by the state shortly after independence. Cuthbert Fanshawe, 'Uncle Cuthers' as Henry knew him, with his equally redoubtable French Seychellois wife, Esme, lived in a typical colonial mansion. Henry remembered, many years back, staring at photos of their white weather-boarded palace, surrounded by the lush vegetation of the tropical rainforest.

"Dear old Esme," he mused, "quite loony of course but great fun." On the infrequent visits she and her husband would make to the UK, they would unfailingly pay a visit to the Fanshawe household to pass on news of the latest scandals to shake St Christol, the small village where they lived on Mahé island. Henry remembered with fondness her extraordinary accent, which managed to combine French, Seychellois patois, and upper-class English. As Henry had been by some way the least reserved of the Fanshawe children, Esme had always been particularly keen on him, and this was reciprocated. For a while after Cuthbert's death they had exchanged letters, though over the last decade or so this had ceased and Henry had almost forgotten about her.

"I had no idea the old girl was still alive," Henry caught himself, "or at least, was alive until relatively recently."

He tried to conjure in his mind's eye the chaos ensuing from an accident involving a tractor and a town bus. None of the images stood at odds with the irrepressible character of Aunt Esme which had so taken him in earlier days.

"Much more fun if she'd gone doing something truly bananas." Henry remembered with a smile the day that she had driven her hired Bentley into the lake at Glyndebourne, after a misunderstanding with the reverse gear, and then dived in after it during the interval to retrieve the picnic. As the party tucked into soggy cucumber sandwiches and smoked salmon, her only remark was, "Well, kept the champers nice and cold."

He re-read the letter, wondering aloud what the matters of great interest might be, when the phone rang. It being Saturday, Henry had set the phone to answer machine in order not to disturb his day of rest, and more particularly his leisurely breakfast and attempt at the *Times* crossword, which usually took him most of the morning.

"I am sorry, but Henry Fanshawe is out at the moment. If you would like to leave a message, please speak after the tone."

"Henry. Are you there? I know you are! Pick up the bloody phone, for God's sake!"

The plummy barked questions that issued from the machine identified the caller immediately as Henry's elder brother Charles, a man with whom Henry enjoyed a cordial enough, though sometimes strained, relationship. This was in part due to the fact that, as second son, Henry had inherited little of the Fanshawe estate and wealth,

9

whilst Charles enjoyed the life of a country squire in Rutland. Henry was in no mood in his current delicate condition to enter a conversation, so he kept quiet while his brother droned on.

"Charles here. Your brother Charles. From Rutland. Have you had a letter about Aunt Esme? Sad news I suppose, though I could never get on with the old bat!"

In a moment of irritation, he almost reached for the phone but thought better of it. Charles had not been born with much tact and had worked hard all his life on eliminating any which remained. Henry decided to let it go.

"Anyway, see you on Friday at the Reform, three pm. This lawyer chappie from the Seychelles is coming over to see us – must be about the will I suppose. And please, Henry, do be on time! Over and out."

"Sometimes my elder brother is such an arse!" Henry found himself speaking out loud. He was used to being told what to do by Charles, but at fifty plus, the urge to obey was wearing a little thin.

Though, Henry figured, he was probably right about the will. He shovelled the last of his toast into his mouth, took a long gulp of coffee, then settled back in his chair, ballpoint in hand, riffling through the *Times* to find the crossword.

2
Henry Nearly Loses It

It was a perfect English summer's evening. The long shadows from the turrets of the Pavilion lay stretched like black icicles across the pitch. The sun was sinking slowly behind the rows of mansion flats that surrounded Lord's, the air was still, and the shouts of the crowd had fallen to a low murmur. All eyes were on the incoming batsman.

Henry Fanshawe strode down the Pavilion steps and through the famous white gate. The crease before him seemed to lie at the end of a long tunnel. He felt like a deep sea diver, taking slow, measured steps, under the weight of several fathoms of English expectation. "Concentrate, man," he muttered to himself as he walked past the glaring Aussie faces, "just five runs to make, and the series is ours."

Then he was taking his guard, eyeing likely spots for a quick single. Towards him, a little speck growing larger by the second. Dennis Lillee, the famed destroyer of the lower order. How could he, Henry Fanshawe, until recently a company team left arm spinner, stand up to the terrible onslaught about to be unleashed? In seeming slow motion, the cricket ball left Lillee's hand and flew unerringly towards Henry's not inconsiderable midriff.

Praying to whichever God held cricket dear, Henry shut his eyes and threw his bat in the general direction of the speeding ball. There was an ear splitting crack, then, as he opened his eyes, a short silence followed rapidly by a shout of applause from the crowd, willing the ball to the boundary.

Henry took a deep breath and was preparing himself for the next ball when he noticed that the bowler had not moved back. In fact he was now bearing down upon the crease, nostrils flared, eyes screwed up with rage.

"What the fuck do you think you're playing at, Fanshawe?"

It was then that Henry noticed the remarkable similarity of Dennis Lillee to his nemesis, Ryan Pikeworth.

"Wake up, you lazy bastard!"

The idyll of Lord's vanished like the morning mist as Henry focused his eyes, only to see the contorted face of his line manager staring at him from the end of his desk.

"My office! Now."

Henry rubbed his eyes and stared at the retreating figure. A late night out had taken its toll, and he found that, with age, the period necessary for recovery had lengthened. He shuffled to his feet and followed Ryan into the glass office.

Outside, at the ranks of desks that sat in the main trading floor of Fanshawe and Co. Global Securities, salesmen manning their phones attempted not to look interested in the scene unfolding within. There was obviously quite an argument going on. Inside, Ryan was losing his cool.

"Six thousand, seven hundred and fifty pounds!"

Henry winced as his manager's fist came thumping down on his preternaturally tidy desk, causing the pencil tidy to quiver perceptibly next to the perfectly aligned out-tray.

Ryan continued, waving a memo, "Expenses for the first day at the Lord's cricket match last Friday – six thousand, seven hundred and fifty pounds? Who did you invite, the Household Cavalry?"

Henry knew he was on weak ground. His legendary generosity with the firm's money was well known, and the tab after his corporate day out at Lord's had broken a few rules and some records.

"Well, we did see a lot of clients there, Ryan. You know how it is."

"Whose names I presume you have noted for Compliance?"

It was also a well-known facet of Henry's character that he didn't do detail. Ryan knew he possessed the advantage when querying any aspect of Henry's administrative acumen. He continued to push.

"And invoices of course!"

"Of course!" Henry breathed a sigh. He knew when he was beaten. It wasn't that he disliked the man opposite him across the desk. He very rarely took dislikes. But Ryan had taken against him and seemed determined to pull him up for any and every breach of the company's new guidelines.

These had been handed out following the latest reorganisation with Global Securities of Des Moines, Iowa, in what, without a trace of irony was called a 'booklet', though Henry had seen and read many Russian novels of less weight.

"And you missed the seminar on desk tidying and correct use of corporate filing systems."

"Yes, there's always a silver lining, isn't there."

"Henry, there is nothing funny about Keep your Desk Tidy Day."

Henry, sitting in front of Ryan's desk, in a slightly lower chair especially prepared for confrontations such as this, could not help smiling. Ryan was in full flow.

"You may be the last Fanshawe in the firm, but you must get rid of the detritus which surrounds your workstation! It offends me, Henry."

Henry shifted his slightly rotund figure in the chair,

"Ryan, many things that you do offend me. But I don't go off on one."

His new line manager had been a constant thorn in his side since an away day (how he hated that phrase) where Henry had questioned the worth of MBA courses at backwater polys. Ryan, ablaze with righteous indignation, had leapt to his feet, declaring that, "he would not be where he was today without the knowledge he had gained at Bracknell Polytechnic – or the University of Heathrow, as it was now called."

It was a dreadful combination, thought Henry. Extreme enthusiasm for bureaucracy coupled with an entirely defunct creative urge. This made rapid preferment in a bank a near-certainty. It was not long before Pikeworth's inexorable rise through middle management left him as Henry's boss, free to exact revenge in all ways available to those in possession of the dreaded co-role as Head of Human Resources.

Henry considered his position and saw that retreat

was the best option. "Look, Ryan, sorry about the tidy desk stuff. I'll have a go this afternoon, promise."

"See that you do, Henry, see that you do."

The public flogging was clearly at an end, so Henry rose and exited the glass-fronted office to return to his seat amongst the serried rows of traders. As he passed by, there were the usual murmurs of condolence from his friends, which was by and large everybody. Many of them had been trained for a while on Henry's desk, where his avuncular but original programme had provided the stepping board for their later careers. All in the firm liked Henry, or 'Old Spice' as he was known. He had been there since pre-Big Bang days, from that golden era before the American takeover. Now, ploughing a homely furrow on the Spice Retail desk at Fanshawes Commodities, Henry had shown himself equally good at making friends and money, selling flavours from the Orient to the seemingly bottomless pit of Anglo-Indian curry houses in the UK.

He sat down at his desk and looked at the pile of papers in front of him. He had always meant to tidy it up some day, but the day never came. Maybe he should show willing and try. It had, after all, been ages since he had last done so properly. And he had been at this desk for some years, since the move to new open plan offices in the 90s. It might even be a good thing, he mused, to see the actual desk again once in a while.

Henry looked back on old days with some nostalgia. With the American takeover had come, inevitably, the Americans. Henry liked the Americans. They arrived as a breath of fresh air in the hidebound London of the 80s. However, there were downsides. Liquid lunches became a thing of the past. Human resource departments blossomed, absurdly complicated computer trading systems took over from the old market floor. A wave of immigrant MBA students from across the pond introduced complex financial models, Microsoft PowerPoint presentations, and softball in the park on Sundays. This irritated Henry, who had made a point of talent spotting in the East End schools, where he ran a cricket club, and training them up in the City. Now these jobs were being inexorably squeezed by the inflow of overseas talent. It didn't seem right.

'That was when the rot really set in,' Henry mused, 'all these keen Yanks in chinos – outrageously expensive coffee shops, everyone doing 'high fives' in the office and talking about windows in their time frame. Then, to cap it all, the undiluted awfulness that was Dress-Down Friday. The idea of not wearing a suit to the office was so completely foreign to Henry that dress-down rules had little effect on his apparel. Occasionally he would arrive on Fridays in brown shoes, as a concession to policy, and once on a mad whim he had worn a yellow tie. But to cross the hallowed entrance hall of Fanshawes, walls festooned with bearded ancestors staring down at him, in anything but a suit was unthinkable for Henry.

Fanshawe Global Securities was the result of an unlikely 80s merger between the old and sleepy commodity traders of Fanshawe and Co. who traced their lineage back to the East India Company and the brash Des Moines Global Securities Investment Bank. Sir Digby Fanshawe, an eminent financier and philanthropist whose portrait dominated the entrance hall, had in the late eighteenth century started trading commodities from the Orient, mainly in order to finance his divorce settlements. Whilst his current wife resided at their stately home in Rutland, Sir Digby would stay in London to manage the firm. This had allowed him to indulge his two favourite pursuits: horseracing and West End actresses. It was a habit continued by many of his male heirs. As a result, the Fanshawe family tree looked more like a circuit diagram for a complicated electronic device, as it would appear to someone with a bad case of multiple vision. Generations later, Henry was the latest and possibly the last Fanshawe of the line to work in the old firm.

He had started moving things around on his desk in a rather desultory fashion when the phone rang. He picked it up, "Henry Fanshawe, Fanshawe's Commodities, can I help you?"

"Hi Henry, it's Mike. Fancy a spot of lunch?"

"Well, I had promised Pikeworth I'd do a bit of desk tidying." Henry waved at the figure some ten yards away who was phoning him, probably to avoid being spotted talking to the condemned man.

"Come on Henry, when have you ever refused? Sweetings, on me."

"Oh, go on then. See you outside at twelve."

When a plate of fish and chips beckoned, desk tidying would have to wait.

3
Henry Really Loses It

So it was that, later in the afternoon, Ryan Pikeworth once again found Henry with his eyes closed and a smile on his face.

"For God's sake Fanshawe, are you ever awake?"

Flustered, Henry attempted to retrieve some of the high ground, "This is my lunch hour. I am quite entitled to spend it as I wish."

Ryan drew himself up to his full five foot three inches, "It's half past three, you arse! My office in fifteen minutes!"

The manager stormed off to his glass fronted office at the side of the trading floor. Henry could see him glaring in the general direction of the spice trading desk where he worked. One of the major disadvantages, in Henry's mind, to these new-fangled open plan offices, was the inability for the rank and file to nod off quietly after a decent lunch. He remembered with some nostalgia the days of the old partnerships.

* * *

When a short while later Henry entered Ryan's office, he was surprised to see the Head of Compliance sitting next to his diminutive manager. His surprise turned to concern when the gentleman stood up and with a policeman's demeanour turned to Henry, "Good afternoon Mr Fanshawe. I wonder if you wouldn't mind coming with me?"

Without preamble he walked out followed by Ryan and a confused Henry. Marched like the condemned man along the rows of desks, they exited the trading floor, and as soon as they were outside, Henry stopped his two grim faced colleagues and exclaimed, "Can someone tell what the hell is going on?"

The Head of Compliance looked back at Henry and replied, "I am not at liberty to discuss this here, Henry. But please come with us and all will be explained very shortly." He pressed the lift button to the executive boardroom floor.

When Henry entered the boardroom, he gasped in spite of himself. The entire board was present, and many turned to look at him as he entered, with faces varying from pity to anger. At the head sat Sir Godfrey Plumborough, ex senior partner, and now Chief Executive of Fanshawe Global. From the mahogany panelled walls, a number of hirsute ancestors stared mercilessly down. Henry shivered.

Sir Godfrey affected examination of his notes, before looking up and adjusting his glasses. "Ah, hello Henry," he murmured in a neutral voice, "please sit down." Henry was ushered by Ryan to a chair positioned slightly away from one end of the boardroom table. He sat, feeling for all the world like a prisoner in the dock.

Sir Godfrey rocked back in his chair and polished his glasses for the fifth time. "So, Henry, tell me, how has business been this year?"

"Pretty good," replied Henry, honestly. "It's amazing how much spice these restaurants get through. Why the other day, the Taj Mahal from Birmingham put in an order for…"

He was cut off by another board member. "Good, you say!" There were muffled comments from those seated, none of which sounded positive to Henry.

"So a profitable year in prospect," went on the Chief Executive.

"I would think so," replied Henry.

"Yes, you've always made a decent amount for the firm."

"Quite."

"Which is why we are frankly quite surprised with the performance this year."

The room was quiet, and Henry felt himself redden. "What do you mean?"

"Well, the figures seem to indicate you have not performed to your usual standard."

"What?" Henry's hackles were rising and he half stood up.

"Yes. There seems to have been an alarming drop in revenue."

Henry was nonplussed. He knew he had done as much as normal, if not a bit better, this year. What was going on?

"An alarming drop, Henry, almost as if…" Sir Godfrey let the sentence hang in the air.

This was the cue for the hiss of indrawn breath from a number of board members and more whispers. Henry thought he made out the word "skimming" from a loud American in the corner.

Sir Godfrey addressed his next question to Ryan, "These are the correct figures, Mr Pikeworth?"

Ryan adjusted his grey suit and replied, "Absolutely, I checked them myself."

The CEO refixed his steely gaze on Henry. "So either you aren't doing as well as you thought, or…"

Henry could hardly contain himself. He jumped to his feet, "You're not suggesting…"

Sir Godfrey readjusted his glasses. "That will be for our auditors to ascertain. Now, in view of the serious nature of this affair, and given that you are the last of the Fanshawes in our employ, I think, Henry, that you should consider your position."

Henry did not know what to say. Having worked in the City for many years, he was well aware of how much revenue he generated, and there was no way he could be doing that badly. Something was happening, something of which he had until now been blissfully unaware. Something had gone wrong, and he was being lined up as the scapegoat. He knew all the signs.

As he rose to plead his case, Sir Godfrey cut him off, "That's all Henry, you can go now."

Speechless, the last of the Fanshawes was led away by Ryan and Compliance back to the trading floor. In the silence of the descending lift, Henry glowered at Ryan. "You had something to do with this, didn't you, you little shit!"

For once Ryan kept his cool. If anything he appeared satisfied. He and Henry had always disliked each other, and it appeared to Henry that the man was almost enjoying this.

Henry continued, "I know I made at least as much this year as last!"

"Don't blame me," replied the grey suited executive, "I don't produce the revenues; I only count them!"

At this point, the Head of Compliance put his hand on Henry's shoulder. Henry angrily shrugged it off. "And you can piss off too, you little Hitler!"

"Mr Fanshawe," the Head of Compliance attempted to look sympathetic and failed. "Mr Fanshawe, I am bound to ask you to clear your desk immediately and vacate the building within half an hour. We will be in touch with you once our investigations are complete. I will send the relevant documentation to your home address shortly. Now, if I can have your pass card please?"

The lift doors opened and the Head of Compliance flew out backwards, followed by an irate Henry, in mid bellow, "And you can shove that pass card anywhere you want!"

Ryan and Henry entered the floor without speaking to each other.

* * *

Henry had managed to appear relatively calm upon entering the trading floor, but on returning to his desk, his situation got the better of him. Arranging the office bin in its most efficient position, he started removing his files and dropping them into it one by one. Having finished with his files, the thought occurred to him that he would probably never enter this floor again, or indeed have anything to do with the world of commodities that had been his life for the past thirty years. As his colleagues watched and began to work out what had transpired upstairs, Henry's behaviour became a little more erratic. He shifted his attention to the TV monitor screens in front of him. First he began calmly to rip out the cabling, then to pull the monitors from their mountings. This equipment followed his files into the bin. Then, a nearby coffee machine. As he eyed up whether the new colour printer would also fit, a colleague realised it was time to stop laughing and act before matters escalated.

He stood up and walked over to his friend, "What's up Henry? I'm no mind reader, but I get the distinct impression that something's bugging you."

Henry paused, holding the colour printer in both hands above his head. The spell was broken, and he suddenly realised that he looked rather foolish. Bringing the printer down onto the desk with slightly more force than was necessary, he stepped back, adjusted his tie and turned towards his friend.

"Sorry about the screens, old boy. Got a little over excited." Henry caught himself. He didn't want to broadcast the true reason for his exit. His mind whirred and quickly settled on a plausible story, "Fact is, they're closing down my section and I've just told our Obergruppenführer to stuff his alternative job offer up his…"

"Henry, ladies present," warned Ted.

"Big fat suburban rectum," continued Henry loudly.

23

"As a result of this altercation, ladies and gentlemen," he now turned to address the growing number of colleagues who had gathered round the desk to witness the scene, "I will be holding court in El Vino's from now until they throw me out. You are all welcome to join me."

There was a muffled cheer and, as Henry placed the last of his personal belongings in his briefcase, a number of colleagues came forward to show quiet sympathy, clap him on the back and generally try to cheer him up. But at this point Henry knew there were only two things likely to cheer him up. One of these carried a mandatory life sentence and the other was red, came in green bottles and could be purchased just down the street from Fanshawes offices. He sensibly decided to pursue the second option.

Henry arrived in El Vino's as the barman was preparing for the evening session. If ever there was a symbol of the old City, El Vino's was it. The walls and roof were stained dark with layers of tobacco smoke, some no doubt exhaled by Samuel Johnson centuries earlier. There had been an outcry when a landlord had decided to repaint the walls white. The small sample section had to be quickly covered with brown paint, to match the murky shade of the untouched original.

On the walls hung paintings in various stages of decomposition. In some one could vaguely recognise an outline of a landscape or some old City dignitary. Others had not worn as well and there was one celebrated picture in the corner which was entirely black save for a few holes where the chemical smog generated by the establishment had eaten right through. The floor was covered in sawdust and the plain wooden tables were surrounded by chairs of differing style, from utilitarian wood to large leather. It was to his favourite of these that Henry headed.

"Afternoon, Charles. Having a small party tonight. Can you leave this bit free for me?"

"Of course, sir."

Charles had been the landlord here for as long as Henry could remember. A white-haired gentleman of impeccable manners and extremely good taste in wine, he also had a right hook renowned throughout the City. This ensured that arguments, and there were many of these as evenings progressed, were quickly settled.

"May I ask the nature of your celebration, sir?"

"Been shafted," Henry snapped, "told the manager to shove his job up…"

"Of course, sir. You are welcome to move the tables aside here for your party." Charles's manner managed to combine sympathy for Henry with delight for an evening that promised to be an excellent earner.

Henry sat down in his habitual position and examined the room. It was a place that had almost become a home from home. In the corner there were two retired brokers who resolutely returned for lunch every Friday, though they had long ceased to work in the City. He nodded a greeting. On another secluded table, a headhunter was plotting with a gentleman where to move next. Henry recognised the gent as a client, and waved at him.

"Moving again, Joe?" he shouted,

"Not so loud, Henry, please," grinned his friend. "Walls have ears, you know."

"Might need your headhunter's number, Joe. Just been canned!" Henry tried to put a brave face on it and remain his normal, jovial self. But it was starting to sink in, and to tell the truth, he was feeling fairly low.

"Charles, a couple of bottles of the Angludet 2002 and some cheese and biscuits, please."

He settled himself down and waited for his friends.

News travels quickly in the City, and nothing travels quicker than news of a leaving party. It was not long after five when the first cohorts of friends and acquaintances that Henry had developed over thirty years started arriving. In the normal City fashion there were the briefest of expressions of sympathy, a pat on the back, and wishes for good luck in finding something else. This was followed by a rapid move towards the waiting glasses to get down to more serious matters.

Henry moved in and out amongst the crowd taking these titbits of consolation and trying to appear cheerful about it. He had lost count of the times that he told colleagues that 'he had a few irons in the fire' or 'he had been thinking of a move to consultancy for a while'. In truth he had no irons, no fires and no idea of what being a consultant actually entailed. He was stuck the wrong side of fifty, and worst of all, everyone knew it. And shortly they would know about the real reason for his dismissal. He realised that he had been framed but by whom? His only plan of note was very short-term: to drink as much of the 2002 Angludet vintage as possible before either closing time or unconsciousness.

He was gratified at least by the amount of people that turned up to his wake. Through the years Henry had become, unbeknownst to himself, something of a celebrity. His refusal to accept the dress-down concept and his scorn for Health and Safety directives in general, and the Clean Desk policy in particular, had provided a rallying point for others less vocal in their opinions. And his willingness to help colleagues, sometimes to his own detriment, and to mentor younger blood, had made him very popular.

After a while, Charles the landlord put out a sign announcing *El Vino closed – private party*. The crowd packed themselves in to the already full wine bar. Still people kept coming, spilling out on to the cobbled street outside with their wine glasses full and their voices set at maximum bray. At one point, as Henry's boss walked out of Fanshawe's building to his bus, they started an impromptu rendition of the conga to serenade him. He stood in the queue for some time to the strains of "Ryan is a wanker, Ryan is a wanker, la la la la, la la la la" in the background.

A drunken friend lurched up to Henry as he looked on, "Amazing isn't it? Pikeworth's being serenaded from the pub and he doesn't even realise it's your leaving do!"

"Not really," replied Henry. "Ryan thinks my departure celebrations are on a different day and in a different place. I've just emailed him an invite."

"Where?"

"Deptford Empire, this Wednesday."

"Wednesday?"

"Yes, Wednesday – Tranny night."

He made it through to closing time, just. As the crowds bade him farewell and melted away, he was left paying a bar bill the size of which, Charles remarked, would have supported a small northern town for at least a week.

As he tried with varying degrees of success to connect meaningfully with the card machine, the publican stood patiently by.

"What am I going to do next, Charles?" he asked plaintively. Alcohol had begun to steer him towards maudlin self-pity.

Charles had seen this happen so many times over his forty year tenure of the city El Vino that he had amassed a great deal of knowledge about what to say in such situations. He took off his glasses, polished them studiously and then turned to the unhappy ex-banker, "Don't worry, sir. I am sure something will turn up."

Having dispensed this small pearl of wisdom, he then addressed the emptying room.

"Gentlemen, time please!" Followed by a pause. "So fuck off."

4
The Morning After

Henry stumbled through the door into his flat at around midnight. He had managed, he felt, to negotiate with some distinction the three flights of stairs in the mansion block behind Victoria Street. Unfortunately all this good work had come to nought when he attempted unsuccessfully to let himself into the flat next door. This was currently occupied by a charming though quiet Japanese businessman, whose look of disdain upon opening the door to find an incoherent and drunk Englishman, would haunt Henry for some considerable time thereafter. Chastened, though still lacking in several of his normal motor functions, Henry managed, at the second attempt, to locate his own flat on the landing and some long minutes later to let himself in.

The flat was, as usual, in a bit of a mess. He had a cleaner, a frosty little Scot who tutted her way around, but to her credit managed to repair most of the damage wrought weekly by Henry on his surroundings. It was then pristine for approximately twenty-four hours before the inevitable force of nature that was its owner returned it to a state which he liked to call 'lived in'.

Although somewhat unkempt, Henry's flat was, underneath the layer of detritus, both elegant and tasteful. Each year, some of his bonus would be spent in the auction rooms of Christie's and Sotheby's on his three major passions in life: nineteenth and twentieth century French landscapes, claret, and cricket. As a result, his walls were adorned with a number of exquisite watercolours and oils, from the earlier Barbizon school depictions of the forest of Fontainebleau, to some strident post-Impressionist panoramas of Provence.

In the kitchen, the wine rack (within a glass case at constant temperature) contained the latest batch of 1985 grand cru Bordeaux to be delivered from his cellars at the Berry Bros. And adorning various corners of the drawing room, arrayed against the rich plum carpet and wallpaper, stood cricket bats, some clearly aged, some relatively new, and all sporting various England cricket campaign badges and team signatures. Shelves groaned under the weight of bails, photos and cricket balls. It came as no surprise to Henry that he was constantly being harassed by the MCC to bequeath his collection to the museum at Lord's.

Upon the mantelpiece stood a black and white photo in a silver frame. The picture was of a beautiful young woman on the arm of a smiling man.

Henry often spoke to this photo when he alone in the flat. The wedding day on which it was taken seemed such a long time ago. He had been so happy and excited that day. All the possibilities of a life shared crowded back into his head, as he gazed drunkenly at the two faces smiling back at him "Well V, gone and done it now, haven't I!"

Vanessa had been a friend since childhood, though

for most of his teenage and university years, Henry had been absent from the country manor which was his home. When he met her again, at a ball in London, he had been bowled over by the transformation from gap-toothed tomboy to lithe and beautiful woman. Vanessa had lost none of the irreverence and wit that Henry remembered from years long gone. She had always been the one to get into trouble, usually with him dragged along, unwillingly, at her side.

They had married at twenty-four and had spent a few blissful years in London, he learning the spice trade, she finishing the lengthy training period undertaken in order to become a vet. They were going to move back to the country once she had qualified.

He smiled as he remembered those years. That golden era before the first NHS letter landed on the doormat one day, advising an urgent visit to hospital. They convinced each other that it was nothing. But one test became two, then three. It was impossible to block out the grim reality. Then the achingly awful morning they were both called in for the verdict.

"About a year if the treatment works, maybe three or four months if not." Henry's throat tightened every time he recalled that day. Followed by an awful six months seeing Vanessa waste away. And the guilt he felt, as the fervent wish for just a little more time with her warred with a longing for such suffering to be finally ended.

It was all an age ago, he told himself, such an age ago. Time heals, he had been constantly reminded. Except that it doesn't. The sadness merely gets concealed, overgrown by the rest of life. Like an underground river it continues to exist, disappearing beneath the sands, only to well up suddenly from time to time, deep, cold and strong flowing as ever.

Henry had suffered periods of melancholy, and apart from the odd fling had never really dipped his toes in this pool again. There was one other woman, from his office, which might have gone further, but in the end he reckoned that the potential for heartache and loss just wasn't worth it. So he just carried on, sharing the odd story with the photo if things got hard, which usually provided a modicum of comfort.

By now the ex-banker was staggering from side-to-side, one hand supporting the wall, the other clasped round a doner kebab that seemed to him to be disgorging its contents onto the floor. He pinpointed two large blurred leather armchairs, took an educated guess at which one was the real one, and slumped into its cosy embrace.

"Bugger."

A pause.

"Bugger, bugger, oh bloody buggery buggeration."

Then there was quiet. Henry had run out of things to say on the subject. In fact, his body had given up the fight against the large amounts of wine poured into it over the evening. The room fell quiet for a short while, before beginning to shake in time with the quite indescribable rhythm and tone of his snoring.

* * *

The sun was up and shining straight into his face when Henry awoke. Habit caused him to look worriedly at his watch, then at his suit, then at the remains of a kebab perched on his midriff.

"Bugger."

Sleep had not led to an improvement in vocabulary.

"Oh shit, late for work!"

Henry stumbled towards the bathroom and was standing over the basin, razor poised, when he remembered.

"Oh shit, not late for work. No buggering work anymore."

He continued shaving, all the while removing various items which may once have been in a kebab from his person.

"That bastard Ryan!"

Moments from the previous twenty-four hours began to filter through the haze into his aching brain: in particular, the awful moment when he realised that he was being framed for some attempt at raking off profits. He would never work in the City again, whatever the result. Try as he might, he could not erase the memory of the twisted smile that his opponent attempted unsuccessfully to hide, as he was walking back to office, having cheerfully provided the evidence to dismantle Henry's career.

"The cunning bastard," muttered Henry. "Talk about being set up! Walked into it like a lamb to the slaughter."

He was still reflecting when the phone rang. Henry had forgotten to put the answering machine on, and had to think quickly, which in his current state was not easy. With shaking hands, he picked up the receiver.

"I am sorry, but Henry Fanshawe is out at the moment. If you would like to leave a message, please speak after the tone. Beeeeep."

33

For a moment there was silence.

"Oh for God's sake Henry, you arse, it's Charles. I know that's you, so cut the crap."

Unfortunately Henry's efforts at mimicry had not yet attained a level sufficient to fool his elder brother, the Honourable Charles Fanshawe. He croaked a hoarse greeting into the phone.

Charles got straight to the point, "I hear you're in a spot of bother down at the firm. What on earth have you done now?"

"Some bastard's framed me. I'm out, Charles – finished."

"Henry, sometimes you are a complete idiot."

"At least it's only sometimes, Charlie."

"What do you mean by that?" His brother's voice took on an even sharper tone, "As the last remaining Fanshawe in the business, you have a heavy responsibility."

"So, I got the work and you got the inheritance," Henry replied with a touch of bitterness. "Well, I've had it with that place."

"But what else can you do?" asked Charles. "You haven't any qualifications, and I can't see you getting a great reference from your employers."

"No idea – I rather thought I would take a holiday and see what comes up."

"Typical, bury your head in the sand as usual."

"If it is sand on the French Riviera you refer to – absolutely!"

"Well, your life I suppose. By the way, you *are* coming to the reading of Aunt Esme's will this afternoon, aren't you?"

Henry straightened up rapidly, and then, clutching his head, wished he hadn't.

"This afternoon?"

"Yes, didn't you call them as requested, or get my message last Saturday?" his brother sighed. "I don't suppose you've even read the letter!"

"No, yes, and yes."

"Well, Kirby has flown in from the Seychelles this morning to meet us and I would advise you to be in the Reform club at three pm sharp. He seemed particularly insistent that you be there – can't think why."

"I'll be there – see you then, Charlie."

"Over and out."

Henry replaced the receiver. Charles wasn't really too bad, he thought, for an older brother, but the family settlement, whereby he received everything and Henry next to nothing, still rankled.

'So, the Reform at three.' Henry mused whilst dressing, and, almost unconsciously, working out whether he had time for a quick sharpener in the pub opposite beforehand.

* * *

Donning his coat a few hours later, Henry walked out of the flat, down the stairs and into the street where he managed to hail a cab almost instantly.

"The Reform Club please." He settled back into the cosy black leather of the taxi. "Maybe my luck's in today."

The cabbie was a world expert on the UK economy. His specialist topics also covered Ken Livingstone, roadworks, traffic calming devices, cyclists, and much else. As he wove his way through the London traffic, he was keen to share this knowledge with his passenger, in a stream of banter that would have been described in guide books as 'lively cockney'. Henry, for his part, settled back to think on the forthcoming meeting, whilst remembering to hum notes of mild assent and the odd "Really!" in response to the driver's more insistent points.

The taxi halted halfway up Pall Mall. Henry gave him a generous tip and stepped out beside the large staircase leading up to the Club's entrance. His family had been members for generations, as befitted their status of Victorian liberals and reformers. He walked in, turned his mobile phone off, and paused to wish the doorman a good afternoon. This man, who had stood by the entrance to the Club for all of Henry's adult life, and must therefore be well into his seventies, knew each of the one thousand two hundred and thirty six members by name.

"Good afternoon, Mr Fanshawe. You will find your party waiting in the Small Library."

"Thank you, Hampton."

Henry moved through the capacious neo-gothic central hall of the Club to the grand staircase, nodding the odd unspoken greeting at a member he recognised, settled into large leather armchairs with a post-luncheon digestif and a copy of the *Racing Times*. The only thing missing Henry thought with some regret, was that layer of cigar smoke which used to drift like incense through the hall after lunch. Bloody nanny state.

It was close to the appointed hour, so Henry mounted the stairs and moved soundlessly towards the door of the

Small Library. He was about to open it, when from inside he heard the sound of raised voices, one of which he recognised as that of his brother. He stopped and listened.

"What do you mean he's getting that!"

Then a somewhat quieter response to his brother's outburst that Henry couldn't make out.

Then his brother again, even louder, "Well it's all highly irregular!"

Taking a deep breath, Henry knocked on the door and entered. The Small Library was in fact the size of minor department store. Books donated from members or bequeathed from old collections formed a strange and varied mix on the shelves. Given the breadth of members' interests, it was quite possible to find, between leather bound volumes titled *Reminiscences of the Italian Campaign 1943/4*: Major R.M. Quiver and *Pacifism and its Place in Today's World*: Bishop N. Vestry, and a well-thumbed copy of *Bedroom Capers: My experiences in pre-War Hollywood*: Curtis Lestrange. However, the library also contained works of real interest and value. Some years before there had been a minor scandal when a member had been found 'borrowing' some copies which later appeared in the British Museum library. Apart from his summary expulsion, this faux-pas was believed to have been the main reason behind his failure to attain the post of Prime Minister (at least initially).

Henry strode into the room and headed towards the large mahogany dining table. Next to the lanky and slightly balding figure that was his brother Charles sat a florid man, with curly black hair and a tie which was too loud for the surroundings. Upon Henry's entrance, he rose from his chair and bounded forward towards the door. There was a look of some relief on his face.

"Henry Fanshawe? Jolly good to meet. My client was always talking about you."

"Aunt Esme?"

"That's right. Allow me to introduce myself, the name's Kirby, Xavier Kirby. I have had the pleasure of representing your aunt for many years."

"Representing?"

"Oh, you know, the odd claim for damages, and such like."

"I didn't know Esme had been libelled."

"Oh no, Mr Fanshawe. These were for damages inflicted *by* Mrs Fanshawe, on other people, or to be more exact, on their property. In her car. Your aunt unfortunately never could get used to the concept of a red light or indeed any other road advisory signage. It was in the end to prove her undoing."

"She seems to have been a woman of mass destruction," Charles added ungallantly.

"On the contrary, she was an angel," Kirby's demeanour combined heartfelt admiration and mild reproof. "The village of St Christol would not have lasted without her. We are all bereft. The Fanshawe legacy will be remembered for a long time."

Henry moved to the table and sat down in one of the chairs. A large amount of paperwork had been laid out, and he was anxious to get started. There had not been much time for an aperitif prior to this meeting, and a longing for some hair of the dog was starting to creep upon him. Best get this over and done with quickly, he thought to himself, so I can get out before Charlie asks me to join him for a cup of tea and some totally unwanted advice.

"Can we begin?"

Mr Kirby moved over to join Henry at the table, whilst Charles leant sullenly against the wall in the shadows. Adjusting a large pair of black spectacles, Kirby picked up one impressive looking document, and passed it to Henry.

"LAST WILL AND TESTAMENT OF
ESMERELDA HARRIET JOSEPHINE
FANSHAWE, WIFE OF THE LATE CUTHBERT
DIGORY STANSTED FANSHAWE"

The seal had been broken. Henry looked up enquiringly.

"Your brother has read its contents already," Kirby explained, "but I think that you may find them rather more interesting than he did."

Henry opened the document and started reading:

I Esmerelda Fanshawe of Fanshawe Manor, St Christol, Beauvallon, being of sound mind and body, do hereby bequeath my worldly goods as follows. To my nephew, the Honourable Charles Windlesham Fanshawe, a bound set of Dickens novels, and my copy of How to be an Interesting Conversationalist *by H.V. Fenton, together with the advice to read it thoroughly in the hope that one day he will be able to speak for more than thirty seconds without encouraging suicidal thoughts in his listeners.*

Henry chortled. Out of the corner of his eye he could make out the spindly figure of his brother glaring at him. He could now see why the old chap had been so put out. Aunt Esme never pulled a punch, always referring to Charlie in her letters as 'Death by Conversation'. He read on,

To my nephew, the somewhat less Honourable Henry Stewart Fanshawe, whose company and letters I enjoyed so much, I bequeath the balance of my estate, my house, Fanshawe Manor, its contents and my portfolio of stocks and shares together with any income thereon.

Henry rocked back in his chair, almost unable to contain his surprise at this positive turn of events. His luck most certainly was in today. Whilst hardly wealthy beyond the dreams of avarice, the Seychelles' Fanshawes had been more than comfortable, and family photos indicated a house on Mahé island which was clearly a fine example of the Victorian colonial style. A decent sale would provide Henry with means quite adequate enough for a happy and unproductive future life. Henry turned the page.

The above bequest is conditional upon two matters. First, Henry Fanshawe must agree to live in Fanshawe Manor for a period of at least ten years, and second, he must undertake to continue the fine work of the Esme Fanshawe club whilst in residence.

This put rather a different slant on things. Henry was certainly not averse to living on tropical islands, but for ten years rather than two weeks? And what was the 'fine work' of the eponymous club referred to? Good God, it could be a WI-type affair! Henry imagined himself leading a group of Seychellois women in a chorus of *Jerusalem* before attending a lecture on the finer points of cheese scones. The picture filled him with horror.

On the other hand, he reflected, what was left for him here? No job, and with the stigma of a financial investigation pending, no prospect of moving firm. He had a well-decorated but ultimately inhibiting flat in London. And then there were those awful Christmas lunches with Charles, his haughty wife, Caroline, and their dreadfully spoilt children. Not enough money and too many relations. He would miss the cricket of course, but satellite TV and an encouraging proximity to India should make up for that. And, he mused, for the first time in a while he would not be in the middle of a crowded, noise-ridden city. On Mahé, he could take his saxophone and play outside under the stars, any night of the year, without Mrs Craig from upstairs calling the police. And if he was going down for some trumped up fraud case, he could at least enjoy the interim on a tropical island.

Mr Kirby adjusted his glasses and leant forward over Henry's shoulder. Henry could feel the disconcertingly hot breath of the lawyer on his neck as with barely suppressed excitement the lawyer whispered in his ear.

"Please consider this offer seriously Mr Fanshawe. The late Mrs Fanshawe always said that you could be trusted to make the right decision, and St Christol without a Fanshawe would be like… would be like…."

"Laurel without Hardy?" ventured Henry.

41

"I was going to say Torvill without Dean."

Henry was still trying to work out why Kirby, an islander from the tropics, had alluded to two figure skaters from the Eighties, when the lawyer straightened up.

"I am afraid that I have to catch this evening's flight back to Mahé, and I need to return with your answer. Would you like me to step outside whilst you reflect on the matter?"

"No need, Kirby, no need." Henry got to his feet and clapped a large right hand round that of the lawyer. "The answer's yes – a man would have to be an idiot not to agree to it!"

"Not in your case Henry," Charles interjected from the corner of the room where he stood sulking.

"Excellent, Henry, absolutely excellent!" The grin on the face of the attorney widened to a large and genuine smile, "I can assure you that you will not regret it."

He started rearranging the various papers on the table and packing them into his briefcase.

"And now gentlemen, I must leave for the airport. It has been a pleasure meeting you both, and I look forward to seeing you, Henry, in a short while, back home."

But Henry another question, "Before you go, Mr Kirby, can I ask one thing?"

"Of course, go ahead,"

"This club that Mrs Fanshawe mentioned – what sort of club is it?"

Mr Xavier Kirby paused by the door and smiled again. "That, I am afraid, Mr Fanshawe, is one of the few pieces of information which your dear aunt expressly asked me to withhold. I think that she wanted it to be a surprise for you. Good afternoon, gentlemen."

And with a nod of the head, he exited the room, leaving Henry and his less than contented brother to themselves.

"It's a bloody cheek, that's what it is, a bloody cheek. Never could stand the woman!" Charles paced up and down the room, cheeks scarlet with ill-disguised fury.

"I think, dear brother, that the feeling may have been mutual." Henry found it hard to mask his glee at the outcome of the meeting, but felt that, for the sake of future relations, it might be sensible to restrain from too open a display of Schadenfreude.

"Well, I'm off. Can't be hanging around here doing nothing!"

"Of course, why do nothing here, when you could be doing nothing so much more comfortably at home in Rutland," Henry observed cheerfully.

His brother muttered a cursory goodbye and without making eye contact, strode from the room leaving an almost visible slipstream of disappointment and envy behind him.

Checking the door was closed and his brother departed, Henry stood by the table staring again at the documents lying open upon it. The giggle that had previously threatened could not be held back, and as it gained momentum within him, he found his feet moving into a little jig on the floor. And, as his moves became more animated, restraint fell away ever further. "What the hell!" he muttered, and jumped up on a chair and thence to the table. Clapping his hands in time to an imaginary banjo, and attempting steps inappropriate for a man of his years, he did not notice the door open.

"Will that be all, sir?"

Henry froze in mid twirl and glanced over to see the club butler standing by the door. How, Henry wondered, could this man appear by magic and then transmit such an air of reproach without altering his expression in any way?

"So sorry, Hampton, but I have just received a bit of rather good news." Henry desisted from his routine and stepped down off the table.

"Evidently so, sir." The words, heavy with disdain, emerged and dropped like large boulders into the quiet room.

After an awkward pause, Henry collected his papers together, desperately trying to think of something to say to defuse the situation, "I expect you have seen worse, eh, Hampton?"

"I expect so, sir." And with this, the butler dematerialised in the same mysterious manner as he had appeared.

A few minutes later, Henry walked down the wide carpeted stairs towards the entrance lobby. He collected his coat and strode out into the evening sunlight. Dusk had started to fall over the city, staining the stone buildings along Pall Mall a deep pink. He walked briskly down to Trafalgar Square to find a cab, weaving his way through the commuters headed for their evening train. Unusually, the elation he felt at the afternoon's news did not lead him to the nearest pub. In fact, he didn't really feel like a drink at all. His feet may have been pounding the London pavement, but his mind was already far away, surveying the white coral sand, the clear blue sea, and the lush greenery of a tropical rain forest.

PREPARATION

5
A Fresh Start

Henry awoke with a start. Adjusting to the glare of the morning sun, he sensed that he was not in his normal bed. In fact, he was not in a bed at all. As the world swam into focus, he found that he was looking into the deep brown eyes of a woman with golden skin and a perfect set of white teeth. These facts momentarily confused him.

"Would you like some coffee, sir?"

In a moment of clarity he realised he was still on the plane. The overnight flight to the island of Mahé in the Seychelles was the first step in his new life. It was tolerably comfortable in Business Class and the wine had been adequate, though Henry always found it difficult to sleep in the sitting position. He was now feeling stiff and slightly jaded. Out of the window he could see the rough, arid mountains of the horn of Africa falling away behind him as the plane flew out over the Indian Ocean. Small white clouds, their shadows dark upon the sea beneath, dotted the horizon, but as yet there was no sign of the granitic island peaks which would herald landfall.

"That would be most kind, my dear," he responded.

Over a cup of coffee, and the usual cubist study in grey that was the airline breakfast, he mused on his changed circumstances. It had only been a few weeks previously that life-changing events had taken place. It had not taken long to pack up his flat, taking with him the cream of his beloved cricket memorabilia (the rest finally went to Lord's), his favourite paintings and of course his saxophone. The apartment had been let out to a friend, who promised to keep a spare room for Henry whenever he returned. Aunt Esme's will allowed for occasional trips away from the Seychelles, so long as 'the running and management of the club was not in any way compromised'.

Henry wondered again what on earth this mysterious club entailed. Esme's likes and dislikes had been so bizarre and numerous that it could literally have been anything. He had read and reread the will for clues, but there were none. Esme had evidently taken care that the element of surprise should not be compromised.

Well, won't be long before I find out, he thought, and set to working out the events for which he would return. The first Summer Test at Lord's, next year's performance of *Turandot* at Glyndebourne. He would, he thought, have to put in at least one or two appearances at his brother's place, though, if well timed, these visits might be arranged so as to coincide with the absence of the children, and especially of their violin playing daughter. Henry was devoted to music, and nothing annoyed him more than the sound of a totally tone-deaf child carving out some classical masterpiece on a violin in a fashion which, had it been in public, would have contravened most of the

UK's Health and Safety legislation. His brother's musical soirees were, to Henry, a form of exquisite torture that he would most certainly not miss.

As he sat back in his seat and attacked the item wishfully described as scrambled egg on the tray before him, Henry felt a quiet satisfaction steal over him. He donned his headphones, turned the switch to Mozart and settled back to enjoy the remaining hour or so in the air.

Before long the plane began to bank and lose altitude in its run up to Mahé airport. Henry looked out of the window and could see the occasional smaller island appearing beneath him, and then in the distance a much larger silhouette towards which the plane was heading. As they drew closer, details began to emerge. The island moved from uniform grey to variegated colour. All of a sudden, Henry could make out the deep green of the palm trees and banana plantations, and the red corrugated iron roofs of houses. Trails of white below resolved themselves into ships steaming towards the harbour, and the granite peaks took on a purple hue in the early morning sun. Then, as the sea moved up to meet them, with a light shudder, the plane touched down on the tarmac.

Henry donned his jacket. He stood firmly by the belief that a jacket should be worn at all times when outside, a belief that was about to be sorely tested as the cabin door was opened. He stepped out through the door, and the warm damp air of the Seychelles hit him like a warm wet towel. Within an instant, he was sweating profusely and wondering how on earth his ancestors could possibly have survived here, dressed in their frock coats, ties and top hats. In a move that would have surprised his many friends back home, Henry took off his blazer and rolled up his shirt sleeves, before proceeding into the terminal building.

The Seychelles immigration control department conformed to the general rule that the length of time spent queuing for entry into a country is in inverse proportion to its size. After an interminable interval, Henry made it to the passport control officer and placed his papers on the desk. Without a flicker of emotion the officer examined them. Then, rising slowly from his chair, to a chorus of exasperated sighs from those passengers behind Henry, he beckoned, "Please step this way, sir, there is someone who wants to see you."

Henry fought off the entirely unwarranted pangs of guilt which assail even the most innocent of travellers when called into a private room at an airport. He followed the uniformed figure to a large door in the corner of the terminal, marked Chief of Police. At this point he began to feel more seriously concerned. Had Pikeworth framed him on some trafficking charge? Was his entry visa correct? He opened the door and went in.

"Ah, Mr Fanshawe, we have been expecting you."

Henry looked over at the diminutive and almost skeletal figure of the Chief of Police sitting behind his desk. All that was missing in Henry's imagination was the white cat perched, purring, upon the knee. With a face etched with unmoving blankness, and mirror glasses which gave no clue to the eyes behind them, the chief continued, "My name is René Mahjoud. I am the Chief of Police. You are the nephew of the late Esmerelda Fanshawe, are you not?"

"I am. May I ask what this is about?" Henry was making mental notes on the letter to the British High

50

Commissioner that he would shortly be sending from his prison cell.

The Chief of Police rose slowly from his chair and crossed the room towards Henry. Then he took off his glasses and broke into a wide smile, "Welcome, on behalf of the Government of the Seychelles. We hope you have a very happy time here and carry on her good work."

"You knew her?"

"She was everyone's favourite woman, at least, when she was not driving!"

Relief flowed in waves over Henry. He sat down on a nearby stool and wiped his brow with a silk handkerchief entirely unsuited to the purpose. The chief started pumping him by the hand, and then holding the door open clicked his heels and bowed very slightly. "We have a car waiting to take you to St Christol with our compliments. I look forward to seeing you again soon at the club."

It seemed to Henry that surprising events were rapidly becoming a part of his life.

Henry walked out of the air-conditioned terminal, bags in hand, back into the sweltering humidity. Standing by the kerb whilst his car was being called, he was struck by the immense fecundity of the landscape. Earth of a rich red hue supported a profusion of trees and shrubs, all pushing towards the sun with vitality so apparent that he imagined he could almost see the plants growing. Between the multi-coloured flowers and against the deep green of the tropical foliage, birds of every shade wheeled, filling the air with deafening song. Steam billowed slowly off the road after a recent downpour. Further up, the high mountains at the island's centre were swathed in clouds

51

which occasionally parted to give sudden and unexpected views of the high angular peaks of pink granite.

As Henry, open mouthed, was taking in this scene, a police car drew up beside him and a large friendly female face leant out of the window, "Is you the new Fanshawe?"

"I am, madam, at your service." Henry laid on the old school charm and was rewarded with a hearty laugh from the driver.

"Well, get your butt in here and I'll take you home."

Henry stepped into the car and was about to start polite conversation with his driver when an unknown hand pushed him back against the seat with some violence. He then realised that this was in fact the G force engendered by the car pulling away with a speed that would have graced Formula One. 'If his aunt had been considered dangerous relative to this type of driving', he mused, 'she must have been bloody lethal'.

As terminal velocity was reached and Henry found blood returning to his extremities, he leaned forward and asked the woman how far it was to his aunt's house.

Negotiating the curves at terrifying speed, one hand on the wheel, she replied, "You ain't been here before then?"

"Never managed to get round to it. But I have heard a lot about it from my aunt." Henry decided to lay on a little charm.

"Though she never told me how attractive the women's police uniforms were." The officer was wearing a dress of loud pink peonies on an electric green background.

There was a peal of laughter from the front of the car. "Uniform? This ain't no uniform. I'm allowed to wear a dress because I'm just too darned fat to get into the uniform!" And with this she rammed her foot down on the accelerator, throwing Henry back into the seat again. Giggling like a schoolgirl, she sped along the road out of the airport and towards St Christol.

Despite the startling speed at which the journey was conducted, it still took around half an hour to reach the house. As the car crested the ridge, Henry stared open-mouthed at the panorama which greeted him. Beauvallon was a large and beautiful bay with sand the colour of snow and fringed with palms and tamarisk. The colours, etched sharp against the blue sky, reminded him of the most violently coloured of his Fauvist paintings, currently pitching in some container ship on their trip over.

As he gazed, the car left the coast and turned abruptly uphill, flinging Henry into the depths of his seat again. There seemed, at first sight, to be no houses there at all. But as the road climbed, Henry realised that they were entering a small saddle-shaped valley set into the mountains and invisible from below. The road, never particularly high grade, ran half-heartedly through a hamlet. Henry noticed a sign "St Christol Welcomes Careful Drivers" hanging precariously from one dented support, and thought again of his departed aunt. As they passed a row of little white bungalows with red corrugated iron roofs, the road gradually gave way to two lines of concrete. Then this too ran out, leaving Henry bouncing about over a cart track and pushing through the hanging green fronds of the jungle.

The car slowed, and Henry was able to spot for the first time the house which he had been bequeathed. The road ended in a black wrought-iron gate. Within the tracery of the iron he could make out the words, Fanshawe Manor. Beyond lay a large circular gravelled drive, with a small lawn and palm tree in the centre. From the drive a set of large white stone steps rose towards a veranda.

It looked to Henry as if little had changed since the days of the old black and white photographs his aunt had sent. The house was a perfect example of the grand colonial style prevalent in the final days of Empire and had clearly been well kept. There were two floors, each with a veranda, and the sloping roof was composed of immaculately painted corrugated iron. The weather-boarded walls were spotlessly white and heavy cream curtains hung in the large windows. At the door stood a small figure, arms folded.

Henry bade his driver farewell and hauled his luggage out of the boot, relieved to find it still in one piece, and strode up the gravel to the steps at the front of the house. Although still early, it was already swelteringly hot and he could feel the rivulets of sweat running down his back as he heaved the case up the steps to the black front door. He put it down, breathing heavily, and proffered a hand to the diminutive female figure at the door waiting for him.

"Good morning, Mr Fanshawe. Please follow me." The woman turned and marched into the semi-darkness of the interior, leaving Henry's hand flapping in mid-air. He had not noticed a smile or indeed any other sign of welcome, and so in a bid to humour her, he picked up his case again and hurried inside after the retreating figure.

She paused at the bottom of a fine wide staircase. Henry's eyes had hardly grown accustomed to the gloom but he could see that his greeter was still not smiling.

"Your room is first on the left. I have made up the bed. Bathroom second on the right. Luncheon is at twelve-thirty in the dining room. Over there, through the door by the grandfather clock. Good day Mr Fanshawe."

And with that she was turning to leave. Henry sensed that he needed to move quickly if he was to glean any more information from her in the near future. He proffered his hand for a second time.

"How do you do, Mrs er....er."

"Call me Cilla." She stood stock-still.

Henry lamely removed his large and extremely sweaty hand. "Of course, Mrs... er... Cilla. Please call me Henry."

"Yes Mr Fanshawe." A short pause. "Will that be all?"

"I suppose so, Cilla."

"Then I will see you at luncheon. Good morning."

"Good morning Cilla."

But Henry by then was already talking to thin air, as the housekeeper had vanished through a door on one side of the stairs. He caught a brief glimpse of the old fashioned kitchen behind it.

Left alone, Henry stood by his bags and turned slowly round to review the fine hall in which he found himself. In addition to the large staircase, the hall was panelled and floored in dark tropical wood, clearly polished with loving care until it glowed. Arranged on the walls were portraits of the Seychellois contingent of Fanshawes, and some other ancestors whom Henry recognised from similar portraits in his boyhood home. On either side of the staircase stood two large Victorian earthenware jars in the Oriental style, each holding a majestic fern. Several cabinets and some faux French second empire chairs stood against the wall.

The glass fronted cabinets displayed a range of curios, including one which Henry recalled his aunt mentioning. He had always wanted to see the famous artefact known in the family as 'Esme's shrunken head'. Most of his siblings discounted this tale as a fiction, but Henry had believed, and it was a pleasure to be proved right. He wondered if somewhere he would happen upon the 'stuffed tiger's manhood', that Esme would also describe in a loud voice at dinner parties, usually, and probably intentionally, choosing quite the wrong moment to do so.

He walked to the large double doors on one side of the hall and found himself moving through into the drawing room. Again, this was floored with a hard dark wood of local origin. It was papered with a beautiful oriental blue flower pattern. Large French windows opened onto a veranda at the back of the house. Next to the standard sofa and armchairs stood a large black grand piano. Henry's eyes lit up. He was no pianist, preferring the soft tones of his tenor sax, but he could find his way about a keyboard and had always wished to improve his technique. He moved towards it, laid his fingers on the keys and pressed. The sound that ensued was not beautiful. In fact it was not even of single pitch. Making a mental note to get the piano tuned as soon as possible, Henry turned towards the French windows, opened them and made his way onto the veranda.

The back of the house stood open to the higher reaches of the hidden valley, overhung with lush green vegetation, and spotted with the brilliant hues of tropical flowers. At the end of a large and immaculate lawn, trimmed with herbaceous borders in a most English of styles, stood a mango tree, heavy with ripe fruit. Henry had always wanted to see these tropical delicacies in their natural state and was spellbound. As he walked down the stairs to the lawn, a powerful and pungent gust of spice caught his attention. He followed the scent and ended up standing in front of a tall tree with large shiny green leaves and red brown bark. Henry laughed with delight. It was a cinnamon tree. Next door was a nutmeg in flower. How ironic, Henry thought, that having been closed down as a spice trader in London, he was going to be spending the next period of his life in such close proximity to the real thing.

Henry walked along the scented path, hemmed on one side by exotic shrubs and trees and on the other by the beautifully-kept borders of more recognisable flowers. As he moved, the garden seemed to grow; its corners, like that of the whole valley, hidden until he was almost upon them. There was a large space at the end of the main garden, delineated by a high hedge, and it was towards a white gate in this hedge that Henry headed. It was impossible to see through the abundant foliage and hanging vines quite what lay beyond. There was some lettering on the gate which Henry could not yet quite make out.

As he approached, the words upon it swam into focus.

PLEASE DO NOT WALK ON THE SQUARE
BY ORDER OF THE E F C C

Henry looked around for a square to avoid, but finding none, he tried the gate. It swung open with a loud squeal to reveal what lay beyond.

Some of Henry's favourite childhood books had been those written about the mythical land of Narnia by C S Lewis. In *The Silver Chair*, his personal favourite, there was a point at which, at the end of a school grounds, on a dark wet winter's evening, two children opened a nondescript door in the back wall. Instead of finding the grey, damp country beyond, they peered through the opening into the fabled land of Narnia, whose setting sun drenched their faces and lit up the surroundings in gold. A doorway to another world.

Had Henry any room in his head to think, this is the image which would have returned to him. For through the gate there stood a perfectly proportioned cricket pitch. His mouth had opened so wide there was some danger that he might swallow a significant amount of the insect life buzzing around him. He turned his head slowly left and right, marvelling at the scene. A professional county sized oval lay before him, with the square roped off. Sight boards balanced on large concrete wheels at each end, and at fifteen-yard intervals around the oval, small white markers indicated the boundary. To his right stood a white clubhouse. On the front veranda, a number of deck chairs were stacked up beside a scoreboard and a large pile of black metal slates bearing numbers and letters.

The whole pitch was surrounded with towering and graceful mahoganies, and the severe black-trunked iron wood trees which, together with the narrowing sides of the valley, served to leave the area completely invisible from any viewpoint save that further up the hillside. Henry gazed in silent awe at such unexpected beauty. Barely able to keep himself from running in his excitement, he made his way round to the club house. On a large plaque over the door he found, at last, the solution to the mystery bequeathed him by his aunt. For in bold lettering below a white hart rampant, the heraldic insignia of the Fanshawes, lay the words:

THE ESME FANSHAWE CRICKET CLUB
Nisi terminus sit cor tuum

6
Another Letter

Somewhere in the distance a gong sounded, an unnatural human intervention into the chorus from the jungle. Henry looked at his watch and realised that it was already nearly twelve-thirty pm. He assumed that the gong signified lunch, and given the demeanour of his housekeeper, Henry thought it wise not to be late. Wiping his hands on his trousers like a schoolboy to clean them, Henry hurried towards the open drawing room doors. He took a moment to compose himself and then, as the grandfather clock in the hall chimed in unison with the village church bell in the valley below, he entered the dining room.

In the middle of the room, whose deep red wallpaper was clearly designed for the evening, stood a large mahogany table, set for one. Henry took his seat, and heard from behind him the quiet swish of a swing door being opened. Moments later Cilla's hand deposited a plate, and withdrew. By the time he had turned to murmur his thanks, she was gone. Henry filled his tumbler from the jug of cold water and examined the dish in front of him. Having recognised the meat as chicken and satisfied himself that nothing was still alive, he started to eat. After a few mouthfuls he sat back smiling. In this day of surprises, yet another. Cilla, though scarcely blessed with the art of small talk, was clearly a wonderful cook. This was delicious, and Henry polished off the serving rapidly. He had scarcely put his knife down after the last mouthful when the door swung again behind him, and a hand snatched the plate away. This time Henry was ready, "Cilla, that was absolutely delicious. You have a great talent for cooking."

Did he imagine it, or was there a slight softening in her eyes?

"I do my best, Mr Fanshawe," and then as she left the room, in a softer voice, "thank you."

She returned shortly with a plate of fresh tropical fruit. Henry marvelled again at the directness of everything Seychellois. All the colours were primary, all the smells intoxicating, all the tastes vibrant. The whole island seemed to be bursting with a barely suppressed zest for life and living. Henry had never been one to reflect too long on the darker side of existence. Though, as with everyone, he had periods of melancholy and self-doubt, his innate optimism always won through. The island was a personification of the joie de vivre that, after an exceptionally good lunch, Henry now felt soaring to the surface within him.

Cilla re-entered, and this time presented herself to his right, "Coffee is in the drawing room, Mr Fanshawe."

"Thank you Cilla. I have a feeling I am going to enjoy it here."

"Here is a letter that Mrs Fanshawe left for you." From the pocket of her white apron, Cilla pulled out a large envelope.

"How did she know that I would agree to her terms?" Henry wondered aloud.

For the first time he noticed emotion on his housekeeper's face. She turned and looked at Henry. In a quiet voice she replied,

"Mrs Fanshawe knew a lot of things, sir."

Henry returned to the drawing room, where, upon a small table by one of the chairs, there stood an elegant Georgian coffee pot and a cup. He sat down, poured himself a coffee and turned over the envelope. The spidery lettering on the front read

'For the attention of Henry Fanshawe'

It was his aunt's handwriting, a little more shaky than he remembered. Henry tore open the envelope and unfolded the pages contained within.

My dear Henry,

If you are reading this, then I assume first that I am now dead, and second that you have accepted my offer and have moved into The Manor. I am sure that over the years, you will come to love it, and the Seychelles, as much as I did. Please do not grieve for me, I have had a wonderful life both with and without my darling Cuthers, though just after he left me I was most dreadfully lonely! That is when I had the idea for the club, and it has become the main ambition in my life to see it reach the peaks to which I am sure it is headed. Alas, it seems that I will not now do so, but you will be pleased to hear that I have left the core of an excellent squad.

You will no doubt by now have met Cilla. Don't worry, her bark is worse than her bite, and her cooking is heavenly. She has worked for me for nigh on twenty years, and is fiercely loyal. She will not hesitate to advise you on matters domestic and I would counsel you to take her advice; it is generally good, if a little unsubtle. She also acts as the scorer for the club, and occasionally umpires matches. Her knowledge of the laws of cricket could use some improvement, but she is so terrifying that nobody argues with her decisions.

You will shortly be introduced to the rest of your staff. Clementine is a young girl from the village who helps out Cilla occasionally and acts as a waitress when we have receptions. She's a sweet girl but somewhat lacking in the brain department (everyone in the village calls her the Bungalow - not much up top). Make sure she understands what it is you want her to do, otherwise you are likely to be surprised by some random action. You won't see her much, but her brother Curtley has the makings of a very useful fast bowler, that is, when he can lay off the weed.

You will also have two gardeners, Pierre and his assistant, who I still only know as 'the Boy'. You might find the set up a little bizarre, as 'the Boy' is about fifty years older than Pierre. However, they get along well and the garden, I am sure you will agree, looks beautiful.

Henry paused to look out of the window. Neatly cut lawns and borders carried a profusion of flowers with great drifts of colour floating through them. Every so often a clipped shrub rose from the grass, and in quiet and shady corners classical statues, mottled with mosses and lichens, gazed down upon their surroundings.

Henry, struck once again by his good fortune, read on.

You may be tempted to interfere in the design or management of the garden. Don't. Pierre seems to take great exception to outside advice and he won't accept it at all. I bought him some new cypresses a few years ago and he refused to do anything with them - they ended up withering away in their pots. Pierre is a good supporter of the club and you will see how well he looks after the pitch. One word of warning though, he is a bit flighty, some would say sly, and always has some scheme or other running - not all of which are strictly legal. There is little point in taking this up with him, the last time I tried, I ended up having to replace an entire bed of petunias.

You should meet everyone in the club as soon as possible. Cilla has all the details and there is normally a club meeting every Sunday evening after church (which you will be attending, Henry) during the rainy season. Try and get over to see Sydney, our current captain, beforehand. He lives just down the road. He was a reasonable county player for Surrey who retired here a few years ago - I am sure that you will get along well (make sure he stays off the strong stuff until six pm at the earliest).

Henry wracked his brains, searching for a Sydney in Surrey Cricket club history. Though he was not a supporter, he had visited the Oval on many occasions. He dimly recalled seeing an S. Mason open the batting in the early nineties for the club. Maybe the 'S' stood for Sydney.

He is a charming man and a very useful opener, but has a tendency to melancholia and misses his wife dreadfully (she ran off with someone else a year or so ago - can't say I entirely blame her!). When he gets in one of his moods he does have a rather strong predilection to drink, which makes him a little aggressive. We had a contretemps at the match with Anse Royale last year which ended with the police being called. Just as well the Chief of Police is in our team, otherwise Sidney would probably have been locked up. As it was I had to pay out a considerable sum to clean the walls of the Anse Royale club house. They couldn't replace the head of the founder's statue and the poor chap now stands there like some damaged Greek artefact from the Parthenon. It was when they found the head in the sherry trifle that the trouble really started.

You should go to the vicarage first thing to say hello to the vicar, an engaging gentleman who goes by the name of the Reverend Roger Kitson. He is the sweetest of men and will be dying to meet you and get you into the choir. Not a bad middle order slogger either.

If you ever need anything, the local shop is run by an Indian gentleman called Sanjay. It has everything hidden somewhere in its dark interior, and the shop is always open. He has been a godsend for the club - providing all the kit. He is the official sponsor of the team, and very proud of it! Make sure you say hello to him when you go into the village.

I wish you the very best of luck. It is so sad that for you to be here, I must of necessity be absent, but do not worry, I will be looking down (or up maybe!) and *following every over. I hope you enjoy yourself as much here as I have done.*

Your everloving aunt
Esmeralda

PS Forgot to say - when selecting the batting order never, <u>never</u> put the twins Jean and Louis Kamling together. You will be told why at the first meeting.

PPS Watch out for the Indian teams - they take it very seriously and there have even been rumours of match fixing! Don't believe it myself for a second but they certainly ship in the odd professional from the sub-continent to help them!

PPPS Do look after my darling Frances (Atterwood). He can't play cricket for toffee but he is <u>so</u> keen. You might find his manner rather flowery, but he is a great supporter and was my closest companion in the latter years. I would be very grateful (if I were alive of course) if you could keep him in the team for a long as possible.

Henry put down the letter and, sipping coffee, considered his position. The house was beautiful, and he had an efficient if slightly taciturn housemaid, who cooked excellently. He had gone through the stocks and shares portfolio which Esme had also left to him and was surprised by how sensibly the monies had been invested. There was plenty available to keep Henry in a very comfortable state, and with enough left over to allow for the odd trip home to the cricket or the opera. Probably enough even, if conscience so dictated, to visit his elder brother. And to cap it all, he could now indulge one of his innermost fantasies, and actually manage an adult cricket team. It all seemed too good to be true. There had to be a catch, but try as he might, Henry could not yet find one.

7
Henry Meets the Neighbours

Still contemplating the contents of his aunt's letter, Henry decided to take a nap in the afternoon and visit the village later. In fact, the long plane trip and the rapid pace of recent events had left him more in need of rest that he realised. He carried his bag upstairs and had a quick shower, then lay down on the bed and fell almost immediately into a deep and dreamless sleep. When he awoke, it was not long before he realised that he had slept through the afternoon, evening and night solidly, and it was now just after dawn on his second morning on the island.

He pulled aside the sheets on the large brass-framed bed and padded towards the open window. Outside, tendrils of steam were rising from the damp earth, snaking their way through the layers of green into the clear blue sky. It had obviously rained during the night, and in the morning sun, pearls of water glittered on wide green leaves. Iridescent splashes from the profusion of flowers bombarded him, and from every direction came the sound of the forest. A mixture of bird calls and insects rubbing various parts of their anatomy together produced a mesmeric cacophony, an audio equivalent of the super abundance of brightness.

Glancing down, Henry saw two figures, who he assumed were Pierre and the Boy, tending to the garden. One was pruning a shrub on the lawn, with the younger astride a large old fashioned petrol mower, moving up and down the lawn in strips of Euclidean straightness. It was, he thought, a grand start to what promised to be another interesting day. But first, breakfast.

Henry opened his case to choose the day's attire. He was not and never had been particularly interested in clothes and this showed in a wardrobe which was conservative without ever looking particularly smart. Having little idea what to expect in the islands, Henry had taken the trusted British route, safe but not entirely sensible. He had packed as if he was off to the country for a summer weekend. Surveying the light summer jackets, silk shirts, corduroy trousers and brown brogues, Henry felt, for the first time, that there might have been something in the concept of the City's dress-down day which made sense. Choosing the lightest shirt and suit that he could find, he dressed and then made his way down to the dining room for breakfast.

On the table, again perfectly set, stood a steaming pot of coffee and several large croissants. Henry, realising that he had missed supper and was hungry, pulled the chair out and was about to sit down when he heard a badly suppressed snort. Cilla was standing in the entrance with a jug of orange juice and an unexpected smile on her face.

"Today ain't Sunday, Mr Fanshawe," she chortled.

"I am aware of that, Cilla."

"Ain't no garden party expected."

"So?"

69

"So why you dressed up like you going to City Hall?"

"Well, I don't think I chose very well what to bring with me. I didn't realise it would be quite this hot," he confessed.

"You have your breakfast, Mr Fanshawe, and I'll find some more sensible stuff for you."

She exited and Henry could see her shoulders shaking with mirth as she faded into the dim light of the hall. And despite the reason, he was pleased that cracks had appeared in the severe facade of his housekeeper. Underneath that reserved exterior, there might even be humour and charm. Henry, ever the optimist, devoutly hoped so. He returned to his breakfast and studied the morning paper that accompanied it.

The *Seychelles Nation* earnestly detailed all of the current events on the island. There was a large section given proudly over to progress in all its forms, from the new drainage system in one village, to the connection of another to the National Grid. Henry read through these quickly, and then at the end, found the pull-out for which he was searching. It detailed the coming season, the tenth, of the Seychelles Cricket League. Henry read on:

"Cricket lovers await with baited breath the start of a new cricket season in the Seychelles. This newest of sports for the islands now enters its tenth year and is picking up in popularity all the time. This year's league will be the biggest, with ten teams now competing. For the first time, Anse Takamaka have a village team ready to compete with the big guns, and the marvellous new pavilion, provided through

the benevolence of Mr Chowdrey for his team, the Chowdrey Steamers, has been finished just in time.

Joint favourites for the Championship Title, alongside the Steamers, are last year's winners, the Seychelles Scanners. From the village team challengers, two to watch are St Christol, now under the management of Mr Henry Fanshawe, nephew of the late lamented Esme Fanshawe, and Anse Royale, captained and managed so ably by Major Raymond Sitwell last year. It promises to be an intriguing contest."

Henry read on. The introduction of a cricket competition was a relatively new affair, and teams were still being formed in order to make up the league. There seemed to be a number of teams from factories and businesses, providing in general the better quality, and then a few village and club sides, including his own. The league was made up of one day forty-over matches, save for the final which would be fifty-overs. A Seychelles Cricketing Association had been set up to oversee events, provide umpires and so on. The season was due to start in a few weeks.

* * *

When he returned to his room, he found a selection of large tee shirts and shorts laid out on his bed. Henry was normally quite averse to wearing shorts for anything but sporting pursuits, but in this heat he was willing to make an exception. And anyway, he had already noticed that everybody, the Chief of Police included, wore shorts. It was all part, he decided, of his new approach – the new Henry, though had he stopped to think, he would have realised it was the old approach of 'Do what everyone else does, and don't rock the boat' merely adapted to a new environment.

It was a tropical-look Henry who strode out of the front door on his way down to the village, although he hadn't been able, at the last, to jettison all the old habits. The sandals laid out for him had been eschewed in favour of his comfortable old brown brogues. So he still looked vaguely ridiculous as he walked over the gravel towards the track which led downhill to St Christol. He felt that with time he might even grow to like the sandals, but Henry was always in favour of taking these life-changing events slowly. Overhead the birds wheeled and shrieked as he picked his way along the path, through an avenue of dark green foliage, to St Christol.

The village was only about a quarter of a mile down the road, and in a few minutes Henry had arrived. Houses began to line the route, climbing up the side of the valley some precariously clinging to the slopes which became ever more sheer. Such was the profusion of growth that many were scarcely visible behind a wall of ultramarine horn of plenty, and all that he could make out were their red corrugated iron roofs. Banana trees filled every available gap between the houses, and trails of orange and magenta bougainvillea wound in and out of the fences and gables. In a central position, surrounded by an open area more tamed than most, stood a white-boarded chapel. As Henry approached and walked through the gate past

72

headstones heavy with moss, he heard the clear sound of voices within. He stopped to listen. A choir was practising inside, and Henry could hear the harmonies drift out through the morning air. He was not a particularly religious person but had always enjoyed the musical aspect of church and banged out the hymns with gusto whenever called upon to do so. The pure and ethereal notes issuing from the church hastened his footsteps, and he entered, hoping to catch the melody more clearly.

The church interior was dim after the bright sunlight outside and surprisingly cool. Incense-laden candles burned in various holders placed around the nave, which was filled with rows of wooden pews. There was a sparse rigour to the décor, no artwork or stained glass, and a single large wooden cross betokened the altar. The choir was arrayed in a group by an electric organ and in front of them stood a tall figure with his back to Henry. He was brandishing a conductors' baton and exaggeratedly beating out time. But the musical effect was wonderful, and Henry quietly took a seat in a pew and listened.

The final chord echoed round the church and died away slowly into silence, and the conductor turned round. Then, placing his baton on the stand, and adjusting first his shorts and then his dog collar, he strode rapidly down the aisle smiling, hand outstretched. He was tall and solidly built and devoured the distance between them in a few athletic paces. From behind the large beard he seemed to be smiling, and as he approached, like an inquisitive grizzly bear, his voice boomed over the pews.

"You *must* be Henry Fanshawe. It is *so* good to meet you."

And then he was right by him, pumping his hand energetically.

"Name's Roger Kitson, vicar here. I was hoping you would drop by. There is *so* much to discuss."

Henry felt himself being gently shepherded, by force of personality alone, and followed the vicar as he walked out of the door.

"I see you were listening to our choir. Good, isn't it? We've made the finals of the national competition and we need to hone our act. I just can't *bear* the thought of losing to Belleville yet again."

By this time they were outside, Henry just managing to keep pace with this whirlwind, whose energy quite belied his age. He must have been at least sixty, yet managed to appear unruffled even whilst carrying his impressive frame, not to mention all that facial hair. Unaccustomed to the heat and humidity of the climate, Henry started to breathe heavily. The vicar turned and stopped.

"My dear boy, I am *so* sorry. It does take a while to get used to the heat. And here am I marching you around without a *thought*! Come back to the vicarage for a cup of tea. I have something to show you on the way. I thought that you might like to see your aunt's final resting place."

"Thank you," Henry could manage only two words as he wheezed his way back to normality. Roger Kitson slowed his pace and guided Henry to the graveyard where flowers indicated a recent occupation. At the end of one row of headstones stood a black marble example with golden lettering, as the vicar headed towards it. By the side there was a fine and fresh bunch of lilies.

Henry stood in front of the headstone and gazed at

the writing. A small and unexpected tear made its way down his face as he read:

ESMERELDA FANSHAWE
1940-2011
ELLE SE CONDUIT AVEC LES ANGES

"Driving with the angels," Henry could not help but smile. That should be interesting, he thought. Such a great shame that she was not here to greet him, but even from beyond the grave she had managed to shift his life onto an altogether better course. He felt the large hand of the vicar on his back.

"A great loss to all of us, both personally, and as the spirit of the village. This place was a crumbling shantytown before she arrived. She did so much!"

"She certainly was an unforgettable character," Henry murmured. "I will try to fill her shoes, though I'm not quite sure how."

"Without her, the streets of St Christol will be safer but duller," intoned the vicar, "but I am sure that you, Henry, will be a worthy successor. Esmerelda always chose well."

They walked silently away from the grave, Henry more acutely aware than ever of the weight of expectation on his shoulders. Could he run a cricket club? Could he become the pillar of the village as his aged aunt had done?

His reverie was broken by Roger. They had arrived at the door of a small white bungalow at the back of the church.

"Welcome to the St Christol vicarage! Let's go in, sit down, and have a jolly good cup of tea!"

Once seated, Henry examined the front room of the vicarage whilst the vicar busied himself in the kitchen. Interspersed between pictures on various religious themes, Henry was pleased to see a row of cricket team photos. He got up and moved closer. In faded ink he could just make out the legend under the first photo.

Trinity College Cambridge First XI 1971

From the front row, a much younger and clean shaven version of Roger stared back at him. Now he looked more like W.G. Grace.

"Wasn't a bad player, then."

A voice behind him alerted Henry to impending tea and he turned and moved back towards the chair, "Yes, my aunt mentioned that you were a fine middle order batsman."

"How sweet of her," Roger mused. "I'm not bad, but the running is getting a *little* slow these days. That's why I tend to slog it a bit. Boundaries are *so* much easier on the knees. What's your speciality, may I ask?"

"Well, I played for school and university as a left arm spinner. Got a trial once for Warwickshire, but by then I had been invited into the family firm. Often wondered how I would have got on."

"Well, we have one excellent spinner in the team so it should be interesting to see you compete for the place."

Henry shifted uneasily in his seat, "I was rather assuming that I would be managing the team rather than playing in it."

"If you're better than Rajiv, I would demand that you play!" replied Roger, a face of mock seriousness, dissipating rapidly into a booming laugh. "But I doubt that you are. He really is a find. The son of Sanjay you know, who runs the village shop."

"I must admit I am looking forward to seeing everyone on Sunday. Esme said you had the core of a good team."

"More than the core, Henry, more than just the core!" Roger sat up in his chair, bristling with bonhomie and enthusiasm. Stroking his luxurious beard, he continued, "I really believe we have a good chance this season. Just you wait and see. With good management and some application, the Seychelles Cup may be ours, after all these years. We've heard great things about you, Henry. I'm sure you won't let us down!"

Henry sat back and sipped his tea in silence and with a rising feeling of apprehension. Esme always was a little flamboyant with the truth and it seemed that his abilities had been talked up to the level where the club was expecting Richie Benaud to walk through the door come Sunday.

After a brief chat on the state of English cricket, Henry began to make his excuses to leave. Roger stood up and ushered him to the door, and with a ferocious slap on the back and a handshake that nearly broke Henry's fingers, bade him goodbye, adding, "I'm sure you have, people to see, *lots* to do. I'll let you get on with it. See you Sunday."

Henry realised that he had not mentioned the choir and was contemplating a run for it. He turned away to the garden gate but the vicar's voice was quicker, "Oh, and one more thing, Henry. Esmeralda said you had a wonderful voice. I do hope you will be able to join our choir. Thursday night practice, six pm."

"Of course!" Henry's gritted teeth covered his annoyance at the failure to leave quickly enough. "I'll be there."

As he walked further into the village, mentally kicking himself for such meek acquiescence, he became aware of a small figure running beside him.

"Mr Fanshawe, you must come now. This way!"

A little hand grabbed the bottom of his sleeve and pulled him to the right. The boy of around fifteen was thin and looked Indian. Henry realised he was being led towards the village shop of which he heard and read much already. A number of loud bangs echoed from inside the establishment, and Henry quickened his pace, enough to look concerned whilst not in fact reaching the door before whatever was happening would have happened. Just as he arrived at the doorway, it was flung open, and two laughing children ran out into the road and off down a side street. They vanished almost instantaneously, before an adult Indian man emerged out of the shop, bellowing and shaking his fist. "Just you wait! I'll tell your mother!"

Henry reached the gesticulating figure, "Are you all right, Mr er… Mr…"

The man turned to him. He was a small gentleman, wearing classic khaki shorts and a tee shirt, set off unusually by a straw boater, whose ribbon Henry recognised with some surprise as that of the Old Etonian Rowing Club. The boater was set at a jaunty angle, possibly nudged into that position as a result of the blast from inside the shop.

He readjusted his headgear, wiped his face with a large red handkerchief, and turned to Henry, "Those ruddy boys, they will be the death of me. Imagine, setting off bangers under my melons!"

Henry let him calm down before repeating his question.

The gentleman subsided and replied, "Oh yes, I suppose I am all right. And it is Mr Sanjay Khumri of the St Christol hypermarket." He dusted his shirt off and drew himself up. "Purveyors of fine foods and merchandise to the Seychelles."

"How do you do, I am…"

"Mr Henry Fanshawe!" A wide smile broke over the face of the shopkeeper. "Cilla told me you had arrived. News travels fast in St Christol!"

"You are going to make our cricket club great," the small boy at his side chanted, eyes wide with admiration for the new saviour from England.

"I see you have met my youngest son Davinder. He is a good boy. No bangers under the melons, no thieving of the sweets when I am not looking! Why are not all boys like that I ask you?" He was clearly still fretting over the incident as he guided Henry into his shop.

It was hard for Henry to see in the gloom but he could immediately make out that not a square inch had been wasted. Every available space had shelving on which were piled all manner of foods, hardware, gardening tools, electrical appliances, and almost anything else that Henry could think of. It was like walking into a cut-price Aladdin's cave, and Sanjay was clearly proud of it.

"Welcome to Sanjay's Hypermarket. The jewel of my empire."

"You have other shops?" Henry was still grappling with the concept of a hypermarket existing in a space just slightly larger than his bathroom.

"Oh yes. My brother has the general stores in Beauvallon, and my cousin sells saris in Victoria. We are also in the import export business, 'Khumri Imports'. Only the highest of quality you understand."

Henry's eyes had adjusted to the gloom but this only served to make him more astounded with the sheer volume of the goods on offer. On a shelf behind the counter, he could make out bottles containing all six brands of Pimms gathering dust and numerous Scotch whiskeys, none of which he recognised. Then various novelty liqueurs whose only connection with the Seychelles seemed to be that they were all contained in bottles shaped in homage to the Coco de Mer, as was practically everything else on the island. Hanging from the rafters were chains of differing sizes, ropes, lengths of cloth, and in one corner, several large salami sausages. Goods seem to have been arranged on a geographical basis. Henry was standing in the Mexican sector, which boasted a large array of spices, jars of chilli and salsas, several mounds of fresh tortillas and three large sombreros. Throughout the shop, he could smell the sweet coconut oil, mixed with the all-pervasive scent of Indian spices.

I suppose I should buy something, Henry thought. "Have you any sweets?"

Sanjay pulled aside a curtain to show Henry a shelf groaning under the weight of a number of large glass jars full to the brim with different items, some of which brought a brief choke of nostalgia to his throat.

"I'll have some traffic lights, some gob stoppers and some flying saucers please." A sentence, he reflected, that he had probably not used for at least forty years.

Henry fished out a Seychellois ten rupee note from his

pocket, and then, having taken a traffic light for old times' sake, he presented the bag to the young boy, who began gleefully to ladle handfuls into his mouth.

"That is a very kind gesture sir, befitting of a Fanshawe. I hope you enjoy your life here in St Christol, and if you are ever needing anything, just ask Sanjay!"

Henry emerged squinting into the late morning sun and decided that the temperature was too high and lunch too near for further visits. He decided to put off his final and main task until the afternoon, and turned to walk back towards the house.

The day, hot enough at dawn, had become more and more oppressive as the sun climbed towards noon. The stroll back up the hill, though not particularly long, had Henry wheezing and red faced by the time he walked through the gates into the drive. He entered the house and tried an, as yet, unopened door into what turned out to be the study. Dark panelling lined the walls between the bookcases, and a partners' desk, with an old leather swivel chair, beckoned to Henry. On the ceiling a large fan with blades of bamboo and wicker revolved lazily. It was blissfully cool after the road up which Henry had laboured. He sat down in the chair and closed his eyes, half snoozing, half preparing for the next round of introductions. He had decided to look in on Sydney Mason later in the afternoon.

After a short while in the cool dark comfort of the study, Henry heard the gong announcing lunch. He looked at his watch. It was on the dot of twelve-thirty, and Henry suspected Cilla would be a stickler for punctuality. He roused himself and went through the hall door to the dining room.

81

8
The Club Captain

It was late afternoon when Henry retraced his steps to the village. Hordes of schoolchildren streamed out of a large white building. A queue had rapidly formed outside Sanjay's Hypermarket and occasionally, as he passed, Henry could hear the tones of its owner, beseeching the children with barely suppressed desperation to be quiet, to queue properly, not to be touching anything. Other children were standing in a line by the bus stop. A number waved at him and he waved back. Some pointed at him and started laughing. He chose to ignore this contingent and pressed on to the bungalow where Sydney lived.

After passing the church and the shop, Henry noticed the houses thinning out and gardens becoming neater and more prominent. This seemed to him the upmarket end of town. Some houses sported numbers on their front gates, others gave away the character of those within with some truly awful names. There was at least one Shangri La. Henry was relieved when he finally made the bungalow belonging to his captain, Sydney Mason, to find that it only had a number. It was a little less kempt than the surrounding group. Not by any means ramshackle, but the odd loose board, a gate in need of painting and the uncut front lawn lent an air of neglect.

Henry opened the gate and walked up to the front door. He rang, waited and then rang again. After a few minutes with no answer he began to wonder whether Sydney was out on some errand, and prepared to make the trek back to his house. He had his hand on the gate when from behind him he heard the sound of a door being opened.

It was the Sydney Mason he had recognised from his old Wisdens, but the similarity was strained. The young athlete had been replaced by a slightly tubby and balding figure in his mid-forties, half-opened eyes red rimmed and bloodshot. He appeared to be wearing a dressing gown and as he shambled onto the steps in front of his house, Henry had the distinct impression that Sydney had just woken up. Not quite knowing where to look, Henry stood at the gate and waited.

"Who's there?" Sydney turned slowly, like a mortally wounded bull, towards the gate. "Ah, it's you, better come in." He turned and re-entered his house, leaving the door ajar for Henry to follow.

Henry did consider legging it back to the Manor at that point. Two factors kept him from doing so. First, he was curious about Sydney and wanted to hear his story. Second, the idea of legging it anywhere in this climate was, for someone of Henry's size, laughable and probably dangerous. After a short internal debate, he followed Sydney inside.

Little attempt had been made to keep the house tidy, and Sydney, unlike Henry, clearly did not have the luxury of a weekly cleaning lady to keep a lid on the debris. As he entered, Sydney made a brave but futile bid to clear the main room. Holding a large pile of clothes, old food tins and empty bottles, he looked over at Henry with a slightly guilty face. "Awfully sorry, wasn't expecting you until later. Caught me having an afternoon nap I'm afraid."

Henry knew all the signs. The man had actually just got up from the night before.

"Make yourself at home. I'll just go and get changed." Sydney vanished through a door into a room which, in the split second that Henry was given to peek, looked even worse than the one in which he stood.

He made his way gingerly between various scattered items and after brushing down a chair vigorously, sat down and waited. From the bedroom came the sound of a shower, a few grunts and then after about ten minutes, Sydney re-appeared. He looked much better. Having shaved, dressed and brushed what remained of his hair into place, he reminded Henry a little more of the dashing batsman of old. Though the smile of greeting was still a little guilty, Sydney also seemed calmer as he shook Henry by the hand. "Delighted to meet you at last. It's Henry isn't it? I'm Sydney, Sydney Mason."

Henry smiled, "Yes, I think I remember you from your days at Surrey. Opener there for a while weren't you."

"Four years, averaging thirty-seven or so. Used to partner old Butcher for most of the time. Good days, good days. Unfortunately my health wasn't up to it long term – slightly dodgy heart." Sydney thumped his chest. "Had a marvellous benefit year in 1985. Then played in the lower leagues for several seasons after that... but it's not the same after being at the top. Me and the wife moved over here in late 2000. Found the house and settled down to a happy retirement. It was all going so well…"

Here he trailed off, stared for a while into the middle distance, and then, pulling himself together, looked at his watch, "Half-past four. Would you like a drink?"

Henry, already forewarned of the danger that this comment concealed, replied almost too quickly, "Yes, a cup of tea would be great thank you."

Sydney's face showed a short flash of disappointment, "Yes, yes, quite right, tea, ah, tea, yes, quite right." He headed into the kitchen (Henry did not even dare to look) to put the kettle on.

Henry, anxious to fill the quiet gaps, attempted some small talk, "So, you're on your own here?"

He quickly wished he had not.

Sydney emerged with two cups of tea. "Quiet evenings, she said. Hours spent shopping. But I was completely blind to it. Thought everything was fine. Then she just left. No note. No nothing. I heard that she'd shacked up with a hairdresser in Victoria. That was bad enough but he plays for Anse Royale. We had a bit of a to-do there last season."

Henry recalled the incident in his aunt's letter.

"She'd actually made a trifle for the cricket tea. A bloody trifle! Never did that for St Christol. I'm afraid I lost my rag a bit."

"Yes, I read something about that from my aunt," Henry tried to move the conversation on. "I'm finding out all kinds of things about Esme that I never knew…"

"A bloody trifle. Proper custard, jelly, the whole works!" Sydney shook his head, working himself up.

"It must have been hard to bear," Henry murmured soothingly.

"We were lucky if she made us a few manky cucumber sandwiches. Not even a Victoria sponge. Oh yes, all the signs were there, but I just didn't pick them up, just didn't realise…"

His voice trailed into nothingness and they sat for a while in a silence punctuated only by the sound of the odd motorbike passing the front gates.

Henry tried manfully to fill the void, "I'm sure that given time you will find someone else."

"Oh, I did Henry, then I managed to cock that up too. It was going nicely, we were really happy and then…"

"Yes?"

"Too awkward to mention, Henry, and all my fault for drinking too much and not thinking enough. Don't know if I'll ever get her back." Again he lapsed into silent introspection. The minutes passed, a few more unsilenced motorbikes passed by outside, and then, with a conscious and visible effort, Sydney pulled himself together, "Still, mustn't dwell on the past. We have work to do. I have a few things for you."

He moved over to a bookcase and began rummaging through the shelves, eventually locating and pulling out a large leather bound book, "These are the Minutes of the club since its inception. I've got the scorebook somewhere round here as well. Thought you might like to have a look at them before Sunday."

"Ah, yes," replied Henry, "I wanted to ask you about that. What's the usual form for Sunday?"

"Well, after church and lunch we all used to gather in the clubhouse for a meeting and then net practice. The

86

rains are practically over so the ground should be OK for a bit of a session this time. I'm expect you'll want to see all the team in action."

"That would be very interesting. I've heard good things about them."

"Good. I'll put round the word that we're having a meeting and a practice. I am sure everyone will turn up, if only to meet their new manager."

"Yes. Well, I wanted to ask you about that as well. I love cricket and have played a decent amount but I have never ever managed a team."

"Piece of cake. I'll give you a hand. Shouldn't be a problem. Mostly about team selection, moving speeches and a sympathetic ear."

Sydney was becoming cheerier, talking himself out of the black mood into which Henry had intruded. He went on, "Our manager at Surrey, absolutely useless cricketer, but a wonderful coach. Used to work entirely on inspiration and rhetoric. Like having Winston Churchill egging you on, I used to think."

"And did it work?"

"I'll say, we used to walk out to the square blazing with confidence. That's all you need in this game, confidence. Let me tell about the time…"

Yes – confidence, plus the reflexes of a fighter pilot, a chess player's concentration and unparalleled hand to eye coordination, Henry thought.

Sydney was rapidly throwing off his mantle of gloom and becoming more animated. Henry took the opportunity of a pause in his flow of stories about his exploits at Surrey, and asked, "Why don't you come to lunch on Sunday before the meeting and we can go through the team then?"

"Good idea, Henry. One thing though."

"Yes?" Henry was getting up to leave.

"Best not to tell Cilla who's coming to lunch. She, er, well, she didn't take the affair at Anse Royale very well. That's where she came from originally, you know. Got particularly worked up over some regrettable business with me, the trifle and a statue."

"Any particular reason?"

"The statue. It was her dad."

"I'll bear that in mind," replied Henry as he opened the door. "See you on Sunday."

"Absolutely." And with a brief shake of the hand Sydney disappeared back inside.

Henry headed back up the hill, his mind on the club and its membership. So far he had met a religious middle order slogger with knee problems and an alcoholic opener with a bad case of post-divorce blues. God knows what the rest would be like.

9
The Club Meeting

Over the course of the next week Henry could not resist returning several times to the clubhouse to assure himself that this was not all a delicious dream. He spent many happy hours googling 'Sydney Mason', 'Seychelles Cricket' and 'The Art of Management' to prepare for the forthcoming Sunday. He even started to take a little light exercise. Henry was not, at this point in his life, at the peak of physical condition. He began a regimen of sit-ups and other exercises each morning, building towards the goal of going on a run one day in the near future. As yet this was having little effect on the spare tyre that greeted him every morning, but there was no doubt that the move had reinvigorated Henry Fanshawe. In common with all life on the island, Henry found within himself an energy and an enthusiasm which he now realised had been lacking for many years. He felt better, and he was drinking less, especially since his meeting with Sydney. He now approached the coming club meeting with anticipation rather than concern. Even Cilla seemed to have softened somewhat in her manner, allowing Henry the odd smile and shifting her demeanour from the severe to the merely laconic.

Henry dressed slightly more formally on Sunday morning and prepared himself for the coming ordeal of Church, a habit he had not indulged for some time back in England. The Fanshawes had their own pew in the local parish church back home. Attendance in those days, sitting quietly behind a screen, separated from the rest of the congregation, had been compulsory. His childhood village had a pleasant but mind-numbingly boring pastor, who engaged in sermons bristling with threat of eternal damnation for wrongdoers. Given the amount of fire and brimstone hurled in his general direction, these left Henry surprisingly cold, and as soon as he had left the village for university and then Lo ndon, his spiritual life had withered. Then after his prayers over his wife's terminal condition remained seemingly unanswered, he had given up for good

The only thing he missed was the music. He had decided that for this first time, he would join the congregation and listen to the choir before deciding whether to join, though he knew in his heart that it was a foregone conclusion. And, as befitted his new found joie de vivre, Henry realised with a shock that he was actually looking forward to it.

He left the house at precisely ten twenty and began to walk down to the church. He could hear the bells ringing, and became aware that the road was gradually filling with others headed in the same direction. It became clear that everyone went to church on Sunday in this village, and what is more, they all wore their Sunday best. Women were dressed, peacock like, in bright primary coloured dresses, many with turbans of improbably large dimensions. Girls, all wearing white cotton, leather-bound bibles held tightly at their sides, headed with the boys into the Sunday school next door.

As Henry approached the door, a sense of nervousness returned. He entered and strode down the aisle, feeling all the eyes of the congregation on him. He wondered where he should sit. As he dawdled in the middle of the aisle, he noticed that Cilla was beckoning him over. He shuffled along the pew and sat down next to her with a nod of thanks, whispering, "People will talk, Cilla."

"No, Mr Fanshawe, they won't."

She returned to her study of the service.

The church was full when the vicar walked up the aisle, followed by a choir of at least twenty, dressed in cassocks of white and blue. As they gained their places, they started to sing, and Henry was instantly transfixed. They sang beautifully, voices well matched, and he sat back and luxuriated in the gentle melodies. After a hymn and a reading, the vicar stood up in his pulpit. This was the bit where Henry usually switched off, but he felt duty-bound this time to pay attention, and at least to give some impression that he was absorbing the wisdom being doled out.

Actually, the Reverend Roger Kitson wasn't bad, he thought. Far superior to the doom-laden sermons of his local childhood rector. A smattering of decent cricketing allusions, and the odd joke that was reasonably funny, though only in a Shakespearean sense. He was winding up, when he turned and looked directly down at the pew where Henry sat. Waving his hands towards the rapidly reddening Englishman, he added in a voice brimming with excitement, "And one more thing, my friends, we have a very important new member here today."

'Oh God,' thought Henry.

The vicar continued, "I would like you all to greet Henry Fanshawe, who has just arrived from England. He is going to take on the running of the Esme Fanshawe Club, and the first meeting is this afternoon."

There was a chorus of hoorays, a few alleluias, and a lot of clapping as Henry felt forced to his feet to accept the welcome. A number of people crowded round to shake him by the hand. This type of behaviour, in church, would have sent the old Henry into paroxysms of deep embarrassment. Shaking hands in church, especially with strangers, was a habit Henry associated with the Happy Clappy movement of the Christian Faith. But here it felt entirely natural, and he had to admit to himself by the end, he was rather enjoying it.

After the service, Henry shook hands with a further number of well-wishers, and with the vicar.

"Looking forward to your first meeting this afternoon, Henry?" asked Roger.

"Do you know what, Roger, I think I am. I really think I am."

And, smiling to himself, with a few small boys nipping at his ankles, he turned to make the short climb back to the house for Sunday lunch.

As he entered the drive, he could see Sydney waiting on the steps for him.

"Didn't see you in church, Sydney." he exclaimed cheerily, still overwhelmed with the warmth of the welcome.

"Don't do church much anymore. Didn't do anything to help me." Sydney was a little grumpy and, Henry surmised, slightly hungover. However, he looked more athletic in his whites and had made a definite attempt to smarten himself up for the upcoming meeting.

As they approached the house, the front door was opened. Like a latter day Mrs Danvers, Cilla, still resplendent in her Sunday best, and a headdress which seemed to double her height, stood in the doorframe staring down at them.

"Mr Fanshawe, you didn't tell me that you were inviting Mr Mason to lunch!"

"Er, good morning Cilla," Sydney ventured hesitantly. He was ignored.

"If it wasn't Sunday, Mr Fanshawe, I might say a few things. But the Lord instructs us to forgive, and in Mr Mason's case there is plenty of that to be done."

"I did tell you we had a visitor, Cilla," Henry appealed.

"A visitor, yes, not *this* visitor!" Cilla snorted reprovingly and retreated indoors.

"Told you so, Henry," Sydney muttered. "Sorry for the scene, but she really is a hard nut to crack. I've tried flowers, letters of apology, everything, but she just won't listen. I really didn't realise it was her father's statue. I really didn't."

"Well, come into the drawing room and we can have a drink before lunchtime," said Henry. He hoped fervently that this affair was not going to drive Sydney back to the bottle.

As they entered the room it became clear that there was no chance of such happening. Cilla had cleared away all the decanters and replaced them with a large jug of lemonade.

"It seems that Cilla has narrowed the choice of aperitif somewhat," Sydney commented bitterly. He accepted a glass of lemonade with an attempt at good grace. "Probably for the best. Need to be on form this afternoon."

'Might be good for you, but I really could do with a sharpener,' Henry thought. And then, an idea occurred to him. He wandered over to the door, "Wait here a moment Sydney. I'll just go into the kitchen to calm Cilla down."

Cilla was standing by the kitchen table, chopping vegetables with a dark frown on her face. Henry felt some sympathy for the vegetables. In fact, he thought, it was worrying enough just being in the same room as Cilla in her current state of mind with that knife.

Without looking up from her violent chopping, she spoke, "That man is a vandal, Mr Fanshawe. How could he do such a thing?"

"Apparently it was his wife's trifle." As an excuse Henry didn't expect this to work, but it was all he could think of at that moment.

"I'm not surprised she ran away."

"Now, Cilla, try to understand. The poor man was overcome with grief. I don't think he's got over it yet. Let's put his mistake behind us, shall we? I am sure he is truly sorry."

There was a hurrumph from Cilla who attacked the vegetables with renewed vigour.

Henry ploughed on, "So, Cilla, can we try to remain calm at least while he is here. He is my guest and I expect that he be treated as such."

"Well, I won't kill him if that's what you're worried about."

The thawing of relations between the two was going to be a long and arduous road, Henry realised. "Good, thank you Cilla, it provides some comfort to know that I will not be privy to murder."

Although still going at the vegetables with some zeal, Cilla began to relax. The snorts subsided, and a faint smile touched her eyes.

"You get back to your guest, Mr Fanshawe. We eat in ten minutes. Oh, but before you go…"

Henry followed Cilla's gaze to the kitchen table. There, softly fizzing, was a perfect gin and tonic.

"Cilla, you know my every thought," he said in a heartfelt manner, and quickly downed the G&T before returning to the drawing room.

Over lunch Sydney filled Henry in on the state of cricket in the Seychelles. It was quite a new sport for most of the island. Henry found this strange, in an ex British colony, but as Sydney explained,

"Oh, the Seychelles isn't really very British at all. Never has been. It was colonised by the French, and governed by the French until the end of the Napoleonic Wars, and by then all the large plantations were run by Frenchmen. The language is more French than English. Still mostly Roman Catholic. That's what makes it such an interesting place. It's a real melting pot: English, French, Africans, Indians. The Brits played cricket a bit, and there's an old cricket pitch and square in the middle of town. A couple of the colonial schools that like to ape all things British used to play, but it was very elite and not that widespread. Cricket didn't really catch on until a few years ago, and that was more from the Indians than us."

Every so often Cilla would enter to clear plates or bring the next course. She would give Henry a brief smile, then glare at Sydney. As the meal progressed, his captain outlined the current league system and the opposition.

"We have one big league – not enough teams to separate things out. So the opposition is variable to say the least. One week we will be playing a village eleven, the next we will be up against one of the factory teams – they're the best. All supposedly non-professional of course, but the games are reasonably attended, and I have heard rumours that the Indians run quite a sizeable betting business on the back of it. Maybe that's why our Sanjay is so pleased to be involved."

"And our team?" asked Henry.

"Well, we have been the pick of the village teams for a while now. Our job this year is to see if we can mix it with the factory teams. We managed to beat a few of the weaker ones last year, and I think we have come on tremendously over the past season. See what you think in the nets this afternoon. We'll put them all through their paces for you."

Henry sat back in his chair, awaiting whatever dessert Cilla had planned. She was an excellent cook, and had he not been exercising more, he would have been putting on weight. What, he wondered, would it be this time?

He leant over to Sydney, "Think what you like about Cilla, but she is magnificent when it comes to pudding. High point of the meal."

Sydney, having also eaten well, was feeling a good deal more cheerful. He sat back and joked, "Maybe she will forgive me at last. That would be a result!"

As the door opened to Cilla's arrival, it swiftly became clear that more time was necessary for a complete rapprochement. On the tray she carried was a large glass dish bearing the most lavish of trifles. As she placed it with a flourish in front of Henry, he noticed that the decoration on top consisted of a couple of large sponge fingers set in a 'V'. This two fingered salute had been cleverly designed to point straight at Sydney.

"It's a dish best served cold, Mr Fanshawe," she intoned as she left the room.

Sydney and Henry finished their lunch and wandered up to the pitch and club house. Henry had found it hard to contain his mirth at Cilla's punk trifle, whilst Sydney appeared unsure whether this signified a thaw in relations or not.

Henry responded to his attempts to seek reassurance with a volley of bad puns and carried on in much the same vein, attempting vainly to suppress a chuckle as he came up with yet another, until they reached the club house. By this time Sydney was beginning to feel a little irritated by the stream of pudding-related humour, and turned to Henry.

"Look, Henry, it may be funny for you but to me it's very serious. I just don't know what to do about Cilla!"

"Well," Henry replied, "it is all a trifle confusing." Unable to contain himself, he giggled maniacally as he turned the key in the door

Sydney gave up. It was clear that Henry would not be deflated on a day like this, and his determinedly good-humoured approach had worn the other man down. They entered the clubhouse, Henry bearing the thick brown leather minute book, and Sydney with the list of fixtures in a large brown envelope embossed with SCC and the ubiquitous Coco de Mer. Henry was both impressed by its size and slightly guilty that it should be rather larger than most islanders' houses. A main room with a small kitchen area at the back gave on to two sets of changing rooms, one on each side, marked 'Us' and 'Them'. The wooden walls were unpainted and carried little adornment, save for several team photos placed in a row along one wall. Upon closer examination Henry could see the diminutive figure of his aunt placed in the middle seated next to Sydney and the Chief of Police. In some of the photos there was a large silver cup at her feet, which Henry noticed was identical to a smaller version in a glass cabinet behind him. He turned to stare at the trophy.

Sydney explained, "That's the Best of Villages Cup. We've won it four or five times, so we get a replica to keep."

They busied themselves arranging four chairs along one side of a small table. Henry entered the 'Us' changing room and saw the neat rows of pegs, many with cricket sweaters still hanging from them. By now it was two-thirty pm and various individuals, some of whom Henry recognised, some of whom he only knew from the wall photos, began to file in. Roger the vicar, arrived, spreading cheerful greetings to all and sundry, and sat next to Sydney at the table in the middle of the room. Henry noticed the vacant seat on the other side of the captain and realised that it was his. As he moved to it, the room quietened a little and all present shuffled themselves into a more or less comfortable position, several hunkered down on the floor, others leaning against the wall. There must, Henry thought, be at least thirty people crammed in here.

Looking around, Henry recognised one or two village characters. Sanjay and Rajiv sat on a bench surrounded by boxes containing various cricket paraphernalia, all heavily branded with the Khumri logo. And in the corner, Xavier Kirby, the lawyer he had met in London. Next to him was an immaculately dressed gentleman whom Henry could not place. The gentleman tipped his hat. He looked enquiringly at Roger.

"Ah, let me introduce you," Roger obliged. "Henry Fanshawe, Francis Atterwood."

The two shook hands.

Francis was a rotund older man with an air of the fading 50s film star about him. He was dressed in a perfectly-tailored white linen suit, with a large magenta cravat around his ample neck. He wore a boater, a buttonhole, and a pair of brown loafers with tassels.

"Henry, darling, call me Frankie. There's something wonderfully unisexual about the name, and I much prefer it."

Slightly taken aback, Henry tried to think of a response to this,

"So, Fran... I mean... Frankie, how did you come to be living here?"

"A long story, darling, but suffice it to say that England in the fifties and sixties was not the sort of place for me. I became an air steward on BOAC, and spent most of my life on the way to or back from the Indian Ocean. When I retired, I decided to stay here – much the nicest and most tolerant place I knew – where I could

99

indulge to the full my real love, amateur dramatics. You see before you the impresario of Beauvallon!" Standing up, Frankie performed a quick pirouette to amused applause from the room. He took a long and low bow and resumed his seat.

Henry couldn't quite think of what to say. Finally he mumbled, "I can see that you like to make an impression."

"Well, as Beauvallon's leading man, one has standards to keep up, don't you know."

There was no reply to this, so Henry merely smiled and sat down.

Roger whispered in Henry's ear. "He's great fun, and no-one cares about that sort of thing here, except perhaps for Cilla."

"So Cilla doesn't approve?"

Francis heard this, "My dears, Cilla doesn't approve of fun!"

All present laughed, save, Henry noticed, for Sydney.

The door opened and for a moment Henry thought he was seeing double. Another priest had entered the room, dressed smartly in a light suit with a purple shirt and dog collar. On his freshly-shaven head perched a white panama, and round his neck an improbably large cross hung on a golden chain. He sported a pencil thin moustache which looked almost as if it had been painted onto his café crème skin. He stopped and nodded to all and sundry in a slightly desultory fashion.

"Messieurs, Mesdames, bonjour."

"Simon, how are you?" Roger jumped up and began pumping his hand. Turning to Henry, "May I introduce our dashing Frenchman, Monseigneur Simon de Pelet!"

"But I thought you were the vicar here?" Henry was confused.

"I am, and so is Simon. He bats for the other side, if you know what I mean."

"What?"

"Not here, of course. He is one of that rare breed, a Frenchman who enjoys cricket. From his days in Martinique I suppose. He runs the Catholic side of the village. But we use the same building on Sundays."

"A sort of religious ground sharing?"

"Indeed, highly economical, and most ecumenical."

Simon extended a hand to Henry and, using the other to brush back his imaginary hair, gave a slightly haughty smile, "Enchanté, Monsieur Fanshawe."

That said, he glided slowly to the corner and assumed a Gallic pose.

There were now three seats filled on the table that clearly constituted the committee for the club. Then, the door opened once more and in stalked the gaunt figure of the Chief of Police. Though it was not light in the clubroom, his mirrored glasses remained firmly in place. Henry expected that he would take the fourth seat, and stood up.

"Please take a seat, sir," he beckoned him over.

The head of law enforcement on the island smiled enigmatically, "Mr Fanshawe, in this room we are all equal. Please, no 'sirs'. Just call me Chief. Even in a position as exalted as mine, I would never dare take that chair." He assumed a position next to the door. Then, like a teacher entering the classroom, Cilla walked in. Without a word she headed through the crowd and took the remaining vacant seat.

She nodded to Henry briefly and started, "As the acting secretary of the Esme Fanshawe Club, I declare this meeting open. Good afternoon everybody. Shall we begin?"

Henry was longing to get out onto the pitch with the team and fidgeted in his seat as the meeting progressed. He was formally welcomed again as chairman by Cilla. He thought he detected a faint softening in her manner when she talked to him. Certainly, relative to the club captain on her right, he was close to gaining some kind of approval.

Once the matter of cricket teas had been organised, new kit and transport requirements discussed, and other small matters finalised ("Every man is responsible for his own box!") the meeting disbanded and the team members went to get changed. Henry, already in whites found for him from a trunk containing his uncle's old kit, walked out on to the field amongst the significant number of non-players who had also come to the meeting. He had expected that this would be just the team, but it was clearly more than that. It seemed that most of the village was represented, whether by the large women who dealt with the teas, the children who looked forward to being trialled one day, or the local businessmen, who, like Sanjay, were providing some facet of sponsorship or equipment. Henry discerned the subtle hand of his aunt everywhere, cleverly assigning jobs so as to include as many locals as possible. This was a social as much as a cricket club, and more or less everybody in the village had some role or other. Henry even noticed the two boys, who had let off bangers in the local shop, chatting away merrily with Sanjay's son Rajiv.

Clearly this was an area of neutrality, a little demilitarised zone in the midst of the community, where quarrels were forgotten and wounds healed.

Sydney led the team out of the clubhouse. Pausing upon the steps he noisily cleared his throat and the crowd fell quiet. "OK, now we've finished the formal business I'd like the following to get ready to bat in the nets: the Kamling brothers, Monseigneur de Pelet, Reverend Kitson, and Frankie."

The gentlemen in question started to pad up whilst Sydney continued to read from his list: "Curtley, can you and Rajiv warm up for some bowling. The rest of you, out on the square and the Chief'll give you some fielding practice. Oh, and Henry, do you fancy trying a little of your famous left arm spin?"

Henry noticed that once he had started talking as the cricket captain, Sydney had grown in stature and authority. He had lost his air of nervous guilt, and had quite unconsciously straightened up and stopped shambling. How clever his aunt had been, he thought, in providing the right handhold for those in trouble to pull themselves up.

All concerned trooped out onto the field, where Henry's gardeners had constructed nets and painted white lines round the boundary and the creases. The situation looked idyllic, and could have come straight from a village ground in rural Kent, save for the lush tropical vegetation that bordered the pitch and the unmistakeable sounds of jungle life that emanated from beyond its boundaries.

Those not practising had set up camp in a line of deck chairs in front of the pavilion and were already passing comment loudly on various team members. Henry realised that this was truly a village effort and that Sunday afternoons were as much for the non-players as the players. A large hamper that had been brought by one of the many women was opened and flasks of cold lemonade doled out. Plates of biscuits were passed from one end of the line of deckchairs to the other. Shoes were kicked off and the village settled back to watch its heroes practise.

Henry sauntered over to the nets, where several batsmen in pads awaited the bowlers. Sydney beckoned to him. "Fancy loosening up and giving our batsmen a few balls, Henry?"

He caught the ball tossed to him with some apprehension. Henry had played for his village when on holiday there as a youth, and latterly captained the Fanshawe & Co. cricket team, the 'Unmentionables', in a number of matches on the old artillery fields behind the Barbican in London, a little space of green hidden behind the great glass facades of the surrounding office blocks. But, he thought, with the recent plunge into a new fitness regime, he felt good. Loosening up with a few mild stretches, he turned to face the batsmen waiting in the nets.

First on was the Reverend Roger Kitson. Henry sent down a few looseners and was quite pleased with the speed at which he had regained his cricketing eye. Not that this did any good as each ball was dispatched expansively by the vicar, whose Christian muscularity was all the more apparent when out of his normal dog collar and suit. After a while, Henry got the ball to spin a bit and passed the bat a few times. The vicar was extremely sharp on the leg side, he noticed, but his footwork was a bit lazy, and as he had previously explained, he tended to go for the big hit rather than amass runs at a safer pace. Still, thought Henry, very useful for the middle order when the bowlers get a bit tired.

Second, the Monseigneur, dressed perfectly, sauntered up to the crease. Under his breath, Henry muttered, "For what you are about to receive, may the Lord make you truly thankful," and sent down a ball fizzing with spin. It totally deceived the Frenchman and bounced high off his bat for a certain catch. De Pelet brushed an imaginary speck of dust off his lapel, and glared at the bowler, "You 'ave a formidable weapon, Monsieur Fanshawe."

Henry declined to point out the innuendo. It would probably not go down well with the rather straight-laced Monseigneur. But he went easier from then on and was rewarded with an improvement in Anglo-French relations. And, thought Henry, he's not too bad as a batsman.

After a few overs, de Pelet was replaced by Jean, one of the two Kamling brothers. Henry was getting into his stride now and sending down some good balls. He tried a googly on Jean and caught him beautifully Leg Before Wicket, to some applause from Sydney. As is usually the case, the next ball was lifted high over the nets for a straight six by the scowling boy, stung at the ease at which he had been caught out on the previous delivery. Henry walked back to his mark and waited for the ball to be returned from the lush undergrowth that fringed the pitch.

At this point, Sydney blew an old football whistle and called Rajiv and Curtley over. He wandered up to Henry.

105

"Care to see our two top bowlers in action? I'll go into the nets and let them have a go at me. But send me down a few looseners first, would you?"

With that he picked up his bat and moved into position. Henry saw immediately how, having taken guard, he shifted into an almost trance-like state, showing the concentration that is needed in a really good batsman. Running in he could see Sydney poised, a coiled snake ready to pounce when the shot had been picked. He sent down a decent medium pace ball to middle and leg. With an action that managed to be languid and ferocious at the same time, and with little if any backlift, Sydney swatted it away with ease and at a speed which would have undoubtedly carried to the boundary had the nets not intervened. Henry marvelled inwardly at the timing of this man, so clearly head and shoulders above the rest. He tried a more devious approach, sending down a flipper. It did not change the outcome. Sydney had somehow managed to get into a perfect position without appearing to move at all, and sent the ball flying into the garden. Henry was quite glad when he felt a tap on his shoulder and the diminutive form of Rajiv at his elbow.

"You are a nice spinner, Mr Fanshawe, but that Mr Mason, he plays spin so well. I have to try very hard to get him out. But I have a secret ball that I have been practising for a while. Shall I show you?"

Rajiv took the ball and started to curl his fingers round it. Henry noticed that for a short boy of around eighteen, he had enormous hands, and once he had full hold of the ball it almost disappeared. He watched as Sydney took guard.

The first attempt did not work and Sydney dealt with it easily, whacking it away to leg. Rajiv, frowning with concentration, walked back and then, having carefully adjusted his grip on the ball, turned towards the wicket. His run up was fairly short, and slow, but at the very last pace or two he arched his body and quickened ever so slightly. The ball left his hand quite early, curling in towards the batsman, who was making ready to cut it away. As it bounced, the large bat swung and Sydney having finished his stroke, stood up to see where the ball had gone.

It had in fact turned sharply past the bat and knocked the off stump out of the ground. In an extraordinary trajectory, reminiscent of the famous Warne 'wonder ball' to Gatting, the ball had bounced almost at right angles and then looped through the air back towards the stumps. Henry, who had a decent knowledge of the black art of spin, stood open mouthed at the amount this small boy was able to impart.

"I don't think I will be challenging for the position of spinner, Sydney."

"See what I mean, Henry, he's a real match winner, that boy. Doesn't always get it right and lacks a little discipline, but with a ball like that who wouldn't play him?" Sydney strode back to the wicket and took his guard again. One of the brothers, Louis, something of an all-rounder, was selected to bowl at him and revealed a useful medium pace. Henry correctly identified him as a likely opening bowler. After the ball had been picked from the undergrowth surrounding the pitch for the tenth time, Sydney thanked Louis, and shook himself, did a few stretches and resumed his position.

"Now, Henry, I'm warmed up OK. See what you think of our other secret weapon." Then he shouted towards the outfield, "Where's Curtley?"

The tall languid figure detached himself from the group gathered chatting by the boundary and strolled towards the nets. Curtley's distinguishing characteristic, apart from his lanky frame, was a head of dreadlocked hair, which, if untied, would have come half-way down his back. He reminded Henry of a wild cat, prowling towards its prey, muscles etched against skin and poised to pounce.

"Morning, boss."

"Curtley, send me down a few slower ones, and then I want you to show Henry what you can do."

"OK, boss."

He started trotting towards the bowling end of the nets, and with a lazy style, wound himself up to deliver the ball. The first few were clearly below full pace, though delivered with a speed which would have pleased Henry, had he been a fast bowler himself. Sydney suddenly became more serious in his guard, blocking the balls rather than going for shots. A slight tension hung over the nets as Curtley delivered ball after ball on a very accurate length to the ex-county cricketer, slowly winding up his speed as he did so. Various members of the team stopped their fielding practice and ambled over to see the contest.

After a few more balls, Sydney shouted from the crease. "OK, Curtley, got my eye in. Now show us what you've got!"

Curtley smiled a wide and partly toothless smile.

"OK, boss."

He walked back a little further than before, and as he turned and started to run in, Henry could detect little difference from the previous deliveries. Then, about ten yards from the wicket, it happened. There was a sudden and dramatic change in Curtley's pace, from an easy shamble to a hard sprint. The bowler arched his back further than before and his bowling hand was flung back, almost, it seemed, to the ground. As he drew it over his head his entire body snapped back like a door on a spring. The ball flew out of his hand towards Sydney at awesome velocity. No sooner, it seemed, than it had left the bowler, Henry saw it fly past the batsman at chest height, having pitched just beyond a normal length. The crowd 'oo-ed' and there was a smattering of applause. Sydney, who had been comprehensively beaten for pace, took out his handkerchief, wiped his brow and turned to his club manager with a grin.

"Not bad, eh!"

Henry was still dumbstruck from the speed of the ball, and could merely grunt his agreement.

"We timed him once. The Chief let us use the Island Speed Radar. Regularly came in over ninety! He's a real find, so long as we can keep him off the wacky baccy."

"The what?" Henry always played the innocent in these matters.

"The grass, you know, marijuana, dope."

"Oh."

Curtley, having delivered one of the fastest balls that Henry had ever seen, professional tests included, smiled and shambled off to the boundary again.

And so the afternoon continued, Sydney putting various members through their paces for Henry's benefit, showing him gradually the bones of the team that would take to the field against the first opposition in a few weeks' time. It was, Henry thought, an impressive first day, and he could see why the captain harboured such hopes for the coming season. They had at least four very capable batsmen led by Sydney, and in Rajiv and Curtley, two bowlers with a professional level of venom. The Chief of Police, who acted as wicketkeeper, was a changed man on the pitch, laughing and joking, needling all his surrounding fielders, and fizzing behind the wicket with an exuberant energy which infected all around him. Francis added little in the way of talent to the mix, but his good humour and infectiously upbeat outlook on life kept a smile on all faces. Yes, Henry thought, this could be a very good team indeed.

10
The Problem with Number Five

By the time the last of the picnickers had departed the field, the sun had moved behind the trees and long shadows streaked across the pitch. The four members of the committee and the Chief of Police sat on the veranda discussing the day, and finishing off the last of the sandwiches together with the dregs from a large iron pot of tea.

"Sydney, I have to say I am impressed!"

Henry was keen to discuss the team and its tactics. By his side he had a large unopened letter from the Seychelles Cricket Confederation, which he assumed was the new fixtures list. Everyone was eager to see who the first opponents were to be.

On one side of him, lounging back in two deckchairs, were Sydney and Roger. Stroking his luxuriant beard, Roger was smiling broadly. He and Sydney were both pleased with the way things had turned out.

On the other side, sat Cilla, making sure that she was out of Sydney's eye line.

"We'll need it, remember last year against the Indians!" The Chief leant against a pillar on the veranda.

His mirrored glasses were now back on, and he had regained his professional and icy composure.

Soon, talk moved on to team selection.

"So, I open with Jean, followed by the Monseigneur," said Sydney. "Vicar, you're in at four. Chief, you can fill your usual spot at six, Louis can bat seven, Francis eight, Xavier nine and then Curtley and Rajiv ten and eleven."

Henry remembered back to his aunt's letter and interrupted.

"Is there something about Louis and Jean not batting together? My aunt advised me recently that you would explain." He stopped abruptly when he realised that all present were staring at him.

"It was in a letter left for me."

Sydney leaned forward and put down his cup of tea.

"She was quite right. They are both fine lads and seem to get along together well most of the time. But put them at two ends of the strip and it will always happen."

"What will always happen?"

"One of them will run the other out," interjected Roger.

Henry considered this. "But surely with a little coaching, in how to call and all that, we could iron the problem out?"

Sydney shrugged his shoulders.

"If, Henry, it were a matter of coaching, we could have dealt with it years ago. But it's much more than that. I believe that a few years ago at school Jean ran Louis out for a duck in the house cup final."

Roger thrust his bearded face forward and took over.

"Yes, and that silly bugger Louis has been carrying a grudge since then."

Sydney waited patiently and resumed.

"Last year, we were heading for victory in one game, until the point at which Jean joined him at the crease. The very next ball he played a push shot towards silly mid-off and shouted for Jean to run."

Roger again felt the need to contribute.

"As clear a case of fratricide since Cain and Abel! Jean wasn't more than half-way down the pitch before his bails were off."

"We lost the game," continued Sydney, "and at tea Jean had to be restrained from taking a swing at his brother. Ever since then we have tried to separate the two in the order."

Roger had the last word. "If we fail and they bat together, then one will always try to run out the other. It's as simple as that."

Monseigneur de Pelet, who had been quietly standing by the club house door, waited for silence, "Mon Dieu, these crazy English brothers!"

"Ah." Henry began to realise that, good as this team was, there were, as always, little pockets of lunacy and irrational behaviour that one had to deal with.

One in particular, between Cilla and Sydney, had been exercising him since lunch. He had the bare bones of a plan to effect a rapprochement. He moved on to his next question.

"I noticed in your team selection that you have no number five."

Sydney looked again at his sheet and clapped his hand to his head unconvincingly.

"You're quite right, I must have missed it. Nothing gets past you, eh, Henry!" he tittered nervously.

"Well, when it comes to counting from one to eleven I do like to think I can be relied on!"

Sydney glanced around the other members, who, Henry noticed, were looking as uncomfortable as he was.

"So, number five…"

The veranda fell silent. "The truth is, we currently have no number five," said Sydney.

"But there must be someone we can find to fill the spot." said Henry.

"Maybe, but there was no one today capable enough and there is the balance of the team to consider." Sydney's pomposity did not convince Henry.

"For goodness sake, there must be someone else in St Christol who can bat!"

"There is, Henry, but the problem is …" Sydney was cut off by a hand signal from Cilla, who continued, "She's a woman, Mr Fanshawe."

"And women can't play cricket," the Monseigneur added.

"This one can," muttered the Chief of Police, "and we would be mad to lose her!"

Henry, who had spent years in the city watching women do men's jobs much better than they could, was about to launch into a short speech when Cilla brought her fist down on the table. It made an alarmingly loud sound.

"Yes they can, Chief, but they are not allowed to, and in this case, I completely agree with the rules."

Sydney explained to Henry.

"She played in a match at the end of last year. Brilliantly, as it turned out. We are awaiting an interim ruling from the Board on the matter. There is nothing in the rules about women playing, but there has been a lot of resistance."

"And who is this girl?" Henry asked.

"Mathilde du Pré, and she's a bit more than a girl, Henry."

"What do you mean by that?"

"Wait and see old boy, wait and see."

Cilla cut in, "What he means, Mr Fanshawe, is that she is a loose woman whose effect on the team could be detrimental in the extreme!"

Roger spoke in a pained voice. "Cilla, you do her a disservice. In any case, surely it is our job, by forgiving and accepting her into the family that is the club, to guide her through the complexities of life, and help her to see the right path."

"All you want to see, Vicar, is the length of her skirt!"

"Really, Cilla, you should be ashamed."

"I'm not having that woman on the team."

And so it went on, back and forth, until Henry decided to stop listening and instead began to peruse the large envelope from the Cricket Board in front of him. As he opened it he realised that in addition to the large shiny card with the fixtures for the forthcoming year, there was another smaller letter addressed to *The Chairman, Esme Fanshawe Cricket Club, St Christol.*

As he examined the contents, a smile appeared on his face. He let the arguments flowing around him die out until all that was left was a rather edgy silence and a lot of folded arms. When he felt they were ready, he started,

"Well, gentlemen and ladies, I think this letter may help decide the matter." And then he read,

"Dear Sir,

As you are aware, the Board of SCC has been considering the matter of EFCC's use of a female player, namely Mathilde du Pré, in their match against Seychelles Petroleum CC on November 7th 2010. Mme Du Pre, who batted at number five for EFCC, has been the subject of a complaint by the opposing team manager that as a woman, she is not allowed by the rules of the Board of Cricket to play in the Seychelles League.

This is an area in which the rules of the league are not entirely clear. Whilst there is no specific ban on the playing of women, our investigation of other leagues indicates that it is more often than not the case that women are not permitted. As a result we have decided on the following compromise:-

1. The initial result (St Christol won by 4 wickets) shall stand.

2. The Seychelles Cricket Association will trial a women's cricket team in the next season, with the aim of creating a league in the future. Until this time, women will be permitted to play for any team.

We hope that this ruling will clarify any confusion. It applies from the beginning of the 2011 Season, which starts on Saturday October 6th 2011.

Yours faithfully
Chairman
Seychelles Board of Cricket"

Henry finished reading and looked up at his colleagues. Cilla was sitting, brow deeply furrowed and muttering to herself, carefully using undecipherable phrases of Seychelles patois which he suspected only the Chief of Police and some of the most local of locals could understand.

Roger, on the other hand, was smiling broadly from behind his beard. Even Sydney, with the odd worried glance at Cilla, seemed pleased. "Well, that's the number five problem sorted, I think."

The Chief, who was trying diplomatically to ignore whatever it was that Cilla was chuntering about, agreed. "She is a good batsman, or batsperson I suppose, and we are lacking in that area. I say we go with her."

"Yes, you and most of the other men in the village wish you could, don't you!" Cilla was still distinctly unimpressed, and Henry decided to put a stop to the argument.

"Well, if she's good enough, I see no reason not to include her," he announced, ignoring the barbed glances from his side.

"So, that's the team selected. Now, shall we have a look at what our first fixture is?"

He pulled out the large white card and placed it on the table, whilst the other three stood up and gathered around it to read the contents.

"Oh bugger!" gasped Roger.

"I don't believe it!" Cilla's temper was going downhill by the moment.

Sydney just stared at the page.

Henry pushed in and looked down at the text.

FIXTURES LIST FOR SEYCHELLES CRICKET
LEAGUE 2011
SATURDAY 6th OCTOBER 2011: FIRST MATCH
Seychelles Petroleum vs. Anse Takamaka
Seybrew Scanners vs. HSBC All Stars

In all there were nine matches, and Henry had to read down to the bottom to find his club. Last on the list, he read the words that had produced such an effect in his colleagues, and realised quickly why.

EFCC St Christol vs. Anse Royale (venue to be decided)

Roger Kitson stood, up folded his arms and looked heavenwards.

"Never, in the field of human endeavour, can so much grief have ever been caused by such a trifle!"

FORGIVENESS

11

A Sea Interlude

The meeting broke up with a number of long faces, shaking of heads, and cursing of luck after the first fixture had been revealed. Henry realised he still had four weeks to fix this problem and specifically to deal with the effect on Cilla. She still clearly harboured a considerable grudge over the way that Sydney had treated her father's statue. As the pair of them walked silently back towards the house, he tried once more to lance the boil using a different tactic.

"You know, Cilla, this Anse Royale matter, it really has got a bit out of hand."

He took the grunt he received in reply as a positive and soldiered on. "It's almost a year ago, and you can see how sorry Sydney is for what he did."

There was still little reaction, so Henry decided to deploy his main weapon.

"What would my aunt think if she knew how this little quarrel has dragged on and on and on?"

At this remark, Cilla stopped and turned to him. Was he imagining it, or was there a little tear in the corner of her eye?

"The thing is, Mr Fanshawe—"

"Henry, please."

"The thing is, Mr Fansh… I mean Henry, it was the betrayal that hurt me so. You see…" her voice trailed away.

"Go on, Cilla, your secret will be safe with me."

"Well, Sydney was… well, he was more than just a friend."

Henry was silent.

Sydney.

And Cilla.

The thought of them together took a while to get over. The pair walked on in silence. So this was the relationship that Sydney had alluded to earlier in the week. This was the reason he was so particularly concerned about Cilla's feelings.

Upon reaching the door, Henry, trying hard to break the embarrassed silence, turned to her.

"You know, he really is desperate to make up, Cilla. He just doesn't know where to start."

Cilla, who had regained by now her normal *sang froid*, brushed herself down. "Mr Fanshawe, after what he did in Anse Royale, one rainy season of suffering is not enough. I intend to make him beg on bended knee!"

She marched off home, but her demeanour was a touch lighter, and Henry saw possibilities. Not quite at the pace that Sydney would have wished, but heartening possibilities nonetheless.

In the hall stood a large number of packing cases. His possessions from London. He had not brought much, preferring to keep the old and the new life as distinct as possible. An unconscious fresh start, in a way. But there were some artefacts he could not leave behind in the rain-soaked London autumn. He scrabbled through the cases, opening each until he found his saxophone.

He was all alone in the house – a perfect time he thought, for some melancholic blues. Lifting the instrument carefully out of its case, and placing a new reed in the mouthpiece, he slung it round his neck, and sauntered towards the French windows.

It was already dark. As in all tropical climes, the sun set at much the same time all year, with a speed which often surprised travellers from temperate zones. As he moved onto the veranda, and into the dark wet warmth of the evening, he could feel the jungle exhale with relief at another hot day over. The ever-present chant of the cicadas, laced with cries from creatures he could not recognise, provided the background hum. The sky was clear, far clearer than the streetlight orange, exhaust-tainted air outside his London flat. In its blackness, pinpoint stars glittered, and a cool breeze from the ocean drifted through the trees. 'How could a place which hummed with such activity and anticipation feel quite so tranquil,' he wondered.

He puckered his lips and started playing. Having established that the cicadas moved mainly around B flat, his fingers ran up and down the sax, weaving a melody around this key, throwing in the odd blue note. The plaintive tune ebbed and flowed, occasionally, he imagined, being answered by cries from the jungle. It was a moment to savour, and as he played, the world contracted. Soon there was nothing but the veranda, his saxophone, and the accompaniment of the night. And as the final notes died away, chased into nothingness on the wind, Henry realised that he was happy. For the first time in ages, he was really happy.

* * *

The next morning Henry and Cilla set to unpacking the rest of the cases. He had even discovered some long forgotten relics of a sport he had once also enjoyed. One case revealed an old wetsuit, some goggles, a snorkel and a very ancient pair of swimming trunks. An idea came unbidden to Henry's mind.

"Cilla."

"Yes Mr Fanshawe?"

"Do you know what I am going to do today?"

"I do not, Mr Fanshawe, but I am sure that you will shortly tell me."

"I'm going to go down to the beach at Beauvallon."

"Yes, but…"

"And go snorkelling. I've heard the coral is marvellous."

"They say the best in the world, Mr Fanshawe, but…"

"But what, Cilla?"

"But… with those trunks?"

"What's wrong with them ?" Henry had always rather liked the Hawaiian style.

"Everything!"

He coldly inquired of Cilla where the right area of the beach was. She continued to gaze uncomprehending at his trunks.

"When you get down to the beach," she said, "walk up almost to the end, near the posh hotel. The woods

124

come right down to the shore there, and there is a coconut palm growing over the beach, almost parallel to the sand. Swim directly out from there for about fifty metres. If your trunks make it, then the fish and the corals are there."

Henry could hardly wait and unpacked the rest of his belongings with the speed of the careless. He told Cilla to decide the best place for them.

"That would be the bin then, Mr Fanshawe."

* * *

The beach at Beauvallon was slightly too far to walk, especially in the middle of the day. He decided he would take aunt Esme's old Land Rover, which had languished in the garage by the front drive, but was, according to Cilla, kept filled up and in working order by the gardener. He opened the wooden doors of the shed and, clearing cobwebs as he went, sat down, threw his kit onto the passenger seat, and turned the key. The engine, after a few stutters, burst into life, belching out black smoke and breaking the harmony of the jungle background with a throaty roar. Henry quickly realised that the vehicle lacked a silencer. In fact, it possessed little apart from the chassis, the engine and four wheels. The seats were a makeshift construction of cloth, hung between two metal struts, the dashboard contained the bare minimum of dials, and there were no sides or a roof.

Henry cautiously manoeuvred the machine out onto the drive, trying to accustom himself to the gears, which had an alarming habit of slipping, and the brake which appeared to possess only two settings: nothing and dead stop. He made a mental note to get the thing to a decent dealer as soon as possible, though this minor difficulty would not dissuade him from making it down to Beauvallon Bay. Slowly and carefully he cajoled the car through the gates and down onto the track below. True to its reputation, the Land Rover handled the slope and the potholes with ease, though every single jolt was communicated free from interference to Henry's backside. After proceeding at just a little faster than walking pace, Henry entered the village, the car trailing fumes like a damaged World War Two fighter plunging to earth.

Henry drove on doggedly through the village, with a British stiff upper lip and his eyes on the road ahead. But even he could not help but notice the way that so many villagers had stopped to look on in amazement, some pointing, some running for cover. Children were swiftly snatched up into their mother's arms, pulled inside, and within a few minutes Henry seemed to be passing through a long deserted township. He decided that maybe the communal memory of his aunt's driving still haunted the road, and that the obvious reluctance to remain anywhere near this particular vehicle was an understandable reaction to years of near-misses.

With the Jeep still smoking like a half-finished cigar, Henry rolled into Beauvallon and parked by the souvenir shop. He took out his swimming gear, trying to avoid comparison with the modern versions displayed in front of him. Then, resplendent in his long eighties trunks, he made ready to walk down to the beach a few short paces away. It was all but hidden from sight by the long line of tamarinds, takamakas and coconut palms which fringed the sand, but he could hear the roar of the breakers and the shouts and splashes of swimming children beyond the green wall. He crossed the road and bent down to avoid the low branches and tangles of leaves. The gravel under his feet changed to fine soft white sand and all of a sudden he was gazing out on the heavenly bay.

For a mile to his left, the long curve of white sand extended, caressed by a sea of turquoise. Every so often, a herd of brightly-coloured sun umbrellas gave away the location of one of the few hotels situated along the beach. In the distance on either side of him two headlands fell vertiginously into the water. Directly in front of him, a dark and looming presence, stood Silhouette island, misty and indistinct, some miles away. In various pockets along the beach, people were playing in the water, others snorkelling over coral reefs. Further out, lines of white snaked through the blue. Water-skiers, and for the braver of heart, parascenders, flying high above the boats that pulled them, legs dangling in the air like puppets. He noted with approval some beach cricket, bowlers running in to a stick that served as a wicket, and hurling a tennis ball at some diminutive schoolboy who defended with a small plank fashioned into a makeshift bat.

Henry stepped out of his sandals (he had rapidly come round to this change in footwear) and, almost as quickly, yelped and scrabbled to put them back on again. Under the noonday sun, the sand was burning his soles. In a near sprint, Henry lurched down to the shore. The cool waters flowed blissfully over his feet. Comfortable again, he kicked off his sandals and let his toes sink into the warm wet sand, as the breaking waves spent the last of their energy creeping up the beach to where he stood.

He was contemplating the scene, and working out where the spot for snorkelling lay, when a young female voice startled him.

"Are you looking for the coral, Mr Fanshawe?" the voice enquired. He turned to the source of the interruption.

Henry was rarely lost for words. His innate shyness had been tempered by working in the mouthy, testosterone-fuelled workplace that is the trading floor of a financial institution, and he had quickly worked out that a ready quip or caustic putdown were necessary weapons in that most gladiatorial of arenas. But this time, words wouldn't come. He stared, trying to close a mouth that had fallen open, at a woman in her mid-twenties, whose figure would have adorned any fashion magazine. Long black hair framed a fine and high cheek-boned face the colour of *café au lait*. Large and bewitching green eyes offered silent inducement. A half smile played along her lips. She was taller than the average Seychellois, with long sleek legs, a narrow waist, and shoulders that rippled with suppressed energy. Henry fought against his jawbone, willing it to rise back to its normal position, from where it seemed to have lodged, halfway down his midriff. Attempting to avoid looking directly at her generous chest, barely covered by a bikini top, he concentrated on producing a few words of comprehensible English.

"I don't believe we have met, Mademoiselle... er... Er..."

"Oh, call me Mathilde. No we haven't, but I've heard

all about you!" Mathilde managed to imbue this sentence with a languorous note which left Henry feeling yet more flustered.

"So, are you the Mathilde who plays cricket?" When in trouble, Henry always reverted to tried and tested ground.

"*Oui*," breathed Mathilde. She was standing uncomfortably close.

Henry was getting desperate. "Left-hander or right-hander?" he stuttered.

"I generally bat right-handed and field at slip, though I am comfortable in most positions." This was said with a slight inversion of her lip. God, she's playing with me now, Henry thought. Mathilde continued, "You are looking for the palm tree, no?"

"Palm tree?"

"You know, the palm tree that shows where the coral is?"

The outside world began to filter back into Henry's mind.

"Yes, of course, that's it, er... the palm tree, coral, fishes, that sort of thing."

"Come, let me show you and maybe we can talk a little."

Henry smiled weakly as she walked off down the beach, beckoning him to follow her. Those who looked on (and there were many) would have seen a tall beauty, gliding cat-like across the sand, followed by an old man shuffling, pulled by some invisible lead, for all the world like an old Labrador, tongue hanging out, eyes permanently fixed on the retreating posterior of its owner.

"So, Monsieur Fanshawe, how do you like our island?"

"At this precise moment, Mademoiselle, I think I can safely say that it has bowled me over."

"Please, Monsieur, its Mathilde."

"Of course. And, Mathilde, it's Henry."

"Henri. Such a delightfully English name." Mathilde delivered this in a breathy French accent which had Henry's tongue again tied in knots. When they reached the palm tree signifying coral he was quite sad to leave her. He turned to say goodbye when Mathilde laid a languorous hand on his arm.

"Maybe when you have finished your swim we could have a drink over there?"

Mathilde waved her hand in the direction of a bar along the beach.

"That would be delightful, Mathilde."

"Then I will see you there, Monsieur Henri." Henry watched the slim figure retreat up the beach, and wished that he were young again. The whole hearted approval of the males of the committee, and the equally fervent repudiation by the female was now completely comprehensible. Not just the physical perfection either, he reflected, but that naiveté, and sharp intellect. What a girl!

Henry, still a touch discombobulated, addressed himself to the water, and specifically to the task of putting on his flippers. Flippers were definitely needed, as there was a fair amount of water to be crossed, and more importantly the initial shallows were dotted with the tell-tale black smudges which indicated the presence of sea urchins. Where the sand gave out, the rock itself was uneven and might be sharp. Henry was willing therefore

130

to trade looking like an idiot on land for a few minutes for the advantage conferred in the water. But he had not counted on the difficulty, with his advancing years, of putting the blessed things on. He was not as supple as he once had been, and he had never been very supple. Soon he was rolling around in the surf with his knee up as near to his chin as possible, fingers locked in the effort of trying to shoe-horn on a flipper.

A number of children had gathered round by the time Henry finally managed, with one last grunt, to get the second flipper on. When he stood up, goggles over his head, the small crowd started clapping. He mouthed a few curses, turned away and flapped into the surf.

With the tide in, the water was deep enough to start swimming a few paces out, and Henry launched himself like a newly-named liner into the ocean, creating as he did a bow wave of almost similar proportion. Paddling out slowly with his flippered feet, he looked down at the sea bed beneath him.

At first, it was if anything a little disappointing. Large masses of green weed covered the sea floor a foot beneath his mask, punctuating by the odd rocky outcrop into which sea urchins clustered. The water was sandy and not particularly clear, though the occasional flash of silver darting away from him betokened a moderately fishy presence.

This continued for fifty metres or so, and Henry began to wonder about his navigation, when the weed abruptly ended and the seabed fell to a deeper level. Henry suddenly found himself swimming over rocks encrusted with dead grey coral; interesting, he thought, but hardly the Garden of Eden of which he had read in the guide books. Then, sensing motion to his right, he shifted his head, and entered a new world.

Half a dozen yards away lay a wall of silver. But this wall moved, both as a body and within itself. He realised it was composed of hundreds of little fish, whitebait-like, performing their acrobatic manoeuvres in perfect harmony. All of a sudden the huge shoal would, for no apparent reason, change direction as one, in the blink of an eye, and head off on another tangent. As it moved, shafts of sunlight diluted by passage through the water, would catch certain scales, changing the colour from silver to an iridescent purple or blue. It was a natural light show as breathtaking as any Henry had seen at the jazz festivals he used to frequent. He followed the shoal out to sea, and quickly became aware of other fish feeding on the rocks, which were by now covered with living corals of varying colour, size and shape. He had entered the reef proper.

It was like a miniature forest, with Henry floating above, looking down on fish of all shapes, sizes and colours: large parrot fish with leopard skin markings in green and grey, and Rorschach blots of indigo round the eyes; elegant angel fish the size of dinner plates in yellow and black, trailing improbably long fins; and scores of smaller creatures, each a different hue. Shoals of silver sea bream and rays flicked their way imperturbably through the sea, and a line of almost-translucent squid moved in a Red Arrows V formation. And on the sea bed, corals of all colours, some fern-like with fluorescent violet tips, others more solid in pinks and reds. In between, Henry could make out the small tentacles of anemones, questing for prey, and deeper down, the ominous W-shaped mouths of giant clams in tyrian purple.

He stopped swimming and gazed down upon the scene, transfixed. As he became used to the scale and the light, yet more revealed itself. With a start, he saw a rock move, and then realised it was a turtle, languidly gliding through the water, unconcerned with the onlooker floating above him. In fact, few of the inhabitants seemed to care in the least about his presence. They would flit quickly away if he got too close but would then resume their grazing a few feet away as if nothing had happened. In the midst of all this teeming life, Henry could do no more than gaze in wonder.

He stayed out as long as he could, anxious not to miss one moment of such beauty, and when he finally came ashore, had little idea of how long he had been swimming. But the sun, high in the sky when he had arrived, was already falling almost visibly towards the horizon. When he looked at his watch, he was surprised to see that he had been afloat for nearly two hours. Still exhilarated with his discovery, he walked back along the beach to a bar he had noted earlier. As the dusk approached, Henry settled himself comfortably into a chair and ordered a cold bottle of Seybrew with which to toast the imminent sunset.

The sun dived slowly behind Silhouette island, a motion scarcely perceptible at first, but then, its disc became a semicircle of red and then a magenta crescent. Henry could almost feel the earth rotating underneath him as the sun set. In the warm dusk, as he listened to the sounds and sights of the beach, a chair was pulled up next to him and a slightly more dressed Mathilde appeared.

"*Bonsoir, Henri,*" she breathed and sat down beside him. "It is all very beautiful, no?"

"A perfect tropical island, Mathilde."

"Henri, you will find that it is not perfect. But it is beautiful."

Mathilde beckoned the waiter over and ordered a beer. Henry noticed that he too scurried to obey her request with undignified speed. She really was bewitching. He turned to the ocean.

A number of fishermen had been dragging a large net through the shallows, some on the beach, some out to sea. Looping round, the net was then dragged, bulging, out of the water, and as it emerged, all manner of sea creatures were thrown onto the sand. With speed borne of practice the fishermen sorted through the catch, throwing some back, and keeping the rest for the growing queue of buyers lined up to purchase their supper. Other fishermen could be seen taking to small boats to row out and collect lobster pots marked with buoys, lanterns twinkling on the prows. A few campfires appeared, and the sound of clinking bottles, radios and laughter. Soon it was quite dark save for the dotted yellow flames on the beach, the neon bar sign, and the glow from various hotels.

Bottle in hand, Mathilde turned and looked into Henry's eyes.

"Henri, have you heard from the Cricket Board?"

"Yes. In fact, we got the ruling from the Board yesterday and ..."

"Please tell me it's good news!"

"Well, half and half. You are OK to play until a women's league is formed, for this season at least."

She gave a little clap for joy and smiled broadly in the green fluorescent light.

"That deals with this year. Then we start a women's team, eh, Henri?"

The thought of eleven Mathildes made Henry feel weak at the knees.

"That is an interesting proposal, Mathilde. But first we have this season to contend with. I hope to see you at the meeting next Sunday."

"I will be there. And now I must say goodnight."

"Good night Mathilde."

"Good night Henri. *Á dimanche.*" She downed her beer in one, rose and slipped soundlessly into the dark.

Henry leant back in the warm blackness, savouring the sea breeze and the smell of wood smoke. He would have happily gone on sitting there and enjoying the surroundings for some time, but it occurred to him that he really ought to return home. Cilla would be expecting him and it would not do to keep her waiting. It was hard to pull himself away from this spot, but finally with an effort of will, he arose and ambled back to the car. It was equipped with headlights, though one seemed not to work and the other was trained on a point some five metres up and to the left of the road. Henry carefully negotiated his way back through the quiet village and finally through the gates of the Manor. A figure stood there, framed in silhouette in the doorway.

Anxious to get his excuse in first, he stumbled from the car, flippers in hand. "Very sorry, Cilla. Know I'm a bit tardy, but the time just flew past."

It did not work.

"You're late for your dinner, Mr Fanshawe."

"Yes. Awfully sorry to muck you about."

"How long did you swim for?"

"About two hours I think," Henry felt himself move helplessly back into guilty schoolboy mode. "I really didn't notice the time."

"Two hours? It must have been much longer than that. Did you put some sunscreen on?"

"Sunscreen?"

"You'd better come inside."

Once in the hall, Cilla looked at Henry and her stern face took on more of a concerned appearance.

"Thought so."

She vanished into the kitchen and came back bearing a bottle containing some foul-looking brown liquid. "Better put some of this on otherwise you'll have a terrible night."

"What's it for?"

"Mr Fanshawe, have you seen yourself?"

Henry moved in front of the large mirror in the hall and almost jumped. Staring back at him was a creature with some resemblance to the Henry he knew well, but in a shade of vermillion only seen previously on the most well-boiled of lobsters. The sight was only made worse by the white unburnt areas left by his mask. A lobster wearing a large pair of pale sunglasses. Turning away from the apparition, Henry accepted the bottle from Cilla and hurried upstairs. After a thorough application he returned to the dining room, now resembling a tomato that had been covered in a thin layer of brown sauce. He knew it was not a pretty sight.

Cilla hurried him through dinner, trying to avoid conversation and eye contact as much as possible. She was, Henry thought, still a little embarrassed about the exchanges of the previous evening. He was determined to sort out what he now realised was a lover's tiff, though where Cilla was concerned a tiff might as well be a lifelong blood vendetta. The bones of a plan were forming in his mind. And he would need to consult with potential allies sooner rather than later.

12
A Day in the Capital

Over the next few days Henry settled in, arranging his prize possessions from the London flat throughout his new home. Cilla hovered, to ensure that minimal change was wrought on the current furnishings. Today, they were unpacking pictures. Cilla had removed a silver framed photo and was looking at it.

"Careful with that, Cilla!" Henry snapped with uncharacteristic venom. Cilla froze, still holding the photo.

In the silence, she held out the picture and pointed. "Is that you, Mr Fanshawe? My, you look most handsome. And who is the beautiful women?"

"That," said Henry, "was my wife, Vanessa."

The look on his face prevented Cilla from replying. She quietly passed him the photo and left the room. Henry sat cradling the frame.

"My God, you'd have loved it here," he muttered.

When Cilla returned, Henry had opened the crate bearing his favourite artworks, and with a flourish pulled one out. It was a large Fauvist lithograph of the *Old Port at Nice*, by Dufy.

"This," he announced, "I would like to go in the dining room."

Cilla looked uncomprehendingly at the violent red and purple scene. She was less than impressed with the concept of a landscape picture in any case.

"What is the point, Mr Fanshawe, of a portrait with the main thing missing?"

"But Cilla, it's a Dufy!"

"Used to do better when I was in school."

Cilla was the type of no-nonsense traditionalist who, like the red squirrel, had all but died out in England. A Mary Poppins without the smile, or indeed the figure, of Julie Andrews. Yet brimming with vitality, loyalty, and scarily efficient. At the moment Henry admired rather than liked Cilla, but he felt sure that, over time, he would come to be as fond of her as his aunt had been.

Henry wanted to swap the Dufy with a particularly gloomy portrait of Sir Cholmondely Fanshawe, a fierce looking Victorian gentleman with large mutton chop sideburns. Henry found that staring up every morning at the sneer born of imperial arrogance put him off his eggs.

"Cilla, not only is that portrait awful, but the grimace on the old boy's face does not aid digestion. I don't want him staring down at me whilst I'm having breakfast."

"But this... this... I can scarcely call it a picture. All splodges of colours, and the wrong colours at that. And all this red! He must have been hit by a van while he was painting it."

"How can you say that, Cilla!"

"Or drunk."

"It's a perfect example of Dufy's Fauvist period." Henry was beginning to get a little irritated and this always made him sound pompous.

"Looks like a perfect example of my primary school art period, Mr Fanshawe."

After several minutes of full and frank exchange of views on the relevance and beauty of modern art in the world, Henry gave up. The Dufy was placed in a less central position and Sir Cholmondeley continued for the present to gaze down on the breakfast table. After all his pictures had been hung, Henry reckoned it a score draw, and there was, he figured, always time to sneak in a few changes later. Though he suspected that Cilla was thinking exactly the same.

As they sat with a cup of coffee, Henry probed Cilla about her background. He wished to glean some information for the plan that was beginning to form in his mind. She was surprisingly forthcoming.

"I was born in Anse Royale. My father was Mayor there, you know. He enlisted young and fought in World War Two in Malaysia. When he returned he found the island practically starving. We'd been cut off for most of the war and everything was simply running out. My father, fresh from the army, with a pile of commendations and campaign medals, was able to get into a senior position at Anse Royale and sort out the corruption. I can't say it was comfortable when I was growing up, but we had enough food, not always the case elsewhere. He ended up as Mayor, and used all his ex-army contacts to get Anse Royale what it needed."

"So why the statue on the cricket pitch?"

"That was his other great love. Learnt it from his English friends in India and Malaysia. He always told me there was an English colonel who was not only one of the bravest men he had ever met, but always insisted on challenging the local villages to a game of cricket."

"Cricket? In Malaysia?"

"Oh, half of them didn't know one end of a bat from another. They had hours of coaching prior to the game. But everyone loved it, and the areas he covered were a lot more peaceful than some others after the war. Not that the colonel cared much. He was sacked for advancing more slowly than his orders permitted, and ended up after the war as a cricket master in some English school. Father used to correspond with him for many years."

"So your father founded the Anse Royale club, a bit like Aunt Esme here?"

"Yes, that's how they got to know each other; in fact that's how I got to work here. Your aunt asked him, one year at the Cricket Board AGM, shortly after her husband had died, whether he knew of anyone prepared to keep house for her. I'd just finished at college and was looking for a job."

"It must have hurt to see his statue harmed like that."

"Deep inside, Mr Fanshawe, deep inside. I felt such a rage! All over a trifle. And now the Anse Club are being difficult about repairing it, it makes me so angry. He saved that village, just like Mrs Fanshawe did here."

"I am sure that something will turn up. I am ever the optimist, Cilla."

Cilla turned to him with, if not the full version, at least the semblance of a smile.

"Mr Fanshawe, you may have terrible taste in pictures, you can't look after yourself properly, and you've a way to go on your blues, but I think you're a good person."

And with that backhanded compliment she departed, leaving Henry unsure whether to be pleased or not. In the end he decided to take it positively. He was after all, by nature, a positive man.

* * *

The weekend was approaching rapidly, and Henry was itching to put his peace plan into action. This would have to be carefully managed, for maximum effect, and some preparation was necessary before the Anse Royale game. He needed time in the national archives in Victoria, and most of all he needed to acquire some local knowledge without Cilla finding out. Having left her to finish various less sensitive areas of the unpacking, he picked up his wallet, and walked out into the garden in search of Pierre and the Boy.

After strolling happily over the smooth green lawn with its well-kept borders, he arrived at a little garden shed, which was hidden away behind a large hibiscus. He knocked on the door, and waited. It opened slowly to reveal a large black face, and a smile containing more space than teeth.

"Mr Fanshawe, *viens*. We were just making cha. Like some?"

Pierre's accent was heavy. Henry entered, and in the gloom of the shed could just make out his colleague sitting on a stool in the corner. A kettle stood on a small primus stove and two battered tin mugs were laid out beside it. Pierre ushered Henry over to the work bench, where, after some rummaging around among the piles of tools, pots and old bottles, he came up, smiling, with an old and dusty third mug. After wiping this on his equally dirty jacket, he handed it over to Henry.

"Thank you very much." Henry sat down gingerly on one of the stools, trying to work out if there were time before the kettle boiled to clean the mug he had been handed. He picked it up and gave it a surreptitious wipe on his shirt when the other two were not looking. Pierre smiled his toothless smile.

"Liking it here, Mr Fanshawe?"

"I am enjoying it very much, and may I add that your gardens are beautiful, Pierre."

"Thank you boss, though they aren't *my* gardens of course." Henry felt the gentle jibe as Pierre continued, "Reckon the cricket pitch is pretty good, too. Last Sunday morning, the Boy rolled it from top to bottom."

Henry looked at the figure in the corner and reflected, that for a man pushing eighty, the nickname was far from apt. He replied, "Yes, I thought the pitch was excellent. In fact I've seen county pitches in England which didn't come up to your standard."

Pierre sat back, pleased.

"Pierre, I need something doing very quietly and very quickly," said Henry. "Nothing bad or illegal you understand, but I am keen that Cilla doesn't find out about it."

"Not much round that Cilla don't find out about sooner or later." Pierre was clearly unimpressed, scratching his head with a worried look on his face.

Henry went on, "Later is OK; it's the sooner bit that I want her to be in the dark over." Pierre still seemed reluctant, so Henry decided to play his final card.

"There'd probably be something in it for you."

Two wrinkled twenty rupee notes were placed on the table. At this, a change came over the gardener. The smile returned, and with a wink he replied.

"Then, Mr Fanshawe, I think we have a deal."

"Good, now here's what you have to do…"

A few minutes and some more rupees later, Henry re-emerged from the shed, wiping his lips to try to remove the taste of the tea. Henry did not know how liquid fertiliser tasted, but he would have laid a bet it would have been a bit like the substance he had just forced down his throat, smiling all the while as his oesophagus was being gently shredded.

Still, Pierre had agreed to help in the conspiracy, leaving Henry able to manage without resorting to Sydney. He felt decidedly more comfortable with this state of affairs. Now, to Victoria, to put the first part of the plan into action.

That afternoon Henry walked down to the village. He did not want to attract too much attention and using the Land Rover was akin to hoisting the mainsail in this respect. He had decided to take the bus to Victoria, and made his way to the bus stop, which was peopled with a few villagers. All shook his hands in that semi-formal manner of greeting which is more French than English. Henry loved the friendliness and the overt good nature of his neighbours, and it was hard not to smile and reciprocate in the face of such gentle humour. It reminded him of a long-lost England. Chiding himself for being so hopelessly nostalgic for a sunlit past that probably had never existed, he settled down to wait.

A small cloud of dust on the horizon betrayed the imminence of the bus. When it arrived at the end of its route before turning back to Victoria, everyone on the bus shook hands again, and then with Henry, and then with the driver, after which there was a pause whilst various village matters were discussed. Finally, a quarter of an hour later, the driver, who had introduced himself as George, put out his cigarette on one of the front tyres, and climbed back into his seat.

"Better be getting along. All aboard!"

And off they went like a pre-war factory outing.

The bus left Beauvallon behind and climbed to the brow of the hill. Henry was planning his day. He wished to spend some time in the National Library, combing old newspapers for information about Cilla's father. In particular he needed some decent photographs, but he was also interested in discovering the man who had replicated his aunt's work in Anse Royale. After the war, the Seychelles (or Seven Sisters islands as it was then known) had been forgotten by its colonial masters, who were too busy rebuilding their own country, and it had endured many years of hardship and famine.

It seemed to Henry that in coping with this period, the country forged a national identity that finally led to independence in 1976, ironically, shortly after the British had started to take their responsibilities seriously again, and had furnished the islands with a brand new international airport. People like Cilla's father, Monsieur

Kheda, and, later, his aunt Esme had been the catalysts of this new-found confidence. He wished to see how they had done it, on an isolated collection of islands whose entire population was smaller than many British cities.

The steaming jungle which surrounded the road had changed into rain forest, swathed in mist, as the bus reached the brow of the hill. The engine's roar died, replaced by the shriek of overused brakes as the vehicle now descended along the winding road into Victoria, stopping every so often, sometimes to let a car pass, sometimes for passengers, and sometimes because the driver had seen a friend and felt like a quick chat. Houses were built in a tangle on the most vertiginous of slopes around the road, thrown together at random. Everywhere was entwined with purple bougainvillea and deep blue horn of plenty. Henry looked down to the centre of the capital, a small, low-rise conurbation, and further on, the docks, full of ships of varying sizes, from large tankers to the small fishing boats and yachts of the well-to-do. On the distant horizon he could make out Praslin, the second biggest island of the group. As the descent began to flatten out, the bus stuttered into Victoria proper.

Henry alighted in what he thought looked like the centre and looked around. On one side of him was a loud and garish market, in a very French style, vegetables of rainbow colours laid out elegant patterns on large trestle tables. Next to them stood blood-spattered Seychellois fishermen with a plethora of marine life peering out from the large ice filled boxes in front of them. And throughout, the bewitching smell of spices vied for supremacy with less appetising aromas. He traced the smell to a stall with sacks of every imaginable condiment, open to entice buyers. The coloured powders, dried leaves and seeds had been arranged with an artist's eye and Henry feasted his senses on the palette laid out before him.

Henry had learnt that practically the entire population of the Seychelles lived in Victoria, and it seemed that most of them were at the market. He made his way through the crowd of buyers, and looked around for directions. In the corner was a large sign with a plan of the town in ceramic tiles. Tracing his finger over the map he found 'Marche Selwyn Selwyn-Clarke' (so good they named it twice, thought Henry). From there he plotted his route to the Bibliotheque Nationale, which was to be found in the small enclave of government buildings which lined a rather grander road, Independence Street, a few blocks away.

He left the market behind, turned into Albert Street, the Oxford Street of Victoria (had Oxford Street been thirty yards long). At the end of the street he noticed the strangest monument. The Victoria clock tower, mistaken by so many tourists for a smaller Big Ben, was in fact a full size replica of a smaller monument that resided in the middle of the rather run-down area, adjacent to Victoria Station, and only a minute from his old London flat. In London, Henry scarcely noticed it amongst the large glass towers which now lined Victoria Street. Here, it stood in the middle of the roundabout, unassailed by other buildings, painted in silver, revealing its true 19th century garishness for all to see. Opposite, the beautiful white towered Anglican Cathedral sat amongst graceful plane trees. He turned past the oddly angular, almost Japanese,

Palace of Justice, and various national banks, towards the library.

Once inside, the sounds of the city outside dimmed to a low hum. Henry approached the receptionist.

"Good morning, I was wondering if you could help me?"

The receptionist looked up, adjusted her glasses and assumed the position common to all librarians, body language subtly inferring that contractually she was bound to listen and assist but only at the greatest of personal cost and bother.

"I am looking for your newspaper archives."

"Third room on the left, you'll find microfiches and a reader." With that she turned half away and resumed her reading, of, Henry noticed, a scarcely suitable Mills and Boon.

Henry wanted to scrutinise the press for a number of reasons. He was keen to read up old match reports, to find out a little more about the previous year's clash, and to research Cilla's father. It would be a long afternoon.

After many attempts, he finally located the relevant microfiche and laid it on the reader:

FRACAS IN CRICKET MATCH AT ANSE

The last match in the season at Anse Royale was blemished by an unseemly tussle involving the captain of EFCC St Christol and several Anse Royale team members. It is understood that the captain, Mr Sydney Mason, damaged the statue of the Anse Royale club founder, Mr William Kheda, before removing its head and placing it in a trifle prepared by the home team for tea. This unsavoury incident overshadowed an exciting match which was won by Anse Royale by one wicket. St Christol batted first and amassed a seemingly unbeatable score off forty overs of 256 runs, most coming from an excellent middle order partnership between Reverend Roger Kitson and Louis Kamling, one of twins playing for St Christol. However, the St Christol bowlers were off form, and thanks to a century by the Anse skipper, Major Raymond Sitwell, and some useful knocks from other team members, Anse Royale were left requiring six runs off the final over with two wickets to spare. Curtley Smith, the young fast bowler from St Christol, who many in the game reckon to be a bright prospect, managed to take one wicket with the first ball of the over, but his inconsistency was to prove St Christol's downfall when the next ball went for four byes. There then followed considerable argument about an LBW decision. This would have given St Christol the match. The umpire, Mr Alphonse, from Anse Royale, ruled it not out, and Anse Royale went on to win. Discussions continued after the match had ended, becoming violent after Mr Mason's act of vandalism. The Anse Royale captain commented, "A good match was marred by the type of mindless actions which we associate with football, or worse, English cricket. I devoutly hope this does not catch on in our game."

Henry breathed a sigh and sat back. This mess would take some sorting, he thought, and it was imperative to move his plan forward rapidly. He trusted Pierre to keep to his side of the bargain, and so it was left to Henry to find as many photos of Kheda as he could, in the remaining hour or so of library time. He scouted back through the papers to an earlier year, and was soon rewarded.

ANSE ROYALE STARTS CRICKET CLUB

Following in the footsteps of Beauvallon, Anse Royale has set up a cricket club and hopes to field a team in the forthcoming 1990 Season. The club is the idea of Captain William Kheda (retd), the current mayor of Anse Royale, who tells us that he learnt to play cricket in the Far East during the war. Anse Royale will be having trials on September 16th so if you are local and wish to join, come along to the village hall at 12.30 pm.

Underneath the article, there was a black and white photograph of a gentleman in cricketing whites, with a large handlebar moustache; bat proudly held forward as if defending a ball. Henry did not need to read the legend underneath to recognise a family likeness to Cilla. The same look of concentration furrowed this man's brow, and underneath a set of bushy eyebrows, the steely glint of his stare seemed to Henry to be directed straight at him. This was perfect.

Henry found a few more portraits in the pages of the *Seychelles Nation*. It was just what he needed to put into action phase two of his plan. He left the newspaper room with a handful of photocopies, and nodded cheerfully to the librarian on the way out. There was no reaction.

13
Preparations

Over the next few days, Henry busied himself with learning more about his first opponents. He had a number of meetings with Sydney, some of them useful, others which descended into drinking bouts, leaving Henry with the vague feeling that something had been discussed but he could not recall quite what. Cilla's mood, whilst generally cheerful, would take on a darker note on the mornings after.

"You mustn't encourage him, Mr F, he's such a child when it comes to drink."

Henry agreed with this in principle, and tried to fix times of day when drinking would not be considered, i.e. before lunch. But occasionally circumstances would necessitate an evening visit, and this, Henry knew, lead to temptation which neither of them could resist. On these occasions he took to carrying a notebook in the hope that some sense might be committed to paper before he found himself unable to hold the pen.

Gradually, the tactical plan emerged for the Anse Royale match. The other team had one excellent batsman, who tended to score the lion's share of the runs, Sydney explained.

"He's sharp and a rapid scorer. The other batsmen try just to defend, in the expectation that he will do the scoring. So we target him with Curtley and Rajiv. If we can get him out quickly, then the match should be ours. Their bowlers aren't much to write home about."

Then he delivered a bombshell. "I've been thinking, Henry, on how to atone for last year's behaviour, and I have a plan. If you promise to keep it to yourself, I'd like to discuss it with you."

"Of course, Sydney."

'How many bloody plans are there surrounding this match?' Henry thought. At this rate, enough for a minor Shakespearean comedy. He decided to keep quiet about his own scheme. The situation was complex enough already.

"I think a magnanimous gesture is called for," said Sydney. "One which will show me as a true sportsman to Cilla, and provide Anse Royale with some advantage in the match, though not one large enough to enable them to win."

"What do you intend to do?"

"I intend, Henry, to walk."

"Walk, where?"

"From the wicket, old boy, at the beginning of our innings. I will retire without scoring as a gesture of contrition for my actions."

Henry was silent for a moment as he took this in. "But we could lose!"

Sydney attempted to look pious. "Henry, where matters of such importance are at stake, what is one result?"

"It's a bloody lot, that's what it is." Henry was losing his cool, "It's my first match in charge and you want to throw it!"

"I wouldn't go as far as that, Henry," replied Sydney reproachfully. "We've a strong batting line up. With Mathilde, Roger and the two brothers, more than enough to beat them."

"You think?"

"But imagine how it would look to Cilla. It might do the trick. Anyway, my mind's made up."

Henry made to argue. But realising that Sydney was deadly serious, he thought better of it. "I hope you're right, Sydney Mason, I just hope you're damned right."

"I know I am, just do me a favour and keep it to yourself, eh?"

"I wouldn't dare tell anyone, Sydney. They'd probably lynch you!"

Henry left in a bad mood, heightened by the impending phone call that he needed to make to Anse Royale regarding the location of the match. When he arrived home, the phone was ringing. It was from Anse Royale's captain.

"Good evening Mr Fanshawe, Major Sitwell here," a cultured voice drawled down the line. Already Henry disliked him.

"About the match. I was hoping that you would agree to hold it at Anse again. We wanted to show that there were no hard feelings about last year."

So, thought Henry, home advantage cloaked in a skein of forgiveness. Very clever. He would have objected, but this time it fitted rather neatly with his plans, and in a voice dripping, he hoped, with bonhomie he replied, "Of course, Major, we would be delighted to accept your hospitality again. Though may I ask you, is Mrs Mason aiming to provide any refreshment this time?"

"I thought it would be in the interests of all that she stood down from the Teas Committee that weekend."

"A sound course of action, Major."

"Thank you. It's only a pity that Kheda's statue will not be there to preside over the game this year."

Henry was alarmed, and tried not to show it. "What, has the statue gone?"

"Only to behind the clubhouse, Mr Fanshawe. We haven't got the money to replace the head and it looked rather odd as a torso."

With some relief, Henry sympathised with the financial plight of the club, discussed the severe economic conditions in general, moved to the weather, and after a full exchange of views on these matters, rung off. Then he slunk quickly and quietly into the garden to update Pierre on events, casting around from time to time to make sure that Cilla was not watching. In some ways, the news from Anse had made things easier.

The Season would commence in a fortnight, leaving EFCC St Christol two Sundays to practise and hone their skills. Despite protestations from Cilla, who was none too pleased at hearing that Henry had also met the female in question, Mathilde was pencilled in at number five.

The next Sunday, after a short meeting, it was back to the nets for some batting practice. Henry acted as a rehearsal bowler, sending down his spinning balls first to Sydney and Simon then Roger, until it was Mathilde's turn.

He knew it was Mathilde's turn, not through being told, but because from behind him, as he was walking back with the ball, all conversation was suddenly extinguished. It was as if a radio had been turned off. Looking round, he saw Mathilde exit from the clubhouse and saunter towards the nets. Nothing could be said to be wrong or unusual with what she was wearing, he told himself. All regulation length and the right colour. There was just something in the way she moved in that skirt, was it a little on the short side? No, it was just the born grace of a girl who would have shimmied effortlessly onto any catwalk in the world. The cap on her head, a touch coquettish in its angle? No laws against that, thought Henry. Polo shirt a little tight? Oh God, I'm becoming a dirty old man! How can I bowl to this?

He got to his mark and tried to compose himself. Mathilde took her guard. Running up to bowl, he was momentarily put off by the wide smile she flashed at him. The first ball was disastrously wide.

"Pull yourself together, man, for God's sake" he muttered to himself as he walked back again. "This is cricket!" He turned and ran in again, ready this time for that smile. Imparting a nice touch of topspin to the ball to make it slide on, he bowled and then stood watching as with a truly elegant shot, Mathilde lifted it over the nets for a textbook lofted drive. Her timing was, as Sydney had said, exquisite, and she barely broke sweat as she thumped ball after ball into the nets, cutting one moment, sweeping the next. After a while, Henry's regard for her obvious charms was exchanged for a strong respect for her batting skills. Maybe, he thought, Sydney's desperate gesture will not consign us to defeat after all.

She fared almost as well with the strike bowlers, very much in control of Rajiv's spin and medium fast inswingers from Jean. Curtley beat her bat a few times when on top pace, but as Sydney remarked to Henry, those balls would have beaten most county cricketers. As dusk fell over the pitch and the shadows lengthened on the grass, Henry reflected that the session had been a good one. Apart from the threat of Sydney's lunatic gesture, the team had advanced on all fronts, and with another practice day to come, he felt fairly confident, even without the undoubted batting prowess of his captain.

* * *

That week, Henry spent a large amount of time in the garden shed. He explained one evening to Cilla that he was 'discussing the flora of the Seychelles compared to that of the United Kingdom'.

"Don't believe a word of it," she announced as the dinner plates were swept from underneath Henry's nose. "You're up to something, aren't you?"

Henry, never very good a keeping a secret, ached to tell her, but decided that it would not be prudent at this sensitive point.

"I was particularly interested in the differing growth rates of roses in the two countries."

This met with a hurumph.

Loudly enough so that he could claim later to have told her, Henry shouted after her retreating form, "Oh, and Cilla, I'm going into town this evening. There's a film on I've been really wanting to see."

He had little idea of what was on, or indeed whether there was a cinema in Victoria, but he reckoned it was a strong likelihood. As an excuse it would have to do.

Having spent another enjoyable afternoon swimming around the reef at Beauvallon, this time with sunscreen applied, he returned to the house and started making his evening preparations. He had intended to get the bus back from town again, as the Land Rover would have been quite useless for the subterfuge that Henry planned.

As he walked out onto the drive, from the bushes to his right he heard an unmistakable sound,

"PSSSST!"

He stopped to look around. Next to him, a hibiscus wobbled.

"PSSTT!"

From the undergrowth, like a reverse Cheshire cat, a wide smiling mouth appeared, shortly after to be framed by the face of Pierre his gardener. Then behind, in ghostly silence, the Boy materialised on his shoulder.

"You ready, boss? Got the van down the track for us."

They walked in silence to the track and Henry pulled himself into the passenger seat. Pierre turned the key and as the engine spluttered into life, he turned and gave the widest of toothless grins.

"Anse Royale next stop."

Henry, quite unused to even the most minor of legal infractions, spent most of the voyage staring worriedly at every bend, imagining behind it a squad of crack policemen waiting to pounce. However, the journey was uneventful, and as full darkness enveloped the island, they coasted slowly and quietly into Anse Royale.

Anse Royale stood on the Eastern side of the island, down the shore from the airport. A long sandy beach was protected by a reef further out to sea, over which the Indian

157

Ocean crashed. Inland, along the Rue Les Cannelles, stood the small centre of the village. And just inland, past the takamaka trees that fringed the white sand of the beach, interspersed with palms that stuck out onto the beach at crazy angles, was a tract of flat sandy ground. It was puddled with brackish water, and dotted with the odd salt bush. Some of the area had been drained and planted with tough grass to create the Anse Royale cricket pitch.

"The clubhouse is just over there," whispered Pierre, pointing at a shack about thirty yards away. "We should be able to get along the fence and through there just behind it."

Henry had put on something dark for this occasion, only to find that anything dark was also extremely hot. Dressed in a pair of old black jeans and long brown shirt that he could only have bought in the late seventies, he was already sweating profusely by the time he alighted from the van onto the patch of scrubby broken ground adjacent to the cricket pitch. Pierre hopped down beside him and then, with a surprisingly agile leap, the Boy followed.

The three figures picked their way carefully through the undergrowth tumbling onto the well cut grass of the pitch. They ended up behind a high, light wooden fence that looked easily scalable. It proved to be less so, and Henry in particular laboured hard to get over. After he had caught his shirt on a nail and ripped it for the third time, he lost patience and gave the fence a sharp kick. The sound seemed to carry on for ever, freezing the three companions where they stood. But it produced a large hole through which Henry could just squeeze.

Once through the fence, they made their way to the

158

clubhouse, a large wooden affair with an empty pedestal standing in front. Unfolding the tarpaulin they had brought for the purpose, they quickly found what they were looking for and wrapped it up. It all went, Henry thought, rather well, except for the fence, and in a few minutes they were nearing the van with their prize.

"Shouldn't count our chickens though," he muttered as they approached the vehicle, and, as if on cue, they had just reached their destination when a large and strong ray of torchlight seemed to illuminate not only the three of them, but most of the rest of the surrounding countryside. From behind the dazzling light, a recognisable voice issued forth,

"Stand completely still!"

They froze as the torch bobbed towards them. As it grew closer, Henry put a name to the shadowy figure behind the light. It was the Chief of Police.

"I thought something was up when I heard the van go through St Christol. Policeman's intuition. Followed you all the way here. Now, can you explain to me what is going on?"

Henry, for the second time in a month, was possessed by visions of being locked up in a hot and small cell in the island's prison.

The torch bobbed from one miscreant to the next. It was Pierre's turn to be illuminated first. "Ah, Pierre. You do have a habit of appearing on these occasions don't you, with your lackey," and the light flicked onto the Boy, who smiled guilelessly.

When the torch was trained on the next figure, the Chief affected some shock. "Mr Fanshawe, I am surprised

159

to see you here. Maybe you can spread some light on this affair."

This line was delivered with a slight chuckle which contained no mirth whatsoever.

Haltingly, and with an unconvincing and guilty disposition, Henry attempted to explain. The Chief listened carefully. He was still, Henry noted, wearing his mirrored shades, which must have made it almost impossible to see anything. Henry went over the plan to the Chief, hoping dearly that he would understand, once a fundamentally honest reason had been provided.

When he had finished, the Chief remained silent for a while, as if weighing up the arguments. After what seemed an eternity, he spoke.

"It seems that you have been using rather unconventional means for an end that you feel justifies this law breaking."

Henry pushed his hands forward involuntarily, expecting the cuffs to be produced any moment.

"It was lucky that *I* found you at it," said the Chief.

Henry disagreed fervently with this statement.

"Any other officer would have arrested you straight away."

The chuckle in his voice had assumed a small measure of actual humour.

"But now I know your plan, I think a police escort to the destination would be most sensible."

Henry breathed a huge sigh of relief. Thoughts of a lengthy sentence receded. The Chief helped them bundle the object in question into the back of the van and then drove quietly behind as it was delivered to the pre-arranged address on the outskirts of Victoria. He even offered to give Henry a lift home.

"Would you take me to the Beauvallon bus stop, please? I told Cilla I was going to the cinema," said Henry.

The Chief's smile broadened. "Let's hope she doesn't check your story out!"

"Why?"

"The cinema this week has only one film on – *The Smurf Movie* – I am not sure that even Cilla is ready to believe that this is the type of entertainment close to your heart, Mr Fanshawe."

Henry was duly dropped at the Beauvallon bus stop to await the last bus home to St Christol. As it jolted through the dark jungle, he sat trying to work out a story which, if needed, would convince his housekeeper that he had spent two hours watching a children's cartoon about little blue men taking over New York. Fortunately, Cilla had left some time before his homecoming, and he hurried quickly to bed, adrenaline from the evening's endeavours still pumping through his veins.

THE SEASON BEGINS

14
The First Match

The final Sunday of team practice went well. At the end of the day, Henry gathered the players together and informed them that the venue had been decided.

"It has been agreed that we will play at Anse Royale again. They want to show that there are no hard feelings about last year." He held up a hand as Sydney jumped to his feet to complain.

"And the tea arrangements are to be provided by St Christol."

Sydney sat down again, shifty with embarrassment.

"So, there will, I hope, be no chance of any of the goings-on that blackened our last match."

There was a chorus of dissatisfied agreement round the table, with some comments about umpires' behaviour thrown in.

Henry continued. "Now, Sydney will go through our tactics for the match."

Sydney rose and marched to the whiteboard. His outward demeanour appeared calm, but there was fire behind his eyes. Henry realised that to walk under these circumstances was a sacrifice of huge proportions for the captain. As a declaration of intent, he hoped fervently that it would have the desired effect on Cilla.

Having finished his team talk, Sydney resumed his place and it was Henry's turn to rally the troops. He stood to address the group.

"Ladies and gentlemen, I need hardly say that of all the matches in which I have been involved, this is probably the most important of my life. I came here to try to continue my Aunt Esme's work, and the proof of whether I have succeeded will become apparent next Saturday. She told me of your potential, and over the past few weeks I have seen that potential."

He was shifting into his stride. Interjections of "Hear, Hear" and nods of agreement encouraged him to continue, "This may just be another match to you, but to me it is the start of my future life on the island. So when you walk out onto that crease, do your best for me. And, more importantly, for our dear departed Esmerelda Fanshawe!"

The round of applause silenced him. Henry paused, realising that he had said enough. The speech was becoming Churchillian, and a small village cricket club on a tropical island was probably not yet ready for this. He pinned up the team selection on the notice board.

EFCC St. Christol
Match to be played Saturday 6th October 2011, versus
Anse Royale
Venue: Anse Royale Cricket Club

Team

1. Mr Sydney Mason
2. Mr Jean Kamling
3. Monseigneur Simon de Pelet
4. Reverend Roger Kitson
5. Mlle Mathilde du Pré
6. Chief Mahjoud
7. Mr Louis Kamling
8. The Hon. Frances Atterwood
9. Mr Xavier Kirby
10. Mr Rajiv Khumri
11. Mr Curtley Smith

Scorer: Mlle Priscilla Kheda

Everyone crowded round the notice board, like schoolchildren receiving their GCSE and A level results. Henry left the happy group and tiptoed quietly out of the room. He had a phone call to make. Only the vigilant Chief noticed him go, winking conspiratorially as Henry passed. Looking left then right, Henry leant towards him and, attempting to appear nonchalant, whispered, "Make sure Cilla stays in here for a while. I need to call the foundry."

He walked out onto the smooth green baize of the pitch and took out his mobile phone, adjusting its position to find a signal in this enclosed valley. Pacing up and down until his screen responded, he was about to start the call, when from the bushes nearby there was a very human rustle.

"Mr F!" The bush seemed to be speaking. "Mr F, we have a problem."

Henry could just make out the outlines of Pierre in the undergrowth, brandishing a newspaper. He addressed the bush, "Why don't you come out?"

"Cilla might see!"

"The Chief is keeping her engaged in the clubhouse."

"You don't know Cilla, Mr F. She can see through walls! Anyway, have a look at this."

A grubby hand pushed its way through the foliage holding that day's copy of the *Seychelles Gazette*. A banner headline read,

FURTHER TROUBLE AT ANSE ROYALE

After the problems at the Cricket club last year, it seems that vandalism has again reared its ugly head at Anse Royale. Sergeant Lefanu of the Seychelles Police reported that two vehicles had been seen near the club house, and had left considerable tyre track damage to the parkland surrounding the pitch. He has told us that thieves attempted to break into the clubhouse after damaging some of the surrounding fencing but were deterred by the security and left with nothing. The club plays its first match against EFCC St Christol on Saturday and it was a relief to the club captain Major Sitwell that the pitch itself was undamaged and none of the cricket equipment was stolen. "It is a shame that not even a cricket clubhouse is safe from the crime wave enveloping our nation," he said. Police are now keeping the area under surveillance and are looking for a large middle-aged gentleman in a brown shirt, remnants of which were found near the scene.

Henry mopped his brow with a mixture of horror and relief. Relief, because the police had clearly not looked behind the clubhouse. Horror, as he realised that he needed to get rid of his torn shirt immediately, before Cilla found it. And if the Anse Royale clubhouse was now being watched, how could he carry out the second stage of his plan? He thrust the paper back at Pierre, "We'll have to think of another way of getting it back, Pierre. We have just under a week."

A hand from the bush grabbed the paper and with a final rustle, all became quiet. Dusk was falling and the sun had dipped below the crest of the valley. Henry hurried back to his bedroom, praying that Cilla had not emptied the laundry basket that morning. He found that he was in luck. Snatching the shredded brown shirt from the basket, he pushed it behind the wardrobe. He sat down on the bed, breathing heavily and waited for the club members to disperse before going back downstairs. His phone call would have to wait.

He had calmed down enough to smile at Cilla when she entered the dining room later that evening, bearing a large fried fish which had probably been alive a few hours previously. The smile was not returned. As she placed the plate on the table a little too firmly, Henry tried to make conversation. "Anything the matter, Cilla?"

"I am concerned, Mr Fanshawe!" she replied.

"Concerned? Whatever for?"

"For you. You are hiding something!"

"I can assure you, Cilla…" Henry began weakly, but was quickly cut off by his housemaid.

"You have been spending too long with Pierre in his shed. That man is trouble!"

"We were discussing roses." Even as it came out of his mouth, Henry thought this sounded pathetic.

"Roses? Was that why I saw you chatting to a bush in the garden yesterday? I hope you are not going to end up like old Mr Fanshawe."

"What happened to him?"

"You aristocrats are all the same. Get to old age and you spend all your days talking to the trees."

Henry realised he would have to take extra care over the next week.

* * *

Henry became more and more nervous as the week progressed. This game really was as important to him as he had told his team. And all the surrounding circumstances conspired to add layers of complexity to an already fraught situation. He alone knew of Sydney's plan for the day and had no idea of how the others would react. His own scheme had almost been derailed by events. Worst of all, Cilla had taken to popping out from behind trees as he walked in the garden and to the village, and looking at him in a most disconcerting manner. She had the schoolmistress talent of making one feel guilty, even if one hadn't done anything. And Henry, of course, *had* done something.

The shadowing of his every move by his housekeeper

limited Henry's options in meeting Pierre. He had taken to shouting, loudly enough for Cilla to hear, "About that hibiscus," or "Pierre, can we discuss the azaleas?" Then, affecting deep interest in some plant, gesticulating and pointing for the benefit of his housemaid whose nose was pressed against the kitchen window, they would finalise arrangements for Saturday. The call to the foundry had been made and everything was on track. Only one problem remained. Amidst ever more histrionic gestures in the general direction of the cinnamon tree, he outlined his solution to Pierre, who smiled his gap-toothed smile and with an "OK boss," disappeared to do the necessary.

Then, all of a sudden, it was Saturday 6th October, start of the official Seychelles Cricket season 2011/12. The team met at the Clubhouse and then walked down to an ancient bus, newly painted in EFCC St Christol colours of blue and white. There was a nervous buzz as it pulled out down the narrow street of the village, lined with well-wishers waving on their heroes. As the aged vehicle rumbled slowly down to Beauvallon, the onlookers returned to their own cars and bikes to follow the team to Anse Royale for the first match of the season.

An hour later the unlikely procession entered Anse Royale. First, the large blue and white striped bus, belching fumes in every direction, then a large collection of horn-hooting and flag-waving followers, and finally Pierre in his van, freshly painted with a sign which read "St Christol Catering – Cricket Teas a Speciality" on the side. The bus pulled into the car park by a cricket pitch which looked very different to Henry from that dark night a short while back. Pierre parked the tea van just around the back of the clubhouse. The pitch appeared good, with the boundary rope laid out, though Henry couldn't help noticing, with a touch of guilt, the large plank covering a hole in the fence. He looked at his watch and hoped that the final part of his grand design would work as planned.

It had been raining on and off for the early part of the morning and the green field steamed in the sun, drying out rapidly as the two captains took to the field to toss a coin. There was a strained civility between Major Sitwell and Sydney, who looked preoccupied, though with what, only Henry knew. Then a stiff handshake in front of the two umpires who, given the previous year's antics, had been provided by the Cricket Board. St Christol won the toss and elected to bowl first. Sydney returned to the clubhouse and led his team out onto the pitch where they limbered up, throwing catches to each other whilst the Anse Royale openers padded up. The boundary was gradually filling with supporters from both sides. Deckchairs were positioned and large rugs laid out on the grass. Picnic hampers and cool boxes came out. An expectant quiet fell over the field as the two batsmen strode out of the clubhouse and down the steps followed by a ripple of applause.

Sydney's strategy for the match was to concentrate his efforts on Major Sitwell, a renowned and dangerous batsman who could score quickly and was well suited to one day matches. The Major played at number three and Sydney wanted to get on to him as soon as possible. Curtley was selected to bowl first and, whilst bowling well within himself to the openers, achieved a few tidy overs and pinned back the run rate admirably. At the other end the swing technique of Louis was faring less well, and he conceded heavily. Sydney watched with some concern from the field, willing his bowlers to make the breakthrough to the number three. Anse Royale, he knew, lacked depth and could be skittled out for a low score, if he could just remove the Major. And only he and Henry knew that St Christol needed a low score to chase.

After eight overs during which Anse scored 39 runs, a little high for Sydney's liking, the breakthrough finally arrived. Louis swung a ball beautifully to nick the outside edge of the bat. Chief Mahjoud leapt gracefully to his right and caught the ball in mid-air, rolling over several times on the grass before, with ball firmly in glove, he extended his hand to the sky.

"Howzat!"

The umpire's finger was quickly raised. A muffled roar of appreciation rose from the St Christol section of the boundary and, to the gentle susurration of muted applause, the batsman left the crease and trudged back to the clubhouse. He was ascending the stairs when, with a large theatrical crash, the doors were flung open and Major Sitwell emerged, swinging his bat in a full circle like Botham in his pomp. Henry, watching from the boundary, was impressed despite himself. Had this entry had a soundtrack, he thought, it would have been the Superman theme. The chap was a giant, at least six foot four, and barrel-chested. That weight, thrown behind a bat with at least a modicum of timing, explained the regular centuries that this fellow made.

Next to him, standing on the boundary, Henry heard Francis breathe a large sigh. "Such a heroic specimen, such a… such a… beast!"

True to form, the Major set about demolishing the attack with disdainful ease. He had notched up seventy runs in ten overs, most coming in boundaries, whilst his partners, who were happy to allow him as much of the strike as possible, got out in varying ways, but never quite fast enough to slow the pace of scoring from the other end. After twenty overs the home team were nudging 110 and looked in control.

Henry walked onto the pitch with drinks and drew Sydney aside. "I know what you intend to do is honourable in the extreme, but don't you think you could postpone your noble sentiments for another day – we could do with your runs if we can't get this chap out."

Sydney straightened up. "No dice, old chap. I have decided that this is the only way to get Cilla back and I intend to go through with it. We'll just have to get the Major out sooner rather than later. He is looking worryingly good today."

Henry knew there was only one thing for it. Curtley, Xavier and Jean had all tried and failed. He would have to use his secret weapon. The Major showed little sign of being frightened by speed, and so it was to his young Indian spinner that the manager turned. "Rajiv," said Henry, "soften him up a little with a few easy ones and then give him one of your specials."

The young and quiet boy looked up at Henry with a serious and intense expression, "Very good Mr Fanshawe, sir. I will soften him until he is well and truly soft, and then I will spin him out, with spin of such extreme intensity that he will not be able to be believing it, not even in slow motion replay!" And with that, Rajiv took the ball and prepared for the next over.

Henry watched the softening up process with some trepidation. Rajiv was certainly sticking to the first part of the plan, and for one and a half overs Henry winced as ball after ball was dispatched effortlessly over the boundary, and once over the fence beyond.

"Come on, he must be bloody soft enough by now, Rajiv!" he murmured.

Then came the last ball of Rajiv's over. He winked at Henry as he turned for his run up. The Major was already half-way down the pitch when the ball left his hands, and could only watch as its trajectory moved so improbably in the air, evading any effort to dispatch it once more to the boundary. The Chief was up to the stumps in a moment, ball in glove, bails flying, and gesticulating wildly.

"Howzat! How… was… zat, howzat, howzat, how… zat!"

It was one of his more enthusiastic appeals.

As Sydney had prophesied, this more or less dealt the killer blow to the Anse Royale innings. They stuck at it, and ground out a more than defendable score of 195. But their bowling was known to be weak. St Christol had given themselves a decent chance.

After a short break, the home team strode out onto the field, led by their redoubtable captain. As he passed Henry, and loud enough to be heard, he muttered to a team mate, "Shouldn't have any problems getting this rabble out for 150!"

Henry's knuckles whitened as he clenched his deck chair. After the fielders came Jean and Sydney. As they passed, Henry asked, rather plaintively, if there were any chance of him reconsidering.

Sydney shrugged, "Sorry Henry, but I'm afraid this is the only way."

Walking on with a puzzled Jean, Sydney made his way to the crease, requested middle and leg of the umpire, and took guard.

It all kicked off as the bowler began to turn for his run in. Sydney immediately threw up his hand, picked up his bat, and addressed the surrounding field.

"Members of the opposition," he began, "I realise that last year I may have strayed from the strict and civilized code expected of all cricketers. For this I truly apologise. And in recognition that you have acted most honourably in allowing me to return, I have decided to retire forthwith from the innings."

To the open-mouthed surprise of the opposition, Jean, and supporters of either persuasion, he then swung his bat under his arm and walked from the crease back to the pavilion.

Everyone on the pitch – and off it – remained silent. Sydney would in fact probably have made it to the relative safety of the changing rooms, had the air not been suddenly rent by a string of curses so extreme that some were entirely new to Henry. He looked round for the source, and saw none other than the Reverend Roger Kitson striding up to the opener, cutting off his escape route, and grabbing the man by both shoulders. Roger was a large fellow, and a push sent Sydney hurtling backwards, almost to the ground.

"And just what the FUCK do you think you are doing, Mason?"

Sydney, visibly shocked by this reaction in a cleric, began his explanation. "I... I... well, I thought it was the right thing to do…" He trailed off in the face of a blaze of righteous anger and unclerical language.

"The right thing to do? THE RIGHT SODDING THING TO SODDING DO? Are you on drugs or something? Our first match of the season, our best team ever, and you want to walk? SODDING WALK?"

Henry feared violence and jumped to his feet to separate the two, but the Monseigneur was faster. He laid his hand on the Reverend's shoulder. "Reverend, Reverend, calm down! Remember your teaching. To err is human…."

"Yes, and to retire on zero is bloody loony!"

Henry shepherded Sydney quickly inside to the changing rooms, leaving one man of God to placate the other. Once safely inside, Sydney slumped onto the bench and looked up at Henry shaking his head, "Well, that's something you don't hear every day!"

Henry was not best pleased himself, but he at least had been given a few days to come to terms with the idea. "Yes," he agreed, "I thought there might be a few angry words, but that, and from a priest!"

Sydney continued, "Roger spends so many hours of the day being nice to everyone, that once in a blue moon, it all comes tumbling out. I thought he was going to punch my lights out."

"If we don't win, he might still do so, and I for one would look on and cheer," said Henry. He turned on his heel and exited, passing a breathless Cilla on the way in.

"Mr Fanshawe, I know that was a strange thing to do."

"Less strange, more certifiable, Cilla."

"Don't worry about the Reverend, he will calm down shortly, and will then be struck by a tidal wave of guilt. It is always the same."

Henry regained a little composure, and enquire, "But you, Cilla, what did you think?"

Cilla, who had caught her breath, looked back at Henry with a shy smile, "Me? Oh, I thought it was marvellous!"

And then she went over to Sydney, motioning Henry to leave. The plan was beginning to work. Now, if only stage two could be accomplished, his role as relationship counsellor would be complete.

Outside, play had resumed with the Monseigneur and Jean at the crease. It became apparent that, as with its batting line up, Anse Royale only really had one decent bowler, faster than medium and with some ability to swing. Runs were being notched up, until Jean left a ball which grazed the stumps, out for a modest score. Henry looked to the clubhouse from which the Reverend now emerged. It was clear that the cooling-off period predicted by Cilla had not yet taken place. As he closed the clubhouse door Roger turned back to poke his head inside for one final remark to Sydney, "Now, come out and watch how cricketers *should* sodding well behave!"

With that, the Reverend strode to the crease with the air of a man who has something to prove. The first ball was despatched to the boundary. As was the second. And the third. And the fourth. On the fifth ball, the bowler, who by this time was looking like a man who has just had his blindfold taken off only to reveal that he is in a cage with a hungry lion, tried a bouncer. He might as well have thrown the ball straight over the clubhouse himself, as that is where, seconds later, it ended up. The Reverend turned to his supporters on the boundary, "That's how bloody cricketers behave! They bloody well play bloody cricket!"

The next ball took his middle stump clean out of the ground.

Given the dramas occurring off and on the pitch, Henry had not really been following the score. He now turned to see that St Christol stood at the reasonable though not emphatic 75 for three off eight overs. Thanks to Roger's rapid but ultimately suicidal 22, the run rate was more than decent. But there were only four proper batsmen left, and still 121 runs to make. Henry returned to the clubhouse veranda where the team were sitting. They were joined by Roger, whose bravado had subsided markedly on his walk back from the wicket. He sidled up to Henry with an air of guilt, "Henry, I feel I may have overreacted."

And then to Sydney, "Sydney, I am sorry if, by chance, I offended."

Sydney just looked up at him, and was about to speak, when Henry quickly interjected.

"Roger, I think you would have offended the professor of swearing at the University of Bad Language with that outburst. But I'm more concerned that you threw your wicket away almost as cheaply as Sydney. We aren't, if I may have my turn, a bloody charity!" Then, he turned to address the rest of the team.

"This little piece of theatre has left us with 120 to get and seven wickets standing. It's do-able, but not straightforward. We have plenty of overs left. So, prudence please."

A subdued team watched as Mathilde and the Monseigneur worked away at the total. They were progressing, slowly, and managed to put on a further 60 runs for the next wicket, when Mathilde was caught behind cutting at a ball which bounced higher than she expected.

The Chief of Police now walked out to the crease. He was not the tallest of men, but, with his trademark mirrored glasses he managed to exude a certain air of menace. It seemed as if the bowlers were not entirely comfortable at the thought of bowling out the senior law enforcement officer in the country, and this translated into easy pickings for the Chief. Recruited originally for his wicket keeping skills and organisational ability, he was also a decent batsman, and with de Pelet at the far end doggedly adding singles and doubles, St Christol reached the thirtieth over on 160 for 4, looking comfortable.

Henry had started to relax and enjoy the match for the first time, when, as always, something happened. A large shout for an LBW, upheld by the umpire, dismissed Monseigneur de Pelet on 78, his highest score, and all the more impressive for having been amassed with minimal boundaries. He walked off with a wave to the crowd and a smug expression, which Henry found so typical of those Frenchmen who have done fairly well.

No sooner had Louis Kamling arrived at the crease and taken guard than he was out LBW to an almost identical ball. 165 for 4 had become 165 for 6 with only the batting tail to go. Eight overs remained, 31 runs to win.

Henry looked over to the clubhouse where the rotund but finely-attired figure of Francis had appeared and was now waddling out to the crease. Henry had little faith in his number eight. He couldn't really play any great strokes, he was too fat to run quick singles, or even, come to think of it, medium-paced singles. His fielding was pretty atrocious, and his spin bowling only to be used in circumstances where the rest of the bowling attack were physically unable to walk, and even then only sparingly. However, not only was he exceptionally good company, unerringly cheerful and helpful, but the club was evidently his life. He had been a close friend of Esme's and, given her wishes, Henry could not bring himself to remove him.

Francis took guard in a Shakespearean flourish, and turning to the bowler, put his unique batting strategy into action. This, Henry quickly realised, lay in a type of reverse sledging – remarks timed to dramatic perfection to put off any fielder near enough to hear them.

"Darling, I'm looking forward to dealing with your new ball," and other such innuendo-laden comment, left half of the other side paralysed with mirth and half totally confused. Then to The Chief of Police, his batting partner: "You know, Chief, you really shouldn't be wearing white, it does *nothing* for you!"

This worked a treat. He grabbed 16 valuable runs in three overs before the fielders, realising what he was doing, buckled down and suppressed any further fits of the giggles. Once Frankie had lost the element of surprise, he was dead in the water. The first straight ball was played at and missed, going through to knock out the middle stump.

"Once more unto the shower room, dear friends," Francis, hand on brow, declaimed, and then departed the crease to polite applause. He was replaced by Xavier, with fifteen runs to make and five overs to go.

Xavier Kirby had listened to Henry. He was a lawyer, and lawyers always listen to their clients. In a cheerful and calm way, his innings was a model of common sense, allowing the Chief to knock off the remaining runs and attain the required total in the second last over.

Chief Mahjoud left the field unvanquished, having made 55, and when Henry looked over to the Major, he was delighted to see the glowering figure berating his team mates. Henry sat back, elated. They had won their first game, despite his captain's antics. Now to phase two of Operation Anse Royale.

Pierre and the Boy were ready behind the clubhouse as the teams trooped off to change. Henry, in as furtive a manner as possible for an overweight Englishman, crept away from the post-match celebrations and joined them.

"Is everything ready, Pierre?" he whispered.

"The statue is under the tea table, Mr Fanshawe," Replied his gardener, "but I warn you, it is very, very heavy. We will need some help."

Henry walked over to the trestle table, now covered in a long white tablecloth. He lifted a corner, and there, strapped to the underside, hung a large bronze statue. Tilting his head, he read the new inscription:

Captain William Kheda founder of Anse Royale
Cricket Club
1921–2002
Donated by Anse Royale Parish Council 2003
Repaired by St Christol Cricket Club 2011

Its head had been refashioned using the photographs gleaned from back copies of the *Seychelles Nation*, and Henry was thrilled with the result. The join was hardly visible, and the new bronze head had been aged so as to meld seamlessly into the original torso. Now, if they could only shift it to the front of the clubhouse, under cover of the tea table, then his grand design would be complete.

Pierre and the Boy took one end of the table and Henry and the Chief the other. Together, and with a lot of heaving, they managed to carry it round from behind the clubhouse, with white tablecloth intact and the statue underneath still hidden. Once in place, various supporters, marshalled by Cilla, who to Henry's delight had not cottoned on in the slightest, arrived with plates of sandwiches, cakes, and a large urn of tea. Henry watched as these were placed on the table. All was going to plan.

It was then that Cilla noticed an imperfection in the tablecloth.

"Mr Fanshawe, there's something underneath the cover, and it's making all the cups tip over."

Before Henry could stop her, she had removed the cups, and the tablecloth.

Cilla shook her head, "Someone's forgotten to take the straps off the table." and as Henry looked on in horror, she continued, "Don't worry, won't take a moment."

And with this she undid the buckle.

There was a loud crunch as the bronze of her father hit the ground. Henry could hardly look, as a small round object rolled out from under the tablecloth and into the crowd of onlookers. Sydney picked it up.

"It's a cricket ball, a bronze cricket ball. Didn't that come from…?"

"…My father's statue!" Cilla finished his sentence, and, as Henry held his breath, she leant over and peered underneath the table.

On the ground and thankfully undamaged, save for the dislodged ball, lay her father in bronze. She looked, speechlessly, at Henry.

"It was meant to be a surprise, Cilla."

"Well, you got that right, Mr Fanshawe!"

"We had it mended. Come on, let's get the chap up on his feet and you can see."

A number of volunteers rushed forward and quickly manhandled the statue onto its old plinth in front of the clubhouse.

Cilla stood before it. She looked her father up and down and seemed lost in thought for a long while. Then she turned to Henry. "If I'd known you were up to all this, I would have stopped it immediately!"

Henry cringed as she continued, "But, you know, this new head… You've got the likeness far better than the old one."

Henry involuntarily started to back away as she walked towards him.

"So."

"Yes, Cilla?"

"No harm done then."

Then, to Henry's, and most of St Christol's utter astonishment, she threw her arms around the blushing Englishman and planted an enormous kiss on his cheek, whispering as she did so, "Thank you so much, you dear, dear man."

After this unprecedented demonstration of affection, Cilla retired inside the clubhouse to gather herself, and tea resumed, to universal and vocal approval of the renovated memorial. Even the sullen Major had the good grace to thank Henry for his unexpected generosity.

Sydney grabbed Henry by the arm. "Do you think I should just go in and check she's all right, Henry?"

"I think, that would be an excellent idea."

As Sydney disappeared inside, Pierre sidled up. Henry slapped him on the back, "Thanks Pierre. You were invaluable."

"It's nothing, boss. But if I were you, I would get this over with and get out of here as quick as you can!"

"Why, Pierre?"

"I've just had a closer look at the statue. The head's OK, but I reckon the arms'll fall off any moment!"

15
A Salutary Lesson

Henry and his team were enormously encouraged by their first match. It was a truth universally held, or at least held in the Seychelles cricketing fraternity, that Anse Royale were a quality village team, and to win, despite the bizarre behaviour of their captain, was an excellent result. This confidence carried them through the next match, their first at home, against the lesser challengers from Port Glaud. The result was never in doubt, from the first over, when Sydney managed to score off every ball including two boundaries and a six, to the last, when Curtley took his seventh wicket for 27 runs. In fact the record would have been even more impressive had his radar not deserted him for a short period which cost 20 in byes. And, a week later, against the HSBC All Stars, admittedly one of the weaker corporate teams, EF St Christol performed outstandingly, to seal the match within 35 overs of the scheduled 40. The Esme Fanshawe Cricket club had strolled to another record victory and expectations grew higher and higher. As the *Seychelles Nation* put it,

Whisper it quietly, but in Beauvallon Bay something exciting is happening to Seychelles cricket. The village side of St Christol, founded by the late and redoubtable Lady Esme Fanshawe and now run by her nephew Henry, has been enthralling enthusiasts with its brand of attacking cricket. In Curtley Smith and Rajiv Khumri, the team have two outstanding bowlers – some would say world-class. This attack, combined with a strong batting line up, including the mercurial talents of the only woman in the senior game, Mme Mathilde du Pré, has ensured maximum points from their first three games. This team is one to watch!

So it was in a high state of excitement that the team travelled to meet the Seybrew Scanners, joint favourites for the competition, and last year's winners. The Scanners were one of the founding teams of the league, having been put together by the Australian head of Seychelles Cable and Wireless from a combination of his staff and those of Seybrew, the local brewery.

The Cable and Wireless factory was situated high in the mountains behind Victoria. Its large, golf ball look-alike installation on one of the peaks overlooking the capital added a strange element of science fiction to an otherwise untainted landscape. It had long been presumed that these were listening stations as well as corporate headquarters, and the whole area surrounding the buildings was certainly heavily fenced and patrolled. Within the compound, and commanding an impressive view of the island and the blue seas beyond, was the corporate cricket pitch. The St Christol coach finally arrived, having wheezed its way slowly up the hill. It stopped by the pitch, gave a loud diesel-drenched belch, and disgorged its occupants onto the grass.

Henry, hatless upon a peak in Mahé, gazed silently at the panorama that opened out before him. On the horizon he could see the Praslin and Silhouette, together with the faint outlines of other smaller islands. Closer to, it was possible to make out the broad sweep of Beauvallon Bay, and if a certain licence were taken, a little square of green near to it, which he fancied might be his own venue. Down beneath him, as if looking from an airplane, he could see Victoria, with boats steaming in and out of the harbour. A hive of activity played out silently save for the moan of the warm tropical wind and the ever-present tropical medley of birdsong and crickets.

Henry had seen many beautiful cricket pitches before. The square at Arundel, the Rose, Upper Club at Eton, and Canterbury, with its tree standing inside the boundary. Even his own square back in St Christol merited a mention. But, he reflected, unless there was a similar location in the Kashmir, or Switzerland decided to take up the sport, he had never seen a location with quite such a stunning vista.

The view turned out to be the best thing about the day, so far as St Christol was concerned. The initial run of victories was abruptly reversed by a team of high standards and impeccable discipline. Curtley was off his speediest form; Sydney had a hangover and lasted less than ten minutes. The Reverend slogged out only to be caught cheaply, though he did manage one six so expansive that it cleared not only the boundary, but the cliff edge. As it dropped the few thousand feet to the jungle below, Henry mused on how surprised the fauna would be when a cricket ball landed amongst them from the heavens above.

All in all, it was a dispiriting affair. Having set the Scanners a mere 154 to win, the opposing team knocked off the runs with relative ease and the game finished at three o'clock.

The events of the day were again well summarised in the *Nation.*

VILLAGERS FINALLY BEATEN

How are the mighty fallen! St Christol suffered a rude awakening on their visit to the Seybrew Scanners, currently joint favourites to win the championship trophy. It was unfortunate that a dip in form for St Christol coincided with their toughest challenge to date. Neither the bowling nor the batting was up to the standards we have seen in recent matches, and the team paid dearly. For the home side Maupassant batted at his supreme best and ended the day unbeaten on 65. The long awaited duel between him and Curtley Smith for St Christol was a curiously damp squib. Sydney Mason, currently in the running for batsman of the year, was also subdued and seemed to find it difficult to see the ball as early as we all know he can. All in all, it was a bad day at the office for the village side, and they will need to regain their previous level of excellence if they are to

*stand any chance against the Chowdrey Steamers in
a month's time.*

The coach home was a quiet affair.

Back at St Christol a post mortem ensued where voices
were raised and mistakes analysed, sometimes over-analysed.
Henry had ordered two hours of extra net practice on their
return, which did not go down that well. Reverend Kitson
led the complaints, "Henry, I won't have any time to write
tomorrow's sermon if I have to stay here for two hours."

"Well, maybe that's a let-off for your congregation."
Henry was pulling no punches. He gathered the team by
the nets and addressed them. "I think I can say, gentlemen,
and Mathilde, that today's showing was the most pathetic
and pusillanimous display I have witnessed. Thank God
we aren't meeting the Indians next week. Where was your
fight? Your determination in adversity? I grant you, these
chaps were good but not that good. They spooked you and
you folded."

There was a general nodding of heads as the deflated
team members made ready to begin. The practice session
was a quiet affair, though punctuated by further complaints
about his forthcoming sermon from the Reverend. This
did not go down well with anyone. As Monseigneur de
Pelet acerbically put it. "I don't know why the man is so
worried. It's not as if anyone listens to him anyway!"

* * *

A subdued Henry finally sat down to his dinner around
eight o'clock. He had left the team to clear up the clubhouse,

with a lot of muttering and general tetchiness in the air. No one was happy with being made to stay after school, even if they had not been as voluble about it as Roger.

Henry had been impressed by the discipline of the Seybrew Scanners, and hoped this attempt to instil something similar in his team would not backfire. He hated the confrontation of it all. But, he thought, they had been particularly spineless that day. This needed to be pointed out, and he was the only one who could say it. He carried on fulminating on this until, in unconscious deference to smells emanating from the kitchen, thoughts of dinner intruded.

Shortly, Cilla entered the dining room with his meal, set it down and hovered. He became aware that she had not left the room as usual. She clearly had something to say, and he decided to get it over with quickly. No doubt it would be another moan of some sort.

"Cilla, is anything the matter?" he enquired.

"As a matter of fact, Mr Fanshawe, there is."

"Well go ahead, spit it out."

"That extra practice, Mr Fanshawe…"

"Yes?"

"You managed to annoy quite a number of your team."

Henry was about to tell her off as well, but Cilla ignored him and continued, "But not me, Mr Fanshawe. They were acting like a bunch of naughty schoolchildren, in need of a good slap. Had you not administered that slap, I would have. I have already reprimanded Sydney for being unable to control himself in the bar last night. He has been gated for a week. You men – you only understand one thing!"

She turned and departed, leaving Henry feeling that if this counted as support from Cilla, he couldn't imagine what being told off was like.

* * *

She was of course quite right. At church the next morning, Henry was besieged by various club members approaching to apologise for both their performance the previous afternoon, and their recalcitrant behaviour afterwards. Even the Chief of Police (this must be a first, thought Henry) ambled up as the congregation were leaving.

"Mr Fanshawe, I feel I should ask your forgiveness for my behaviour."

"I thought that is what you had just been doing in church, Chief."

The Chief smiled.

"You are right of course, it is only the Almighty who can truly forgive. But I suspect he may have his plate full today pardoning our vicar for his truly awful sermon."

"Yes. Roger certainly wasn't joking when he said the enforced period of nets would impact badly."

"Anyway, Henry, you did the right thing. Discipline – always discipline. The only way. And of course there was one team member fully in favour."

"Cilla?"

"I was thinking of Mathilde. She told me she loved it when you got angry!"

He walked off, leaving Henry embarrassed, slightly worried, and a little flattered.

16
The Tea Party

After the let-down that was the defeat to the Scanners, no one was particularly looking forward to the next match. This was compounded by the nature and location of their opponents.

Mont Capucins was at the far end of Mahé island from Beauvallon Bay, a good few hours ride on the club coach, the last half of which would be spent crawling slowly on two narrow tracks of concrete through the rainforest, worryingly steeply up and then, equally uncomfortably, rapidly down into the final valley before the island gave way to the warm blue waters of the Indian Ocean. Here, the ocean currents were so strong and beaches so dangerous that little tourism had developed. The land had retained much of its pre-settlement wildness, and it was a wildness shared by the opposing cricket team. In fact, several of the league members had complained about having to visit this outpost of the beautiful game, because of its isolation and the rumours circulating about the habits of the village. For this journey, none of the normal medley of supporters would be accompanying the team coach.

Cilla, over breakfast that morning muttered darkly.

"What's that, Cilla?"

"They say that only last year a shrunken head was found."

Henry pointed out that head shrinking had never been closer to the Seychelles than New Guinea, but Cilla was having none of it. In fact, as they bounced over the potholes on the way to Capucins, only two of the team appeared cheerful about the prospect of the upcoming match. The Reverend Roger Kitson remarked that although civilisation may not have penetrated quite so deeply into this area, there was a single and supreme redeeming factor.

"Henry, old boy," he whispered hoarsely, "I seem to remember that they do the most wonderful teas!"

And Curtley also seemed unduly cheerful, though why, he would not vouchsafe.

When the coach finally inched into the village, the driver switched the ignition off and the engine spluttered a few times before expiring. Henry exited the vehicle and stepped into a museum. Surrounding a large and grassless clearing were a few huts roofed with corrugated iron sheets, the only concession to modernity. There did not appear to be any evidence of electricity or phone lines, and the villagers had gathered round the coach silently counting each visitor off with their eyes. An elder approached Henry and started speaking in a swift and incomprehensible version of Seychellois patois. Dismayed, Henry looked around desperately for an interpreter.

"He says, 'Welcome to Capucins and hopes you will stay for tea afterwards.'"

The voice behind Henry made him jump. It was Curtley, who seemed more at home here than usual. Rattling off in a string of sentences to the elder, the content of which left Henry similarly bemused, he moved forward, and prompted the Englishman, "Offer him your hand, boss, and smile."

Henry did as he was told, and immediately, ice broken, the villagers broke into large grins. They clustered around the team, grabbing kit bags and shepherding the visitors towards one of the larger huts. The elder pulled aside the cloth hanging by its entrance and pointed inside.

"Vizite chanje isit la," said the elder.

"Visitors changing here," translated Curtley.

The man then gestured to the patch of earth where some activity appeared to be taking place.

"Kriket isit la."

"Cricket there."

And moving his hand towards another of the huts, "Te isit la."

"Tea there," continued the fast bowler.

"Thank you," replied Henry.

"Pou gwo aplodi moute le ou pede."

Henry looked inquiringly towards Curtley.

"He said, for big cheer up when you lose, boss."

The elder smiled and departed.

The hard mud flats in the centre of the village were being prepared for the match as the away team changed. By the time they emerged in their whites, to some laughter from the locals, a rough pitch and creases had been painted on the ground, and the boundaries marked out with old petrol cans. Henry noticed that the opposition had forsaken white clothing for a more sensible approach. Their captain, the same elder who had greeted them, approached in army fatigues with ten similarly attired villagers behind him. Mont Capucins won the toss and elected to bowl.

As the pitch resembled little more than a concrete school playground, it was unsurprising that the opposition fielded an attack comprised entirely of fast bowlers. There was a distinct sense of apprehension, almost fear, in the eyes of Sydney and Jean as they strode out to open the batting. Not only would be the ball be delivered at a fearsome pace onto a hard pitch, but it was tricky to pick out the bowler's arm when covered in army fatigues. Henry sat back on a large palm trunk which had been pulled up in front of the changing hut. It was likely, he thought, to be a low-scoring game.

After a few overs it became apparent that, but for some waywardness in direction by the bowlers, it would have been an extremely low-scoring game. The square was uneven and very hard, causing deliveries to bounce erratically, high, and at extreme pace. Batsman's helmets were called for after the first ball pitched up at the throat of Sydney, causing him to bend over backwards so alarmingly that Henry feared he might have injured himself. The single helmet possessed by the club was brought out and handed to Sydney by Henry, with a grimace.

"Just stay in and the extras will do the scoring," he muttered to the captain under his breath.

"Now I know what a rabbit in a headlight feels like," Sydney answered.

The extras mounted up helpfully, but so did the dismissals. Some of the deliveries were simply unplayable, and wickets fell regularly. No batsman got in convincingly, although a sharp knock from Mathilde added twenty useful runs to the score. Then yet another erratic bouncer forced her into instinctive defence, producing a simple catch for the bowler. The innings petered out to a close with St Christol making 137 runs, of which 53 were wides or byes, most of which had travelled straight to the boundary untouched by human hand.

There was much chuntering at the halfway stage.

"Talk about designing a pitch to suit your strengths. If this wasn't the Seychelles they'd be investigated."

"That last delivery nearly took my hand off at the elbow!"

Henry gathered the team around him and expounded his strategy, "Gentlemen, and Mathilde. We must fight fire with fire. We are lucky to have a quickie on our side who is usually accurate as well as fast. No point using the spinners – go for the accurate medium pace of Jean one end and let Curtley chuck his grenades down at the other. We'll skittle them out for nothing at all."

That at least was the plan. And for a while it seemed to be working. Tight fielding and a bowler on fire yielded five early wickets in the opening ten overs at a cost of only 27 runs. The locals called for a round of drinks. Henry could not make out the words, but the worried tone of the discussion reassured him. In fact, he was concentrating so hard on this that he did not notice Curtley slip away from the field. It was not until play resumed that Henry saw that he was missing. He wandered around the perimeter, yelling for Curtley, when out of the bush, the fellow arrived back at the boundary.

"Get on with it, man you're bowling the next over!" Henry seethed.

There was no reply, as the fast bowler shambled on to the pitch. Henry's words seemed not to affect him in the slightest. He was beaming broadly as the umpire chucked the ball to him. He carried on smiling as the ball slipped through his hands onto the ground. Retrieving it, he shambled back to the boundary to begin his run up. Still smiling idiotically, he turned and headed at ever-growing speed towards the wicket. Just as the unnerved batsman facing was taking his guard and, possibly unconsciously, making himself as small a target a possible, the bowler pulled up sharp, and lobbed a slow underarm delivery at the quivering figure.

It worked. Frozen to the spot, the batsman watched as the ball ran along the ground at walking pace with just enough energy as it reached the stumps to gently dislodge a bail. The umpire raised his finger and the batsman, visibly fuming, turned, swatted an invisible fly stomped back to the boundary. The effect on Curtley was immediate. Hands on knees, he started laughing, great choking guffaws shaking his slim frame. He fell over, still giggling uncontrollably, legs bicycling in the air above him.

Henry could not decide whether he was shocked at such a lapse in gamesmanship, impressed by the guile of the move, or amused by the look on the departing batsman's face. He decided that on the whole he was nonplussed by such unusual behaviour. As he looked on, it became clear that Curtley had continued to find the moment hilarious and showed no signs of stopping.

Several of his team surrounded the bowler, first to congratulate him, and then as he continued to roll helpless with laughter on the ground, to beckon Henry over with worried expressions.

"He seems to be having some sort of seizure!" exclaimed the worried Reverend.

Henry peered over the heads of concerned team mates to view shoulders heaving in continued mirth. He sniffed the air.

"Seizure my arse – he's been on the wacky baccy again – can't you smell it!"

Then he pushed through the crowd, dragged Curtley to his feet and unceremoniously marched him to the boundary, where, to a global hiss of indrawn breath he plunged his hands into the man's trousers. He seemed to be whispering in his ear.

Henry was fuming, "I know you've got some hidden there – get rid of it now, and I never, repeat, never want to see you like this again, or you're sacked."

The effects of the last smoke were starting to wear off and Curtley stiffened.

"You have five minutes to dispose of it and get back out there," said Henry.

"OK, boss." He shambled off to one of the huts.

Henry turned to face the umpire. "Sorry about that, our bowler just needs to find a new lace for his shoes – won't be a second."

The face of the umpire registered a certain amount of disbelief.

Curtley re-emerged to finish his over, which he managed badly, giving away a dozen extras in three boundaries, and failing to hit anywhere near to the target. The opponents' score was crawling slowly up to the desired level. Henry brought on the drinks.

"Change of plan – our fast bowler clearly can't see the wicket, let alone take one."

Curtley hung his head in shame, though Henry couldn't help but notice he was still smiling.

"Have you got rid of that stuff?"

"Yes, boss."

"And why are you smiling?"

"I may be smiling on the outside, but inside I'm crying, boss."

"Right, well, whatever, you certainly aren't bowling again. We'll try and restrict them with accurate medium pace and see what happens. At least we are in amongst the tail now. Xavier, you and Jean can bowl out the remaining overs."

As it turned out, he need not have worried. The remaining four batsmen were weak and unable either to score runs or to bat out the remaining time. Gradually the wickets fell until, with a few overs left, the last batsman skied a ball which looked destined to land just where the chastened figure of Curtley was standing.

"Curtley, this is your chance to redeem yourself!" shouted the Reverend. From the boundary, Henry couldn't look.

The ball sped ground-wards towards the lanky figure. It was easy to see that he was nowhere near in the right position. There was an anguished scream from the Reverend.

"The bugger's going to miss it!"

Then, from silly mid-on, Monseigneur de Pelet spun and started to sprint towards the stationary fielder. A hush fell, as all eyes followed the puffing Frenchman as he closed upon his goal.

When the ball reached Curtley, the Monseigneur was only a few yards away. As expected, Curtley's outstretched hands were in quite the wrong position, and the ball missed them completely. Henry groaned.

His head, however, was positioned in exactly the right place. For a split second the ball disappeared into the mane of impressive dreadlocks. And then reappeared, rolling gently down onto a shoulder, as Curtley slumped, semi-conscious, to the ground. The Monseigneur grabbed him as he fell, retrieved the ball from where it had lodged in his overlarge collar, and with a stream of French as passionate as it was incomprehensible, held it aloft in celebration. After a moment's hesitation, the umpire raised his finger slowly and the batsman turned and trudged disconsolately to the clubhouse. From his position on the boundary, Henry could just hear the Reverend add his congratulations, "Well, fuck me sideways, never seen that before!"

As the teams left the pitch, Henry walked over to the barely conscious fast bowler, who was by now sitting up and rubbing his head. His words emerged slowly, "Did I catch it, boss?"

"In a manner of speaking, Curtley, in a manner of speaking." Henry helped the bowler to his uncertain feet and together they made their way to the hut marked 'Tea'.

Inside they were greeted warmly by the opposition and their elders who seemed to bear no grudges. It was in fact becoming a warm and friendly occasion. After a few cups of tea, Henry could feel any residual irritation with his fast bowler ebb away into a more genial bonhomie, a bonhomie that seemed to be extending throughout the party. Henry couldn't quite understand what that the opposing manager was saying to him, but that did not stop him finding it surprisingly amusing, and after a while, quite improbably hilarious. And as he laughed he noticed everyone joining in, guffawing, helpless with mirth in some cases.

After a while Henry, still giggling, exited the tea hut to get some air and a short break from the increasingly raucous party within. He ambled, executing the odd dance step to a hummed tune, when he noticed a disconsolate figure hunched over a small fire. It was his errant fast bowler, and filled with charity, Henry walked over and hunkered down to reassure him, murmuring, "We all make mistakes, you know."

"Yes, boss, and I made a big one."

"You did, but I am sure that this will be the last time."

"It will – the bag broke."

"Not quite sure I follow, Curtley."

"I stashed the bag in the water tank behind the clubhouse, but the bag broke, and it's all been ruined."

Those few cells in Henry's brain that were still functioning normally edged slowly towards an analysis. As he trudged back to the Tea hut, the phrases, 'water tank' and 'bag broke' circulated round his mind. Opening the door, he noticed, to howls of laughter, the Reverend Roger Kitson launching into his imitation of a World War Two fighter pilot, using only cricket boxes as a prop. In a moment of relative sanity, one of his last, he realised why it was that the tea tasted so good.

"Well, sod it, who cares anyway. We won didn't we?" And with that, Henry rejoined the party and all memory of events ceased.

17
The Morning After

When Henry awoke, the sun was pouring in through his bedroom window. He realised that he must have overslept, and jumped out of bed, before freezing almost immediately in his tracks as a large sledgehammer seemed to descend on his skull. Then he padded downstairs in his loud oriental dressing gown.

At the bottom of the stairs Henry stopped, aghast at the scene before him. All around him lay debris from a party he could not remember. Half-open bottles, his saxophone sitting on the piano, ashtrays in various stages of combustion. And the thin, mean smell of old alcohol and smoke. Cilla was nowhere to be seen.

Whilst surveying the damage, and trying to piece together the blurred events of the previous night, he smelled bacon. Henry was firmly of the view that bacon had been provided by God for the relief of hangover sufferers, so he gathered together an armful of glasses, empty bottles and ashtrays, and pushed open the swing door into the kitchen. No further than a yard inside, he froze for the second time that morning. The scene that presented itself filled him with utter horror. Mathilde, in some of his pyjamas, was cooking breakfast.

'Oh God, what have I done,' thought Henry, as she turned towards him.

"Morning Henri, fancy some breakfast?"

Henry could only mumble, standing like a statue by the kitchen door.

Mathilde continued. "I must say, Monsieur, you were fantastic last night."

The blood drained from Henry's cheeks.

"Such a wonderful sense of rhythm."

Can this get any worse, thought Henry. He tried to answer but no sound would come.

Mathilde heaped a large amount of bacon onto a plate, and held it out to him. "I had no idea you were so good at the sax."

Henry felt faint.

"The sax?"

"Yes, the sax… the saxophone. I had no idea you played the saxophone so well. We all loved it. Now go next door, the rest have already started."

Bottles and glasses nearly slipped through Henry's nerveless fingers. He just managed to pull himself together and placed them down on the table before accepting the proffered plate.

"The saxophone you say?"

"Yes," smiled Mathilde, "you had us all dancing like dervishes. By the way, thanks for the loan of the pyjamas and the spare room. The boys, I'm afraid, had to sleep downstairs."

He had only been up for ten minutes and already Henry was feeling mentally and physically drained. He shuffled into the dining room, where Roger and the Chief were tucking in.

"Ah, morning, Henry."

Roger, tucking into a large plate of food, appeared disgustingly well given the obvious excesses of the previous night. The chief, mirrored glasses already on, was quieter and seemed to be suffering. He merely grunted and went back to his bacon.

All Henry could manage was a plaintive, "So what exactly happened last night?"

"Everyone seemed to be in such good spirits when we returned, that you invited us all up here for a continuation," said the Reverend. "Your sax, dancing – it was terrific!"

"And Cilla? She's usually here by now."

"Ah, well, we did spot her leaving with Sydney…"

"And the rest of you?"

"The party broke up about midnight but the four of us were so deeply involved in conversation – can't quite recall what about – that you offered to put us up for the night. I must say, your sofas are jolly comfortable."

The Chief grunted again.

At this point Mathilde entered, having changed back into yesterday's clothes.

"I've cleaned up most of the mess, Henry. Cilla won't approve of course, not up to her standards. But you can always pretend that you did it! I'm off – see you soon," and she waltzed out of the door humming *Summertime*.

The Chief finally spoke. "I think it would be best, Henry, if you we not mention to Cilla that *she* stayed here last night."

All three nodded in agreement. Then Roger rose to take his leave and prepare for the Sunday service. As he prepared to exit, the Chief grabbed him by the arm. "Please, Roger. The sermon today…"

"Yes?"

"Make it a short one."

The Sunday morning service was a quiet affair. To their credit, most of the team made it, and many, as they passed Henry dying in a pew near the back, clapped him on the back, or smiled, with remarks like "Great party, Henry", "Didn't know you could play like that" and mysteriously, "I'm still laughing at that camel story." The Reverend's sermon was mercifully brief, and Cilla came up to Henry after the service and asked if she could be excused from lunch duties that day. He was only too happy to agree, and suggested, to widespread assent, that the Sunday cricket practice would also be postponed to Thursday.

Thank God, he thought as he wondered slowly back to the Manor, now I can go back to bed.

* * *

On Tuesday, feeling somewhat better, Henry set himself to the task of preparing for the oncoming match. This was the big one. The Chowdrey Steamers were the wealthiest club in the league, funded by the seemingly bottomless coffers of their owner. They boasted several Indian professionals and, it was said, a most luxurious clubhouse. Henry decided to wonder down to see Sydney to have a chat and start the ball rolling.

As he sauntered down the path towards St Christol, a voice beckoned from the Hypermarket. Sanjay was waving at him to enter, so he made his way over to the shop and stepped through the bead curtain. Inside, the smell of a thousand spices assailed him.

Sanjay was looking excited. "Saturday is an important day for St Christol Cricket, Mr Fanshawe. To think, we have never beaten the Steamers, and this time we have a chance."

"Do you know Mr Chowdrey, Sanjay?"

Sanjay paused before answering. "I would not say I knew him, but my brother has dealings with him on the shipping side. He is a very important man in the Seychelles, Henry. You need to be careful."

"Careful? Why so?"

"Well, I mean, you should understand that he controls a lot of interests on the island, and that he has the money to do near enough what he wants."

"Does that matter to Saturday's game?"

"Oh no, Mr Fanshawe, not at all." Sanjay gave an embarrassed laugh. "It is just that he is used to getting his own way – he won't like it if we win."

"All the more reason for doing so!" Henry loved a contest, and being English, entering one as the underdog held a strong appeal.

"Of course, Mr Fanshawe, of course. Let us cross our fingers most tightly."

Henry bade goodbye and left the shop to walk the short distance past the white church to Sydney's house. On the odd strip of greenery, a few goats munched the tough grass and studied passers-by. Several women were standing in their gardens hanging out colourful washing and chatting over the white picket fences. In the graveyard he could see Roger indulging in a spot of weeding, a full-time job in a climate where every plant seemed to be straining to outdo its neighbour. It was, Henry thought, a thoroughly pastoral scene. He arrived at Sydney's house.

For a second he thought he might have miscounted. The air of slight dilapidation he had found on his first visit had been comprehensively banished. The fence had been repaired and covered in a pristine coat of new white paint. The gate did not squeak. The flower beds had been weeded and dug. There was a spring clean feel about the place which, Henry realised, could only have been wrought by one person, that one person not being Sydney.

He rung the door bell and stood admiring the makeover, when the door opened and a jolly Sydney presented himself. Clean-shaven, smartly-dressed; the change was emphatic. He ushered Henry to the door and smiled. "Morning Henry. Finally got over Saturday evening I see."

"You look pretty good too. Been getting some help?"

"If, Henry, by help, you mean being told to do things, the answer is yes."

"It's certainly working."

"And you know what," Sydney continued with a smile, "I don't even mind too much."

Henry paused.

"That would be Cilla, then."

"In one, Henry, in one. Don't know quite what happened on Saturday, but it certainly has advanced my cause… immeasurably."

Chalk one up to illegal substances, thought Henry as he entered the house.

The interior had undergone a similar transformation. Henry was able to sit down without at first examining the cushion shortly to receive him. The woman's hand was evident throughout, even though, as Sydney was quick to mention, she was not of course living there… yet. Over a cup of tea, they sat down to plan the attack on the Indian citadel of Seychelles cricket.

18
The Indians

A sense of anticipation pervaded the team bus that morning. Henry had arrived at the clubhouse to find that, unusually, all members had beaten him to it. A nervous tension reigned, with various individuals concentrating furiously on tasks they would never have bothered with for more mundane encounters. Sydney was carefully sponging linseed oil into his bat, repeating the action again and again like a caged wild animal prowling endlessly up and down behind the bars. The Chief was applying further Blanco to a pair of cricket boots which already shone like the full moon. The twin brothers sat in a corner, for once content not to argue about who went in first.

The Reverend Kitson rose to meet the manager. "Well, Henry, this is the big one."

Henry nodded.

"The Alamo, the siege of Khartoum," continued Roger.

"Yes," agreed Henry.

"Our Waterloo, Agincourt…"

"I get the picture, Roger."

Henry left him still reciting great battles and other

world-changing events and went in search of something less dramatic. Unfortunately his next encounter was with Francis.

"Frankie, I don't think your rather unconventional methods will work with these chaps. I am told that most of them are professional."

"You may be right, Henry, but there is still a place for those with amateur talents, and besides…" Francis sat back in his chair, and closed his eyes, "…many's the time, Henry, that I've dreamt of a nice Indian to take away."

* * *

As the bus approached the ground, there were muffled gasps – the Indian team, the Chowdrey Steamers, had the benefit of being funded by Chowdrey Shipping, the largest and most wealthy trading concern on the island. It was run by Mr Kaaliya Chowdrey, whose passions ran, alongside the opulent display of his wealth, to cricket in all of its forms. He had been instrumental in creating the new Seychellois league and was determined that this ground should be its Lord's.

No expense had been spared. The green outfield stood level, grass recently cut and rolled to within a millimetre of perfection. Of Euclidean accuracy, the square could have been used for billiards. But the square could not prepare him for the Baroque glory that was the Club Pavilion. Henry looked and marvelled.

Maybe the intrepid traveller, catching his first sight of the Taj Mahal in the light of a full moon, or a passenger staring from the deck of the Queen Elizabeth II at the approaching

Manhattan skyline. Perhaps a desert nomad mounting the brow of a dune and coming face to face with the Pyramids, would have been similarly affected. It was stunning.

It seemed to Henry that the architect had seen the Pavilion at Lord's once, in some old and tattered magazine, and using this vague memory as a base, had then attempted to recreate that Victorian red brick grandeur, but with elements from his Indian heritage. The Pavilion had been adorned with various figures in poses both natural and, to Henry, unnatural but interesting. Where square towers and turrets would have sat in the London Headquarters of cricket, there were large domes and minarets, inlaid with gemstones and gold leaf. At the door stood, motionless, two large Sikhs bearing full battle dress complete with turbans and long scimitars.

In a large box, which had been decked out in silks of green, white and orange, the team colours, there sat a suited individual who rose quickly and marched down the steps and over to where Henry stood in bedazzled silence.

"Good morning Mr Fanshawe, I am so pleased to meet you at last. We have a real game in prospect!"

Mr Chowdrey had made every effort to improve the large but short body which fate had bestowed on him. His hair, though greasy and dyed jet black, had been perfectly cut. His smile revealed an immaculately white set of teeth shot with the odd glint of gold. His suit was of Parisian origin and shirt ironed to starchy perfection. His shoes gleamed darkly in the sun.

Chowdrey threw an arm round Henry's shoulders and guided him resolutely towards the pavilion. "So, what do think of our ground, Mr Fanshawe? I had it renovated at the end of last season – though 'renovated' may be something of a euphemism." He giggled self-consciously, "I'm afraid some people think I went a little over the top!"

Henry was about to answer untruthfully, but luckily for him Mr Chowdrey was now in full flow. "I wanted it to be a statement – a call to arms for the cricketing people of the Seychelles. We have created this from next to nothing over a few short years, and I must say, Mr Fanshawe… Henry, if you will allow me to call you Henry, your aunt was most helpful in spreading the word."

Henry allowed himself to be guided into the box. On the pitch, St. Christol won the toss and elected to bat. As the Indians marched onto the pitch, resplendent in their whites, Mr Chowdrey leant over. "Now we will see how good your batsmen are."

As the match progressed, it became clear to Henry, that this team was very good indeed. Well-drilled fielding and strength in bowling, evidenced an organisation of depth and serious buying power. Henry doubted that many of the side's incumbents were actually employed for their prowess in the world of shipping, but they were undoubtedly, and by some way, the finest team he had yet encountered. Henry silently decided this match was a lost cause and watched on.

St Christol were batting as well as could be expected and though the opening pair managed to withstand the initial onslaught of a large and fast pair of bowlers, the breakthrough looked inevitable. In the fourth over, Jean got an edge which flew at waist height to first slip. There was no mistake about the professional catching ability of the Indians and Jean trudged back to the pavilion having added only five runs to his account. At the other end, Sydney was faring better. The professional atmosphere surrounding his foes seemed to bring back the form which took him to county status many years earlier, and though not scoring prolifically, he looked comfortable.

This was just as well, because his partners came and went with some frequency. No one seemed to be able to get their eye in before being removed, and within fifteen overs, St Christol stood precariously at 47 for four.

As Mathilde strode out onto the pitch, to the usual tut-tutting of some of the opposition, Henry was mentally rehearsing a rousing speech for the bus home, pointing out the positives to take from the inevitable drubbing. Caught up in this world of reflection, he did not see her dispatch the first delivery faced with aplomb, pulled elegantly towards the leg boundary. The sound of polite clapping woke him from his reverie, so he did catch her second boundary. The fizzing square cut was travelling at some pace even as it bounced over the boundary rope. As a spectator retrieved the ball and tossed it back to the fielder, Henry was musing as to why the game of cricket could turn in such a compressed and instant fashion between two outcomes. It was like balancing a marble on an upturned bowl, an unstable equilibrium, where any slight move would send the pattern of play careering off in a new and unexpected direction. This looked like a good partnership, both batsmen in form, and in shot-making mood. Henry put his speech on hold.

Over the next hour, the partnership proved its worth, with Sydney reaching fifty by dint of a massive six off a spinner who saw the ball returned over his head, then the boundary, and then some cars parked along the periphery. It took some minutes to retrieve the ball from the jungle into which it had fallen.

"Ah, quality will out, quality will always out, will it not Henry?" commented Chowdrey, as the girl again guided a slightly wide ball, with a beautiful late cut, to the boundary. This brought up her 50, a partnership of 85 with Sydney. For the first time in the match the momentum began to swing towards the visitors.

"What a marvellous cut she has!" continued Chowdrey. "You know, Henry, I really thought she was in the team for another reason entirely…" followed by a schoolboy snigger.

Henry decided to ignore this.

The pair had reached 140 for four when disaster struck. A quick nudged single was on offer and Sydney made as if to run. Mathilde, backing up, duly set off down the pitch only to see Sydney change his mind and return to his crease, arm uplifted and hand splayed in the universal 'Go back' gesture. It was far too late, and Mathilde could only turn to stare at the bowler catching the throw and whipping off the bails in exultation.

By the thirty-fifth of the allotted forty overs, it was all wrapped up. Curtley, whose batting had never really achieved the heights of his bowling, or for that matter, any heights at all, managed a welcome six which seemed to surprise him as much as anyone else, being six more than his usual score for that season. But by dint of deciding to bowl at the stumps, the Indian pace bowler rapidly removed him thereafter. St Christol had made a total of 157.

Easily within the reach of this outfit, pondered Henry, as his team prepared to take their places in the field. The pitch looked well rolled, flat and fairly benign. Not much for spinners, and not really quite hard enough for out-and-out pace. Chowdrey had clearly done his homework on Henry's side, a compliment in itself, Henry thought. Not that this would be of much comfort in a few hours' time.

Curtley opened with his usual wayward first over. Luckily, the speed of his delivery was such that little was lost. The opening batsmen, not yet attuned to the pace of the pitch, left the balls to fly harmlessly to the Chief keeping wicket, and in one case, to the boundary. At the other end, Jean was finding it harder to contain the batsmen. His fast medium pace was adequate for most sides, but to this squad it was an invitation. After three overs at eight per over, he began to look ragged.

After fifteen overs, the result was looking a foregone conclusion. But for one careless stroke that presented Xavier with an easy catch, and a run out, the Chowdrey Steamers had appeared faultless, and of a quality well above that of the normal Seychellois league. They had put on one hundred runs and were coasting to an early victory, when Sydney decided to change his tactics and employ his spinner at one end whilst keeping the tiring Curtley at the other. For a pitch that was so flat and dead, the result was both surprising and immediate. Maybe an element of over-confidence had crept into the opponents' play, but on his first delivery their opener, until then a calm and ruthless destroyer of the bowling, marched up the pitch, bat poised to slog for a huge six, and completely missed the flight of the ball. He was only able to turn round to see his bales fly into the air as the leg stump was rattled by the delivery. And the incoming batsman fared little better, facing two balls nervously before stepping back to defend and being caught plumb LBW.

Suddenly, from the edge of the abyss, hope returned. Fielding became sharper, Curtley became perceptibly quicker and more accurate, and Henry's side managed to contain the batsmen to a meagre three per over for the next ten overs, with further dismissals at both ends. 130 for six after twenty-five overs, still nowhere near a winning position, but not quite the drubbing that had seemed likely earlier on.

Both Henry and his host walked out to their teams at drinks.

"This team's got more bloody ringers than my local campanology society," the Reverend Kitson complained bitterly. "Half of them come from the Indian leagues for the season; they're not even proper Seychellois!"

Henry looked up and noticed that Rajiv had been collared by his father Sanjay, who seemed to be lecturing him intently.

"What was that about, Rajiv?" he inquired as the boy sauntered back to his team. With less than his normal ebullience, the young spinner kicked the grass.

"Business with my father, Mr Fanshawe. Just business."

They returned to the team talk.

"We're defending a low total – they only need 28 off the next ten overs, and that's a big ask. But let's keep the fielding as tight as we can and trust to Rajiv and Curtley to work some of their magic. Remember, we've bowled sides out for less."

"And of course, we have at least one God on our side," added Rev Kitson with a nod in the direction of Monseigneur de Pelet, "whichever of us is right."

"We may have one God, but I regret to say that the Indians have at least fifteen," answered his Catholic partner.

"And a manager who thinks he's bloody Jesus Christ," exclaimed Sydney. "I'm surprised he hasn't had a lake put in as well to take his morning constitutional on!"

Back on the field the total mounted inexorably if slowly, due in part to some excellent fielding and tight bowling by St Christol. Then Jean had managed to produce a fine outswinger which resulted in a wicket. The spin of Rajiv had provided a further scalp, but there were so few runs to play with. As the final over loomed, the score stood at a precarious 154 for eight. Four runs for victory, with one decent batsmen still in and the other spot occupied by the fast bowler.

Quiet fell as the ball was thrown to Rajiv for his final over. He looked distinctly ill as he took the ball. Nerves, thought Henry, as he turned to bowl. His first ball was dispatched to the boundary and would have won the match, save for a surprising turn of speed from the Monseigneur, whose excellent throw restricted the score to two runs. As the next ball came down Henry groaned inwardly. It was terrible, slow and straight. Henry closed his eyes and waited for the inevitable six. Nothing happened and then a roar from the visitors. He opened his eyes to see a disconsolate batsman trudging back to the pavilion. It appeared that he had raced up the pitch and missed it completely. The stumping was a formality. 156 for nine.

Henry scarcely dared watch. Four balls remaining, two runs needed. One wicket still standing. How on earth had it become this close? The next delivery bounced harmlessly and was padded away. Three balls to go. Henry starting muttering, "There's a deathly hush in the close tonight," but that was all he could ever remember.

The next delivery afforded a quick single. All square with two balls to go and one wicket. Up and down the boundary various spectators could be seen indulging in forms of prayer, knuckles outlined in white against the mahogany of their deckchairs. A few could not look, heads buried behind their hands. All was quiet as the second last ball was bowled.

What happened next would be reported best in the Seychellois press.

AN EXTRAORDINARY RESULT FOR ST CHRISTOL

In a split second, one of those wonderful sporting miracles occurred. From a seemingly unwinnable position, the David of the Seychellois league came back to bloody the nose of the current Goliath. In the rays of the sinking sun, Rajiv Khumri, St Christol's young spinner, provided the delivery, the second last of the innings, that comprehensively beat Chowdrey Steamer's tailender to level the score and the match. Draws in limited over cricket are rarer than black pearls and this was particularly exotic, given the total dominance achieved by the Steamers for most of the match.

Henry was up off his feet and running towards the bowler, arms outstretched. The rest of team let out a whoop of joy and crowded round their hero. Rajiv looked almost dazed and strangely ill at ease to Henry. Claps on the back and hearty congratulations followed.

Henry felt a hand on his shoulder and swung round to see the beaming face of Mr Chowdrey. He felt his hand grasped and pumped up and down. Chowdrey, who seemed quite unruffled by the way his team had capitulated, was fulsome in his praise. "Many congratulations, Mr Fanshawe, Henry. Wonderful show of English phlegm and determination from a Seychellois team."

"Yes, most surprising given the… er… quality of your side, Mr Chowdrey."

"I am dismayed – yes, a little – but every cloud, as they say, Henry, has a silver lining. You see, I bet on a draw." And with that he retreated, moving over for a whispered conversation with his captain, and leaving Henry to ponder his last words.

Henry had been dimly aware that betting happened in the Seychelles league, but thought it a small affair, and in any case mostly confined to the Indian sub-continent. But before he could reflect further on the extraordinary outcome, Mr Chowdrey reappeared and guided him firmly in the direction of a large red and green tent where tea was being served.

"With of course, cucumber sandwiches. One of the best features of the British Way of Life which you exported so successfully to your once great empire."

Henry couldn't quite pin down the rudeness in this statement but felt sure it was there somewhere.

19
Indian Take Away

Still confused from the improbable draw with the Chowdrey Steamers XI, Henry decided that he needed a night out. He informed Cilla, received the normal pursed look of disapproval that inevitably accompanied such conversations, and taking the Land Rover down to the beach, parked up and began to wander along the sand. Around him a few families and couples prepared barbecues and lit camp fires; radios were turned on, broadcasting soft Seychellois beats across the sand, old Sega and the newer Seggae, old rhythms re-interpreted by the island's Bob Marley. Clinking Seybrew bottles were set down, the laughter rose, with shouts and children's cries, and permeating all, the steady continuo of the forest at night. Out to sea, twinkling lights betrayed the presence of small fishing boats. Along the fringes of the beach, restaurants switched on their fluorescent signs.

The ambiance would normally have cheered Henry, but this evening was different. Something was wrong. His team had played as well as they could, but they were up against the acknowledged giants of Seychellois cricket. Given a small target to defend, the bowlers had reacted manfully, but it was clear that the outcome would never be in doubt. Right up until the final two overs, the visitors were coasting to victory with wickets in hand and four runs required from twelve balls. The odds against a draw in one-day cricket were astronomically high. So why the sudden collapse when victory was within their grasp? Losing one wicket in an over was, as Wilde nearly once said, a mistake, but two wickets? And so tamely given. Rajiv was a decent spinner, but to take two for three runs in a final over of a limited overs match was a miracle. He remained profoundly uneasy. Something was not quite right about the lame capitulation of a batting line up acknowledged as the best on the island.

Still wrestling with his thoughts, Henry wandered further along the beach. By now he had left Beauvallon village behind and the coastline cafes had given way to dense forest. In the distance a well-ordered string of lanterns fronting one of the more luxurious resort hotels was just visible. Around Henry there were only dark shadows, the blackness of the interior, and a phosphorescent sea lapping at the shore. He did not notice, as he passed by, two of the shadows detach themselves and follow him. He was all but oblivious to the quiet sound of footsteps on sand behind him until a voice jolted him from his reverie.

"Mr Fanshawe?"

Henry ignored the address and quickened his step. He was about four hundred yards from the hotel. Another voice.

"Please, Mr Fanshawe, our friend would like a word with you."

And then a large hand on his shoulder. Henry stopped, affecting a calm demeanour. Inside his heart was pounding.

"Good evening, I am afraid I cannot stop – dinner, you see, over there." Henry pointed to the hotel.

"I am sure they can wait for a few minutes. Please, Mr Fanshawe, follow me." This spoken in a tone which brooked no dissent.

"A few minutes?"

"They will not be knowing you are gone, sir."

And with that the two large figures, hats pulled down over their faces, ushered Henry into a clearing in the forest where a large Bentley was idling. One of them walked over to the car, opened the door and motioned Henry to get in. He felt a momentary pleasure at sinking into the plush interior, before his greeters entered the car on either side of him. In the front, in black silhouette, a large gentleman shifted his body.

"Good evening, Mr Fanshawe. I hope we have not inconvenienced you."

Henry's innate courtesy urged him to assure them they had not, but as he opened his mouth to speak, a large and evil smelling handkerchief was thrust over his mouth. He struggled to breathe, but then an unexpected sense of pure relaxation intervened. Before he had time to say anything, the blackness of the surrounding forest crept unbidden into his soul.

* * *

When Henry came round, he was sitting on a chair. Head pounding, he became aware that his arms and legs had been loosely tied. In the darkness in front of him he could just make out two men standing by a third who was seated behind a desk. He could not see the face of the seated man, who spoke first.

"I must apologise, Mr Fanshawe, Henry, for the surprise we have caused you. But it was very important that we see you urgently."

"What on earth is this all about?" Henry attempted to keep the panic out of his voice.

"Cricket, Henry, it is about cricket."

The two standing men glared as their boss continued, "You see, Henry, although the game is young in these islands, it has already ready attracted some attention."

"From whom?" Henry asked

"From us. We are most interested in its development. Especially in, how shall I put it, in the potential for gambling. Our masters…"

"From India I presume."

"Maybe. Our masters are using this season as a trial run for their business. I am sure that you realise how important this makes the results. And how important it is that they are fair and above reproach."

Henry realised where this conversation was leading.

"You mean, *seen* to be fair and above reproach."

"I mean exactly what I just said!" The voice became a little firmer and less polite. "Yesterday you seem to have had a miraculous result."

"Now I know why."

"It was written in the stars."

Henry said nothing.

"Who knows where fate may strike? It may even happen again. And that, Henry, is what I wished to

226

discuss with you. There may come a time in the not too distant future when you and your team will embark on the most important game of your career. The final of the Seychellois league tournament."

Henry's sense of realism intruded.

"Can't see us making that."

"Oh but I can, Henry, I can. We have high hopes for you. We think you will make the final, to face the Chowdrey Steamers once again. After a thrilling match, you will go down fighting. It will be admirable, but in the final analysis, just a step too far for a team of village amateurs. You will gain the fame of having played in a national final. We will have made a considerable fortune."

"But that's not cricket!"

In the gloom Henry could make out the white teeth of his smiling adversary. "I think you will find, Henry, that 'cricket' is exactly what it is. We will be in touch. Good evening."

A handkerchief was again pressed over Henry's mouth and all went black.

* * *

Awaking for the second time, Henry felt a moment of panic when he opened his eyes and found all was still dark. He quickly realised he was back in the Bentley, blindfolded. His arms and legs had been tied and he was lying on the black seat between the two men. He let out a low moan, and from the front the voice apologised.

"I am afraid you may be a little late for your dinner reservation, Mr Fanshawe."

His two comrades laughed mirthlessly.

"But there is always tomorrow evening. Providing our agreement works as expected."

Henry sat up groggily.

"What agreement?"

"Why, your agreement to lose the National Final. Surely you remember that?"

"But that would be cheating." Henry silently cursed himself for replying as the car lurched forward.

"Sometimes, Mr Fanshawe, one has to choose the lesser of two evils, don't you think? I feel sure you will make the right choice."

The large car, after driving for an hour or so round the island to disorientate him once more, stopped at Beauvallon beach close to where it had picked him up earlier that evening.

"Goodnight, Mr Fanshawe. I do hope we have made ourselves clear."

"Quite clear." Henry swayed unsteadily on his legs as the cords were released. He was given a push and staggered out of the car down onto the beach, silent now in the small hours of the morning.

"We will speak again when we have need of your assistance."

The door closed and the car sped away. Henry could not make out its number plate. He stood gazing at the tail lights as they disappeared into the distance, and, shaking violently, sat down on the sand to massage his aching legs and make sense of the episode. A sick and bitter taste pushed its way up Henry's throat and into his mouth. The sudden discovery of evil in such a seemingly innocent place made him gag. For though they had made every effort to remain anonymous, his captors had not been able to disguise the smell of the room where he had been held – a heady aroma of spices, Indian and Mexican, instantly and unmistakeably recognisable, to anyone from thereabouts, as that of Mr Sanjay Khumri's Hypermarket.

MID SEASON

20
Another Visit to the Capital

Henry gazed as the tail lights of the car disappeared round the corner, and then set to walking up the beach back towards the Land Rover he had left in Beauvallon. He looked at his watch. It was two o'clock in the morning.

Once he had started the Land Rover, he left the headlights off. Save for the usual hum of jungle nightlife there was little sound, and only moonlight to guide him up the dark track. With the aid of a full moon, he passed quietly through the village and eventually back to his house as discreetly as possible. Thanking his lucky stars that Cilla had left for the night, he let himself in and marched immediately to the drinks cabinet in the drawing room. Two stiff whiskies later, and calmed slightly by the strains of a bluesy CD, he sat in his usual armchair and reflected on the events of the evening.

He had been left in no doubt that he was expected to throw the final, if and when his team made it. And that the price of not doing so would be undoubtedly painful and possibly terminal. He was equally sure that the Indian fraternity were running the show, probably through the dislikeable Mr Chowdrey, and worse, that Sanjay and the Khumri family were involved in some way.

Before the combination of alcohol and residual chloroform sent him to sleep where he sat, Henry toyed with the idea of telling the police. But Henry had no idea who he could trust, and he knew it would play very badly indeed if this got back to his captors.

* * *

Cilla stood above him, arms crossed. Henry woke, with a fruity snore, still slumped in the armchair. He had a thick head and an incipient foul mood. Normally, an innate politeness would have stopped him from losing his temper, but the expression on Cilla's face and her first question provided the perfect excuse.

"Haven't you been to bed, Mr Fanshawe?"

"None of your damned business, Cilla."

"Well! You needn't take that tone with me!"

"I may not need to, Cilla, but what if I want to? Have you thought of that, eh?"

With a hurrumph that ranked high on the list of her all-time best, she turned her back on him and walked away. Henry rose and followed her into the hall, but not quick enough to stop her from diving into the kitchen.

Henry stood in front of the still swinging door. "And now I'm going out to town. Don't know when I'll be back either!"

Feeling slightly better, if a little guilty, Henry readied himself for another trip to Victoria. There were a number of questions which needed answers, and he felt sure that the answers could be found in the capital.

As he drove down the narrow track to St Christol, Henry decided to start his investigation in the local hypermarket. He wished to check two points. Affecting a need of some general groceries, he parked by the shop and wandered inside. Behind the counter, a familiar boater bobbed up and down.

"Good morning Mr Fanshawe, and what can I be getting for you?"

"Don't worry, Sanjay, just need to pick up a few things, don't let me keep you."

He wandered down the aisle looking to see if there was anything that might connect the shop with the events of the previous night. The smell of the place was strongly reminiscent. But that was all. There were no marks, footprints, or signs of anything out of place that could be construed as proving any of his theories. Nevertheless, he still harboured suspicions.

Sanjay, who seemed unwilling to let him out of his sight, asked again if he needed something in particular, and Henry could see that he was not going to achieve anything useful. He sauntered up to the counter, affecting nonchalance. "Could I have a packet of disposable razors – and that bag of wine gums please, Sanjay?"

"Of course Mr Fanshawe, that will be four rupees fifty."

"Thank you Sanjay. Well, what did you think of the match yesterday? Great result!"

Sanjay paused a moment to think. "I feel it was a gift from God, Mr Fanshawe. Rajiv excelled himself."

"An expensive gift, Sanjay."

"Priceless, I would say, Mr Fanshawe. We now have a hope of making it to the final."

This verbal jousting was making Henry uneasy, so he changed tack. "Were your family there, Sanjay?"

"All of them, all cheering for our wonderful little club."

"Even your brother from… from… what did you say the company was called?"

"Khumri Imports, Mr Fanshawe."

"Yes that's it, Khumri Imports. Based, of course, in the Seychelles?"

"Indeed."

"And registered here, I would suppose."

"That is so."

Sanjay's voice had taken on a shade of suspicion. Henry realised he had gone far enough. He moved to the doorway, and in one final attempt to glean some knowledge, replied, "Well, they must have all been very proud, as must you, Sanjay."

"Rajiv is a good boy, Mr Fanshawe. He always does what he is told."

"Good day, Sanjay."

"And to you, Mr Fanshawe."

Once in Victoria, he returned quickly to the library. The same receptionist greeted him, with her usual reserve, though Henry was pleased that she was now reading *Jane Eyre*. He inquired as to the whereabouts of the Companies Records, and made his way into a smallish and rarely-used room at the back. One wall was lined with filing cabinets marked 'Company Reports'. Henry opened the cabinet and riffled through the files, searching under 'C' and 'K'. Eventually he spotted what he sought, pulled out the last few years of reports and placed them on the desk.

After an hour of painstaking analysis he found what he was after. On the desk in front of him, he had, two sets of reports from 2010, replete with Post-it notes in various pages marking specific facts and figures. The Chowdrey Shipping Annual Report stood open in his hands in the Notes to the Accounts section. Henry read,

Mergers and Acquisitions 2009/2010:
15th May 2009: Hollis Engineering.
27th Sept 2009: Kanu Motor Corporation.

And then the item for which he had been searching

31st October 2009: Khumri Imports.

He took a copy, and sat down at the desk to add a few written figures, and the address of Chowdrey Shipping. Then he stuffed it in his pocket, and left the room.

Once outside, Henry strolled back up Independence Street and into the shopping area of Albert Street. After a short search he stopped outside a shop named VG Optics and entered, to be greeted by a man in a white lab coat.

"Good morning, do you sell binoculars here?" asked Henry.

"You are in luck, sir. We have an excellent selection. May I ask for what purpose you would be needing them?"

"I'm looking for… for…" Henry racked his brains, and found inspiration, "for birdwatching, the… the… black parrot."

"Ah, the black parrot. Birdwatching. On Praslin."

"Yes, yes, on Praslin."

"Then," said the man in the white coat, bending to reach under the counter, "I think these would be most suitable."

Henry paid quickly.. "Oh, and could you tell me the way to the docks... for the ferry?"

"Of course, sir."

Thus equipped, he made his way out of the shop and down towards the sea.

Nothing was more than about five to ten minutes away from the centre of Victoria, and it was not long before the stink of fish and diesel alerted Henry to the fact that he was near his destination. He began looking for a good vantage point with which to study the area.

On the rising road to the left of the port, Henry could make out patches of undergrowth that would hide even him reasonably well. He did not want to be seen doing what he was about to do – not by the port workers, nor indeed by any passers-by, who might get quite the wrong idea. So he made his way past the port gates and turned up the road towards Glacis and the north tip of Mahé, looking for a route into the bushes which he could to use as cover.

After a few hundred yards, he noticed a small path down into the undergrowth on his right. This, he figured, would be a perfect viewpoint overlooking the docks, and private enough not to arouse suspicion. He looked behind him, left and right, and then, with nobody watching, plunged into the bushes.

Once he had moved a few yards down the narrow path, he guessed he was invisible enough to commence operations. Pulling the case from his back, he unpacked the binoculars and trained them on the port area, scanning the buildings in the hope of finding what he was looking for.

It did not take long. On a large warehouse right by the waterside, Henry found his subject. The building in question was a long low warehouse, fringed with cranes bordering the waterfront. Along both sides ran, in large letters, a sign:

CHOWDREY SHIPPING COMPANY – 'WE TAKE ANYTHING, ANYWHERE'

How true, thought Henry, scanning along the building for the main entrance. As he did so, he noticed a smaller building adjoining the warehouse, marked KHUMRI IMPORTS. The connection was obvious. Items of all shapes and sizes were being downloaded from a tanker. Large, refrigerated containers for food, and, as if to outline the opulence of the enterprise, a group of new red Porsches, driven off and parked on the quayside. Then, as he watched, he noticed some movement further along the wharf. It was Mr Chowdrey. He walked up the wharf with a small number of outriders and turned towards a door which Henry took to be the main entrance. Chowdrey was gesticulating and seemed to be in argument with one of the hangers-on. On gaining the entrance, he disappeared inside, leaving two of his posse on the door.

Henry studied the two men deputed to stand guard. With a cold shock, he realised that one of them bore a close resemblance to a captor from the night before. The more he looked, the more sure he became. And this certainty grew when, some minutes later, a car drew up. It matched perfectly that in which Henry had been abducted.

Henry carried on studying the area for some time, hoping to recognise more characters from the night before. However, very little seemed to be happening, and he was just about to give up, when he noticed a door open on the smaller Khumri Imports office. Moving his binoculars over, he studied the figure now emerging onto the wharf.

It was Sanjay Khumri. After closing the door to the Khumri office, he made his way down, under Henry's gaze, to the Chowdrey Shipping foyer. Henry's worst fears were realised. Sanjay shook hands with the guards, made some joke, judging from the heaving forms of the bodies, and then entered the warehouse.

Henry waited around for Sanjay to reappear at the door. When he did, some ten minutes later, he emerged with Mr Chowdrey. The two shook hands and Sanjay climbed into a Khumri Imports van parked nearby and headed out of the gate. It was clear to Henry that whatever was going on, Sanjay and his family were inextricably involved.

21
A Watery Encounter

Henry got up bright and early to greet the Saturday morning of the next match. There was some mystery about this encounter, which entailed travelling by boat first to the nearby island of Praslin. The opposition was the only team on this island and the game was treated half as a proper fixture and half as a wonderful excuse to cross the short stretch of Indian Ocean between the two islands, for a grand village day out. Extra buses had been laid on and a ferry booked from Victoria. The locals were clearly keeping something from their manager, and all sorts of half clues and impenetrable witticisms vouchsafed to him over the previous week.

"It's the only offshore match in the calendar, Henry."

"You'll have to be careful about moisture on the pitch at this one."

And so forth.

At nine o'clock the buses rolled noisily out of the village belching the normal black smoke with even more of a carnival atmosphere than normal. Breasting the hills towards Victoria, Henry could see, set against the deep blue of the port, the white ferry destined to carry them the ten miles to where Praslin stood in hazy purple silhouette. The island was said to be even more beautiful and laid-back than Mahé – which in Henry's book would make it both very beautiful indeed and almost supine.

They bustled from the bus to the gangplank, women resplendent in billowing multi-coloured dresses, bright parasols and large wicker hampers. The club flag was carried, furled, by Sydney, who was already dressed in his whites with an old Surrey blazer, looking every inch the visiting test cricketer. Cilla looked quietly on, checking every now and then that her scoring book was in her large carpet bag. Henry thought he saw a little glow of pride on her otherwise severe face.

The ferry terminal was adjacent to the commercial port, and Henry felt a pang of cold discomfort when he saw a ship from the Chowdrey fleet moving into the harbour to dock. He had bought his binoculars for this moment, and once aboard the ferry he trained them as before on the harbour side offices of Chowdrey Shipping. He spotted the burley Indian whom he had recognised from his impromptu stake-out the week before. The man looked up at the ferry and straight back at him. Henry shivered and pulled the binoculars away smartly.

Soon the boat was ready to leave. A few deafening blasts of the foghorn and they were away, skimming over the sea, which changed from green to a deeper blue as they left the harbour behind. Overhead, seabirds wheeled, and the odd helicopter bearing the über-wealthy to the discreet and fabulously expensive resort hotels on Praslin buzzed through the clear skies.

Henry stood leaning over the prow, face occasionally freshened by a sharp and salty plume of spray from the bows, and thought – Indian betting syndicates excepted – how his luck had changed so abruptly, how rapidly he had fallen in love with this island and its inhabitants. When things get big, he mused, they invariably go wrong. Small is beautiful, and not a Human Resource department or Health and Safety manager in sight. He wondered how Ryan Pikeworth was doing, back in the gloomy fluorescent lit trading floor, managing the trade in spices and commodities produced in little paradises such as this. Without, he realised, a second thought as to their provenance. Intent only on maximising their monetary worth.

In the middle distance the island of Praslin loomed, its hazy outline becoming more defined, the uniform dull purple giving way to the greens of the forest and the occasional man-made splash of white or red as the villages became visible. Whatever the surprise he had been promised was, Henry mused, it would be worthwhile, just for this journey.

Upon landing in Praslin the team and their considerable entourage made their way down the gangplank to be greeted by three large tractors pulling trailers into which the crowd surged. Stepping off an aged Massey Ferguson, the opposing manager, a large and genial Dutchman who doubled as the manager of a nearby resort hotel, ambled towards Henry with hand outstretched. "Ah, Mr Fanshawe, such a great pleasure to welcome you to Praslin. My name is Hoof, Eric van Hoof. Our team may not be quite in your league but I'm sure we'll make a game of it and, of course, there are the extra delights of our ground."

There were a few sniggers from the team which only served to heighten Henry's curiosity. He grasped the Dutchman's proffered hand and tried to appear unconcerned. "Pleased to meet you, Mr van Hoof. Delights, you say?"

More sniggers, and the manager effortlessly batted away the comment, "Ah, Mr Fanshawe, I see they have not told you. I think we should keep you guessing."

Leaving Henry's question hanging in mid-air, he bounced back onto his tractor and motioned the cavalcade to begin the journey. It was slow progress, as the caravan processed through several small villages, before halting finally at a long white beach on the far side of the island. Henry looked around in some confusion. The scenery was stunning, with lush rainforest bordering the purest white fine coral sand, shaded by coconut palms overhanging the beach at the craziest of angles. But there was a marked lack of anything that remotely resembled a cricket pitch. He stepped down from the trailer and tried to appear as if he was not surveying the horizon in every direction for clues.

Mr van Hoof loped towards him. "So, do you like our ground, Mr Fanshawe?"

The look of puzzlement on Henry's face led to another round of giggles from those in the know. "Well, Mr van Hoof, I have to confess that I am finding it a little difficult to pin down the exact whereabouts of your pitch."

There was more offstage mirth. The Dutchman smiled, "Please, call me Eric. And, Mr Fanshawe, if you look this way, all will become clear." He motioned towards the sea.

By now totally bemused, Henry followed the pointed hand out into the bay. As he looked, he thought he could make out a spit of sand in the middle of the blue semicircle of water. He took his binoculars from the case hanging about his neck.

"Those might help!" suggested van Hoof.

Henry trained the binoculars out into the bay. He located the spit of sand again. In the middle of the oval shaped island, there lay a darker and elongated rectangle of what looked like seaweed. Upon further examination he saw that this area had what looked suspiciously like wickets at either end. The seaweed resolved itself into dark green matting.

"Our only offshore fixture, Henry," chortled Sydney.

"A marine encounter," added the Reverend.

Henry turned to his number four. "I presume we will be taking a boat and you will be walking there."

The Dutchman beckoned over some of the small fishing boats to a small jetty near where they stood. He turned to Henry. "So, Mr Fanshawe, what do you think of our pitch? There's always been a little patch of sand that emerges at low tide. They used to have tribal meetings there – a neutral venue for disputes. Then my predecessor put in the strip – it's the perfect size you see, and beautifully flat. The only problem is we have to restrict the overs to twenty per team. We were in fact the first 20/20 venue in the world!"

The fishing boats stood ready and the two teams plus umpires embarked. Some were possessed of old outboard motors but many relied on oars, and Henry watched as Sydney stepped into a boat to be greeted by the toothless but genuine smile of his ferryman who then proceeded to row him to the pitch, which had now also risen Atlantis-like from the sea, marked out in buoys which lay idle on the sands. On the closest area of the beach, a few deckchairs and a parasol stood waiting for him, Cilla and the Dutchman. The rest of the supporters sat behind them, and a fortunate and prescient few had also brought binoculars to watch the action.

Eric leaned over. "This is less a match than a barbecue, Mr Fanshawe, but it's always nice to have the cricket in the background."

The strip had dried rapidly in the sun, though the surrounding sands were still a little sticky. St Christol won the toss and decided to bat first, hoping that a dry strip might work better for their bowlers later in the afternoon. In truth, the strip was uneven, still wet in places, and Henry realised that this would be more than the usual lottery. The openers were despatched with instruction to slog anything that moved.

Sydney agreed, "All we can do is hit out and hope we get more runs than the other side."

The ever laconic Monseigneur, his opening partner, nodded. "As ever, Monsieur Mason, you have a refreshing and original style of stating the... how do you English say? The bleeding obvious!"

There was a certain *froideur* between the pair as they made their way to the crease. Most of the field had removed cricket shoes and pulled up their whites. The scene resembled an Edwardian day on the beach, with only the knotted handkerchiefs missing from the heads of the participants.

It was not long before Sydney returned. Two mighty sixes in the first over, and then a ball which pitched quite unexpectedly, having hit some unfortunate element of marine life that scuttled across the crease at the last moment. An edge provided their first slip with an easy catch. Still chuntering, he was ferried back to where Henry sat, and hunkered down in the sand next to Henry's deckchair.

"Totally impossible to tell what the ball's going to do. Especially with a bloody hermit crab running across the wicket like that." He moved over to share his disgruntlement with Cilla who shooed him away.

"Not now, I need to concentrate."

It was indeed hard to keep up with the action. Any thought of quick singles had to be abandoned as it became clear that upon hitting the wet sand, the ball generally stopped dead. Only airborne shots stood any chance of scoring, and catches came thick and fast. It was clear that 20/20 really was the only possible type of cricket to play on this surface. Here, the unreconstructed schoolboy slog ruled, and as a result, the art and style of the opening batsmen was of little to no use.

Matters brightened for the tourists when the Reverend Roger Kitson strode to the crease with the score on 36 for two. The Reverend was a natural born schoolboy slogger. Carrying the bat more like a baseball player than a cricketer, Roger was determined to put his talent to good use. Ball after ball was despatched for six, or, if it did not reach the boundary, remaining motionless in the wet sand, for at least two. He was scoring at the rate of ten per over and together with Jean had added a further 65 by the time a miscued effort was nicked to the slips. His lead was followed by Mathilde. She was less successful, possessing far too classical a style for this venue. But the Chief managed to put on another 28 runs. After Jean's departure for a solid forty runs, mirrored glasses gleaming in the sun, the policeman was left to shepherd the tail-enders until the allotted number of overs ran out. At the end of their innings, St Christol had made 142 for eight.

The changeover was a rapid affair. It became clear that even with the shortened innings, haste was needed to ensure that the full number of overs could be bowled. The tide had turned and the waves were now lapping yards from the boundary. It would not be long before the Indian Ocean would again cover this unusual pitch. And it became clear to Henry that any delays would put paid to the chance of winning which they now possessed thanks to the Reverend's innings – referred to by an irreligious Sydney as a 'demon knock'. Henry looked skyward, sensing that there was the distinct possibility of delay from the weather.

He had recently read in a guide to The Seychelles that it had two distinct seasons, a Rainy season and a Dry season. The book added that these descriptions were simplistic and should be taken with a pinch of salt. Henry agreed. To call the wet season 'Rainy' does the god of rain an injustice, he thought. Imagine standing under a large water tank shedding its entire contents in a matter of seconds. Clouds serenely floating on the prevailing winds over the Indian Ocean, amassing water as they progress, hit the islands and unleash inches of rain in minutes. And when, as always, the monsoon subsides and the sun reappears, it is to an island glowing with wet green foliage and rivers of blood red sediment washing down from the mountains into the sea.

Next to this, the 'Dry' season is relatively dry, with strong emphasis on the word 'relatively'. The rain is less torrential (though by British standards well into the cloudburst category) and considerably less frequent. However, by no stretch of the imagination can it be described as 'dry' in the normal sense of the word. And being an island, the weather is apt to change sharply and without warning.

The buses had departed Beauvallon in warm sunshine and clear blue skies. This clement weather had continued, right up until the changeover, but Henry, from his deckchair, could now see dark clouds scudding across the sea towards the island. The temperature of the wind had dropped quite dramatically, and on the field of play, there were a number of anxious skyward glances from the fielders. An attempt was made to hurry Curtley, but his temperament did not lend itself to haste. Henry realised that this game was running out of time.

The skies grew darker, the wind picked up and within ten minutes Henry felt the first drops of rain. He turned towards Eric van Hoof. "We're going to have to stop this match – look at the lightning out to sea!"

As they gazed at the approaching deluge, and mesmeric forks of whiteness playing across the horizon, the earth shook to a clap of thunder. Henry jumped to his feet. "Get the boat out, for God's sake, or one of them is going to get fried!"

Cilla looked up from her scoring book. "Don't worry, Mr Fanshawe, it's only a shower. It'll blow over soon enough."

"A shower? A shower! Behind us, in the jungle, the animals are at this moment pairing up and putting on their wellies. Anyway, even if it blows over, we won't have enough time to complete the innings before the tide comes in – look, it's at the boundary already."

Cilla and Henry surveyed the scene – the players had stopped and were now huddling together in the middle of the sandbank. The tide was moving in quickly, lashed by the offshore winds. And lightning flashes continued to play along the reef.

Cilla turned to Henry. "You may be right, Mr Fanshawe. But they won't get the boat out in this. They'll have to swim for it."

Whilst making gestures to the players to return, Eric was attempting to persuade the flotilla of little rowing boats to put to sea. However, the fishermen, wiser to the ways of the ocean than he, would have none of it. Henry remembered that Sydney had bought his mobile phone, and praying that he had it switched on, dialled and was rewarded by an answer from the rain sodden captain.

Sydney was not happy. "Get those bloody boats going – it's like the wreck of the Hesperus out here!"

"They won't move – they say it's too dangerous." Henry looked over at the immobile ferrymen.

"Too dangerous? Too dangerous! I've seen higher waves in the Serpentine for God's sake. What do you expect us to do? Hitch a ride on the Rev's shoulders and get him to walk back?"

"I'm afraid you're going to have to swim for it, Sydney." And as Henry watched, he saw that most of the players had already struck out to the shore.

"I'm going to charge the cost of a new phone to the club expenses. This is the most ridiculous game I have ever played in!" and with that Sydney rang off. Henry saw him remove his cricket cap and stride into the water.

Some of the more thoughtful supporters had grabbed towels and stood at the water's edge welcoming incoming swimmers in a parody of the end of a marathon. Once all had been accounted for (many without sweaters and other accoutrements which had been jettisoned in the swim for home), one of the more adventurous fisherman was paid generously, to retrieve the flotsam and jetsam of jumpers, cricket bats, pads, wickets and bails, which threatened to be lost at sea now the storm had calmed a little. Then there was a meeting to discuss the result.

It transpired that the Duckworth Lewis method had not yet made its way onto the rulebooks in the Seychelles. Henry attempted to explain the reasoning and maths behind the calculation, but, since he himself hardly understood how it worked, trying to convince a Dutchman and a group of islanders proved a task beyond him. Before long, he gave up and asked for other suggestions, adding reflectively, "Never has the Duck in Duckworth Lewis been more apt."

The suggestion of using run rate was firmly vetoed by Eric van Hoof. "How can you compare the rate from our seven overs to your twenty? We had no time to get our eye in!"

Henry's observation that no one had bothered for more than one ball to 'get their eye in' fell on deaf ears. In the stand-off that followed, tensions were not eased by the Reverend's one line contribution,

251

"Bugger Duckworth; we annihilated you!"

Finally, amidst a lot of poring over the rule book, and an air of slight resignation, they decided to call it a draw.

In a spirit of reconciliation, Henry murmured to Eric afterwards, "Maybe the fairest result Eric, and I have to say, this has been a match I will never forget!" And Henry thought the tea afterwards was magnificent.

* * *

By the time the bedraggled group had returned to the ferry port in Praslin, night had fallen. On the road back to the port, Henry marvelled at the surroundings, even more unsullied than the delights of Mahé. Over the sea, he could make out the main island, a starless lump in the dark sky where the lighthouse, whose gently rhythmic beam swung round every few seconds, marked the entrance to Victoria Harbour.

The ferry left Praslin in almost complete darkness. Henry leant over the deck rail to watch the sea scudding by. At the back of the boat, phosphorescence traced a light turquoise path back to the island. Save for the thrumming of the ferry's engine, and the rush of water passing, all was quiet. Most of the team and supporters were sat on deck, chatting quietly or sleeping off the effects of the splendid tea. The odd clink of bottles, a short burst of laughter. This he thought, was about as close to earthly paradise as one could find. Pity about the draw of course.

When the boat docked in Victoria harbour, Henry, trying to avoid staring too much at the floodlit activity of the Chowdrey compound nearby, disembarked and headed towards the waiting coach. It halted outside the church an hour later in the warm damp dark of the tropical night. The team, with the odd back slapped and cheery goodnights, melted into the gloom. Henry was left to walk up to the Manor.

Upon entering the house, he noticed that an envelope had been put under the front door – marked 'Urgent – for the Attention of Henry Fanshawe, manager, Esme Fanshawe Cricket Club'. It bore a crest of some tree which he could not quite pinpoint. He opened the letter and read its contents:

Dear Fanshawe,

Apologies for the hurried nature of this note. You may recall that your next fixture is against us in a week's time. However, a situation has arisen which I think we will need to consider with some urgency before then. I cannot, I am afraid, be more explicit about the subject in this letter, but would be most grateful if you could visit me at the Club tomorrow morning.

Can I impress upon you the need to keep this letter and its contents strictly between us for the moment?

Many thanks in advance for your forbearance.

Yours sincerely,
Colonel John Farrer (Retd)
Chairman, The Cinnamon Club

Henry folded the letter and put it in his pocket. The events of the last week had left him suspicious and shaken. And now a mysterious letter from the team's next opponents. Strolling into the drawing room, he fixed himself a large gin and tonic, and sat down in the chair that, having conformed quickly to his generous contours, was rapidly becoming his favourite. To the background of nocturnal jungle rhythms, he sipped his drink and wondered what on earth was going to happen next.

22
Skulduggery at the Cinnamon Club

Not many vestiges of colonial rule remained in the modern island state of the Seychelles. However, on the main road out to the airport (the only dual carriageway on the island) nestling amongst the emerald foliage and set on a lawn of geometric perfection, lay a building of the deepest brown mahogany. It seemed to have been designed by an architect with one foot in the South Seas, and the other in an Alpine chalet. A large bronze plaque announced to visitors that this was the home of the exclusive and mysterious Cinnamon Club.

Rumours about goings on in this exclusive club abounded. Whispered stories of bizarre initiation rites for new entrants, its astronomical membership fees, bacchanalian parties, and abuse of several prohibited substances had filtered through to Henry over the past few months. So it was with some curiosity that he arrived at the gates on his way to meet the chairman, who was the manager of the next cricket team St Christol were due to play.

Henry swung open the large black iron gate, and walked up the path to the main door. He could not help but feel admiration for the extreme uniformity of the cut grass on either side of him, or indeed for the rows of marigolds, flawlessly linear, which bordered this billiard table. In the midst of the perfectly manicured carpet stood the tree which gave the club its name. An old cinnamon, with bark the hue of dark plain chocolate, and a rich smell that reminded Henry of hours back in the City spent sitting in Starbucks with a spiced latte and a hangover.

He strode up the wide steps to a large black door and knocked twice with the imposing brass coconut which faced him.

In the minutes that followed, Henry could see the lace curtains at the front of the building twitch in sequence, as someone approached. Finally, to the sound of a large bolt sliding back, and hinges that squealed as if they were auditioning for a part in a Hammer horror movie, the door moved about six inches and a rather sad face presented itself.

"Good morning, sir."

"Good morning. My name is Henry Fanshawe, I have come…"

"The tradesman's entrance is round the back." The door began to close.

Henry, with a surprising turn of speed, stuck out a left foot and jammed it in the doorframe, thanking God that he had decided to wear his walking boots.

"Kindly, remove your foot, sir. I cannot recognise you and you therefore cannot be a member of this club."

"But I am a guest of the chairman!"

"That may be the case, sir, but it does not change the fact that you are not a member, and only members may enter by the front door."

"That is the most ridiculous rule I have ever heard. So, if I were a member you would let me in then?"

"No, sir."

"Now I am confused. Why ever not?"

"You are not wearing a tie, sir." And with that the door opened a touch, Henry's foot was levered out, and the door closed again.

Henry stood on the veranda in a haze of indecision. He considered walking round to the back of the building to find the tradesman's entrance. He was also very tempted to shout some expletives through the letter box and then storm off in a huff. However, the chairman, who seemed a pleasant if rather stiff fellow, had been most insistent that they meet. Indeed, Colonel Farrer had sworn Henry to secrecy about the rendezvous, and he was quite curious to find out why.

In the end the choice was made for him. After the sounds of muffled argument behind the closed door, it swung open once more. Standing, framed in the doorway, was the Colonel, whose ruddy cheeked and laughter lined face sported a handlebar moustache of a length that Henry thought long since extinct. Next to him, in the shadows, lurked a rather disgruntled looking butler.

"Awfully sorry about that, Mr Fanshawe. Felix is a bit … literal in his interpretation of the rules of the club."

"Please, call me Henry." He could not help but warm to the round and jolly countenance of his host.

"Of course, Henry, and you can call me Colonel. Now, do come in – we'll need to find you a tie of course but that can be arranged." He turned to the glum retainer. "Run along Felix, there's a good chap, and fetch our guest a tie."

The diminutive figure retreated into the background, muttering in an incomprehensible French patois. And that, Henry decided, was probably a good thing.

The Colonel leant towards him. "He has a bit of a thing about the English. It's his French ancestry you see – very proud of it – claims his father fought with de Gaulle and his grandfather fought with Marshall Petain etc. etc."

"His family doesn't seem to have got on with anybody," replied Henry.

After a few seconds of thought, the Colonel gave a large guffaw. "Very funny, sir, very funny – just like your dear departed aunt. Life and soul, don't you know, life and soul!"

Henry was taken into a large drawing room which could easily have been situated in Henry's London club. Smooth leather armchairs bore the shine and impression that can only be gained from years of polish by a succession of eminent posteriors. The pictures on the wall were of variable quality, and uniformly portrayed stern men with large amounts of facial hair. Some of the individuals seated were studying the newspapers, cigars feeding a thin vertical pillar of smoke from the ashtrays beside them. Others snored gently. The Colonel headed towards a door marked 'Chairman' and ushered Henry through.

Once seated at the large mahogany desk which dwarfed most of the other furniture in the room, the Colonel leant backwards and tugged at a long bell pull. From a smaller door behind the Colonel, the recalcitrant French doorman reappeared, bearing a tray set with the finest porcelain, and a plate of cucumber sandwiches, cut to a right-angled precision which would have impressed Pythagoras himself.

The Colonel rose. "I'll be mother – do have a sandwich, Henry."

Henry settled back into an armchair, balancing his tea and a plate full of sandwiches on his lap, and commenced pre-business pleasantries, "So, Colonel, how did you come to be living here?"

The Colonel took off his glasses and polished them, relaxing into the chair and assuming a storytelling pose that slightly worried Henry.

"Well," he started, "it is a rather strange tale."

Henry made himself as comfortable as possible and put on his interested face.

"First time I came here I was just out of the army, and doing a job for a friend," said the Colonel.

"A job? Sounds mysterious,"

"Yes – in fact it should have been a lot more mysterious than it turned out to be. We were mercenaries, from South Africa, and we had flown in to help in a coup. Trouble was, everyone knew about us before we arrived. Landed the plane at the international airport. Jumped out of the hatch ready to storm the palace and fell straight into the arms of a rather large policewoman and several chaps with Armalites. Ended up spending the first year of my time here in prison."

"So why did you stay?"

"Well, when they let me out, I realised that I had come to like the place and its people. They were all very nice to me and frankly I didn't want to leave. That was over thirty years ago."

"Isn't there some type of syndrome that has those symptoms?"

"Yes. Thoroughly Nice Place Syndrome!" The Colonel paused to chuckle at his wit and continued, "You must have felt it too, Henry. Enjoying yourself here, what?"

"Colonel, I don't think I need to tell you that I'm having as much fun as I can ever remember."

"Yes, it does have a habit of sneaking up on you here, doesn't it?"

"Doesn't what?"

"That calmness. The sense of wonder. At the scenery, at the people. So easy to just sit back and let it wash over you. And who is to say that's wrong?"

Henry suspected that this was a rhetorical question.

The Colonel leant forward, his face shifting from the bluff to the serious. "But not all is what it seems, Henry. They have a prison here, just like everywhere else, don't you know. Now, Henry, you may wonder why I have asked you here in advance of our match."

Henry nodded. The Colonel went on, "Well, the fact is, and I have to say it has shaken me to the core, the fact is, Henry, that I have had… advances."

"Advances?" Henry was not quite sure where this conversation was going.

"Yes. Advances. Very suggestive advances at that."

In Henry's mind a distinctly unattractive picture was forming.

"Guess what the suggestion was, Henry."

"I have no idea, Colonel."

"They wanted me to throw the game. I mean, can you believe it?"

As the words sank in, relief rapidly turned to dismay and a hollow feeling of dread. Henry decided to keep his immediate suspicions to himself. Affecting ignorance, he replied, "What, you mean to lose our game on purpose – but who would suggest such a thing?"

"Not quite sure, old boy, it was a phone call late at night; no names, but sounded like an Indian voice to me – I'd had a few and thought I might have been dreaming – but there was a letter here the next day."

He opened a drawer in his desk and drew out a page of paper on which, in classic criminal style, words from newspapers had been stuck, laying out an ominous warning.

FOLLOW LAST NIGHT'S INSTRUCTIONS.
LOSE THE MATCH AND YOU WILL NOT BE
HARMED.

"What are you going to do, Colonel?"

"I'm not going to do anything. Whoever heard of throwing away a game? Why, it's just, it's just—"

"Not cricket?"

"Precisely – it's an affront to the noble game. How dare they! They don't know who they're dealing with – I was on the first boarding craft onto the Falklands. Not going to let a bunch of gangsters dictate terms to me."

The Colonel had visibly reddened. Small veins were standing out on his neck as he worked himself up. "This is just between us, Henry. I'll deal with it myself and I wouldn't want word getting out to the players."

"That's very brave, Colonel, but may I make one suggestion?"

"Of course, Henry, go on."

"Let me at least take the letter to give to the Chief of Police when I see him at net practice on Thursday. He might be able to help."

"Capital idea. Get the local plod onto it."

Henry was not sure that the Chief of Police would be entirely happy with this description, but he took the letter and shoved it in his pocket. He was keen to close the matter down before too many questions were sent in his direction. Luckily the Colonel seemed to have a short attention span and was now moving into other areas.

"Jolly good to meet you at last, Henry. Always a great fan of your aunt, you know. Life and soul, life and soul. Such a tragedy…" He tailed off and starting gazing wistfully through the window at a large mango tree that sat in the middle of the back lawn, dark green against light green. Then he shoved the remainder of the cucumber sandwich he was holding into his mouth, stood up and walked to the window.

"It's almost allegorical isn't it?" murmured the Colonel.

"Allegorical?"

"Or metaphorical."

"Metaphorical?"

"Yes."

A pause hung in the air while Henry struggled to catch up.

"What?"

"Sorry?"

"What is metaphorical?"

"Oh yes, where was I, metaphorical…. Or possibly allegorical."

"Yes, Colonel, but what was metaphorical or allegorical?"

"Damned if I know, old boy. Just long words to me!"

Henry was now lost, and remained quite silent while the colonel worked his way back to the real world.

"Look outside into the jungle, Henry. All that beauty and profusion. Takes the breath away doesn't it?"

Henry joined him at the window and gazed out at the greenest of greens, the most striking of flowers, and listened to the evocative birdsong. He nodded.

The Colonel strode across the room to the door and, opening it, turned back to Henry. "But we all know that it hides snakes, my boy. Best remember that."

Henry was shown out by a reluctant Felix, who, after the return of the tie, bundled him through the front door, unconsciously scanning the street for anyone who might have noticed this transgression of Club rules. Once on the veranda, Henry turned to offer diplomatic thanks, but the door had already been closed in his face. He walked away from the building irritated, worried and muttering. It was maybe this state of mind which distracted him from noticing that, as he exited the establishment, a large van marked Khumri Imports had drawn up in the car park behind him.

* * *

The Thursday evening practice session started smoothly enough, but Henry's mind was not really on the cricket. He was waiting for a chance to collar the Chief of Police, and when the clubroom had cleared of the various hangers on and junior members of the team, he sidled up and surreptitiously beckoned the man outside.

Once on a quiet patch of ground underneath a large takamaka tree, Henry removed the scrap of paper from Colonel Farrer and handed it over.

"I thought you should see this."

The Chief of Police looked at the sheet, stiffened and immediately grabbed Henry by the arm and almost frogmarched him off into the undergrowth. "Where the hell did you get this, Henry?"

"Colonel gave it to me. The Chairman of the Cinnamon Club."

"And I presume he is refusing to be intimidated?"

"Yes."

"This is a delicate matter, Henry. Don't tell a soul about this. I will take it from here."

For a moment Henry thought of telling the Chief about his own experiences, but something inside stopped him from doing so. In a way, he pondered, this was a lucky break for him – a means to inform the police about what was going on, without implicating himself or his club. So he remained silent and nodded.

They rejoined the others and then sat chatting about the next day's match with the Cinnamon Club. Pierre had cut and rolled the square to a near-perfect state, a large postage stamp of lighter green that became darker in the outfield, leading into the profusion of jungle that encroached on the boundary.

There must, Henry thought, have been an enormous effort put in to level this area prior to the pitch being laid. The hillside fell off rapidly on one side and climbed equally rapidly on the other. The house, its garden, and the pitch, lay on a level spit of ground which had been extended over the years. Since then, the jungle had regained some dominance, leaving the house and its surroundings all but invisible from below. But from the pitch, Henry could look out over the trees to the graceful curve of Beauvallon Bay, and the precipitate headlands plunging into the water that defined it.

* * *

It was the tradition to have a large village barbeque on the night before the final home match. So, as the practice ground to a halt, he could see large numbers of villagers and their families filtering into the ground through the white gate and laying out bright fabric picnic rugs behind the boundary.

In a corner of the field, next to a large pile of grass clippings, there stood a small hillock of wood and cardboard, covered in a tarpaulin. As the sun briefly outlined Silhouette island on the horizon in a blaze of orange before dipping rapidly beneath the sea, the cover was pulled off and the bonfire lit. Large ice-filled plastic dustbins were loaded up with bottles of Seybrew. Cilla had set up a small stall from which she dispensed the drinks. She was keeping a beady eye on the consumption by locals, especially Sydney, who seemed to be enjoying himself. Up from the coast arrived fishermen with long sticks, off which hung fish of all shapes and sizes, some still flapping feebly as they finally gave up the ghost. The bonfire was allowed to burn down and the sticks were thrust over the embers. The sound and smell of the fish cooking made Henry's mouth water.

He walked up and down between the various families camped on their colourful squares, savouring the aroma of the wood smoke. Frequently he was called over to some gathering, to shake the hands of each member of the relevant family ensconced there. There was an end of season feel to the occasion.

As he walked back towards the house, the Monseigneur rose from his blanket and beckoned Henry over.

"Henri, I recall that you play a mean saxophone. You like the great jazz, my friend."

Henry nodded, and Simon continued, "I too play jazz – have you had your piano tuned? It used to be terrible." Simon rolled the 'r' to emphasise his dismay.

Henry straightened up. "Of course, Monseigneur. I could never allow such a thing to continue. Why?"

The Gallic exterior of the Monseigneur softened. "Do you not think that this would be a perfect occasion to, as you British say, jam?"

Henry usually reserved his playing for when he was on his own. But after the famous Capucin match, when they had all returned unwittingly high as kites, he had apparently entertained the team with an impromptu and acclaimed medley. As with many musicians, his love of showing off had to be correctly primed before it caught fire. He remained reticent.

"Well… I don't know, Simon. Are you sure?"

"Of course I am, Henri. Get your sax out and I will accompany you *au piano*. I am feeling, how you say, tres groovy!"

Henry did not need to be asked twice. They returned to the house and threw open the French windows which overlooked the back garden. Simon seated himself by the piano and ran a few times up and down the keys.

"*Moi*, I am more of a classical man, Henri – impressionist – Ravel, Debussy. But just now I think a little Oscar Peterson would not be wrong yes?"

"Why not?"

"Or maybe Fats."

And without stopping he launched into *Honeysuckle Rose* with a verve and technique that left Henry speechless.

De Pelet explained, "Before I took to the church in Martinique, Henry, I lived a rather less ascetic life. My interest in matters spiritual was, at that time, concentrated on spirits of a different kind, if you understand me. I used to play the piano in a bar in downtown Fort-de-France. To make enough money for the drinking."

"Do you miss it?"

"Not the drinking, really – but I do miss the jazz." And with this he executed a final flourish to general applause. Turning to Henry who by now had his sax at the ready, and smiling with genuine excitement, he held his hands poised above the keyboard.

"Blues, Henri, in G, I think. Ready?"

"Ready."

And off they went.

23
The Cinnamon Club Match

Henry woke up early on the morning of the match. It was the penultimate of the league section and the winner would most probably qualify for the final four knockout. The loser would probably finish fifth and miss out. There was still a mathematical possibility of qualification for the loser, but the run rate required in the last game would be dizzyingly high. This match was in effect the quarter final. It seemed to Henry as if the heavy tropical atmosphere hung expectantly in a steamy mist around the house and gardens.

Players and supporters had started to drift up from the village. Some seemed to have stayed overnight after the barbecue of the previous evening. The square was rolled once more by the Boy. White lines were being applied precisely by Pierre. Others hefted the large boundary rope from the clubhouse and began to pull it into the ellipse that marked out the playing area. In the midst of this industry, Cilla sat with her scorebook inscribing the names of the team and opponents in meticulous copperplate. Beside her stood a large blackboard and an equally high pile of square metal plates inscribed with numbers, and the odd phrase such as RUN OUT and LBW. It was the job of Pierre and the Boy to man the scoreboard, taking instruction from Cilla who sat at a desk under a large flowery parasol, barking orders at them.

Shortly before midday, the coach carrying the Cinnamon Club team pulled into the drive. The local supporters, who were now processing up the track from St Christol, were noisily chanting and clapping their team, in expectation of a thoroughly enjoyable afternoon's sport.

The Colonel stepped down for the bus and grasped Henry's outstretched hand. "Who'd have thought it – us two playing for a place in the semi-finals? Damned exciting, eh what!"

Henry liked the Colonel. He may have been a slight caricature of the stranded colonial bemused by the new world order and railing against the changing of fashion, but Henry was sure that underneath the bluster there was a fine man. The captains tossed a coin, and the Cinnamon Club elected to field first. The Colonel turned to Henry.

"Wait 'til you see our opening bowler, old boy. He's a devil!" And with this he ushered his team out onto the pitch, full of chat and backslapping.

As the opposition marched onto the green swathe cut into the middle of the jungle, Henry noticed Cilla making final preparations to Sydney's attire before he entered the arena. They were getting on well again, much to Henry's delight, as it made for a less depressive Sydney and a milder Cilla. As he gazed, his housekeeper even gave Sydney a peck on the cheek. Not much in today's climate of easy morals, Henry thought, but quite daring for Cilla.

Like a yacht whose sails have just been caught by the wind, Sydney walked out onto the field of play with

Jean beside him. Looking every inch the captain, chest puffed out, newly pressed white shirt ruffling gently in the wind, he swept up to the crease. Once stationed, he called for middle, prepared his guard, and then, in the time-honoured tradition of all opening batsmen, had a little walkabout, prodding the ground gently with his bat and taking in the field placement. A few stretches with the bat followed, and Sydney was ready to face the opening ball.

After such a grand entrance, everyone expected the first applause to have been for a delightful shot. But the shout that went up was from the fielders. The opening ball from Cinnamon's heralded bowler was indeed a devilish delivery. Fast and pitched up, it caught Sydney completely unawares. Hopping in an attempt to get the bat to the pitch of the ball, he was caught hopelessly square. His bat missed the oncoming delivery and the ball thumped into his pads. It was as plumb an LBW as could be imagined. Being honourable, Sydney didn't even wait for the raised finger of the umpire. He shouldered his bat with an exasperated groan, echoed by the crowd, and walked off the crease. St Christol zero for one.

It did not improve. Henry sat on the boundary, feeling that he was watching a car crash in slow motion. The Reverend came and went, falling cheaply to the pace attack of the Cinnamon Club. The local support went quiet as the third wicket fell, when Monsignor de Pelet was caught beautifully by a diving slip, and Mathilde entered the fray. St Christol 28 for three.

Mathilde, with Jean toiling at the far end, managed to stop the haemorrhage of wickets for a few overs, and the score began to rise to more a acceptable level. When Jean was finally bowled, St Christol stood at 75 for four after twenty agonising overs. Not nearly enough, Henry thought, from his deckchair. He watched, as the Chief of Police, padded and ready, rose from his deckchair and strode up to the wicket, mirrored glasses gleaming in the tropical sunshine.

The reaction of various bowlers to being faced with the Chief of Police had varied through the season. Some were apt to slow their pace a little, provide easier balls, hoping to bank a few little favours for the next time they were stopped in the process of some illicit undertaking. But for others, the sight of a policeman at their mercy was sufficient inducement to take entirely the opposite course, sending down balls much faster than normal, pitched on occasion to play the man rather than the stumps. And unfortunately for Chief Mahjoud, this was one of the times where the temptation of doing injury to a senior member of the constabulary proved just too great.

In his first over, the Chief was liberally peppered with balls clearly designed to remove his head rather than to take a wicket. He fended off the deliveries, jumping about the crease like the proponent of some new breakdancing craze, but after a few near misses, a ball finally got through. There was a loud crack as it hit the single helmet owned by St Christol, and the Chief went down, poleaxed, falling backwards straight onto his own bails. St Christol 75 for five.

Henry had his head in his hands as the Chief, having only slightly recovered, crumpled into a deckchair beside him.

"Never liked that man, Henry. It's the same every year. Ever since I caught him speeding he's waited to get back at me. Half of those balls were closer to throws!"

"The policeman's lot is not a happy one," murmured Henry.

"Well, two can play at that game," the Chief stood up unsteadily, and made his way over to a line of parked cars. "I'm going to check his tyres. Never fails."

* * *

Though Mathilde responded valiantly to the continual loss of wickets around her, there was no respite for St Christol. The Cinnamon Club had been exceedingly well drilled by Colonel Farrer, and their sharp fielding restricted any kind of recovery from the position in which Henry's team found itself. Wickets continued to fall regularly, and by the thirty seventh over, a straight delivery passed between the bat and the pad of Curtley, signalling the end of the innings. St Christol had reached a lamentable score of 127 all out. In the clubhouse, Henry gathered the team around him, at a loss for quite what to say. In the end he sighed, "Well, we need to field as well, and bowl better, than they have."

"An astounding insight, Henry, quite astounding!" Sydney was not in a good mood.

"We must put our faith in the Almighty, and field like the very devil," intoned the Reverend Kitson, stroking his luxuriant beard.

Sydney was not having this either. "I'm not sure what the Good Lord can do about this. Can't remember anything in the good book about his talent for slip fielding, you pious old fart."

For a second Roger looked as if he might retaliate, but, drawing himself up to his full height, he gave Sydney a hard stare, and then marched off into the corner to rearrange his kit bag.

Henry turned to his bowlers. "You are going to have to bowl your hearts out today. Keep it tight, and let's have a good go at them."

He watched the team take to the field. Their heads were down, and he could not imagine them winning from this dispiriting position. He returned to his deckchair and sat down to watch.

It did not start too badly. The bowlers were tight for the first few overs, and the fielding efficient if uninspired. Sydney put down a tricky catch at slip, which did not improve his mood. Henry could sense his grumpy demeanour, even from behind the boundary rope, and it had infected the team. And although the runs were coming slowly, St Christol had not yet achieved a breakthrough with the ball. There would come a time soon, Henry thought, when this pair could begin to accelerate their scoring as the bowlers tired, and the game would be gone.

The next over was encouraging. Jean swung a ball away from the opener, who had started to play at a few of the more risky balls in an attempt to quicken the scoring. It was a mistake, as the ball nicked his bat and flew into the wicketkeeper's gloves. Cinnamon Club 12 for one after five overs. And three balls later, another good delivery caught the incoming batsman cold and unprepared. As the umpire raised his finger for the LBW, Henry dared to hope.

Looking back on the match afterwards, this was probably the last time that optimism reared its head that afternoon. The Cinnamon Club were well drilled, efficient, and stubborn. It became clear that they were not going to forfeit the chance presented by the bowlers. Each wicket was defended strongly, and although runs came slowly, the rate required was so low that it soon became clear it would be achieved. Milestones came and went; 30 runs for three off ten overs, 75 runs for four off twenty overs, and by the thirtieth over, the Cinnamon club stood at 110 for five.

Henry brought out the drinks. "Seventeen runs off ten overs. We need a miracle!" He looked unconsciously in the direction of the two vicars. This was noticed by a glum Frankie.

"No good trying there, darling. Loaves and fishes, yes. Water into wine, no problem. A constitutional on Lake Galilee, just watch me. But five wickets for 17 in ten overs. Not a chance!"

And in the following half hour, he was proved entirely correct. The remaining runs were knocked off in five overs by the incumbent batsmen. And then it was finished. As the last ball of the innings was dispatched theatrically for four, the Cinnamon Club team rushed onto the pitch to congratulate the scorer, and then each other. Colonel Farrer, less fleet of foot, strolled over to Henry where he sat in a state of resigned gloom.

"Well played, old chap, jolly good game."

'But it wasn't,' thought Henry as he rose to shake the proffered hand. 'We were rubbish.'

The Colonel tried to sound sympathetic. "Caught you on an off day I think! That's lady fortune for you, eh what?"

"Miss Fortune for us I think." Henry's attempt at

humour, which sounded lame, even as he heard himself say it, was taken in good part by the Colonel.

"Miss Fortune... Miss Fortune, that's a good one Henry, ha ha. Capital!"

A slap on the back followed which nearly removed Henry's teeth, and the Colonel was off, shaking hands with all and sundry, proffering words of comfort to the losers. Tea afterwards was a quiet affair. All knew that the win put the Cinnamon Club ahead in the league, into fourth position. Though St Christol had one game in hand, their batting average was significantly inferior. They had thrown their chance away. Henry attempted to inject some cheerfulness into proceedings, but even his forced joviality could do little to enliven the mood. Sydney was inconsolable in the corner, and well on the way to getting drunk. Cilla had retreated to another corner to fume silently. Henry strolled over to a silent and ruminative Reverend Kitson.

"It's only a game, I suppose, Roger."

"That, Henry, is what I keep telling myself. But there remains the question."

"The question?"

"Yes, the question, Henry. If it *is* only a game, why am I so bloody miserable?"

There was no answer to this. Henry left the cleric with his thoughts and sat down next to Sydney.

A mournful face turned towards him.

"Pass us another beer, Henry, there's a good chap".

FINALS

24
The Last Game

There was one game left in the league, before the final knockout commenced. After the loss to the Cinnamon Club, a simple win would not be enough to move St Christol into fourth place. The team would need to significantly improve their batting average, and only a phenomenal score would move them up the table enough to qualify.

However, this was not beyond the bounds of possibility. Anse Takamaka, their final opponents, were one of the weaker village teams, so a win was the overwhelmingly likely outcome. St Christol would have to bat first to make the necessary total, and then bowl them out to amass the points which they needed. Everyone would have to be on form, and highly disciplined, a fact he had hammered home at that week's practice. By Saturday, with thoughts of the recent loss consigned to the past, Henry was confident that all possible preparations had been made.

He was up early on Saturday morning to ready himself. Over breakfast he went once more through his notes, disregarding the *Seychelles Nation*, which lay unopened on the white tablecloth beside him. He didn't even bother to look at the banner headline on the front page.

CHAIRMAN OF CINNAMON CLUB INJURED IN BREAK-IN

The passage to Anse Takamaka necessitated a long drive down the east coast of the island, through Victoria, along the dual carriageway past the airport, and down to the south, before climbing west over the mountainous interior. The coach battled up the roads and past the tea plantations which by now lined the route. The jungle had given way to a slightly cooler rainforest, much of which had been cleared to grow tea. In the fields, pickers in bright saris bobbed in and out of the waves of green bushes, spotted paniers on their backs like a swarm of feeding ladybirds.

The road fell away after Quatre Bornes and the coach was soon heading along the western coast to Anse Takamaka. The village stood adjacent to a beach which was considered too dangerous to swim from. It was fringed by a long line of the eponymous trees, and boasted a little shack rumoured to serve the best lobster in the Indian Ocean, if not the world.

The pitch was small with a close boundary, a good omen, thought Henry. As the coach disgorged the team, a diminutive figure walked out of the shack that served as a clubhouse, to greet him.

"Good morning Mr Fanshawe, a fine day for a game of cricket."

The opposing captain was a rotund and jolly Ceylonese. He reminded Henry of Danny DeVito as he bustled out, shaking hands and smiling broadly.

"Good morning Mr... Mr..."

"Vengasurwinath. But everyone calls me Danny."

"You must be from Sri Lanka, Danny."

"Ceylon, when I left it, but yes. Came here decades back to run the tea plantation. Then, with the Tamils and everything, seemed better here than back home."

How full the island was, Henry thought, with those who had come for a short stint and stayed forever.

Danny hopped from foot to foot excitedly. "You find yourself in an interesting position, I believe."

Henry flinched, then realised that his opponent was remarking on the fight for fourth position, rather than the darker aspects of the game to which he had been recently introduced.

"Yes... of course... the points situation. Couldn't be closer, Mr Veng...Vengasur... Danny"

"It will make for an exciting game. We know you will have to hit out – maybe we will be able to take advantage." Danny smiled infectiously and disappeared into the shack.

The St Christol team followed him and were ushered inside to get ready. Henry entered, and in the dim interior began to expound his game plan. It was not complicated.

"I've done the maths. We need over 322 runs in forty overs to make the run rate we need. That's a tall order, I know, but Anse Takamaka are new to the league and they've been pretty well beaten by most teams. We need to bat first, and slog any ball that deserves it to the boundary."

281

The Reverend Roger Kitson, pulling on his cricket boots, echoed the instruction. "Slog, boys, slog with all your hearts, and the Almighty will be slogging alongside you!"

Thus heartened, the team began to move for the door, which was opened by Danny who entered with a more concerned face than previously. He cornered Henry. "We have a problem, Mr Fanshawe."

Ushering Henry out of the door, he pointed at the square. The creases were well marked and the wickets stood proudly to attention on the close cut green. All looked perfect for a day's play, save for one aspect.

In the middle of the strip lay a very, very large cow. As Henry looked on, several of the opposing team members were trying, half-heartedly, to shoo it off the square. Their efforts seemed to be having little if any effect. Danny, standing beside him, looked worried. "Evelyn has escaped again, Mr Fanshawe. She loves it here and whenever she gets out, she always comes here. It is the very devil of a job to move her."

"She must be quite heavy," said Henry

"Heavy?" Danny mopped his brow with a large white handkerchief. "She's a giant among cows! She's won 'Cow of the Seychelles' three years running. And once she's settled down she just won't budge."

Now Henry was concerned. With the rapid tropical sunset at six o'clock, there was never a massive amount of spare time to play with, and any shortening of the match could cause problems with the run-count.

"Surely someone can get her to move?" he pleaded.

"Yes, Mr Fanshawe, that would be Old Monsieur Ledouche," replied Danny.

"Well, why don't we get hold of him and sort this out?" Henry's temper was starting to fray.

"If only it was that easy. You see, Old LD may be wonderful with animals, but his treatment of humans is less charitable."

"So?"

"He got into a fight yesterday at the Takamaka Bar – again – and is currently in jail."

Henry thought about this, and then in a flash of rare and rapid brilliance, exclaimed "Which jail, Danny?"

"Anse Royale."

"And if I can get him out and back here, you'll let us bat first?"

"Are you planning some sort of jail break, Mr Fanshawe?"

"Just leave this to me, Danny."

Henry walked back to the team and pulled the Chief to one side. "Chief, I need a favour."

"Yes, Henry?"

"That cow over there. She will only respond to one man, and he's currently banged up in the police station at Anse Royale."

"Henry, I understand you perfectly." The Chief pulled his phone out of a pocket and dialled a number. After a few pleasantries and a short conversation, he put the phone back and turned to Henry. "I have informed Monsieur Capitaine Picquet of Anse Royale force of our predicament. He will be here shortly with Old Monsieur Ledouche. It shouldn't take long to get here from Anse Royale with a police escort."

"Thank God for that, Chief!"

283

"One thing, Henry, I need 200 rupees off you for the … bail money."

A small price to pay, Henry thought, as he handed over the cash. And the Chief was as good as his word, for it was only fifteen minutes later when, sirens blaring, several police cars screeched into view along the coast road and into the car park, halting in a cloud of red dust. Out stepped several extremely smart policemen, and one dishevelled old man, dressed in a kaftan that had seen better days, the better days in question probably being the early 1960s. He was pushed towards the waiting teams, advancing somewhat reluctantly and occasionally turning to mouth some obscenity at his jailers.

Danny turned to Henry. "Old LD keeps himself to himself. Doesn't like newcomers much, and to him, anyone who arrived after about 1930 is a newcomer."

Henry smiled. "Just so long as he moves that bloody cow, Danny!"

A short conversation between Danny and the old hippy, laced with promises of alcohol and cigarettes, seemed to do the trick. Still surrounded by police, he was taken out to where the cow still lay luxuriating on the grass. Kneeling down beside the huge animal, and dwarfed by its bulk, the be-kaftaned figure pulled up a large flapping ear and whispered something into it. The result was spectacular and immediate. The cow, belying its size, leapt briskly to its feet. Ignoring all spectators, it then walked slowly to the edge of the pitch, where it lay down again in the shade and continued to gaze calmly at nothing in particular.

Danny ushered the old man off the pitch into a waiting police car, and then returned to the clubhouse.

"I don't know what he says, Mr Fanshawe, but when it comes to cows, Old Monsieur Ledouche has one hell of a way with words."

After a short interval, Anse Takamaka, led by their diminutive DeVito look-alike, took to the field. They were followed quickly by Jean and Sydney, clearly pumped up and in a hurry to get started. Sydney took his guard and turned to face the first ball. From the boundary, Henry whispered a quiet prayer to the Gods of cricket and watched on.

Sydney began with a flourish, a drilled cover drive to the boundary of exquisite timing evading the hands of the diving fielder by inches. There was little time for lassitude when they were chasing around eight runs an over. With Jean looking solid at the other end, he set about the bowling in a dispassionate and deadly fashion. Henry purred in admiration at this exhibition of shot making. It was going well, he mused, as St Christol put on 35 runs in the first six overs. Nearly the required rate.

The captain remained at his professional best until a stroke of bad luck. Departing for a quick single in the seventh over, he slipped and fell. A loud shout of pain had Cilla rushing on with the trainer's medicine bag and a worried face to where he lay rolling on the grass. Fielders gathered round the body, hands on hips, and Danny, after a quick look, gestured to Henry.

As Henry hurried over, the team parted, to reveal a very grey looking Sydney, head cradled in Cilla's lap.

"I'm hurt, Henry," he whispered plaintively.

"What have you done to yourself, old boy?" asked Henry.

Cilla looked up and replied, "It's the ankle. He obviously went over on it. Not broken, thank God, but a nasty sprain. No more cricket for you today."

Now Sydney looked downcast as well as injured.

"Rats, just as I was getting my eye in. Could I have a runner do you think?"

Cilla was not in the mood for any dissent. "For a runner to work, dear, the batsman needs to be able to stand. You cannot stand. Therefore a runner will not work."

"I suppose if you put it that way, Cilla," replied Sydney.

"I do."

And, to subdued applause, Sydney was hefted into a standing position and, grabbing onto the shoulders of Henry, more or less carried off the pitch. It was a blow, thought Henry, not a mortal blow, but certainly a setback.

Sydney reached the sanctuary of the deckchair and slumped into it off Henry's arm muttering gloomily, "Let's hope the others can get there."

With the weak bowling from Anse Takamaka, Henry remained confident that the unlikely target of 322 could be achieved, and for the next period of the match, St Christol remained well in touch with this target. The only concern for Henry was whether they would run out of batsmen. For in their haste to hit out, wickets were falling on a slow but regular basis. Monseigneur de Pelet spooned a catch to the bowler to leave St Christol on 125 for two, then after a fabulously rapid and carefree knock, The Reverend followed him back to the pavilion having made 35 runs in four overs. St Christol 183 for three after twenty-two overs.

Jean, unnoticed, was batting carefully at the other end, and amassing a good score. By this time he had passed his half century, and looked impregnable. So long as he remains, thought Henry, we have a chance.

Mathilde was next to bat, and provided her usual exhibition of stunning shots and thinly disguised coquetry to push the score on through 200. When she departed, to be replaced by the Chief of Police, it was clear that the chase was on. Henry unconsciously gripped the struts of his deckchair, playing each shot in his imagination alongside the facing batsman.

In this tense atmosphere, milestones continued to fall, 225 for four, then 250 for four, then 275 for four off 34 overs. Sydney turned to Henry, pain almost forgotten as a result of the growing excitement, combined with a dose of painkillers and several large pink gins, "You know, Henry, we might do it. We might just bloody well do it!"

Henry shared his excitement, but when the Chief was bowled by the first decent delivery of the day, he looked over to the pavilion and saw Louis making ready to take over. Alarm bells started to ring in his brain, and in an instant he was on his feet, running towards the hut, hands waving. "No, Louis, no – I want Frankie on first."

Louis was not pleased. "Why, boss? I'm much better than he is!"

Henry tried to find a suitable rejoinder. "It's er… it's… it's what Mrs. Fanshawe would have wanted."

With very bad grace, Louis disappeared back into the clubhouse, and the dapper figure of the Honourable Frances Atterwood appeared, smiling and waving to friend and foe alike.

Henry returned to his seat and turned to his injured captain, "That was a close one, Sydney. Nearly broke Esme's first rule."

"Which was?"

"Never let the Kamling brothers bat together."

Sydney nodded, "Of course, but I fear, Henry, that you have only delayed the inevitable. Unless our mate Frankie performs way beyond expectations, he'll have to bat sooner or later."

"Let us hope it is later, Sydney."

It was not later. Frances batted with his usual skill and aplomb, that is to say not much skill and very little aplomb, and was out after scoring five runs. Henry had arranged for Xavier to come in next, and was trying to subdue a by now thoroughly irritated Louis. Xavier, like the calm and sensible attorney he was, stuck to his appointed task well. This allowed Jean to accrue runs and pass his century, to loud acclaim from the pockets of away supporters who had come for the day. St Christol 307 for six off thirty-eight overs. Fifteen runs to make off twelve balls.

Then Anse Takamaka struck to remove Xavier with the first ball of the second last over. Henry was faced with a terrible dilemma. Louis was a good batsman, far superior to Curtley or Rajiv. But would he conform to type and cause some problem with his brother? It was extraordinary, Henry thought, that the two, who got on so well normally, would have this blind spot when it came to facing each other on a pitch. Rajiv was sent on, only to return almost immediately, having left Cilla untroubled in her role as scorer.

"Surely he won't muck this up?" Henry said to Sydney, as he finally beckoned Louis on. The immediate hush from the on-looking crowd of St Christol residents was no comfort.

Louis took guard. As the spin bowler sent down the third ball of the over, he waltzed a few yards down the pitch and flung his bat at it. There was a resounding crack as the ball flew to the boundary, dropping behind the ropes for a six. Nine to make off nine balls. Henry breathed a sigh of relief. "As long as he just scores boundaries and sixes, we don't have a problem, Sydney."

And as if to order, the next ball was also despatched for a four. St Christol, five runs to make off eight balls. The result was in their grasp. After blocking the next delivery, the final ball of the over was pushed to mid-on by Louis.

"Run!" shouted Henry from his seat.

The two brothers gazed at each other, each resolutely unwilling to be the one to make the first move. Leaving five runs to get off the final over.

"That was an easy single. What are they thinking!" Henry slumped back in his deckchair, drained by the tension of the moment.

The final over was indeed a nail-biting affair. Anse Takamaka had done their homework and realised that the total required for qualification was achingly close. The best bowler was on, the field was set to minimise run scoring, and the crowd watched on as Jean took guard.

The first two balls, yorkers, were only just kept out. The bowler seemed to have found extra pace from somewhere and was causing real problems for the two nervous batsmen. Henry could hardly watch. Then another pushed ball crying out for a single which was not run.

By this time Henry was on his feet gesticulating like some football manager. "For God's sake, you've only got three balls left. Run!"

Jean faced up, and guided the next delivery beautifully through a gap in the on field.

Henry was by now jumping up and down on the boundary.

"They must be able to run this – two at least!"

And, as he watched, Jean gave a loud cry of "Yes" and set off down the pitch.

There were undoubtedly two runs to be had. As the fielder pursued the ball which had flown past him, Jean sprinted towards the other end and turned to head back.

Louis however did not move. Looking up, Jean, his momentum still carrying him forward, started screaming at his brother.

"Run, Louis!"

Louis showed no signs of moving and, with a large hand raised, responded, "Go back!"

Caught in an agony of indecision, and marooned in the middle of the pitch. Jean finally decided to turn back. But it was too late. By then the fielder had the ball, and with a throw of some quality, sent it hurtling towards the bowling end. The run out became a formality.

Henry threw his hat to the ground and started jumping on it, and in the middle, Jean had to be restrained from taking the matter further with his brother. Finally, shoulders hunched and looking neither left nor right he marched off into the clubhouse and did not re-emerge.

Louis and Curtley, together for two balls, were not able to conjure up the remaining runs. St Christol ended their allotted forty overs on 319 for nine, three short of the target.

Sydney leant over to Henry as they sat on the boundary watching Louis returning with Curtley from the crease. Jean had exited the clubhouse and stood waiting beside them with a look on his face that was decidedly unfriendly.

"He's going to kill his brother when he gets back to the pavilion!"

"Not if I get there first!" A puce Reverend Kitson strode out towards Louis, who slowed his already snail-like pace of return and winced, involuntarily, in expectation of the tsunami of Anglo Saxon invective that was shortly going to wash over him.

In fact, the Reverend was strangely quiet, which if anything was even more terrifying than the usual barrage. He had half dragged Jean with him and stood the two together before commencing, "Louis?"

"Yes, Reverend."

"Jean?"

"Yes?"

"This has to stop."

"But he was the one who ran me out!"

"I don't care. And if either of you pull that stunt again, I'll… I'll…"

Roger was now getting into his normal stride. "I'll break your bloody legs!"

He turned and marched off but not before one last outburst.

"And I'll tell your mother!"

The result was never in question, a resounding victory to St Christol, who, anxious to get away, had bowled and fielded in exemplary fashion and dismissed their opponents for 95 in thirty overs. But the ride back was a thoroughly dispiriting affair. The coach wound quietly through Victoria, and over the pass to Beauvallon, followed by the various supporters' forms of transport, more in the nature of a cortege than a victory parade. It had been so near, and Henry was still steaming. The twins had effectively cost St Christol its place in the semi-final. Roger sat next to him, fuming. The two miserable teenagers huddled together at the back, shunned by the others.

The coach and its entourage pulled into St Christol. There was to have been another party that evening, but it seemed that no-one had the stomach for it. Sydney tried half-heartedly to inject some more cheerfulness, reminding everyone to be at the clubhouse that evening at seven-thirty, but the majority remained stonily silent, aware of how close they had come to clinching fourth place and how thoughtlessly it had been snatched from them.

Henry surveyed the scene with a sinking heart. He, as a true supporter of sport understood the depths of depression which set in on such occasions. He didn't really feel like a party either, but all had been prepared and he guessed that many would get over this immediate despair and recover sufficiently to take advantage of the food and drink offered.

Sydney turned to him. "You know, Henry, I just want to get up to the club and then get totally pissed."

Henry replied, "For once, Sydney, I quite understand the urge. But we are better men, no?"

He was about to walk back up to the Manor, when a small van marked Khumri Imports tore into the village, skidding to a stop in front of the hypermarket. Out jumped the diminutive figure of Sanjay, holding a copy of the *Seychelles Evening News* and jumping around pointing to the back page. "Everyone! Listen! Have you seen the news?"

Henry looked at the back page article shoved under his nose. His eyes widened.

"Good God!" he murmured.

Sanjay jumped back up on the coach's lower step and flung out his hand for silence. Everyone stopped and looked towards him.

"This is extraordinary!" He began to read out the article to the assembled crowd.

BIZARRE TWIST IN CRICKET LEAGUE PLACINGS

Today's results have filled the last place in the semi-finals of the Seychelles championship. It was expected that the Cinnamon Club, having beaten gallant St Christol, would occupy this position, as St Christol who play Anse Takamaka this afternoon, would need a miracle to achieve the average run rate required. However, in an extraordinary and dramatic about turn, the current acting manager of the Cinnamon Club has withdrawn his team from the competition, in consideration of the very serious nature of the injuries sustained by the club's chairman, Colonel Farrer. The following announcement was made to the Seychelles Cricket board and the Evening News *this afternoon,*

"Due to the grave nature of the attack on our Chairman and the critical condition in which he now resides, in Victoria hospital, the Cinnamon Club feels that it is unable to compete in the Semi Finals of the Seychelles Cricket Championship, and resigns its place forthwith. As a result, fifth placed St Christol will play the Seychelles Scanners next Saturday in the semi-finals."

"What attack?" Henry was suddenly a very worried man.

Frankie turned to him, "Didn't you read the paper this morning, Henry?"

"No, why?"

"There was a break-in at the Cinnamon Club yesterday."

"A break-in?"

"Yes, and Colonel Farrer was unfortunately the only person there. He must have caught them at it. Got pretty badly beaten up. He's in hospital in a coma."

"Oh my God!" Henry felt the blood drain from his face. A queasy feeling overtook him, and he had to place his hand on Frankie's shoulder to steady himself.

Frankie was concerned, "Are you quite all right, Henry darling? You look completely white!"

Henry didn't know what to say or do. He needed to sit down somewhere quiet to take in this news. Wishing fervently that Frankie would leave him, he muttered, "Nothing to worry about, Frankie. Just the heat I expect."

"Quite understand, darling! Plays havoc with the makeup doesn't it." Frankie moved off, leaving Henry shivering in spite of the evening warmth.

There was an awkward silence as competing emotions of sympathy, surprise and elation worked their way through the crowd. Then a sudden outbreak of noise as everyone began to speak at once. This was stilled as the Reverend Roger Kitson jumped up onto the step next to Henry, grabbing his hand and raising it heavenwards. His words boomed forth like Moses addressing the Red Sea. "We're in the semi-finals. We're in the bloody semi-finals!"

A massive cheer rang through the crowd. If there was any guilt about the nature of their path to the knockout phase of the competition, it had been rapidly consigned to second place by all but Henry.

"See you all at the club at seven-thirty," said Roger.

At the back of the crowd, a few of the more observant souls might have noticed twin brothers hugging each other. They might have also seen the figure of their manager retreating into his house, unable, for reasons known only to him, to partake in the general mood of celebration.

25
The Semi-Final

The coach wound its weary way for the second time up the tortuous and narrow road to the peak then rolled downhill, puffing into the car park to meet the Seybrew Scanners. Henry's attention was caught by a shiny new red Porsche parked up next to the coach. He was racking his brains to try to remember where he had seen it before, when out stepped Don Travers, the Australian manager of the opposing semi-finalists.

"Good Morning, Mr Fanshawe."

Was there a touch of guilt in his voice?

"Looking forward to the match I hope," blustered Travers. "Should be an excellent contest."

"I am sure everyone will put their heart and soul into it," replied Henry. Excellent as the result might turn out to be for St Christol, he reflected, he was unsure if it would actually be a real contest at all.

As a good size crowd arrived in various forms of transport from St Christol, Henry walked onto the pitch, which seemed to be in a decent state, despite the rains which were becoming more frequent as the wet season approached. He noticed at the far end of the field, a helicopter, primed and just about to take off. His suspicions grew as it swung into the air, exposing the words 'Chowdrey Shipping' written in large green lettering on one side of the tail. Straining his eyes, he imagined he could make out the diminutive dark skinned figure of Mr Chowdrey at the controls. He knew what was about to happen.

The Scanners won the toss and elected to bat first.

Henry's worst fears about the likely outcome of the contest were quickly realised. Unlike the first time that they had met, the opponents seemed reticent and confused. St Christol bowled and fielded well, but not well enough to justify the ease with which batsmen were dispatched back to the pavilion. It seemed to Henry that, having played themselves in and after adding a few runs, practically all of the Scanners' batsmen managed to throw away their wickets in a show of ineptitude that was quite out of keeping with their reputation as favourites. Easy catches were spooned to waiting fielders, shots were played and theatrically missed, and on one particularly obvious occasion, the stumps were taken off by a flailing bat clearly aimed with that in mind.

When the innings was over, and a target set for St Christol of 165, Henry was the only member of the team not smiling. Sydney led his side off to loud cheers from the onlookers and grinned at his manager. "Don't know what got into them, Henry! They played like rubbish today."

Henry kept silent, attempting to match Sydney's cheerful demeanour. He knew exactly what had got into them. Threats, a large amount of money, and a shiny new Porsche.

The Scanners' efforts in the field confirmed his fears. Harmless bowling and a few spectacular misfields allowed St Christol to amass 100 runs off twenty overs with some ease and without losing a wicket. It was all too simple. Even when a moment of proper cricket, a sharp and accurate throw, resulted in Sydney being run out on 60, the result was never in doubt. The away team coasted past the required total with five overs left. The winning stroke was provided by the Monseigneur, who let out a Gallic shout of triumph. St Christol had beaten the pre-season favourites comprehensively. Henry watched the resigned faces of the fielding team as they returned to the clubhouse. The only man smiling was Don.

Henry was anxious to get away. He was the only man in full possession of the facts and felt isolated from the happy team surrounding him. Though a glance from the Chief of Police as he left the pitch suggested Mahjoud shared his views.

Mr Travers made his way through the crowd of players towards him, hands outstretched. "Congratulations, Mr Fanshawe. I believe this is the first time that a village team have made it to the finals. I am afraid that we didn't do ourselves justice out there today."

Henry responded carefully. "Yes, you did seem a trifle off form. It must be exasperating, for you to play so well through the season and then misfire at such a crucial moment."

"Yes, Mr Fanshawe, sometimes the dice are just loaded against us, aren't they?"

"I try not to play with loaded dice, Mr Travers." Henry was finding it difficult to cover up his disgust.

Don glanced at him strangely for a second. "It's Don… but I wish you all the best in the final, anyway."

Henry stiffened. "We will try our *honest* best, Mr Travers."

Now Don was trying to leave, but Henry would not let him go. Placing a firm hand upon the man's shoulder, he steered him gently out of the crowd, and waved his hand in the direction of the car park. "Nice car, Don. That must have cost you a pretty penny."

"I got lucky, Mr Fanshawe."

"You certainly did."

Henry had remembered where he had seen the car before, and was replaying in his mind's eye the view from his binoculars of Chowdrey Wharf, and the three sleek motors parked along the quayside.

Worse was to come. When Henry got home, Pierre the gardener was standing on the veranda, waving a letter in front of him.

"Mr Fanshawe, someone has left this for you." He handed Henry the letter.

"Thank you Pierre."

"And, boss, he left something else as well." Pierre gesticulated to his left, and Henry noticed, in the dark and parked just alongside the house, with its boot showing, the back of a shiny new red Porsche.

Without saying anything to the gardener, who stood admiring the new car, he walked inside and threw the envelope onto the hall table. It could wait, he would read it tomorrow. After all, he already knew what it was going to say.

26
A Strange Twist

Thursday morning found Henry grimly reviewing his options over breakfast. The letter received a few evenings before had been straightforward and unequivocal.

He was to lose the final by putting Sydney, his captain, in to bat down the order. Mathilde was to be 'rested'. He was to use Curtley 'sparingly'. Rajiv, his spinner, was to bowl extra overs, proof, Henry surmised, of Khumri's complicity in this grubby affair. These changes, together with the undoubted superiority of the Steamers, would almost guarantee them a win.

He gazed at his toast with a sinking feeling and put his head in his hands. It was an impossible position. Even if he agreed to carry out such changes, there was no certainty that either Sydney or any of the others would accept. And he had been expressly informed not to tell them. What if they won anyway? Would he be the next casualty of the 'burglars' who had so nearly finished off the Colonel?

He was roused from his reverie by the telephone ringing. It was an old fashioned Bakelite object, one which would probably have been viewed as attractively retro in Islington and other arty London environs.

Picking up the earpiece, Henry remained silent, fearing that it might be a call from his tormentors.

A female English voice sounded in his ear. "Mr Fanshawe, is that you? Henry? Are you there?

"Fanshawe here. Who's speaking?"

"Ah, Henry, it's Polly here. Don't you recognise me?"

Rusted wheels began to turn in Henry's brain. "Polly… Polly Farrer. What are you doing telephoning me?"

"The very same. I've been promoted. I'm PA to Sir Godfrey now."

"Congratulations, Polly, I'm so pleased for you."

"And how are you, Henry?"

Henry dissembled. "Couldn't be better, Polly. Loving it out here."

"Yes, it's a super place – you never know I might come and see you one day – I have family there."

Many years previously, after the death of his wife, Henry had fallen for Polly. It had really been the only serious affair since those dark days. In his youth she was one of the price girls at Fanshawes, marking up changes to commodity values in red and blue pens on a large white board at the end of the old dealing room. Polly had the knack of cheering Henry up and for a while it had looked as if it might progress further. But Henry could never quite bring himself to make a serious move and in the end it had all petered out amicably. She had gone on into secretarial work. Henry was impressed that she was now PA to Sir Godfrey Plumborough (pronounced 'Pluff'), senior partner of the firm, and noticed a small frisson as he talked to his one-time lover. It was a sensation he had not felt for many years.

"How's the cricket team going?" asked Polly.

"Good and bad. Well, it's a long story, Polly. Anyway, why are you phoning? It must be costing a bomb."

"You're right, Henry, and no time for small talk, enjoyable as it is. Sir Godfrey would like to speak to you on a matter of some importance. Can I put him through?"

"I suppose so, though it would be nice to know wh…"

"…Fanshawe, that you there?"

Henry stepped back unconsciously and almost fell over his chair as the bellowing knight barked out over the line. Recovering his balance and his composure, and holding the handset some way from his ear, he replied. "Yes, Sir Godfrey, Henry Fanshawe here."

"Good. Now listen very carefully, Fanshawe, this could be your lucky day!"

Thoughts and suspicions crowded into Henry's mind. It was not difficult to listen carefully to Sir Godfrey. Quite the opposite in fact. Not for nothing was the head of the firm known as the Sergeant Major. Henry suspected that he might have been able to hear the fellow talking even without the convenience of a phone line between them. But as to why he was being called out of the blue like this, he had no idea.

Sir Godfrey continued, "Now, Fanshawe, do you remember Ryan Pikeworth?"

"I find it hard to forget him, Sir Godfrey."

"Don't get flippant with me, Fanshawe!"

"Why not sir? You may remember that I ceased to be an employee of yours some months ago."

"I am fully aware of that fact, Fanshawe. Indeed, that is precisely why I am calling."

"I don't quite follow, sir."

There was a muffled cough on the line from London, tinged with shades of embarrassment. "Now look here, Fanshawe… Henry… Old boy. The results of the auditors' investigation have just come in. It's led to a spot of a reorganisation back in London. Found out a few things. Had a bit of a rethink. Ran a few ideas up the old flagpole. The upshot being… "

"Yes?" Henry had forgotten that the ear splitting volume of his ex-boss was matched by a complete inability to get to the point within an average human lifespan.

"… the upshot being, that an apology is due."

"I'm not apologising to that ill-mannered little twerp."

"No, no, Fanshawe. An apology to you. And what's more, we would like to offer you your job back."

This time Henry really did step back and fall over his chair. Picking himself and the receiver up off the floor, he tried to reply. The result came over as an extended gurgle.

"What was that, Henry?" asked Sir Godfrey.

Henry was still lost for words.

"Speak up man!"

Henry finally managed to frame a sentence. "Where does Ryan fit in to this?"

"Oh, you needn't concern yourself about Pikeworth. In fact, he is the reason you are being asked back."

"What, he wanted me to return?"

"Not exactly. It is Mr Ryan Pikeworth who is wanted… by the City of London police."

If it were possible, Henry would have been even more dumbfounded by this information.

Sir Godfrey continued, "Yes, it seems he was siphoning all the profits made on your desk into his private account. That's why we fired you, Henry. We thought you had your fingers in the till. As it turns out, Pikeworth did. You ran one of the most profitable areas in the whole firm. So much so that we would be delighted if you were to return. Double the salary of course, and you'd be upgraded to a main board director."

Henry continued to make frog like noises and open and close his mouth needlessly. Finally, and hoarsely, he managed a brief reply. "Sir Godfrey, I will consider it most seriously."

"Well don't delay, Fanshawe. Remember, time and tide. Time and tide."

"Time and tide?" Henry was getting lost again.

"Don't bloody well hang around waiting for anyone!"

"Of course, sir. You will have my answer within the day."

"Fair enough, old boy. Make sure it's the right one."

Sir Godfrey rang off, leaving Henry still sitting on the floor with the handset held frozen to his ear. It was in this position that Cilla found him, a far-away look upon his face. "Are you all right, Mr Fanshawe?" she asked, with some concern in her voice.

Henry shook himself and rose unsteadily to his feet. "You know, Cilla, I am not quite sure. I really am not quite sure."

"Was it the phone call… bad news?"

"On the contrary, Cilla. Not bad news. Not bad news at all."

"Can I do anything for you?"

"No Cilla, I don't think you can. I just don't think you can."

Cilla scooped up the breakfast dishes and headed for the door. "Well, in that case, Mr Fanshawe, I'll leave you alone until you have stopped repeating yourself."

Henry was left sitting at the table musing. This was it, he thought. The perfect escape. Just accept the offer, jump on a plane, and within a few days he would be back in his flat, working at his old desk, as if the past six months had never happened. No Indian mafia on his case, no broken bones, no having to carry out instructions. Just a taxi to the airport that evening (he was fortunate that Thursdays happened to be the weekly date of British Airways' single flight to London). It was, as many of his soon-to-be renewed colleagues would have said, an absolute no-brainer.

So why, he wondered, did he feel quite so bad about it? He knew that there was something wrong with his plan when he realised that he was avoiding looking at his wedding photo.

As he stood up to leave the room, headed for an hour of surreptitious packing, the phone went again. He let it ring.

"I'm sorry I am not in at present but if you like to leave a…'

"Oh, for God's sake, Henry, stop fooling around!"

The familiar tones of Charles Fanshawe, his elder brother, rang through the dining room. Henry, already in a state of some confusion, decided that a conversation with his brother was not going to help matters. As Charles began, Henry exited the room and closed the door.

"Well, if you aren't there, I need to speak with you. Urgently! Some problems at home. But don't worry, I'll see you soon. You see, I'm currently in the transfer lounge at Dubai. The plane to Mahé leaves in half an hour. I'll be on it."

Important news indeed. But by then, Henry was out of earshot and hadn't heard a single word.

* * *

That afternoon, Henry stood in his bedroom and gazed at the open overnight bag, containing the barest essentials for life. Staring back at him was the silver framed picture of his wedding. He would have to leave most of his belongings here in the Manor and was only packing one suitcase with items necessary for the first few days of his return to London. He had purchased a ticket for the evening flight and was hurrying to get ready before Cilla returned from her shopping. He could not bear the thought of meeting face to face. His guilt at taking the easy way out would shine forth, and Cilla was an expert at locating the slightest element of cant. He closed the bag and left it by the front door. Then, as downcast as he could ever remember, he fished the rapidly scribbled letter to Cilla and placed it on the main table, propped up against a large bowl of mangos. The content was not lengthy, nor anything to be proud of:

Dear Cilla,
I am going out. I may be some time.
Much love,
Henry Fanshawe

He turned, took one look around the hall, then grabbed the overnight bag, his smaller saxophone case and finally the keys to the new Porsche. He pushed open the door with a shoulder, and walked out into the drive where the aged Land Rover stood. He was busy throwing his belongings into the back and was about to drive off when one final thought came to him. Furtively, and checking that the gardeners were not present, he walked as quickly as he could over to the cricket pitch gate. As it swung open, Henry gazed with an intense sadness at the beautiful green swathe cut into the darker greens of the jungle behind. He stared at the white clubhouse, paint still fresh from the final match there; at the geometric perfection of the lines indicating the crease and the boundary. He would, he thought, have done almost anything to avoid leaving this behind – save, that is, throwing a cricket match, or not throwing it and putting his life in danger.

He knew he had little time before the sound of footsteps from the village path would herald the approach of his housemaid. So he returned to the car, paused once more to look back at the frontage of the house, and then jumped in and turned to the key. The engine spluttered into motion with the usual strangled coughs and belches of black smoke from the exhaust. He gingerly put it in first gear and, with a lump in his throat, drew away and cruised slowly out of the gate. By the time he reached the village, his cheeks were wet with hot tears.

Henry negotiated the half-hour trip to Victoria without incident. He had managed to avoid being spotted by anyone he knew, as he passed through St Christol village, then Beauvallon and the capital itself. He made a brief detour to the docks, to hand in the keys of the Porsche together with a short note instructing Mr Chowdrey where he might like to put them, and then continued on to the airport. The Land Rover was parked and Henry turned to walk towards the main terminal. He noticed, as he entered its high roofed interior, the BA jet on the runway, already disgorging its contents onto the tarmac. The sight took him straight back to that day, only six months previously, when he was one of those jaded travellers, with no knowledge of how extraordinary the next few months would prove to be. All of the wonderful characters he was about to meet. The unconditional friendship shown to him by all and sundry. Cilla's dry wit. Cilla's excellent cooking. The beautiful house and its accompanying cricket pitch. The team he was about to desert.

Unbidden, the team motto came into his mind:

"Nisi terminus sit cor tuum."

When he had asked Roger Kitson about this, he had been told that it was an elegant little punning play on words (by Roger Kitson of course), a Latinisation.

"Let your heart be the only boundary," Roger had chortled, stroking his beard.

He had never checked the translation. But now, with time on his hands, he felt possessed by a sudden urge to try. As doubts roiled through his mind, he took a seat at the nearby computer terminal.

His shaking fingers keyed into Google translate Latin to English and then input the motto. As he watched, the answer appeared on the screen in front of him.

The only limit is your heart.

In that instant, amongst the great milling crowds around him, the airline announcements, the ever-present wildlife, Henry felt the world go perfectly still. Held in this trance for what seemed like an age but was probably only a few seconds, he realised, in a rush, that he could not possibly go ahead with this flit. The tickets fell unnoticed from his hands as he sat there, coming to terms with his decision.

But what of the death threats, his logical side argued. What of the dark deeds required of him by the Indians? There was no way out.

Still wrestling with these intractable problems, Henry did not notice that the first British Airways passengers were beginning to exit the customs hall loudly marvelling at the heat and the profusion of sound and colour, just as Henry had. So it was unsurprising that he jumped high into the air when a large English hand was laid on his shoulder and an equally large English voice boomed in his ear. "Henry! Wonderful to see you!"

Henry had, earlier that day, jumped some distance upon being offered his old job back. That jump would qualify as little more than a neat step compared to the great leap of surprise that he now took. His coffee was sent flying over the computer terminal and his luggage over the surrounding floor, and he almost head butted his brother as he snapped to his feet.

"What the hell…?" Henry started.

"Glad you got my message. Good of you to come and pick me up."

"Message…?"

"Haven't brought much. Won't be staying for too long, circumstances permitting."

"Staying…?"

"Cocked up rather. Lots to talk about, Henry, but not here. Where's your transport?"

And with that Charles picked up his case and stood gazing expectantly at Henry awaiting directions.

There are times when the phrase "Didn't know what to do" is merely the mask for a more truthful "Knew what to do, but didn't want to do it". This was not one of those times. Henry really didn't know what to do. His plan of escape, such as it was, had been mortally compromised by the appearance of his brother. Even had his logical brain overwhelmed his conscience, which was looking increasingly unlikely, he could hardly get on the evening flight now. And the next would be after the final game in any case. He was stuck. Stuck without any hope of ducking the issue. Worst of all, he was stuck with his garrulous sibling.

Wearily he motioned towards the car park. "It's over here, Charles. The Land Rover. A bit old, but it will get us home."

"So this is home now, Henry?"

"It seems so, Charles. It seems so."

They drove back to the Manor in silence. Charles occasionally attempted to strike up conversation but was eventually worn down by the monosyllabic replies of his brother. They arrived at the house in the dark to find Cilla waiting for them.

"Good evening, Mr Fanshawe."

"Good evening," both brothers replied in unison.

"You must be Mr Fanshawe's brother. It is lucky that I listened to the phone messages today. Your brother mentioned nothing of this in his letter."

"My letter?" began Henry before remembering the brief and guilty note he had left some hours earlier.

"Yes. Your rather short and unhelpful letter, Mr Fanshawe. Why did you not just tell me you were going to pick up your brother?"

Henry mumbled something indistinct.

"I have left a cold supper for you in the dining room. I am late and must be on my way home this moment."

Cilla pulled her shawl round her shoulders and marched past the two brothers and into the dark. They could hear her muttered comments dying slowly into the distance as she returned to St Christol.

Charles dropped his bags in the hall and stretched. "So, here we are."

Henry looked up. He was still not sure whether to hate his brother for ruining his escape or to thank the man for cutting short a plan which had so little in the way of morally redeeming features. He settled for just being irritated. "Charles, I have had a long and difficult day. You could have given me more warning than five hours, and I really don't want to lose a minute talking about your predicament when it could be spent asleep. You go and have something to eat. I am going to bed. We will talk in the morning. Spare room is second on left. Breakfast eight-thirty. Goodnight."

And leaving his brother trying to frame a reasonable riposte, Henry turned and went immediately up to his room. Once inside, he fell on the bed and rolled into a small ball, a position from which he did not move for several hours.

27
Kidnapped

Breakfast the next morning was a strained affair. Whilst Charles seemed almost desperate to appear cheerful, Henry made no effort to disguise his misery and irritation with the world in general and his brother in particular. Conversation was a distinctly one-sided affair.

"Beautiful morning, Henry."

"Is it?"

"Well... excellent breakfast anyway."

A grunt from opposite.

"Henry?"

Silence.

Charles tried again. "Henry, I suspect you might be wondering why I suddenly pitched up here."

More silence.

"I mean, it was rather out of the blue. Didn't know myself until last Monday."

Henry realised that ignoring Charles would, as usual, not work. With a pained sigh, which was louder than strictly necessary, he put down the newspaper.

"Do go on, Charles," he said in a tone which inferred the opposite. "I'm all ears."

Charles reddened a little. "Well, it's a bit awkward really, a tad embarrassing to tell the truth. Thing is… well, the thing is… I've been chucked out."

Henry, having been prepared to switch off, was now suddenly and truthfully all ears. He leant forward. "Chucked out?"

"Yes, chucked out, given the heave-ho, marching orders…"

"All right, Charles, I get your drift. Chucked out of what?"

"The house."

"The house?"

"Yes, my house Henry, the old homestead, where the Fanshawes have lived for over four hundred years. By Caroline."

"By Caroline! Can I ask why?"

Charles's face blushed deeper and his voice dropped a few decibels.

"Well, bit of a cock up really – all rather embarrassing. Do you remember Audrey?"

"Ah, Audrey." Henry did remember Audrey. She was the woman who Charles had alluded to over the past decade as his 'friend' in London. Henry had been asked many times to confirm Charles's stay over at his flat, when in fact he was nowhere to be seen.

"That sort of cock-up, Charles."

"No need to be vulgar, Henry. Fact is, Caroline decided to go shopping in town last week and bumped into us having lunch."

"That must have been a surprise!"

"For both of us – I had told her I was in New York on business."

"What happened?"

"Well, after I had removed the soup plate from my lap, I tried to think of something to say; but you know how difficult it is to come up with a good story when your wife has you pinned to the wall."

"As it happens, I don't, but then of course I am not married to Caroline."

"She's like the Spanish Inquisition when she gets going, Henry; I didn't last a minute. Anyway, she flounced out, and when I got home there was a suitcase outside in the porch and a note telling me to get out."

"So, what are you going to do?"

"Not really sure. Lie low here for a while and then try to sort it out with C when the dust has settled. Could be a while."

Secretly thinking that hell would freeze over before Caroline changed her mind about anything, Henry nodded sagely and kept quiet. It was clear that Charles would be a house guest for some time yet, and so there was little point in getting off on the wrong foot. He sat back. "Well, now you are here, fancy helping a bit with Aunt Esme's club?"

"I suppose beggars can't be choosers. What can I do to help the old bat's memory?"

"Less of the old bat, Charles, or your suitcase will be on the porch first thing tomorrow."

Charles looked down at his feet and gave a sheepish shrug. "Sorry Henry, force of habit. Still rankles a bit, that will business. Anyway, Esme's club…"

Henry interrupted, "Esme's *Cricket* club, Charles. In case you did not know, the Esme Fanshawe St Christol

Cricket Club competes in the final of the Seychelles Cup for the first time in its history."

"Cricket you say? She really was a nutcase wasn't she! Reminds me of the time…"

A note of warning in Henry's demeanour stopped Charles momentarily. He paused and changed tack. "Ah, cricket… yes… well… not one of my greatest strengths. More of a boxer at school, you remember."

As chief punch bag during his early childhood years, Henry could hardly forget. "Well, I'm sure we can find something sufficiently exciting for you."

A grunt from his elder brother signified grudging assent.

Henry finished his toast, and stood up. He now knew what to do. Clapping his brother on the back he managed a smile. "Now, go and get yourself ready. I just need to make a phone call and then we can take a trip round the island."

Charles left the room and Henry paused for a final sip of coffee, framing in his mind the conversation he was shortly to have with Sir Godfrey Plumborough.

* * *

"Good Morning. Fanshawe Global Securities, how may I help you?"

It was that desperate cheeriness, and the soprano trill on the word 'help', that always reminded Henry there were worse things to life than not working in a bank.

"Good morning. May I speak to Sir Godfrey Plumborough, please?"

"Just putting you through. Who's calling?"

"Henry Fanshawe."

"*The* Henry Fanshawe?"

"I suppose so."

"We're all looking forward to seeing you back again, Mr Fanshawe."

Henry felt both touched by the sentiment and appalled that everyone seemed to know about his re-appearance. The next voice was that of his old friend Polly.

"Just putting you through, Henry." Henry extended his arm to hold the phone as far as possible from his ear.

"Morning Fanshawe, Godfrey here!"

"Good morning, Sir Godfrey."

"So, phoning to give me the good news I expect. When can you start?"

"Ah, yes, well… that is the reason I'm calling."

"Of course!"

"I have given the matter some thought overnight, and… well…"

"Come on man, spit it out!"

"I have decided that, with regret, I cannot accept your kind and generous offer."

"WHAT!" Sir Godfrey's retort echoed through the drawing room, whilst outside, birds took to the air in panic. "ARE YOU MAD, FANSHAWE?"

But Henry was quite calm now. "No, Sir Godfrey, I am not mad. In fact, I have never been less mad. I have some unfinished business to attend to, and a large number of my friends are relying on me. I could not possibly leave at this venture. It would be… a betrayal."

"Betrayal – but you're a banker for god's sake, Fanshawe, you're supposed to be amoral!"

"Maybe so in the past, Sir Godfrey, but not this time."

"Well, Fanshawe," some measure returned to Sir Godfrey's voice, "you're being a bloody fool about this. The job's not going to wait for you, you know."

"I am well aware of that, sir, and I would like to thank you for your kind offer, which I have unfortunately…"

Henry was in mid flow when he realised that Sir Godfrey had already hung up and he was talking into thin air. He replaced the phone and put his head around the door and shouted upstairs. "Charles, that trip round the island. Fancy getting going?"

Charles emerged from the spare room in an altogether unconvincing Hawaiian tee shirt and shorts. "Absolutely! Been looking forward to the guided tour."

For the remainder of the day, Henry, Charles, and the most environmentally-unsound Land Rover in existence chugged around Mahé taking in the sights. Even Charles, to whom the concept of nature's bounty was generally confined to grouse flying slowly into his gunsights, was caught up in the wonder of the island.

"I say, Henry, this really is the most fabulous place. Maybe I could prolong the stay a little while."

Henry stiffened at the wheel. "Charles, whilst your company is welcome just at the moment, an extended visit might have consequences."

"Consequences?"

"Consequences. Injurious to the health."

"Health?"

"Yes. My mental health, and shortly thereafter, your physical health."

"Oh." Charles turned away to look out of the window, and instantly forgot this put-down, "I say. Look! Are those tea pickers over there? Takes me right back, to those pictures of Ceylon in my geography book at prep school."

By lunchtime, they had reached Anse Takamaka. Despite his occasional problems with Charles, and his greater worries, there was no reason, Henry figured, not to use the visit as an excuse to sample the delicacies at his favourite restaurant. The Land Rover was deposited in a sandy car park next to the beach and he jumped out and beckoned his brother to follow him down a little dusty track to the headland.

"Where on earth are we going, Henry?" Charles was hungry and had been buffeted from side to side during the tour to such an extent that felt bruised all over. His previous bonhomie had started to evaporate.

Henry pointed to a tumbledown shack further down the beach. From its crooked chimney rose a plume of white smoke. "We are going to heaven, Charles."

"Heaven?"

"Well, a variety of heaven that comes in pink shells covered with a delicious chili and lime sauce."

"I am none the wiser, Henry, and I'm also famished."

"Which is precisely why, Charles, you are about to sample the greatest lobster ever served."

Charles' mood leapt a good few notches, and his pace quickened, "Lobster you say?"

"Yes, lobster, Charles, but not as you know it."

* * *

As they skirted the white beach at Beauvallon on the way back, Charles leaned over to Henry. "Been meaning to ask. Why are we in a clapped out old banger when you have that beautiful new Porsche sitting in the drive?"

Henry was quiet for a while before replying. He did not want to involve his brother in this mess, but he was longing to tell someone about the problems which beset him, if only to get them off his chest. In the end he muttered, "It's not the sort of car I would wish to drive."

"Why not – looks great?"

"Not so much the car, as where it came from, Charles. You see, there have been some odd things going on in the cricket world here, and the car forms part of them."

"What sort of odd things?"

"Suspicions of Indian match fixing, bribes, and a manager who was beaten up when he refused to play ball."

"Goodness, sounds serious. Have you mentioned this to the police?"

"Yes, and they are dealing with it – so not a word to anyone, understand?"

After Henry had elaborated a little, Charles sat back in his primitive chair, trying for the hundredth time to get comfortable. "A rum do, Henry. So, I guess the Porsche was an inducement."

"It was. An inducement I have rejected. I returned the keys yesterday."

"Very admirable, Henry." Charles was being quite genuine.

"Thank you."

"Pity though – would have loved a ride in it first."

Charles went to bed early that night, suffering from the delayed effects of the twelve hour flight. Before too long the muffled sound of snoring could be faintly heard from the study where Henry was taking a last look at the notes that he and Sydney had made for tomorrow's final.

So engrossed had he become in the plans for the final that Henry did not hear the crunch of gravel in the drive as a large van drew quietly up outside. Nor, a few minutes later, did he notice the curtains shifting by the open window behind him. He was thus taken completely unawares when one pair of arms snaked round the chair to hold him tight whilst another clamped an evil smelling and not entirely pristine handkerchief over his mouth. Henry gasped for breath and in an instant he was transported by the smell back to that dark beach a few weeks earlier. A gentle stupor quickly drifted into his mind, and he slumped unconscious into the arms of his night visitors.

When he awoke, he found himself in a dark and airless room, tied by his hands and legs to a chair. From a small window high in one corner, a grey light suggested that it was close to dawn. Of his kidnappers, or anyone else, there was no sign.

28
The Final Morning

Whilst Henry was languishing in his airless cell, the morning was getting underway at Fanshawe Manor, where Cilla was perplexed and not a little irritated. "Today of all days!" she muttered as she laid out breakfast on the table for an absent Henry and his brother.

"Surely he cannot have forgotten and overslept."

After waiting a further five minutes, she could not help herself and marched up the stairs. When a polite knock on the bedroom door evinced no response, she gave it a more robust hammering and shouted through the keyhole.

"Mr Fanshawe. Are you still in bed? Do you know what time it is? Breakfast is waiting."

Still no answer. Cilla, who had never once in the previous six months entered Henry's bedroom in his presence, was by now in a state of some panic and when another attempt to awake the sleeping figure behind the door failed to elicit any response, she decided that more direct action was called for.

Opening the door with a loud cry of "Mr Fanshawe? I'm coming in!" Cilla entered the bedroom. To her shock and surprise, it was completely devoid of any sign of Henry. On further rushed inspection, so was the adjoining bathroom.

She ran out onto the landing and practically fell into the arms of Charles, on his way down to breakfast. He side-stepped and smiled, "Good morning Cilla."

"Mr Fanshawe, oh Mr Fanshawe! Something has happened!"

"Something has happened? What has happened?"

"Mr Fanshawe."

"Yes?"

"No, the other Mr Fanshawe… Henry. He has disappeared!"

Together they re-entered the room. Not only was Henry nowhere to be seen, but it was clear that his bed had not been slept in.

After a quick search of the house and garden revealed nothing, Pierre the gardener was despatched to alert Sydney, the Reverend and the Chief of Police. Soon they were gathered in the drawing room.

"What on earth has happened to him?" asked Sydney. "For God's sake, it's the morning of the final. Not the sort of time you would normally pick to go out for an all-night session."

Cilla looked over witheringly. "He cannot have been on an all-night session, Sydney."

"Why not may I ask?"

"Because you are here."

Sydney relapsed into silence.

A voice from behind them joined the conversation. "If you will allow me, I may be able to shed some light."

They all turned to look at Charles. He carried on, "Last night, Henry mentioned something about an unusual *accident* after a previous match."

"I am guessing that would be the break-in at the Cinnamon Club when the Colonel was attacked," ventured the Chief.

"Correct. He didn't spell it out in so many words, but he inferred that it was no accident. He suggested it was more an act of revenge."

"Revenge? For what?" asked Sydney.

"Not quite sure," Charles continued, "but I think it was for not losing the match. He said there was some sort of Indian betting syndicate behind it."

The Chief immediately stiffened. "*Not* losing the match, Mr Fanshawe?"

"Yes – *not* losing, having been *told* to lose, if you get my meaning"

"I do, Mr Fanshawe, I do. And did he say anything else? Anything at all?"

"Well, not exactly, but I got the strong feeling Henry was worried that something similar might happen to him, and…"

"And now, on the morning of the final, he has just vanished into thin air." The Chief finished Charles' sentence. "This is more serious than I thought. You see, a few weeks ago Henry informed me of a phone call and letter received by Colonel Farrer of the Cinnamon Club, from an unknown source, more or less ordering him to throw the match. He, of course, refused. When he won the match he was brutally attacked in a break-in at the club, which I always suspected was a cover. But we could prove nothing. Henry never told me he was subject to similar threats, but it does make sense."

Charles stiffened, "So, some match-fixing bastards have nabbed him. Nabbed my brother!"

"Well, we don't *know* that, Mr Fanshawe," said the Chief.

"Of course we do! And everyone knows about illegal betting syndicates – Henry told me all about the last time you played that Indian shipping company team and got that remarkable draw. He's probably holed up in some horrible little hovel as we speak. We must get out and look for him."

Sydney looked panic-stricken. "But we can't go out searching for him now. We have to leave for the match in five minutes. And that means you as well, Chief. I am not going to forfeit the final for anyone!"

As Charles opened his mouth to castigate Sydney, he was silenced by a hand from Cilla. "And, gentlemen, remember. Mr Fanshawe wouldn't want us to." She turned to Charles, "Of course, this does not mean that *you* cannot look for him – and I have an idea that the Chief may know of a good place to start."

The Chief removed his shades for a polish and pondered the situation. Having replaced them, he turned to Charles and replied, "I think, Mr Fanshawe, you should start with the St Christol hypermarket."

In Henry's continued absence, it was down to Cilla and Sydney to rally the team. After a short update to its members, and in a quiet and subdued atmosphere, the coach then made its way out of St Christol to Victoria, followed as usual by a flotilla of smaller vehicles.

The supporters, who had not been told of Henry's disappearance, were in good voice, waving from their transport at the string of well-wishers who lined the road as they passed through Beauvallon. It was clear that by making the final (the first village team ever to have done so) a type of FA cup fever had overtaken not only the immediate environs of St Christol, but most of the north of Mahé. As the coach entered Victoria, further crowds were there to greet the team with ungrammatical but eye-catching banners proclaiming their support for the underdogs.

It should have been festive, mused Sydney. Instead, the whole team were tense and worried. Sydney could not motivate with the natural ease of Henry, and the ex-Surrey opener found himself missing his manager. Not only because of his concern for Henry's well-being, but also because he had become unused to planning strategies without the man there. Cilla, noticing the worry lines on his face, took hold of his hand and squeezed it hard. She gave him a brave smile as he turned.

* * *

Somewhere else in Mahé, Henry tried to stretch his legs as far as possible given the ropes that bound him. He managed to bend his neck and twist his arms enough to read his wristwatch and found that it was ten-thirty am. His whole body ached from being held in the sitting position for the previous ten hours. Outside, he thought, the coach would be on its way to the match. Carrying a team with high hopes, and absolutely no idea about what was going on, or any intention of not winning the match. He had done nothing about the instructions left him by his captors, and he feared the worst. He found it indescribably sad that Sanjay was caught up in this, whether on purpose or by coercion. He hoped it was for the second reason. As he was thinking about the local shopkeeper, there was a noise at the door and Sanjay entered with a mug of water and a rather old looking hunk of bread. "Mr Fanshawe, I have brought you some breakfast."

Henry did not reply.

"Mr Fanshawe, I advise you to eat it. It may be all there is for some time. All the guards have gone to the match and I must follow."

"Judas!" muttered Henry under his breath.

"Please, Mr Fanshawe, eat," begged the Indian. "Here, I will undo your arms."

Sanjay loosened the knots binding Henry's arms until he was able to hold the mug and the bread and take them to his mouth. "Now, Mr Fanshawe, I must go to join the others at Chowdrey Park. Everyone will be there."

"How could you, Sanjay? Betraying your own village… your own son."

Sanjay turned to Henry with a piercing stare. The barb had hit home. "I will forget you said that, Mr Fanshawe. But just remember, not all is as it seems."

It was only after Sanjay had left, that Henry realised that the jailer had forgotten to re-tie his arms.

* * *

Charles Fanshawe's brain had swung ponderously into action from the moment the word 'hypermarket' passed the Chief's lips. He had stopped in the village briefly the day before and had even been subjected to Sanjay's views on various global topics whilst shopping.

Charles could never have been called sharp, but there was a certain dogged quality to his reasoning. Once the team coach had left, he had jumped into the Land Rover and taken off down to St Christol. He had slowly absorbed the hypermarket concept, and then, wheels grinding, connected it firstly with the fact that Sanjay was clearly of Indian extraction, and secondly with the undoubted Indian genesis of the betting ring, which had hospitalized the Colonel and now, it seems, had kidnapped his brother.

"That bastard shopkeeper. I'll get him. Kidnapping my brother – a Fanshawe!" he was shouting to himself as he drove.

The Land Rover ploughed into St Christol and screeched to a halt outside the shop. Charles jumped out and ran inside. The village was practically deserted as all had left for the match, but the odd stray dog and one or two infirm grandmothers looked on in surprise as the sound of breaking crockery and worse issued from the door of the shop. After a few moments a slightly dishevelled and flour-covered Charles re-emerged.

"Where is he, that bastard?"

Charles took a deep breath, attempted to calm down, and then re-entered the shop. His random approach had not thrown up any clues, and Sanjay was nowhere to be seen. A more rational and deliberate strategy was needed. He started at the front of the shop and began to search the place in a restrained and orderly fashion, still chuntering about the sheer cheek of treating his brother, a Fanshawe, in such a manner. Then, between the Mexican section and the Indian spice shelves, he noticed a small door in the wall. It was almost hidden behind hanging fronds of dried chilli peppers and tins of coconut milk. The door had been bolted and padlocked, and Charles quickly looked around the shop for the necessary opening implement. Having availed himself of a large axe from the ironmongery counter, he set to, and in a few moments the door was hanging from its hinges, revealing an unlit staircase.

The stairs were of uneven tread and covered with various sacks and tins, and at the bottom Charles found himself looking down a corridor, where only a small skylight illuminated the gloom. There was another padlocked door at the far end. He attacked this with as much vigour as the first one and it was not long before the hinges gave way and the door swung slowly open. Charles rushed in, shouting for Henry, and then stopped. In the middle of the floor was an overturned chair surrounded by various lengths of rope, a half-eaten piece of bread, an empty mug and broken panes of glass. Looking up, he located a smashed window. It was the only one in the room, and stood high up on the far wall. And although a number of torn lengths of cloth hung in shrouds from the ledge, of Henry there was no sign.

* * *

As the coach lurched along the road from Victoria to the grandest of cricketing venues Sydney's demeanour rose a little. He was the captain, he told himself. The captain of a fine team, possibly the finest village team that had ever graced the Seychelles, and the first ever to compete in the final. Not much maybe, given that cricket was only a decade or two old here, but a milestone nevertheless. The unexplained disappearance of his manager and friend served only to stiffen his determination.

By the time the coach passed through the large white gates and onto the tree lined drive to the mini Taj Mahal that was the Chowdrey clubhouse, he had rehearsed his team talk one hundred times. There was no doubting it. Sydney was ready for action and what was more, he was ready for a scrap. The coach pulled up to its allotted parking bay. All present rose and were about to make their way to the door when Sydney jumped to his feet.

"Silence please, and don't move." It was almost a shout, and transfixed every soul on board. Sydney went on, "Now, you've all heard about Henry's mysterious disappearance this morning. We have reason to believe that he has been kidnapped by a gang who wish us to lose this match on purpose, so that they can fill their grubby little hands with some betting profits."

There were mixed groans, shouts of 'shame', and questions from the team. Sydney again raised his hand for quiet. "We don't know where Henry is, but believe me, we are doing everything we can to find him. The Chief has policemen combing the island. But for now we will just have to do without him."

More groans, and the odd comment.

"The Lord have mercy on their souls," intoned the Reverend Kitson, adding under his breath, "and they'll need it if I ever get my hands on the bastards!"

But Sydney was warming to his task. Glancing down at Cilla, who smiled back, he placed one foot up onto the arm of the seat he was standing in, striking what he felt was a combative and inspiring pose. "Though Henry is not with us, his spirit is still here."

There was a half-hearted cheer from some of the onlookers. Sydney grew in stature. "We have to ask ourselves, what would he do? What would our brave and honest leader Henry Fanshawe do?"

The cheers grew more insistent.

"Would he ask us to give in and throw the game, or would he ask us to fight on?"

Cilla gazed up with a look approaching outright admiration.

Cries of "Fight on" and clapping erupted from the ranks in front of him.

"So team mates… we fight on!"

The coach emptied, leaving Curtley, always the last off, sitting in his chair, taking in this turn of events. After a few moments, he also rose to leave.

Sydney held the door for him. "I know you'll bowl your heart out today."

Curtley stopped and for once he looked serious. "Anyone touches the old boss, I'll get them, new boss."

* * *

Somewhere else on Mahé, thoughts of cricket had for the moment been banished far from Henry's mind. After realising that he had been left untied, and squeezing through the small window onto the roof, he had grabbed a nearby tree vine and launched himself off the roof into a green and tangled mass of vegetation below. It was unexpectedly soft and cushioned his generous rear with greater comfort than he had anticipated. However, it did not represent actual terra firma, and quickly gave way, depositing Henry some yards lower onto much harder soil.

Henry groaned in pain and lay there for a few moments. Then, feeling himself gingerly all over, he decided that nothing was broken and sat down to plan his next move. On the plus side, he had escaped and got off the roof without breaking his neck. On the negative side he felt bruised all over and still had no idea where he was. And, whilst lying on the ground, Henry became aware of a third and peculiarly insistent negative. Like a displaced Wild Man of Borneo, shouting and screaming, he leapt to his feet, flailing around with his hands in all directions.

Henry had landed on an ants' nest. As a burning sensation progressed up his legs to a more intimate area, he ripped off his trousers and, slapping his legs like a mad thing looked around for a source of respite. Above was the tin roof from which he had fallen. Gazing around desperately, he noticed a small stream running down through the jungle. In a dash to make it before his insect tormentors performed the most basic of castrations, he bounded up the incline and leapt into the pool.

Blissful relief washed over him as the ants fell away, and in the cool clear water he began to consider his position. He needed to find out where on earth, or at least on Mahé, he was. He did not dare go to the front of the house in which he had been held captive for fear of guards.

The jungle trees were far too high to afford a view of the surrounding area. Henry decided that the best course would be to head uphill, in the hope that he could reach a vantage point which would give him some clue as to his whereabouts. Retrieving his trousers, and giving them a thorough shake, he started pushing his way upwards.

It was hard going. Without a machete or any clearing implement Henry was getting cut, bruised and increasingly desperate, and the jungle showed no sign of thinning out. After an hour of this, he was exhausted, and found an old branch where he sat down, wheezing, hot, bothered and still completely lost.

He gazed around at the dense green forests that hugged the mountains in Mahé. Undeniably beautiful, but not when escaping from kidnappers. The pink granite of the higher peaks, teeming with dazzling flowers and birds took Henry's breath away in a much more brutal fashion. The heat and humidity bore down on him. Henry began to feel lonely and rather afraid. He knew he had to get away from his place of captivity in case the gaolers returned. But he had no idea of which direction to go. He was close to giving into his characteristic passivity, just to hunker down and see what happened.

It was in this dark mood that a slight change to the constant hum of the jungle alerted Henry's senses. As his hearing became attuned to the constant throaty chirruping of birds and the drone of insects, he could now make out a deeper roar. It seemed to be coming from his left, slightly up the hill. He summoned up the last dregs of his energy, and stumbled up in the direction of the noise, which was growing louder and more mechanical minute by minute.

And then, clothes ripped, body covered in mud and quite without warning, Henry staggered into a place he knew very well indeed. Breathing a heavy and profound sigh of relief, he found himself gazing at the pristine beauty of the Esme Fanshawe Cricket Club pitch, onto which he had strayed. Pierre was busy with the lawnmower powering away in one corner. He was close to collapse as Pierre noticed him and jumped off the mower. "What happened to you, boss? We've been looking everywhere."

Helped by his gardener, Henry made it to the house.

His gardener moved over to the drinks cabinet and poured a large scotch, which he then proceeded to down in one, before filling another glass and bringing it over to Henry.

Between mouthfuls of Talisker, Henry recounted the tale of his abduction. Pierre listened and shook his head slowly, "These are bad people, Mr Fanshawe. You'd better go quick. Get off the island!"

"But how can I?" Henry replied bleakly, "I couldn't leave while the team is actually playing. I need to get there. They'll have started by now. The team needs its manager!"

The effect of the whisky kicked in. He collapsed on the sofa and lay staring at the ceiling quite undecided as to what else he could possibly do next.

His reveries were cut short by the sound of crunching gravel and screaming brakes in the drive. Seconds later, a red faced Charles hurled himself through the door and rushed over to the sofa. "Henry, my God, you're OK. Thank Christ for that." And, kneeling down by the slumped figure, he gave Henry a big bear hug.

Had Henry not been in a state of near-complete exhaustion, he would have been more than surprised. This was possibly the first time that Charles had ever shown anything approaching concern for his younger sibling. Shows of affection, along with any sort of physical contact, had been bred out of the Fanshawe dynasty in the early part of the seventeenth century, and this outpouring of filial love was unprecedented in living memory.

"We've been combing the island for you. Chief has most of the force on it. Couldn't find hide nor hair, until he suggested I look in the back of the hypermarket. Since then I've been up and down the hills around here in the Land Rover trying to spot you."

Henry was touched. "Thanks for trying, Charles. Captivity disorientates you – I had no idea of where I was either until I walked into the cricket pitch."

"Well, no time for relaxing. We need to get you to the match!" Charles had recovered some of his normal reserve and subtlety. "Get upstairs, have a quick wash – you absolutely stink by the way – and change out of that filthy stuff. I'll be waiting in the Land Rover. And you, Pierre— "

"Yes sir?"

"Phone the Chief. Tell him that the boss is back."

29
The First Innings

On the field of play, the two captains, with barely disguised animosity, had tossed a coin, and St Christol elected to bat first. The captain of the Chowdrey Steamers stuck out his hand.

"May the best man win, Mr Mason."

Sydney grasped it, squeezed harder than he should have, and pulled the captain close, "Yes, he just might, you fucking cheat."

He left the opposing captain nursing his fingers and marched off to pad up.

Shortly afterwards Sydney and Jean, his opening partner, marched onto the pitch, and at the appointed hour of eleven am, the Grand 2012 Final of the Seychelles Cricket Championship began.

As with many finals, the initial skirmishes were tense, and of mediocre quality. Everyone was nervous, though in this respect Sydney had the advantage. He had, in his day, played at Lord's for Surrey in a number of one day finals. And although one of the bowlers was clearly an Indian professional, the man's form had fallen away since their first encounter. Moreover, through Sydney, there coursed the fire of righteous indignation. Jean held out bravely, defending whilst being peppered with bouncers (far more than the allowed amount, thought Sydney – maybe the umpires were in on it, too). By the tenth over, St Christol had crawled to 35 but as yet had not lost a wicket.

Eventually the Chowdrey bowlers made the breakthrough. Jean was out LBW to a ball that turned late and was shortly followed by the Monseigneur de Pelet. But not before he turned to the bowler as he left the field of play. "In Greenland, they have fifty different words for 'snow'. In France, my friend, we have fifty different words for 'shit'… and you are all of them!"

Roger Kitson had a more successful time at the crease. His partnership with Sydney added 77 runs in rapid order, and by the time he was finally caught on the boundary for 48, St Christol's total stood at a reasonable 125 for three off twenty-five overs. Next to bat was the Chief. Sydney had wished to keep Mathilde back for the later overs in the hope that her stroke play would add valuable runs at the death. The Chief played his typical tight innings, giving little away but not scoring at a great pace. Luckily, Sydney, now with an eye thoroughly attuned, was starting to accelerate, and the fall of the Chief's wicket was only achieved at the cost of another 35 runs. 160 for four off thirty overs.

His replacement Louis did not last long, and in the thirty-first over, Mathilde took the field. Sydney was on 74, and batting with the pomp and style that recalled his earlier days at Surrey. There was a grim determination outlined in his stance. The bowlers were beginning to weary as Mathilde turned to face her first ball.

* * *

At long last, the Fanshawe brothers arrived at the long tree-lined entrance to the Chowdrey Steamers ground. Henry directed Charles round to a small patch of bare ground just beyond the gate.

"I think we should arrive without a fanfare," said Henry.

"Yes, give them a bit of a surprise and see how they react."

A small boulder by the walls allowed the pair to scale the barrier and enter the grounds unnoticed. Slipping from bush to bush as quietly and discreetly as they could (which given their age and size was not very), they made their way to a large storm drain which led directly to the cricket pitch.

Henry eventually found himself not more than five yards from where Cilla was seated at a table. He waited until the end of the over, and then gave as quiet a whistle as he was able.

"Cilla."

She looked around for the source of the noise, saw nothing, and turned back to her book.

Louder. "Cilla!"

This time Cilla got up and walked around the table towards the ditch where the two brothers were hiding.

"Cilla, down here."

Finally, she caught sight of the two large muddied men staring back at her. "Mr Fanshawe and Mr Fanshawe!" she cried.

"Shhhh, we don't want to be seen just yet."

"I should think not, in that state! What are you doing down there?"

"Keeping out of sight. Now, listen. Go and get the Chief, and bring some dark glasses and floppy hats back with you."

Cilla disappeared into the ornate clubhouse, while Henry tried to work out where the match had got to. St Christol were batting first, and Mathilde and Sydney were in. The score stood at 200 for five off thirty-five overs. Not bad at all, thought Henry.

Cilla returned with two large Mexican sombreros, two pairs of dark glasses, a poncho, and the Chief of Police. Once attired, Henry and Charles pulled themselves out of the drain and followed the Chief over to the car park. Standing in the corner was a large van marked Khumri Imports. The Chief beckoned them over, opened the back door and motioned for the pair to enter.

Henry felt he had entered a spaceship. He was confronted with a great battery of electronic panels with lights flashing, and TV monitors, manned by figures in police uniforms and headphones.

"This is our centre of operations, Henry," said the Chief. "From here we can monitor anything that is being said or done within a mile. And we can listen in on all the phone calls. There's been quite a lot of activity between here and India this morning!"

"So you knew."

"We had our suspicions, Henry. Ever since that odd result here earlier in the season. And then of course that letter you showed us before the Cinnamon Club game."

"Why didn't you do something – I've just had the worst week of my life!"

"Not enough evidence – we need to catch them red handed. In fact, I am glad that we found you, Henry."

"Er. I think *I* found me, Chief."

"Quite, quite. Anyway, now you are here, we can set up the perfect honey trap for Mr Chowdrey and his accomplices. Henry, I want you to do something for us."

Henry had a sinking feeling. "Would this something involve any danger, Chief?"

"Not at all, not at all."

"Really?"

"Well, not very much danger. Hardly any danger really."

Henry turned to his brother. "Charles, welcome to the Seychelles, land of coral beaches, dusky maidens, and staggering understatement."

The Chief ignored this remark. "Henry, we are going to wire you up."

"Set me up, more like."

"When you are spotted and taken by Chowdrey's hoods, we will be able to hear everything."

Henry stiffened.

The Chief attempted to reassure the nervous Englishman. "Do not worry, Henry. We will be shadowing you."

"Closely I hope."

"As close as a well-fitted suit."

So it was that a few minutes later, a van marked Khumri Imports pulled out of the car park and drove around to the back of the clubhouse. Anyone observant would have been surprised to see two Mexicans step out, followed by a cricketer dressed in whites sporting a policeman's cap. But since all eyes were glued to the match, no-one spotted them, at least initially.

Henry and Charles made their way round to the front of the clubhouse. Once positioned in full view of as many people as possible, Henry threw off his sombrero, cupped his hands to his mouth and, waiting to the end of the over, gave a loud shout to the batsmen.

"Well played, Sydney – only five for your century!"

Sydney, Mathilde, and the rest of the St Christol team immediately looked around for the source of the shout. When they spotted Henry and Charles there was an involuntary cheer, and suddenly all the spectators were staring in their direction, whispering to each other and pointing. Henry looked up at the balcony where Mr Chowdrey had risen and pushed to the front. He was gesticulating wildly to a number of large suits and pointing down to where he stood. It wouldn't be long now, he thought.

Sure enough, as Henry walked around the boundary, shaking hands with a number of the St Christol supporters, he became aware of two large Indian gentlemen following him. He was not in a mood to make things easy, so he allowed the Indians to close in, but continued round the boundary rope keeping just out of reach. He had practically finished the full circuit when he noticed two further suits moving to cut him off. Waiting until they were nearly upon him, he turned to greet some more villagers sitting on a large blanket and toasting their side each time a run was scored. One of them proffered a cold bottle of beer. He sat down as the suits, eyeing him from a moderate distance, waited. After a while their patience ran out. One sauntered up nonchalantly to Henry, and leant over to whisper in his ear. "I wonder if we could have a word, sir?"

"Fire away." Henry was almost starting to enjoy this.

"Mr Chowdrey would very much like to invite you to his box."

"Would he now? Have you a written invitation?"

"Maybe this would suffice, sir," The suit in question moved his jacket lapels minimally to reveal the glint of a large knife.

Henry took the hint. "That will do nicely. Tell him I'll be up in a tick."

"He was keen to see you right away."

"Can I just finish this beer? Shame to waste it."

"Right now, sir."

Henry realised that he was on the brink of going too far. He rose, bid his hosts goodbye and moved off towards the clubhouse, hemmed in by four large guides.

As Henry entered the balcony box surrounded by his minders, Mr Chowdrey rose to greet him.

"Mr Fanshawe, it is a surprise to see you here. We thought you would be enjoying a nap in the room we so carefully selected."

Henry remained silent as Chowdrey continued, "It is a great shame you chose not to agree to our terms. As it is, we will probably win, but you… Well, you are, strictly speaking, expendable."

Grabbing him by the collar, Chowdrey thrust his mouth up to Henry's ear. "They have an old saying here. The Seychelles is deemed so beautiful, that life is particularly valuable. *Lanmor I voler*. Do you know what that means, Henry?"

Henry shook his head, hoping vehemently that the wire was picking all this up.

Close to his ear, the Indian whispered, "It means *Death comes as a thief*, Henry."

Then, disengaging himself, "Though in your case I suspect the *man overboard* approach a little more likely. Now. Let us return to the match, you and I."

Henry felt hands on his shoulders pull him to a chair and force him down into it. Silently praying that the Chief was on his way, and acutely conscious of the two heavies who had sat down on either side of him, he turned to watch.

Had he the stomach to follow the game, Henry would have been pleased with the progress his team were making. Unlike the league, the final was a fifty over match and both Sydney and Mathilde had bested the bowling attack. As the final overs approached Sydney had come alive and was slogging boundaries to every corner of the field. Even Chowdrey, despite his guest, was forced to applaud some of the strokes.

With his usual menacing politeness, he turned to Henry. "Your opener is batting like a man possessed, Mr Fanshawe."

Henry remained silent. He had some idea of what Chowdrey intended to do in order to fix the result, but it clearly did not involve either of the current batsmen. A silent but intense pride suffused him as Sydney moved effortlessly, first through his century and, it seemed

342

without pause, to approach 150. Mathilde's delicious stroke play was a joy to watch, as she pushed her total up to 50.

At the commencement of the final over of their innings, Esme Fanshawe's village team stood at 288 for five. Sydney finished his mental preparations, turned to the clubhouse, and waved at his manager. Henry made to stand up, and raised his arm to acknowledge the salute, but found it pulled back roughly behind the chair, with a hand on his shoulder forcing him down.

"Now, now, Mr Fanshawe, I thought the English above such vulgar displays of emotion."

There was no doubt that Chowdrey was becoming rattled by this turn of events.

Henry prayed devoutly that all of this conversation was being monitored back in the van and tried to start an incriminating conversation with his captor. "Doesn't seem like my team has taken your shilling, Chowdrey."

The man obligingly replied. "For your sake, Henry, I hope the next innings will prove you wrong."

Chowdrey was about to continue when a large cheer erupted from the crowd. Sydney had hoisted the first ball of the over for a stupendous six which carried to the clubhouse and narrowly missed the box, removing on its way the trunk of a large gilded elephant attached to the magnificent building. The Indian's mood darkened, and he smacked his chair arm. "He will pay for that!"

The last over provided two more boundaries for Sydney, a snatched single, and then, for the final ball of the innings a scything cut boundary by Mathilde, which caused joyous uproar by the drinks tent, where the loudest area of St Christol support lay. St Christol ended their innings on 307 for five, with Sydney (152) and Mathilde (51) applauded loudly by spectators, and clapped reluctantly off the field by the opposing team.

Henry, sensing his opportunity to tease some more incriminating evidence from his captor, stood up and shouted over to the pair, "Well done St Christol – you pulverised them!"

Again, heavy hands pushed him back down to his seat, but he continued to goad. "Can't see you coming back from here, Chowdrey. Never thought I'd see a score like that."

Chowdrey glowered at him, "I advise you not to count your chickens, Mr Fanshawe."

"How are you going to do it though? We have a good bowling attack, and no-one's ever got close to that number of runs against us."

"With a normal team, Mr Fanshawe, I would be inclined to agree with you. However, I have invited a few friends from India to join our batting line up. And of course, some of your team's bowling may not be up to its normal standard."

He gave a short theatrical laugh. "Form, Henry, is temporary, but money is permanent."

"You cheating bastard!"

"Enough!" Chowdrey's temper finally snapped. He addressed his henchmen. "Tie him up. I don't want him going anywhere until his final cruise into the sunset, courtesy of Chowdrey Shipping."

Henry felt his hands being pulled behind the chair and, for the second time in twenty-four hours, bound roughly together. He slumped back, wondering when the cavalry would finally arrive and save him from this situation. Surely enough had been said by now to warrant an arrest? Surely he would not be forced to watch the next innings in this position? With a sinking heart, he saw the St Christol team take the field, Chief of Police included. It seemed he was here for the long haul.

30
The Indians Reply

As Henry sat bound and sweltering in the plush box of Mr Chowdrey, the two opening batsmen walked out of the pavilion and, to deafening applause from their supporters, strode out to the crease. Their whole manner and gait defined them as professional sportsmen with a lithe prowl, alert to the slightest of movement. These were, Henry guessed, the recent imports from India.

Their skill became clear in the first few overs. Both defended well against Curtley's speed and dealt comfortably with the medium pace of Jean. Runs flowed freely from the bat. With immaculate timing, balls were despatched in all directions, and even in the face of tigerish fielding by St Christol, the required run rate was being achieved.

Despite his position, Henry could not help but give the odd murmur of appreciation for some of the shots. He fell into a reverie. Why was it that, despite being in mortal danger, he was still carried away by the sublime pace and beauty of a cricket match? He remembered his old school teacher, for whom the sport was not such a great attraction, when he had once asked for time off to go to a match.

"Cricket, Fanshawe? Hours of boredom punctuated by moments of sheer hell!"

But for Henry it was not hell – it was a perfect microcosm of life. It was the longueurs, where nothing seemed to happen, that made the massive and sudden shifts in fortune so entertaining. And even when play was quiet, one could still admire a stroke for its beauty, quite divorced from the direction in which the match was headed. And then one could discuss this happily with a neighbouring spectator, whoever he or she turned out to be. Henry remembered once chatting merrily away at the MCC enclosure at Lord's, only to turn and find that he had been conversing for the past hour with Mick Jagger. On another occasion, in the Fanshawe box in the new Mound stand, he noticed John Major beside him, separated by a length of rope. When he turned again surreptitiously, the occupant had morphed into Jeffrey Archer. There must be a moral there somewhere, thought Henry.

What was it about cricket that Henry so loved that he was prepared to go such lengths to protect it? It wasn't just the traditions which surrounded the sport. Not just the complex rules. Had it been a matter of complexity or nostalgia, he would have taken up golf. It wasn't the fact that one could play for five days, end up with no result, and still feel that something had been achieved. It was not even the very English importance of the weather on proceedings. No, thought Henry, it was the innate sense of fair play, that other English habit. And where this fairness was impugned or perverted, Henry could not idly stand by.

He was jolted from his daydream by a loud shout from the field. After some deliberation, the umpire's finger was raised. St Christol had made its first breakthrough, a viciously fast delivery from Curtley which kept a little low, catching the batsman LBW. Chowdrey Steamers 47 for one off six overs. And as Henry watched in quiet pride over the next few overs, Curtley enjoyed a purple patch. He reminded the captive manager of a West Indian paceman in his pomp, ripping balls down towards the hunched batsmen in a blur of motion. And he quickly added a second scalp, uprooting the leg stump of the number two who, having been peppered with balls for an over, seemed to have decided to give up the fight. Chowdrey Steamers 57 for two off eight overs. The fourth batsman trudged up to the crease to face the last ball of the over from a now thoroughly pumped-up Curtley. The St Christol crowd, roaring with volume which increased as the bowler approached the wicket, were on their feet. Once again the ball left Curtley's hand in a blur, and this time it was a bouncer pitching up at the new batsman's throat. It was clear that this batsman was no ringer and equally clear that he could not cope with such a turn of speed. He shied away instinctively, with bat held up to ward off the blow. The ball disappeared skyward in an almost vertical trajectory. As the crowd watched, it slowed, reached its apex, and resumed on the downward trajectory to where Francis was waiting, eyes wide with horror.

From the box, Henry groaned. "Anyone but Frankie," he muttered as the panicking figure run this way and that, trying to position himself under the ball as it hurtled earthwards. Frankie's unblemished attire gave notice of the effort he generally committed to fielding, and his catching ability, or lack of it, had long passed into local cricket folklore. The supporting crowd knew this and voices were quickly hushed, the quiet punctuated by the odd shout of encouragement and prayer.

At last Frankie chose his spot. Face turned skywards, and hands held out, he waited for the ball to arrive. And then it did, hitting his outstretched arm and bouncing back up into the air. Frankie instinctively withdrew his hands and started to shake them in pain. He seemed destined to put the catch down. But at the last moment, as the ball resumed its earthbound journey, he snapped out of his trance and threw himself to the ground, one hand managing to get under the ball just before it hit the grass. A massive shout erupted from the Chief, who by then was flinging his gloves off and running towards Frankie, arms outstretched.

"Howzat, howzat, how... was... zat!" he screamed, losing, for a moment, all of his legendary reserve.

The umpire raised his finger and the fielders clustered around Frankie who had struggled back up, ball held in hand, posing like Hamlet and his skull. Sydney clapped him soundly on the back. "That, Frankie, was the best catch I have ever seen you make!"

"Sydney, darling, that was the *first* catch you have ever seen me make. And it's absolutely ruined the crease in my trousers!"

At the end of the eighth over the Chowdrey Steamers were 57 for three. "Game on," thought Henry.

As always, flow was followed by ebb for St Christol. The two batsmen dug in as Henry's bowlers began to tire. Runs accrued more and more easily off the bat, and by the twentieth over, the Steamers had moved to 122 without further loss. Mr Chowdrey, having become noticeably more irascible as the wickets started to fall, had now calmed down.

He turned to Henry. "It appears that we might not need to call on help to win this match in any case, Henry. That would certainly avoid any further unpleasantness. Except for you, of course."

Henry was growing increasingly concerned. For all the assurances of protection he had been given in the back of the Khumri van, there seemed little sign of any rescue party amongst the crowds, and Chowdrey had taken considerable care to choose a number of the largest and meanest looking henchmen he had ever encountered.

As the match progressed, the full seriousness of the predicament in which Henry found himself began to dawn. Worse still, his team were being put to the sword by the batting pair. Having lost another wicket to a rather messy run out (there was a hint of an outstretched foot from silly mid-off, over which the batsman inevitably tumbled) the new partnership had grafted, and then broken away, adding 50 runs in seven overs. Steamers 182 for five off twenty-seven overs.

The bowlers were slowing, and Henry watched in horror as Sydney took the ball from Jean and passed it to Rajiv. He noticed that Chowdrey, stretched out on his seat, hands on the back of his head, was smiling again.

The Indian turned to Henry. "I have always made it a rule, Henry, never to leave anything to chance. We'd probably win anyway, but with some help from young Rajiv, it might be finished by teatime."

Henry saw his chance, and devoutly hoping that the wire sitting in an altogether uncomfortable crevice of his anatomy was still working, he sat up. "What do you mean, with Rajiv helping?"

"Mr Fanshawe, Khumri Imports is one of the companies in which I own a significant share, and I always demand loyalty from my employees and their families. Rajiv's father, Sanjay, has been kind enough to convince him, on my behalf, of the need to allow his undoubted talent to shine a little less brightly today."

He chuckled and sat back to watch.

Rajiv's first ball was dreadful, a slow full toss, walloped back over his head for a huge six. The following balls of the over were little better. By the time Rajiv flicked the ball to Xavier, on in order to give Curtley a well-earned rest, the over had cost nineteen runs.

"A feast of cricket, eh, Mr Fanshawe!" Chowdrey could hardly contain himself.

At the other end, the news was a little better for St Christol. Xavier had never been a star bowler, but was useful in containing the batsmen, with a metronomically accurate pitch and speed. After a few overs, and more in frustration than anything else, the batsman nudged at a ball that swung away a little, presenting Sydney at first slip with an easy catch. Steamers 250 for six off 37 overs.

Fifty odd off the next 13 overs, roughly four an over, thought Henry. Very get-able, but with the batting tail falling away, still hope. Though he was worried about Rajiv. Was the young boy following his father's orders, or was he just not bowling very well? That end was haemorrhaging runs, and there were too few to play with. The last over before tea began.

Rajiv picked up the ball and wondered back slowly to his mark. Turning towards the crease, and twisting his body into the most ungainly of shapes, he released the first ball. The last proper batsman of the opposing team danced up the pitch intent on smashing it away as he had so many others. Henry closed his eyes, waiting for the cheer as the ball crossed the boundary. The cheer came, but when he reopened his eyes, he noticed it issued from the St Christol supporters. At the crease, the Chief was gesticulating with the ball in his hand, and the bails lay in the grass some metres away.

"Howzat!"

The umpire lifted his finger. Stumped, after the ball turned and was missed completely by the oncoming batsman. The team crowded round Rajiv to congratulate him.

"Not over yet, eh, Chowdrey?" said Henry.

"He has to give some appearance of trying, Fanshawe. I can assure you the result will still be the same in the end."

After two dot balls, Rajiv turned again to face the new batsman. The ball was pitched up and hit the rough on the leg side just in front of the bat. Turning viciously in and bouncing higher than seemed physically possible, it careered off the bat and into the hands of short leg. Steamers 250 for seven.

Chowdrey's mood had rapidly changed as he turned and called over one of his cronies. "It seems that our young friend has decided not to use common sense. Maybe his father should have another talk with him at tea. Fetch Sanjay for me – now!"

The teams trooped off for a short tea break, leaving Henry secretly elated and glowing inwardly with pride at his team's performance. Three wickets versus 54 runs, in 12 overs. Finely poised.

His thoughts were interrupted by a commotion at the door as Sanjay was pushed through it by two large figures. Chowdrey rose from his chair and walked over to where the shopkeeper stood. "Mr Khumri, may I remind you of our deal?"

"What deal would that be, Mr Chowdrey?"

"Don't joke with me, Khumri! What's got into you? Get that boy of yours to bowl rubbish like we agreed, or you and he will be joining Mr Fanshawe on my little cruise!"

"Are you threatening me, Mr Chowdrey?"

"Too damn right I am. Now, get out there and do what you are told!"

Sanjay made to turn to the door, but in a rapid and unexpected shift, he darted off towards Henry, kicking out as he did and putting one of the bodyguards on the floor of the box.

"Now!" he shouted.

Everything happened very quickly, though Henry afterwards always recalled it in slow motion. The door burst open and the Chief of Police and a number of constables surged into the room. After them roared a bristling Charles Fanshawe.

"Get the weapons!" shouted the Chief.

Sanjay had made it over to Henry and was trying to undo the ropes holding him whilst fending off a bodyguard. Henry felt the knots go loose around his hands

353

and stood up, catching, as he did, a glint of steel from the attacking guard. The man stood in front of him with an unhealthy smile, playing with a long and vicious knife in his hands. As he stepped forward to administer the thrust to an immobilised Henry, there was a blur of movement to his right. A long white arm extended, hands in a fist, and connected squarely with the jawbone of the oncoming attacker. The smile on the face disappeared. It was replaced, first with confusion, and then with a blissful peace, as his eyes closed and he slumped to the ground. Henry looked round to see his brother striding forward, nostrils flared. "No-one threatens a Fanshawe while I'm around!"

At that point, and probably for the first and only time in his life, Henry could have kissed his brother Charles.

It was over as quickly as it had started. Various employees of Chowdrey Shipping lay on the floor, pinned to the ground by policemen. Mr Chowdrey was handcuffed to his chair by the Chief of Police.

"Mr Khaaliya Chowdrey, I am arresting you on suspicion of fraud, kidnap, conspiracy to commit murder, and match rigging. You do not have to—"

"You've made a big mistake, Mahjoud. I'll have your arse for this when the President hears."

"But the President has already heard, old fellow. It was he who gave us permission to monitor your communications. I think we now have a fairly cut-and-dried case against you. The last few hours have been most instructive." The Chief turned to Henry. "Thank you so much, Mr Fanshawe, your help has been invaluable in giving us the last pieces we needed to put this man away for a long, long, time."

As he spoke, a bell rang out from the clubhouse.

The Chief turned to Mr Chowdrey. "Now, sir, you will excuse me. St Christol have a cricket match to finish." Leaving a few policemen to guard the prisoners, he exited, appearing some moments later on the pitch to join the rest of the team that were trooping out for the final twelve overs.

Henry, Charles and Sanjay were left standing in the box together, in an almost embarrassed silence. No one really wanted to start, but after a few moments, Henry, eyes on his feet made a slightly ham-fisted attempt to slap his brother on the back and, clearing his throat, muttered, "Thanks, Charles, really helped me out there."

Charles was dusting himself off, and, equally unwilling to show emotion, replied with a hint of a smile, "Don't mention it. Always told you that boxing was my real strength."

Sanjay chimed in, "And that was a punch amongst punches, if you are not minding me saying that, sir."

"Thank you, Mr Khumri."

Sanjay proffered his hand to Henry. "I am sorry, Mr Fanshawe that I could not tell you earlier, but we had to make it look as realistic as possible. I am a reserve police officer and I have been undercover on this case for six months. I couldn't afford to blow it by telling everyone – not even Rajiv."

They turned and looked as Rajiv began to bowl. The eyes of the crowd returned to the cricket. Henry took Sanjay by the hand and pumped it up and down. "Now, Sanjay, Charles, let's get down to the boundary to see what your talented son can do!"

The match was indeed finely poised. The run rate

required, at around four per over, was easily achievable, but all the decent batsmen were now back in the pavilion. Xavier had finished his allotted overs with good figures, and only Curtley and Rajiv remained with six overs each. Henry and Charles made it to the boundary by the time Rajiv was running in for his third ball. As they both appeared by the rope, a huge cheer went up from the crowd, and Sydney turned from his slip position to wave manically.

Having given away a handsome amount of runs in the spell before tea, Rajiv was now becoming much more economical. The slower pace restricted boundaries, and the ball was starting to move unpredictably out of the rough patches that had grown around the crease. He finished the over, which provided only two singles for the Steamers. And they were definitely getting rattled. Glances up to the box where Mr Chowdrey sat stony-faced between two uniformed policemen. Muttered conferences were held mid-wicket after each ball, voices were raised.

"Looks like you've got them on the run, old chap," observed Charles to his brother.

"Still have to bowl them out though – otherwise they'll make the total."

Henry sauntered over to where Curtley was standing on the boundary.

"Glad to see you back, boss." The large and lanky figure seemed almost consumed by his wide smile.

"Glad to be back, Curtley. Now, go out and take them apart."

"That, boss, is exactly what I was going to do." Taking the ball from the Chief, he jogged back to his starting position, which had been moved, if anything, closer to the boundary than usual. There was no doubting the look of fearful anticipation on the face of the opposing batsman, as Curtley steamed in for his first ball.

Over the next ten minutes, Henry, the crowd, and most of the watching press would unleash and exhaust almost every cliché known to the world of cricket. Curtley Smith was, according to the *Seychelles News*, "on fire", and bowling "like a man possessed". The balls he sent hurtling down towards the luckless figures were unplayable and left them rooted to the spot. Suffice to say that, apart from a ball so rapid that it was missed by the normally reliable wicket keeper, and went for four, he roughed up the batsman in a fashion so brutal that when the over was called, neither seemed particularly keen to continue. And after the brief respite of an over of spin by Rajiv that yielded three runs, there he was again.

If anything, the second over of this spell was even faster. Something had to give, and sure enough on the fifth ball, a vicious low bouncer, the batsman turned and flailed at the ball with his bat, trying merely to avoid being caught in the chest for a second time. The ball cannoned off the hilt of the bat and flew back at a perfect height to be grabbed out of the air by the Chief. Steamers 259 for eight, 44 runs to get off 55 balls. The tension of the encounter had quietened the crowd, who were now following each ball avidly and silently, willing the batsman to block, or fail, depending on their loyalty. Curtley had retreated to his mark by the time the tenth batsman arrived at the crease, taking guard in a manner that suggested he would rather be almost anywhere else but where he stood. Then the bowler, with a theatrical pawing of the ground, returned to deliver his next ball.

It was a perfect Yorker. The batsman had instinctively raised his bat to fend off the bouncer and could not get it down before the ball had slipped under and knocked the middle stump out of the ground. A roar erupted from the St Christol supporters, leaving the disconsolate batsman to turn and make his way back to the pavilion.

One wicket left, and still 44 to make. The tide had turned, and even with some heroic defence, edged boundaries, and lucky breaks, the final pair looked doomed. It fell to Curtley four overs later to administer last rites, with the score on 275. A cleverly disguised slower delivery left the batsman swinging far too early and the catchable ball was spooned up to mid off, where the dependable Monseigneur de Pelet took it, before hurling the ball in the air with a very un-Gallic rush of excitement. He then took off towards the Chief, jumping and leaping and shouting "Vive St Christol" at the top of his voice. A large swathe of the crowd had invaded the pitch, and various members made a beeline for Sydney and Curtley, who were hoisted on four large shoulders and carried to the boundary to join the emotional figure of Henry.

Charles had grabbed his hand and was enthusiastically pumping it, "Never thought I'd say this, Henry, but I'm bursting with pride for you. Simply bursting!"

Henry didn't really know what to think. He had never really believed this moment would arrive, and he was having some trouble taking in the victory. Those who watched carefully might have noticed that he was having some trouble with his glasses, which seemed to have steamed up.

Sydney arrived, jumped off his carriers, and threw himself at the manager. Henry found himself encompassed in an all-consuming bear hug. "We've done it, Henry, we've only bloody gone and done it!"

Curtley, still smiling his wide smile, fished something from out of his back pocket. It was the match ball. "This is for you, boss."

Some yards away, Mr Chowdrey, shepherded by a policeman towards the approaching Chief, was twisting against the handcuffs and shaking his head.

The teams made their way to the front of the clubhouse, where, on a table, covered with a pure white cloth, ironed to within an inch of its life, stood the Seychelles Cricket Cup. The President of the Seychelles Cricket Association, with a wide smile on his face and a can of Seybrew in his hand, beckoned Sydney onto the rostrum. He seemed blissfully unaware of anything that had transpired at this most eventful of matches.

"Ladies and gentlemen," he intoned, then shouted to make himself heard, "LADIES AND GENTLEMEN!"

The crowd quietened.

"I think you will agree that today's match has been one of the most exciting witnessed on these islands."

If only you knew, thought Henry.

"A hard and well-fought game, and a credit to the teams involved, and I would like to hope, to the Seychelles Cricket Association. Now, it falls to me to present the Seychelles Cricket Cup 2012 to the winners. Ladies and Gentlemen, The Esme Fanshawe St Christol Cricket Club!"

Henry felt he would burst with emotion as Sydney claimed the trophy and held the large silver goblet above his head. How could he have ever thought of leaving

359

these shores, these people? This wonderful place where happiness lay deep in the soul, and beauty radiated from every leafy corner. And he had done the right thing, at some personal risk, and come through. All was well with the world.

Outside, Henry wandered over to where the Chief was holding Mr Chowdrey, now a forlorn-looking figure, seemingly broken by recent events.

Henry shook the policeman's hand. "So, what happens now, Chief?"

"We win it again next year, Henry, of course!"

"No, I don't mean the cricket. What happens to our friend?"

"Ah. Yes. Well, Interpol seem quite interested in some of his other activities, so I do not think Mr Chowdrey will be bothering us again for a while, will you eh, sir?"

The Chief was unlocking the cuffs and pushing Chowdrey towards the car. In a split second, the man saw his chance. As his two henchmen were being ushered into the back seats, he suddenly squirmed out of the grip of the Chief, ducked under his elbow, and pushed him to the ground. Then he was off, sprinting towards the large helicopter at the side of the clubhouse, whose rotors were still idling. He had a head start, and it quickly became clear to Henry that he would get away. The Chief jumped back up and began the pursuit, shouting for all to follow, but he was no match for the desperation of a man showing a turn of speed that belied his mass.

Henry looked at the two retreating figures, and pondered. In his earlier life, one of his special skills was a rasping and accurate low throw which, in his playing days, had amassed a number of run outs which still stood as a record in his university cricket club. Now was the time. Around him, the sounds of the world began to dim. He was entering, he thought calmly, a trance-like state where all his attention began to be focused on the cricket ball nestling in his hand. In a slow and deliberate motion, looking first at the receding figure of Chowdrey and then at the cricket ball, he arched his back, pulled his arm behind him, then turned and let loose.

The ball arrowed towards its quarry. There were only a few yards before Chowdrey would be in the helicopter and away to safety. Seconds before collision, the fugitive turned to look back at his pursuer, and in that instant, the ball connected, smacking him squarely on the forehead. Mr Chowdrey went down, pole-axed, with a look of surprise on his face. The Chief arrived seconds later, and bestriding his prey, pulled out his cuffs, dragged the man's hands behind his back and clicked the lock shut.

Pulling the Indian up by the scruff of his neck, Chief Mahjoud glared at his captive and sneered, "As I believe they say in England – you're nicked!"

A semi-conscious Chowdrey was led back to the waiting car, where he was pushed into the back with his dejected henchmen. The opposing team were summoned into their changing room for questioning by Chief Mahjoud. Henry strode to the helicopter, located his match ball, and returned to the crowd amidst much cheering and back slapping. He felt elated, but more than that, he felt relieved. Deeply relieved.

He was immediately cornered by a glowing Reverend. "This, Henry, is what makes me believe in God!" And then, in a more secular vein, "Fucking amazing throw, old boy!"

All over the ground, groups had gathered into impromptu celebrations. A put-upon groundsman was trying unsuccessfully to stop some of the St Christol children making off with the stumps. As Henry surveyed the scene, he noticed Sydney and Cilla, arms entwined. And Frankie, already replaying his one and only catch of the season in full dramatic style to a crowd of enthusiastic onlookers. The cup was filled with champagne and handed round for all to take the traditional draught, though as it reached Rajiv Khumri, Sanjay appeared from nowhere to promptly remove it.

And as he watched, Mathilde took the trophy and, beckoning the others to follow, shimmied towards Henry. "Monsieur Fanshawe, this is for you."

Henry held out his hands to accept the cup, and was a little surprised when she put it down on the grass, encircled him with her long and elegant arms, and leaning a little towards him, planted a soft and sensuous kiss on his lips.

"You are not only an attractive man, Henri, you are a *brave* man," she whispered, and Henry felt a large blush suffuse his face. "It is a pity you are not a young man as well."

And with that, she disengaged, picked up the cup and upended its dregs over the nonplussed manager.

Turning to the crowd, and waving the cup in the air above her, Mathilde shouted "Three cheers for Henry Fanshawe!"

The sound echoed round the pitch. Even the Gallic poise of the Monseigneur had been left behind, as he led the cheers. Turning to Henry he proffered his hand, "Now Monsieur, you are a true Seychellois."

It was a compliment that Henry found almost too moving. He made to speak and round him the crowd shushed to hear his words. But the words wouldn't come. In the end, after a pause which was becoming unbearable, all he could do was whisper, in a choked voice, "Thank you. Thank you for everything."

And that was all he could say.

As the parties started in earnest, Henry wandered over towards the Chief, Sanjay and the Reverend, who was being given the whole story behind the day's extraordinary events. The policeman halted and motioned to Henry to join him.

He took off his mirrored glasses and polished them. "The thing was, we had absolutely no evidence apart from what Henry had told us. Sanjay of course had been providing information, but nothing good enough to stand up in court. We had to catch Chowdrey and his goons in the act."

Replacing his glasses, he went on. "So, Henry, the need to play it out as if we did not know, and to do nothing which would arouse his suspicions. I really am deeply sorry it had to come to an abduction, but believe me, it was the only way."

Henry sighed. He had nearly fled the country, he had been drugged, gagged and bound. He had been attacked and nearly emasculated by ants while escaping from the Black Hole of Calcutta. On the other hand, he had won the cup with his closest friends. His brother had come to his aid without a second thought. And he had apprehended a cricketing villain with a throw which ranked as one of his best ever.

EPILOGUE

A few mornings later, Henry was reading the paper, still reliving the events of the past week in his mind. The first court hearing had been held. The telephone rang in the corner of the room and he rose to answer it.

It was Chief Mahjoud. "Hello Henry. Have you seen the press this morning?"

"I have, Chief, though I wish they wouldn't make quite such a fuss – I mean, 'as good as any wicket-taking throw I have ever seen'? The reporter obviously doesn't know about Mike Gatting."

"Henry, Henry, do shut up!" the Chief was chortling down the line, "You are a hero. Enjoy it. Chowdrey's going to be put away for a very long time indeed, and it's in no small part thanks to you."

Henry glanced at the photo of his wife and smiled. The long departed Vanessa seemed to be looking particularly happy this morning.

"Well, it is nice to be recognised."

"That's better – and now I have some other good news for you."

"Yes?"

"Colonel Farrer has regained consciousness and expressed an urgent desire to see you."

Henry breathed a great sigh of relief. "Now that really *is* good news. Tell him I'm on my way."

Pausing only to grab his jacket and a slice of toast and marmalade, Henry rushed out of the house to the Land Rover and drove off.

Half an hour later, he was walking through the antiseptic tainted corridors of the hospital past various posters warning of the many dangers besetting the human race, interspersed with drawings from local schoolchildren. When he entered the Colonel's private room, Henry was shocked by what he saw. The old man in bed had aged in the weeks of his coma, and lost enough weight to give him a skeletal appearance. His head was still a mass of bandage and livid bruising.

However, as he walked towards the bed, the Colonel's head turned, his eyes opened as wide as they were able, and a ghost of a smile began to play over the patient's lips. "Henry, how wonderful to see you."

Henry took the thin proffered hand and shook it gently, "And I you, Colonel, and I you. We were all very worried for a while there."

"Oh, we military chaps are made of sterner stuff – it'll take more than a few baseball bats to finish me off, what!"

"Clearly, Colonel."

"And did you enjoy your first season in the sun?"

"It was quite an experience, yes."

The Colonel struggled into a sitting position on the bed. "Now, Fanshawe... Henry, do tell me..."

"Tell you what?"

"While I've been out cold – has anything interesting happened?"

Henry found a chair, sat down and made himself comfortable. Then he took a deep breath and began.

The Colonel listened in rapt attention to the story, occasionally interjecting with "Man's a complete bounder!" and other less printable remarks, and once or twice a laugh followed by a quick wince. When Henry had finished, he was smiling broadly.

"Well, you showed them, Henry – never underestimate an Englishman, especially one who plays cricket, eh? Money's not everything, is it!" Henry blushed as the Colonel went on,

"You know, Henry, that I never had much to do with finance or the City. We were more the forces type, though I had a niece who once went into it."

Henry formed the distinct impression that this conversation was heading somewhere.

"Yes, until recently she was PA to quite a senior character. The funny thing is, when I came to, there was a letter from her. Apparently she had recently resigned her position and wanted to come out to the Seychelles to look after me."

"Well," said Henry, "that sounds like a wonderful idea. You will need some looking after for a while."

"That's what I thought. Anyway, she's due here in a few minutes, so do stay around. I think you two might get along rather well."

Henry was about to ask her name when the door handled rattled and in walked a slim attractive woman in her mid-forties. She stopped at the door, her hand moving quickly to her mouth in shock at the thin apparition before her. The Colonel laughed and wheezed as he looked at the equally shocked face of Henry, who had risen from his chair in politeness and stood rooted to the spot.

"Henry, may I introduce you to my niece, Polly Farrer."

"No need, Uncle dear, I know him already," said the woman standing by the door.

"From the City," Henry added, somewhat redundantly.

Polly brushed off an imaginary speck, walked over to give her uncle a peck on the cheek, and then sat down. "I heard about Uncle Jim and decided to come and look after him, Henry."

"Yes." Henry couldn't really think of how to respond.

Polly looked him up and down. "You've lost weight, Henry! You're looking ten years younger, you know. Must be all that exercise."

She continued, beginning to grin. "I didn't realise you were friends. I suppose we will be seeing quite a lot of each other."

Then Henry smiled as well. "I am sure that we will, Polly."

And because his back was turned to the Colonel and his attention firmly focussed upon the new arrival, Henry quite missed the long and theatrical wink which Uncle Jim now bestowed on his favourite niece. Nor, deep in thought, did he catch the old man's muttered quip.

"Aah, the wonderful and mysterious Seychelles. The moment one conspiracy is over, the next begins…"